The Terror of Constantinople

By the same author

Conspiracies of Rome

RICHARD BLAKE

The Terror
of Constantinople

HODDER &
STOUGHTON

First published in Great Britain in 2009 by Hodder & Stoughton
An Hachette Livre UK company

1

Copyright © Richard Blake 2009

The right of Richard Blake to be identified as the Author
of the Work has been asserted by him in accordance
with the Copyright, Designs and Patents Act 1988.

A CIP catalogue record for this title is available from the British Library

Hardback ISBN 978 0 340 95114 9
Trade paperback ISBN 978 0 340 95119 4

Typeset in Plantin by Hewer Text UK Ltd, Edinburgh
Printed and bound by Clays Ltd, St Ives plc

Hodder & Stoughton policy is to use papers that are natural, renewable
and recyclable products and made from wood grown in sustainable
forests. The logging and manufacturing processes are expected to
conform to the environmental regulations of the country of origin.

Hodder & Stoughton Ltd
338 Euston Road
London NW1 3BH

www.hodder.co.uk

To my dear wife Andrea and to our daughter Philippa, without whose patience this novel would never have been written

ACKNOWLEDGEMENTS

The two quoted lines in Chapter 24 are from *Antigone* by Sophocles (Author's translation)

The two abusive epigrams in Chapter 31 are by the Author

The quotation in Chapter 32 of the lines from *Oedipus the King* by Sophocles is from the translation by Francis Storr (1839–1919)

The translation in Chapter 36 of the lines by Sappho is by the Author

The quotation in Chapter 43 ascribed to Euripides is from A.E. Housman (1859–1936), *Fragment of a Greek Tragedy*

The poem in Chapter 59 ascribed to Simonides is by A.E. Housman, *More Poems*, 1936, XXXVI

PROLOGUE

Monday, 16 April 686

'Why are you crying, Master?' Bede asked me this morning. Though knocking as usual, he'd brought in the hot water before I could sit up properly in bed and compose my features.

'A complaint of age, my child,' I replied with a weak stab at the enigmatic. The absence of light coming through the shutters confirmed it was raining again. That's all it ever seems to do in Northumbria. It falls in a gentle mist that blurs the landscape and soaks you before you can notice. I can hardly remember when I last spent a whole day reading in the sun.

In silence, I washed my hands and face, and stood shivering as Bede stretched up and rubbed at my frail, withered body. Time was – and not too long ago – when that would have banished all misery. Nowadays, the most solitary pleasures often evade my grasp.

'I've missed morning prayers again,' I said, to break the silence.

'My Lord Abbot said to leave you sleeping. He told me you were late to bed.'

So Benedict had noticed that jug of beer I'd grabbed off the dinner table. I grunted and held my arms apart so Bede could start dressing me.

'There is fresh bread today, Master,' he added. 'Even so, I made sure to steep it well in the milk.'

'I thank you, my child,' I said. I ran my tongue over sore gums and wondered how long before I was entirely confined to curds and stewed fruit. When you reach ninety-five, there are very few teeth you haven't outlived. 'But I'll eat shortly. For the moment, let us proceed with your lesson.'

I

I thought briefly, then recited a passage from Cicero at his most rhetorically florid. I paused at every natural break in the flow, letting Bede keep up with me as, eyes squeezed shut, he committed the text to his own memory. This done, I let him continue in the time-honoured manner – parsing and analysis of grammar, rare or difficult words explained, their etymology given, and so forth. Whenever he stumbled, I intervened with just enough explanation to set him right again. My interventions grew decreasingly frequent, and then only on points that would tax a much older student than Bede.

He's a bright lad. He reminds me of myself. If he lives, he'll be the glory of his age.

As the lesson moved smoothly on like a carriage in the grooves of a much-travelled road, I began to feel better. I hadn't at first been able to remember why, but I had woken crying. It was the dreams, you see. They'd been in sharper colours and more painful since I arrived here. Memory isn't like a religious text, where passages are separated into chapters and sections. You can't have one memory called to the front of your mind and expect all the others to remain buried in the oblivion of time.

I looked up again. Bede had mistaken two words close to the end of a sentence. There was an arguable ambiguity about this particular *clausula*, but I took the opportunity to remind him about quantitative prose rhythms that we moderns don't always hear.

'It is as you say, Master,' said Bede with downcast eyes. 'Forgive my slip.'

'It is a pardonable error, my child,' I said. 'You will be aware that words are important – their choice and meaning can turn the world from its expected course. Pray continue, however, with explaining the double accusative construction.'

Bede was still looking down. 'Is it true, Master,' he asked, lapsing into English, 'that you will be leaving us?'

For the first time, I smiled. I'd seen him yesterday with the other boys and the monks, looking anxiously in through the open doors and windows of the great hall. As discussions had been in Greek, no one could have known about the Emperor's pardon – witnessed by the Patriarch himself – or about the restoration of my property and status. But the shortest overland distance from Constantinople to Jarrow is two thousand five hundred miles. You don't have two senators and a bishop turn up with Easter greetings.

They had arrived the day before yesterday. They'd outrun the message of warning Bishop Theodore had sent out from Canterbury, and had caught me as I was finishing Advanced Theology with the novices. No journey is kind on the baggage, and the finery they had taken care to put on before knocking at the gate would have raised eyebrows anywhere east of Ravenna. But in Jarrow it had set the whole monastery and school afire with wonder and with concern.

'What do you suppose I shall do?' I asked Bede in Latin.

'I suppose, Master,' he replied in a small voice, 'that you will return to the Great City at the end of the world.'

End of the world! That isn't how they'd see it back in Constantinople. But I let that pass.

'Bede,' I said, still smiling, 'for all that I have lived in the Empire, and become great in its councils, I was born like you in this land of England. And it is to England that I have returned at the end of my life.'

That's the truth so far as it goes. I wasn't going to admit that nothing but extreme necessity could have parted me from my snug palace and the company of my books.

I got up and pulled one of the shutters open. It was still raining, but the sky was growing brighter.

I turned back to the boy.

'What would you have me do?' I asked. 'I can see the Lord Bishop Alexius lurking under cover in the yard. He'll be on me the moment I step out. Speak openly, my child – what would you have me do?'

'I would stay, Master,' Bede straight away replied, now fierce and looking up at me. 'I'd stay among my own, and be looked after and always revered.'

That was all this morning. It's now much later in the day. I'm back here alone in my room to gather my thoughts and set them down in

3

the privacy of Greek. I know I should begin with Alexius and the exact nature of his promises. But those words of Bede keep coming back into my mind: '*I'd stay among my own.*'

Well, who are 'my own'? Is it these monks and semi-barbarians in the rain-soaked wilds of northern England? Or is it a pack of shifty Greeks who only want me back because the Saracens are on the march again?

Age hasn't answered the question for me. Alexius may be telling the truth for the first time in his career when he talks about the state of the roads to Marseilles, and the comforts of the armed convoy riding there at anchor to take me 'home'. Even so, I'm barely worse for travel now than when, two years ago, I hobbled here alone through the ruin and desolation of the West.

So do I stay among those who love me? Or do I go back to a world I thought I had lost for ever?

What was it I said to Bede earlier? '*Words are important – their choice and meaning can turn the world from its expected course.*'

God, how right I was.

I

I first saw Constantinople on Monday, 6 July 610. I was twenty at the time. We'd set out from Rome by barge, changed to a ship at Ostia, and then to a larger ship at Naples. We'd stopped for supplies at Palermo and again at Corinth, where the ship had been dragged across the narrow spit of land. I'd fancied a further stop at Athens but the Captain was muttering something about prevailing winds and his 'instructions'.

Most likely, I'd said to Martin, he was scared of putting in anywhere north of Corinth. The Slavs were now raiding at so many points that almost nowhere could be counted safe. Every night, after we'd passed Corinth, the sky was lit up by the fires of captured cities.

Once, sailing north along that silent coast, we'd come upon a whole band of Slavs together with their booty and their captives. They'd raised their spears at us and shouted something incomprehensible. We'd tried to shoot at them with our bows, but always without success. After that, we'd made sure to stand well out from the shore at night, with guards posted on the main deck.

From Euboea, we'd struck out for the East, straight through the Aegean. Every day, the sun had burned down from a sky of darkest blue on to still waters of blue and silver. We'd then entered the main shipping lanes, and were passing trading ships and fishing boats and war galleys. We'd passed little islands, sometimes putting in to shore. On some I saw abandoned temples gleaming white in the distance, and monasteries and fortifications of various kinds. To the bemusement of the crew, I'd scampered about the remnants of more civic and more populous ages, chasing away the queer lizards that darted all over the ruins and filling my head with details of inscriptions and building styles.

5

On days when we hadn't landed, I'd swum in the warm salty waters, with Martin's voice calling out every so often he might have seen another dolphin. Despite the clear assurance of Aristotle and of the sailors stood beside him, he couldn't be brought to believe the things weren't dangerous.

There had been a quickening of the traffic as we passed into the Hellespont, and a fair crowding of it as the channel widened out into the Propontis. It was now, looking left across the water, that I first saw the great City. Piled on to a high, central hill, its public buildings looked down over walls of a size and magnificence that came close to topping my wildest dreams. These surround the city, guarding its landward side with a triple fortification that no enemy has ever breached, or can ever breach. The two lengths of wall that front the sea are less elaborate but still provide adequate protection.

Even if you aren't allowed inside, the walls give an idea of how vast is Constantinople. The two sea walls are each about three miles long. The land wall is another three miles or so. Beyond the walls, suburbs – though mostly long abandoned – stretch some way into Thrace, and cover the neighbouring shore.

When I first arrived, the whole blunted triangle and its dependencies may have contained a million people. Even today, it must remain the biggest and richest city in the world.

'Behold the ancient city of Constantine,' said Martin, sounding glum beside me.

'Come, now,' I said, ignoring his mood, 'you know much better than that. Just three hundred years ago, this was a dumpy little town without walls, called Byzantium. Compared with Rome, it's a thing of yesterday. It was only when the Great Constantine established the Faith, and then wanted a capital he could fill with churches and with better access to the frontiers, that this place became anything at all.'

Ignoring the challenge to debate, Martin continued leaning on the rail and looked bleakly across the diminishing expanse of water that separated us from the City walls. The conversation of flags between ship and shore was ordering us closer in; I supposed it was to avoid the more important shipping in that crowded channel. Built on the far edge of Europe, the city faces Asia across waters narrow enough to swim, but for the treacherous tides.

'Three hundred years,' he said at length, 'is long enough to bring every vice and every crime to ripeness. You wait and see.'

There was a sudden shouting behind us. Men were running all over the ship, pulling on ropes. The sails came down, and I heard the dull beat of the drum as the rowers took over from the wind and we turned left into the Golden Horn – the long, sheltered harbour that washes the north-eastern sea walls and makes Constantinople a greater commercial centre even than Alexandria.

I'd never seen so many ships before. Some crowded along the docks that lined an unwalled stretch at the city's edge and that were repeated on the opposite shore. Others stood out in the channel and little boats darted between them and the docks. On land, I could see row after row of vast warehouses of the kind I'd seen in Ostia. But those were mostly abandoned, crumbling away beneath their vaulted roofs. These were bursting with all the produce of the world – foodstuffs, textiles, spices and drugs and aromatic goods, manufactures of all kinds, works of art. Whatever can be bought and sold, you'll find in those warehouses.

The Captain was shouting orders to his men and greetings to other ships as we navigated our way slowly and carefully across the harbour. No longer responding, his signalman was intent on the rapid waving of flags onshore. Every time the message was reported, the Captain would bark another set of orders. Since they all spoke Syriac to each other, I had no idea what was being said.

From a few hundred yards out, I could see the swarming crowds on the docks – naked porters fetching and carrying, officials and their secretaries consulting lists, men and women of every condition and colour. I made out a line of slaves all chained together, still wearing the clothes of their northern home, their skins red from the burning sun.

Beyond the docks the land rose upwards. Here, I allowed myself a sight of a jumble of glittering buildings. Some of these looked

7

quite old – at least, they were in the ancient style of the Greeks. The larger buildings were all in the modern Imperial style. I strained to see more of them, but the afternoon sun was in my eyes and it dazzled me. I also couldn't explain the little dark projections at regular points along an inner wall.

Partly to rest my eyes, I looked down into the water. Further back, the oars were breaking it into a white foam. Where I stood at the front of the ship, I could see my own reflection, clear but distorted by the parting of the waters. I had put on my best robe for the occasion – yellow with a dark blue trim that gave me a vaguely official look. Because I still wasn't up to growing a proper beard, I'd let my hair grow very thick and had bound it with a ribbon into a mass of gold.

I gave myself a little hug as I leaned forward over the rail and looked down at that beautiful reflection. Behind my back, people might well be asking about the exact nature of my citizenship. None could deny that, visually, I was among the most glorious objects they had ever seen. I was like an old statue, with all the paint and gilding still fresh upon it. As ever when I caught an unexpected view of myself, I could feel a stiffy coming on.

Still beside me, dressed in a suitably contrasting grey, a hat to keep the sun off his milk-white, freckled skin, Martin cleared his throat. It was one of those noises he made when somewhere between moderate concern and paralysing fear.

'We're putting into the Senatorial Dock,' he said flatly.

Certainly, we were going straight past the place where I'd seen all the activity. Still shouting orders I couldn't understand, the Captain was pointing to some other landing place round a bend in the shore.

For the hundredth time that day, Martin reached up to make sure his hat was in place. Hair as red as his doesn't long survive a thirtieth birthday, and I knew Martin was approaching that age faster than he wanted.

'Our things', he added, 'will still need to clear customs, but it shouldn't be as searching as I expected.'

'Well,' I said, trying to keep my voice neutral, 'let us be grateful for that.'

Martin had warned me how the Greeks like to check everything when you land, and even try to levy duties on your personal effects. I hadn't liked the thought of that. If we could avoid it, I'd not object to a little change of plan.

I looked again towards the shore which was approaching fast. With the crowds behind us, we were putting into a small landing faced with blue marble and overlooked by buildings of restrained grandeur. Leading up to the main city, there was a wide avenue lined with trees.

Following Martin's glance to the landing place, I could see a small, though very fat man dressed in a robe with a purple border. Beardless, of indeterminate age, he seemed to be wearing a wig – or perhaps it was a full head of hair dyed black. It was hard to see the details at that distance or in that terrible glare of sunlight. A secretary stood beside him, his face cast down. Behind him, at a respectful distance, stood various retainers, some of them armed.

'That's not the Permanent Legate, or his people,' Martin hissed, his grip tightening on the rail. 'It's a *Gloriosus*. There's a really senior official waiting to greet you. You only see people of that status come down to greet foreign ambassadors.'

My stomach turned over. The scared speculations I had pushed out of my mind on that hasty, midnight rush down the Tiber came crawling back. With the shore getting closer and closer, I felt like a man who falls from a high window and sees the ground rushing towards him. Even if I'd dared to ask, would the Captain have turned back?

I wanted to say something reassuring to Martin. All I did was reach out to him under cover of the rail. He took my hand in his. It was cold and sweaty, but firmer than my own. We stood close together as the ship covered the last hundred yards or so.

'He'll be expecting our total deference,' Martin whispered with a slight nod at the official. 'You address him as "Your Magnificence".'

I had a speech rehearsed for the Permanent Legate's agent. I had a variation ready just in case the Lord Silas should deign to meet us in person. I had nothing prepared for this.

9

It might be a mistake, I told myself again and again. The Permanent Legate's people might be waiting at one of the general docks. Perhaps an ambassador's ship was even now being inspected by those customs men, and there'd be red faces all round. But I thought it best to assume that the traffic-control people in the city knew what they were doing, so I put an open smile on to my face and made a gentle bow in the official's direction. He bowed in response, touching his forehead in the Eastern manner.

As the oars swung suddenly upright and we coasted the last few yards into dock, I glanced up again at the inner wall. I could now see that those dark projections I hadn't been able to make out were iron gibbets. There must have been dozens of these clustered round the Senatorial Dock. Each held a corpse in various stages of decay.

The corpses looked sightlessly down at me, twisted in their death agonies, blackened by the sun. Some were naked. Others had shreds of clothing that scavengers and the shifting winds hadn't yet torn away. Here and there, though faded, I could make out the purple border of the senatorial classes.

Martin cleared his throat, directing my attention to the open mouth and outstretched arms of the official.

'Executed traitors,' he whispered again with a momentary glance at the gibbets. 'You should pretend not to notice them.'

As I stepped ashore, the official hurried forward to embrace me.

'Greetings, Alaric of Britain,' he called in a voice that might have been a woman's but for its great power. His flabby, painted jowls shook with the force of his greeting. 'I bid you welcome after your journey from the Old Rome to the New. Welcome, Alaric, welcome to the City of Caesar!

'I am Theophanes, and I represent the Master of the Offices himself. In the name of His Glorious Excellency, and in the name of the Great Augustus whose benevolence shines upon us as a second sun, I bid you welcome. Yes, young and most beautiful Alaric, I bid you a fond welcome.'

Theophanes must have seen my furtive look beyond him to the jumble of attendants. He continued:

'His Excellency the Permanent Legate is sadly indisposed. Rather than send down a subordinate from the Legation, he took up our suggestion of an official greeting. It was no less than we could offer for a scholar of such pre-eminent qualities as yourself.'

He paused and put a slight emphasis on the elaboration of the flattery: 'A scholar whose qualities are no stranger to the city – though we were unprepared for such personal beauty to be so artlessly combined with youth and learning. Please regard me throughout your stay as entirely at your service.'

His face creased into a smile and he spread his arms as if about to begin a declamation: 'All that you require for your mission – all that you may desire for your convenience – you will look to me to provide.'

He spoke in good Latin, though with an accent that wasn't quite Greek. I answered in my best Greek, praising the Emperor for his forethought in all matters and thanking Theophanes for his own eminent goodness of heart.

So there was no mistake. I was indeed the object of this fuss. The Emperor's most senior Minister had taken an interest. He had sent one of his own most senior officials to greet me.

As we drew back from our second kiss and were about to begin a new round of mutual flattery, the breeze shifted. The perfume that hung like a suffocating fog round Theophanes gave way to a smell of death from the gibbets above our heads. I resisted the urge to gag at the sudden stench and controlled my features. In a moment, the breeze shifted again and the smell of ropes and tarpaulins filled the air.

We moved towards the litters placed for our service, and the armed men lined up into a guard of honour. Behind me, I could hear Martin giving subdued but curt orders for the unloading of our luggage. The customs officials who'd been hovering behind Theophanes and his entourage had given up hope of inspecting this and were dispersing.

That ship had been our home for what seemed an age. I never looked back to it.

2

Oh, but this will never do! The ancient poets may have opened in the middle of things, working backwards and forwards as they felt inspired. You can do that when writing a diary. I seem, however, to have begun a regular chapter in the history of my life. One day soon, when I'm gone to a place condemnation cannot reach, I like to think Bede will take this up and further practise his Greek. I'll need to do a great deal better than I have to explain myself.

Let us, then, leave things as they were on the Senatorial Dock – no one left frozen there is likely, I think, to complain – and go back to the real beginning of the story.

That was a month earlier in Rome, where I'd now been living for a year, and life was sweet. It was the morning after the Feast of Saint Rubellus, and the bodies of some of those who hadn't recovered from their stupor had not yet been taken away by their next of kin. Fortunately, the Lombards were on the prowl again, and there were fewer pilgrims than usual. I was making my way down to the financial markets. The fortune I was hoping to make on some Cornish tin had taken an interesting turn, and I needed a meeting with my associates. I was so busy keeping my new shoes from getting blood on them that the monk's greeting took me by surprise.

'His Excellency the Dispensator would be glad of the citizen Alaric's company,' he said, looking down at me. If he was trying for a grand effect, it didn't work. As he spoke, the heap of rubble on which he was standing gave way, and his last word ended in a squawk as he landed at my feet.

I could have laughed – especially at the dull sound of the corpse that broke his fall – but didn't. As you might imagine from his name, the Dispensator's job was to oversee the Papal charity that bound people materially to the Church. In fact, he had for some time been doing rather more than this. Now he was sinking deeper into his illness, poor old Pope Boniface signed whatever the Dispensator put before him, and did whatever he was advised. The Dispensator ran the Church. The Church ran Rome. If he wanted me now, my time was his.

So, having sent my slave on to the financial district with my excuses, I found myself for the first time since Christmas in the Lateran Palace.

'I can find my own way in, many thanks,' I said to the monk. He was plainly glad of the chance to go and get cleaned up before anyone saw him.

I turned left out of the lush beauty of the main hall and made as if for the Papal apartments. Then I took another left turn down an unlit corridor and found myself in the decidedly unlush waiting room outside the Dispensator's office. I nodded to the clerical monk who kept order and walked past the various supplicants who waited there in silence.

After a while of sitting alone in the office, I heard the door open behind me from an inner room. With a rustle of linen and his usual dry cough, the Dispensator was with me.

'Do feel free to remain seated,' he said in a tone that barely hinted at my impertinence. I twisted round and smiled at him. Paying no attention to this, he paused before one of the overstuffed filing racks that had lately taken up what little room was left in the office. He raised his hand to a sheaf of documents but thought better of taking anything out. He sat himself on his side of the desk and looked intently at his manicured nails.

'I must thank you, Alaric,' he began, 'for having come so promptly. I appreciate that you have much else to occupy you at the moment. But it is on a matter of the highest importance that I have called you here.'

He fell silent as another clerical monk shuffled into the room with more papers. He picked up one of the larger sheets of papyrus and read its contents with slow deliberation. At last, he signed it and rolled it up and sealed it.

'Get this to a courier at once,' he said. 'I want it on the first packet out of Ostia. Do not send it overland via Ravenna,' he added, a finger raised for emphasis.

The clerk bowed silently and left the room.

While he was reading, I had a good look at the Dispensator. He was even thinner than at our last meeting. The weatherbeaten look his face had taken on gave him still more the appearance of a dried stick. But he was wearing a very nice robe, of a cut I hadn't seen before. For a moment I thought of asking for the name of his tailor, but decided not to push my welcome.

As the door closed and we were alone again, he continued. 'You may be aware that it is now twenty years since the Spanish King abandoned the damnable heresy of Arianism that his barbarian ancestors introduced into the country. He and his successors have been ever since firm in the true Orthodox Faith of Nicaea.'

I was vaguely aware of the fact. But whether Christ was One *with the Father* or merely *of the Father* had never much troubled me. Nor was I much concerned what view any of the barbarians who'd planted themselves in the old Western Provinces took of the matter. When both parties to an argument scream incomprehensible formulae at each other, and threaten any observers with hellfire unless they fully agree with one against the other, the time is for men of sense to make their excuses.

But I knew it was the Dispensator's duty to stand up for Nicaea. For all that it had started as an argument among Greeks, the Roman Church had for centuries been defending the Creed of Nicaea against anyone who presumed to doubt it. This had raised troubles in the West where most barbarians had – accidentally – converted to the wrong side. More importantly, the further argument over the Single or Double Nature of Christ had turned the Greek and other Eastern Churches upside down, and kept them from uniting against Rome. So I nodded and tried to look interested.

'You will be aware then', he continued, 'that an insignificant but vocal minority in Spain have persisted in the darkness of heresy. The secular authorities have exhausted all the loving care at their

14

disposal to win them over. Here in Rome, therefore, we have arranged one last meeting between the Orthodox and the spokesmen of heresy. These latter are to attend under a flag of truce. They may yet be brought over without need of a truly disruptive severity.'

'And you want me to go to Spain', I broke in, 'to complete the work you began there of dishing out bribes to, or gathering dirt on, the Arian bishops?'

I thought this an inspired stab. A Spanish trip would have fitted my Cornish plans, and a mission for the Church would have been a fine cover. Mainly, though, I just wanted for once to break through that smooth, bureaucratic exterior.

No such luck. The Dispensator gave me a withering look and went on with his exposition.

'Our problem', he said, 'is that one of the leaders of the Arian party – I do not, by the way, think "Bishop" an appropriate title for a heretic – is a person of some pretence to learning. He has raised questions regarding the procedural regularity of the Councils of Nicaea and Constantinople, and of the authorised Latin translation of their Acts. In particular, he notes that the Holy Ghost is said in the Creed to proceed only from the Father and not from the Father and Son. Making use of this alleged ambiguity, he denies that the Creed truly expresses what we have always taken it to mean.

'These questions must have been raised at least once in the past three centuries, and doubtless fully answered. Sadly, neither we nor the Spanish Church have been able to find any discussion useful to our purposes.'

That must have been embarrassing, I thought. Forget theology – this was politics. If you're English, you'll be used to the fact that our churchmen look directly to Rome. Our secular authorities aren't up to much at the best of times, and only get attention out of politeness or when something is wanted. It was different back then in the French and Spanish Churches. Of course, they accepted the spiritual primacy of Rome but they looked to their local kings much as they had to the Emperor when there was still one in the West.

This annoyed Rome like nothing else. Its ambition was to be *Omnium Orbis Ecclesiarum Mater et Caput* – the Mother and Head of all the Churches of the world. From the Pope down, the words hung on every pair of lips in the Lateran.

Now it was faced with an admission that it couldn't flatten some heretical Goth on the meaning of the Creed. Yes, most embarrassing.

But the Dispensator hadn't paused to give me time for a gloat. He put down the lead seal he'd been toying with and looked straight at me.

'I therefore need someone competent in theology and in Greek', he said, 'to travel to Constantinople to consult the libraries and the religious scholars of that city.'

Well, you could have buggered me with a bargepole and I'd not have noticed. I think my mouth fell open. I sat for a while looking at him and trying to gather some reply.

'According to what I've picked up on the Exchange,' I said at last, 'the Danube frontier has collapsed and Slavs are pouring into the Balkans. The Persians have invaded Mesopotamia and may already be in Syria. The Exarch of Africa is in revolt against the Emperor, and his people have taken Egypt. These are all converging on Constantinople and it's an open bet who will get there first. Whoever does get there will find an emperor who is incompetent for every purpose but murdering anyone who might have some ready cash to steal, or who may have given one of his statues a funny look.

'I'll not deny, My Lord Dispensator, you have some right to my services. But you'll need to try a lot harder to get me into that shambles. The two of us may have agreed that certain events here and outside Ravenna never took place last year. I hardly think Emperor Phocas considers himself bound by our agreement.'

The Dispensator gave me one of his bleak smiles and motioned me back into my seat.

'Of course, Aelric,' he said – as ever, when he needed my services badly enough, with a failed attempt at pronouncing my real name – 'I have no means to compel you to do anything. You are a free agent. Our rule is one of persuasion and love, not of force. But do consider that you came here with Father – but I correct myself! with *Saint* – Maximin to gather books for the mission library in Canterbury. Now, think of the great libraries of Constantinople. Think of the entry to these that the Church could obtain for you. I can offer you all the learning of the ages – books the like of which haven't been in Rome for a hundred years or more.

'And you will be under the full protection of the Church,' he added, 'and our Permanent Legate in the City will watch over you at all times.'

'So,' I asked, trying to ignore the thought of those libraries, 'why not get His Excellency the Permanent Legate to do your research? Isn't it for that sort of thing that he gets paid?'

'No, Alaric,' came the reply. 'The Lord Silas has many excellences, and comes from one of the very best families in Rome. But his Greek is not sufficient for our purpose. And we do not think a local agent would be appropriate.'

So it was the usual nepotistic stitch-up. The best job in the Church, short of a really juicy bishopric, and it had gone to another duffer who had to transact all business in the Imperial capital – a few formal occasions apart, where Latin was still used – through an interpreter.

'What makes you suppose I'm any better as a scholar?' I asked again.

The Dispensator's smile broadened till it bordered on the grotesque.

'But Alaric, I have from both Rome and Canterbury the most glowing reports of your scholarship. Only last month' – he took up a sheet of papyrus from one of the trays on his desk and squinted over the writing – 'you were praised in an oration to His Holiness himself as "the Light from the North; the beauteous young barbarian drawn here by the gold of our learning, not of our palaces".'

I can't say I'd seen much learning in Rome, or many palaces that weren't half-ruined slums. Nor can I say I liked the bit about being a barbarian. At the time, though, I'd found the notice flattering. It made a change from all the complaints the Church authorities had been getting about my talent for shady finance.

Good as I was in Roman terms, that hardly fitted me to rub shoulders with the tenured intellectuals of the greatest centre of learning in the world. What mattered most, though, was that the Dispensator seemed to think otherwise. Rome hadn't yet been flooded with refugees from the Saracen invasions. Back then, Greek had become a rare accomplishment.

But there was no point debating any of this. My mind was made up.

'I won't go,' I said firmly. 'You must accept my apologies for declining your invitation. But nothing you can say will make me go.'

I rose. I was starving for my breakfast and I had to get to that meeting about the Cornish tin. There was no saying what my associates would agree without me there to keep them in line.

The Dispensator ignored my preparation to leave.

'I am asking a favour of some considerable importance,' he said, his voice now silky smooth, his annoyance discernible but not evident. 'I know you have persuaded His Excellency the Prefect to "recognise" your Roman citizenship, and your having reached an age that my sources assure me you have not. But there is more than a chance that success in Constantinople would bring a grant of senatorial status – just think of the social privileges, the legal immunities. Surely you would want that for yourself. If not for yourself, then for your unborn child?'

So he had heard about that. Was there anything he didn't hear about? Still standing, though, I decided to end the conversation with a direct snub.

'What you are offering only the Emperor can grant. And you can't get him to grant Boniface the title of Universal Bishop. Since he murdered his way to the top, you people have been splashing flattery on Phocas as if it were mud thrown up by a cart. I can't imagine how much gold you've slipped his way these past eight years. And all he's done for the Pope is call him Universal Bishop in a correspondence that stops short of a formal grant.

'And you're offering me senatorial status? I really think, my Lord Dispensator, you will need stronger incentives than that to get me within five hundred miles of Phocas.'

I looked back as I left his office. For once, I had actually brought colour to the wretched man's face. Yes, he was the most powerful man in Rome. But hadn't I already done enough for him and his Church?

I missed the tin meeting. By the time I got to the financial district, all my associates had cleared off, and it would take at least another ten days to get them together again. As I passed the Forum on the way back, I dodged into a wine shop in what used to be a diplomatic archives building and drank myself into a better humour with the world.

'Fucking cheek!' I said to no one in particular as I looked out of a window at the roofless shell of the Temple of Isis. Beyond that lay the Forum, where, towering atop its column, the statue of Phocas lately set up by the Church was shedding its gilt.

'The bloody, fucking cheek of the man!'

3

My good humour continued about fifty paces beyond the wine shop. All the bodies had now been cleared away, and the streets around the Forum were littered only with the usual filth. But there was now the beginning of a small riot between me and the Caelian Hill.

'Anathema on the traitorous Exarch,' someone at the front of one of the two opposing mobs bellowed. He wore a hood but wasn't a monk, and spoke Latin with an accent that was neither Roman nor barbarian. 'And on the Exarch's son and on the Exarch's nephew who would challenge our Lord Caesar Phocas for the Purple,' he added. There was a ragged cheer behind him.

'Anathema, much rather, on the tyrant Phocas,' someone shouted back at him, 'and blessings on the young hero Heraclius who, even now, journeys to Constantinople to heal the Empire's grievance.'

More cheering, and a few howled insults.

And so they carried on at each other. For the moment, it was just more of the ritual shouting that had been getting on Roman nerves for the past six months. Both sides in the civil war had their embassies here, each negotiating for the blessing of the Church – which would bring the support of the whole West and a fair bit of the East. And while the Church stayed aloof but formally loyal to the Emperor in possession, each side had its hired mobs to fill the streets with noise.

For the time being, as said, it was just more of the shouting. At any moment, though, it might proceed to the throwing of dead cats and rotten vegetables, and then to actual violence. It was all a matter of what directions came from the covered chairs lurking just beyond each of the groups.

I hurried past the smaller of these groups. Someone clutched at my arm.

'Will you sign our letter to His Holiness?' he rasped, breathing garlic and bad teeth at me. He waved me in the direction of some other piece of scum who was carrying a suspiciously clean and expensive sheet of parchment.

'Piss off and sign it yourself,' I snarled. As he stood back, I took my sword half out of the scabbard and let him see its notched edge.

That got me past without any stains on my tunic. But as I walked towards the Caelian Hill my ears burned at the abuse they had called after me. I could just about stomach it from persons of quality. But to be called a barbarian by these verminous out-of-towners really was the limit. I was inclined to turn round and tell them that I was a man of considerable wealth and learning, and that I could trace my ancestry through a line of nobles and kings that reached back – my mother had assured me – to the Tribal Gods of Kent.

But I resisted the urge. My face turning redder and redder as I hurried past some of my neighbours, I went home and called for more wine.

I sat in my library much later. It was that time of day early in a Roman summer when the light is fading but there is no need yet for lamps. The preserving oil had now dried on the book racks, and the main smell in the room was of the dust my slaves hadn't yet managed to clean entirely off the books. These were still mostly in their crates. Piled up beside me was an edition of Saint Jerome I had bought cheap at auction and was planning to send off to the Lateran scriptorium for copying and dispatch to Canterbury.

I should have been going through this, making sure the pages were stitched in the right order and that there were no obvious copying errors. Once in England, copies would be multiplied with great enthusiasm, but with no critical awareness. It was up to me to ensure that we'd send no cripples or bastards into the world.

Instead, though, I was going again through the rebuilding accounts. My requirements had been specific. I wanted something large and solid and readily defensible by just me and a few armed slaves. At the same time, the house had to be low enough on the Caelian Hill to receive water from the one aqueduct that hadn't yet been cut. I was looking forward to having one of the only working bathhouses in Rome.

I'd known that would come at a price. Apart from the financial district across the river, the Caelian was now the only decent part of Rome to live in. All the best people were there or trying to buy their way in. Most of the few habitable buildings that came on the market were being snapped up long before they got to auction.

I'd been glad enough when the agent had found me this place. It had needed new floors throughout and much new plastering, but had been sound in its externals. So why were those swindling beasts putting in bills for new roof tiles? Indeed, bearing in mind the perfectly good tiles that could be harvested for free from the derelict properties at the foot of the hill, why charge at all for the things?

'I suppose they think I was born yesterday,' I sneered to myself. The more money you have, I can tell you, the more careful you become about giving it away. I took up a stylus and scratched through that part of the bill. There was room enough at the foot of the waxed tablet for some nasty comment. I looked up and tried to think of something cutting but simple enough for the owner of the building company to understand.

My slave Authari knocked and put his head round the door. 'The Lady Marcella and her man of law beg to be received,' he said in the pompous manner he'd got from his last owner.

'Do then show them in,' I said, rising from my desk. 'And do send in wine and cakes,' I added. 'We have important business to transact.'

He stepped fully through the door. 'Begging your pardon, Master,' he said, 'but the good wine is all spoiled.'

He stood in a late ray of sunlight that slanted through the overhead window. Except that the battle scar on his face shone more livid than usual, his expression remained as bland as the

Dispensator's. As I opened my mouth to speak, Marcella came into the room. She wore a confection of silk that might have harmonised with the fresh blackness of her hair, but for the green tinge she'd taken of late to adding to the lead paste that covered her wrinkles.

'Well, young Alaric,' she said, not waiting for the formal greeting. 'You've certainly brought this place on. My dear husband – the Senator, you know, or would have been had God spared him – couldn't have done no better himself.'

'Dearest Marcella,' said I, 'you are always welcome in my house – just as I was in yours. If you are no longer my landlady, I rejoice daily in your friendship.'

I settled her into a chair and sat down opposite. The lawyer began fussing with his satchel. He wasn't the jolly little man who'd drafted the terms of the agreement, but someone new – a big creature with a mass of brown hair and with bags under his cold, glittering eyes.

Another slave entered carrying a tray. The wine was an embarrassment but, served in those nice glass cups the builders had dug out of the basement, no one had any right to notice.

'The provisional agreement', said the lawyer, still on his feet, 'was made on the Kalends of May between the Lady Marcella, relict of the sub-Clarissimus Porcinus, official in the Imperial Service, and Alaric, citizen from the presently alienated Province of Britain. The citizen Alaric, believing himself to have got with child one Gretel, a slave in the household of the Lady Marcella, has offered a price to be agreed by further negotiation for the sale of the said Gretel. He has further offered to continue paying rent on his suite in the house of the Lady Marcella until such time as the said Gretel shall have been transferred to his ownership and until such time as his own house shall be ready to receive . . .'

And on and on the man droned, going through all the formalities of the sale. I thought back to that winter afternoon when the first upper rooms in the house had been ready for occupation and I'd sent off with an excuse to get Gretel to come over. She'd said to be careful as I ripped at her clothes and pulled her on to the new bed. But I'd

23

been too drunk on unmixed wine and self-love to pay attention. Sure enough, my seed fell on good ground and did yield fruit that sprang up and increased. As I watched her belly take on a firm roundness, my joy and excitement had passed into a fixed intention.

The droning came to an end and I pulled myself back to the present.

'So,' I said, 'we need to agree the price, and then we can sign the contract. I believe the practice is to name an arbitrator in case of disagreement – though I hardly think that will be necessary.'

I leaned forward and poured another two cups of wine.

A look flashed between the lawyer and Marcella. Before anything could register in my mind, I could feel the sweat breaking out on my upper back. I sat up and looked properly at her in the fading light. She wasn't quite her normal self.

'I apologise if I have not made myself plain,' the lawyer took up again. 'Allow me to explain further. The provisional agreement was that you were buying the slave Gretel for the purpose of marrying her and acknowledging her child as your own. We have, however, received information that you are already married – to a barbarian woman in the Province of Britain, on whom you fathered a son before settling in Rome.'

For the second time that day, my mouth fell open. That Edwina had given birth to a son was more news than I'd been able to get out of Canterbury. My repeated letters to Bishop Lawrence had either gone unanswered or received evasive replies.

And married to Edwina? Well, if Ethelbert, that murderous royal shitbag, had confirmed my noble status and let me marry the girl, I'd never have had to leave Kent.

What was going on? I closed my eyes and commanded the winey clouds to disperse.

'The Lady Marcella must be aware', I said, 'that I am not married, in Britain or anywhere else. I am prepared to swear to that in any church she cares to name. She is misinformed.'

'I must insist', the lawyer replied, 'that My Lady has her information from an unimpeachable source. She cannot possibly consent to a sale that would enable fornication. In a word, the

24

contract is void, on the grounds of fundamental immorality in its subject matter. Such I am instructed to argue for my client in any legal proceedings.'

'That's right, young Alaric,' the old witch broke in. 'That Gretel is a right hot-arsed prick-teaser – if you'll pardon my Greek. You don't know that trash in her belly is yours. You just forget her and send for that nice girl you left behind in Britain. I'm told she's very well-born, even if a barbarian. And she must be fair pining for you after such a long time away. As for that tramp Gretel, I curse the day I let her bring you washing water.

'Tomorrow morning, first thing, I'm selling her to the brothel I shouldn't never have saved her from when she was brung to market from the Lombards.'

I ignored Marcella. I turned in my chair and spoke directly to the lawyer.

'You will inform your client, or at least the Lady Marcella,' I said coldly, 'that whatever information may have arrived from Britain is false. I am not, nor ever have been, married. I have negotiated in good faith for the sale of Gretel. It is my intention to marry her the moment I have freed her.

'One way or another, the agreed transfer will go ahead. It may be by friendly consent. It may be on the judgement of the Prefect. It may be following some other process. Until such time as that happens, the Lady Marcella will retain Gretel in her own household and will continue to allow her all the indulgences we agreed when her pregnancy was confirmed. Do I make myself clear?'

Marcella glanced away from me. She looked suddenly a good fifty years older than the eighty I'd always taken her for. The lawyer looked back at me, unimpressed.

'I understand the slave's child is due in October,' he said. 'You will be aware, I have no doubt, of the great length that legal proceedings can often reach. You will equally be aware that, unless the mother is freed at any time between conception and birth, the child will also be a slave. Even if subsequently freed, the child will suffer certain disabilities. This might not count much in the case of a girl. Boys, however—'

25

'I know the law perfectly well, if you please,' I snapped. And I did. If I couldn't be father to Edwina's child, I'd not pass up the opportunity Gretel had presented me. I would be a father, and my child would have everything a father could give. You can't give looks and intelligence: those come from Nature. But you can give education and wealth and status. No one this side of the grave would stop me from giving those.

I looked at the fresh tiling on the library floor and stood up. There was nothing more to discuss with these people. That much was plain. What further business I had lay elsewhere. With frigid politeness, I asked Marcella if she needed an escort back to her lodging house. The streets would soon be far too unsafe for the elderly slaves I imagined she'd brought with her.

'You're a good boy, Alaric,' she whispered once the lawyer had left the room ahead us. 'You know, by myself I'd never do nothing to hurt you—'

She broke off. Then: 'Oh, this wicked world surely can't be for much longer,' she sobbed gently. 'It must surely be the end of times when—'

She broke off again. Then: 'Oh, my poor husband the Senator. Why couldn't I be carried off with him?'

I was once more alone. I'd paced up and down in the library until no light came from overhead. I'd crossed over the courtyard to the main part of the house and walked around the rooms on the upper floor. Fresh paint and woodwork, restored mosaics and frescoes – things that until then had cheered me and filled me with confidence in the future – now seemed a kind of mockery. Of course, I'd bought the place with only myself in mind. But I'd soon got used to the idea of a growing household with me at the head of it. I'd shown Gretel where her quarters would be. I'd ordered furniture for the child and looked into the procedure of buying the right sort of wet nurse.

Back in the library, I shouted for Authari. 'Get me an opium pill,' I told him. 'I rather hope you've not been dipping down those as well. I have a meeting at the Lateran just as soon as the dawn

26

comes up. With time to get down there, I want you to wake me with enough hot water for a bath and my pink robe – the one with brown roses embroidered on the front. For what I'm about to do, I want to look my best.'

4

I was so angry as I stepped out into the square that I almost missed the flash of steel. But there's a difference between almost and not at all. Probably before even managing to nick my arm, he had my sword sticking six inches out of his back.

For a thief, he had the etiquette all wrong. It's at night, you see, that you kill and then grab. By daylight, you grab and run, and only pull out the knife if you can't get away. But that was his problem. He was the one on the pavement, gurgling out bloody froth as he sped into the final darkness. Though breathing hard and not altogether with it, I was still on my feet.

'Hey, you can't do that here!' It was one of the armed church-wardens, come up beside me. He pointed down at the now dead man, outrage in his voice. 'This is Church property.'

He was wrong. I was just outside the Lateran precinct. Here, it was a matter for the Prefect – if for anyone at all.

But I wasn't up for debate. And Authari had now lumbered up beside me.

'Fuck off, you!' he snarled. 'You leave my master alone – or else.'

'That will do, Authari,' I said weakly, putting a hand on his sword arm. I wanted no more trouble that morning. Inside the palace, it had been 'Aelric this' and 'Aelric that' from the Dispensator, who'd almost wet himself at his triumph. He'd been waiting with his – unsigned – letter of clarification for Marcella regarding my 'marriage' in Kent, and with his undertaking to act in my place regarding Gretel if I should be delayed past her time of delivery.

I didn't fancy another trip into that office. Not over a matter like this.

'But you're bleeding, Master,' said Authari.

I looked down at my forearm. So I was. That had been a savage little knife. It was the sort of weapon that had Murder written all over it. Luckily, the man had got me below the hem of my sleeve. You couldn't get new silk that year in Rome for love or money.

Authari pulled me across the square to the side not yet reached by the sun, and sat me on a stone bench. He called for wine and biscuits from one of the hawkers.

'I would have come sooner, Master,' he explained in a panicky tone. 'But those friends of his were all about me, jabbering something about His Holiness.'

He sat down heavily beside me and drank half the wine straight off. While that settled another of the fits of shakes that had made me leave him outside the Lateran, I followed his vague pointing. A hundred yards off, the churchwarden was still fussing over the bloody heap. He'd been joined by a couple of monks. Every so often, he was pointing across at me.

Over to their left, there was another crowd of those petitioners. Even as I looked, they melted into the smaller alleyways that led from the square.

Deep beneath the shock and the after-effects of what might have been a shade too much opium, I felt a faint stirring of alarm, and of what now was a creative anger. This wasn't a matter of thiefly etiquette. The man hadn't looked at all like a thief. And he'd been far too swarthy for a native: an African, perhaps, or a Sicilian?

I turned back to Authari, whose babble of explanations was now descending into his native Lombardic.

'I am entirely satisfied you did your best,' I said firmly, trying to shut him up. 'Indeed, you may have done me quite a favour. Had you been with me, they might have gone for me some other time and with more success. As it is, forewarned is forearmed.'

Unconvinced, Authari fell silent, his face still dark with shame and the fear of a slave who has slipped up in his duty. I leaned back against the still cool bricks of the wall behind me and gathered my thoughts.

'Tell me, Authari,' I said, sipping what he'd left me of the wine, 'do you know which side it was that grabbed you? And do put your sword away. The only trouble we might have now is from those monks over there.'

He gave me a look of rather vexing stupidity and replied that the men had been talking about His Holiness.

I sighed, but kept my temper. 'You do know', I prompted, 'there's a civil war in the Empire?'

He didn't.

'It doesn't normally affect us here,' I continued. 'Since your people turned up in Italy, the Emperor's Exarch doesn't control much more than Ravenna. Under His Holiness, Rome is effect-ively an independent city-state.

'Yes, a city-state,' I mused. 'After fifteen hundred years, Rome ends its experience of empire more of less where it began.'

But I pulled myself back to present matters. I didn't want to lose Authari.

'It's a revolt got up by the Exarch of Africa. And he's winning. Because of that, Emperor Phocas is piling on the pressure in Rome. He needs His Holiness to excommunicate Heraclius the father and Heraclius the son and Nicetas the nephew. That won't count for much in the East. But Africa is part of the West. A formal denunciation from Rome would cut the rebels off from their base.

'The problem is', I went on, summarising what I'd picked up on the Exchange, 'that the only thing Rome wants of Phocas as the price is something the Eastern Churches wouldn't allow. The Pope must be made "Universal Bishop". There must be an irrevocable statement that he stands above the other Four Patriarchs of the Universal Church. Constantinople and Antioch and Alexandria and Jerusalem must all bow down before Rome.

'That needs a sealed patent for advertising in the East, and shoving under the nose of every bishop and king in the West.

'There is a further problem. Even if the Eastern Churches could be bullied into assenting to such a patent, neither Pope nor Emperor trusts the other. Neither will make the first move. And it may now be too late. Heraclius, the son, or his cousin will soon show up outside Constantinople. Whoever gets there first will be Emperor himself before Christmas. That means all Rome needs do is wait, while extracting whatever concessions it can from both sides.

'That brings us to the petitioning mobs. Were the people who stopped you for or against the Emperor? I'd like to know who wants me dead.'

But I had lost him. I might as well have asked him about forward contracts on the price of tin for all the sense I could get out of him.

I dropped the matter. Had I been more with it, I'd have skipped the lecture and stuck to questioning. Even so, I might have all the information that I reasonably needed for what I now had in mind.

Looking back across the square, I could see that the body had now disappeared. It would never do for pilgrims to have that in their first view of the Lateran. In its place stood a huddle of clerical monks. Behind them, on the Lateran steps, stood the Dispensator himself. He had the sun in his eyes, and I wasn't sure if he could see me. But I could just make out the abstracted look on his face.

'Heresy in Spain?' I muttered – 'my arse!' Well before the close of business that day, I swore to myself, I'd have this out with His Excellency the sodding Dispensator. This time, I'd be in control of the exchanges.

For the moment, though, I had some urgent preliminary business.

'Authari,' I said in my firm, master's voice, 'go back home and get some rest. No more to drink this morning. I want you washed and looking respectable for when I send you to fetch the Lady Gretel for her inspection of those Cretan tablecloths.

'No,' I said still more firmly, 'I'll face no more trouble this morning. And it's probably for the best if you aren't with me where I now have to go.'

Sveta took me into the kitchen of the little house and poured me a cup of wine.

'But you're bleeding!' she said with a still more suspicious look at my forearm.

'Do forgive me,' I said as she called her woman for hot water, 'but I didn't notice.' I really should have gone home first for a bandage – that, or something with longer sleeves.

It was a surprisingly deep cut, and I winced as the slave woman massaged in the salted pork fat.

'I believe your husband is teaching?' I asked.

Ignoring my pleasant smile, Sveta pulled her eyes away from the trickle of blood on to the kitchen table and nodded.

'Martin will come as soon as he can end the lesson. I went to tell him as soon as I saw you at the door. But it is his best student – he's the natural son of the Lord Bishop Servilianus, you know.'

I didn't mind waiting. Servilianus was as influential as his bastard was thick. Martin needed more pupils like that if he was to keep up this go at being independent. I drained the cup with my good arm and held up the other so the slave could do a proper job with her bandage.

'So, Martin,' I asked with an attempt at cheerfulness, 'I take it you don't fancy Constantinople at the moment?'

He looked up from the letter of instruction. 'Not now. Not ever,' he said, his voice most emphatic for a man who'd just nearly shat himself. 'You know what happened to me when I lived there. Now there's a civil war about to reach the place, you can't imagine how it will be.

'Rather than go back to the City, I'd sooner be taken by the Lombards, and kept this time. I'd sooner go back to Ireland, passing through every village in your own land while speaking in Celtic. Either would be death. But the City would be death as well – death, and before that . . .'

I waited for him to finish. The baby began crying in an upstairs room. I felt a pang of envy as I heard Sveta go up the external staircase.

I waved at the letter of instruction. 'Well, I don't want to go there either,' I said. 'So you just save your complaints for the Dispensator. He's the one who says you know Constantinople. He's the one who says I need an assistant I can trust absolutely. He's the one we need to get round if we aren't to go anywhere at all.'

Martin smiled sadly. 'After all we've been through,' he asked, 'you still think you can negotiate with the Dispensator? You can no more talk your way out of these instructions than you can reason with the tides on Dover Beach.'

'There's every chance we can get out of this,' I said in a reassuring tone that was as much for me as for him. 'Either we can get out of it altogether, or we can get it put off till later in the year. At least we can go in better circumstances than seem presently intended.'

I pushed my cup towards him for a refill. Martin poured to the halfway mark. I took it back before he could reach for the water jug.

'I'm seeing His Excellency again this afternoon,' I said. 'I'll need you with me for support.'

Martin ignored me. 'I did pray', he said, self-pity now replacing alarm, 'that I might live to see my child grow up. But happiness was never my fate. "The Lord giveth and the Lord taketh away. Blessed be the Name of the Lord." '

He looked upwards – possibly for God, more likely worried that Sveta might be listening through the floorboards. There were degrees of martyrdom beyond even his present mood.

But this was getting us nowhere. I changed the subject.

'I bumped into your landlord as I came down the street,' I said, dropping my voice still further. 'I took the liberty of settling your rent arrears. Next time you can't pay the wretch, do come and tell me. I think the two men with him were baliliffs.'

Martin looked up again. There was a heavy tramp on the upper floor, and the muted sound of a baby being comforted.

'Thank you, Aelric,' he said, a burden plainly coming off his mind. 'I'll tell Sveta when you've gone. She does respect you greatly. And she's as grateful as I am for all you've done already to help. Sadly, I can't persuade her to trust you. She says you only ever get me into trouble. She thinks – she thinks that you might be an atheist . . .'

'Think it a token of the great affection I bear you and your family,' I said quickly. No fool was Sveta. She deserved better than Martin.

I pushed the cup forward again. Martin looked around.

'You came alone?' he asked. 'Does that mean . . .?'

'Does it mean', I answered, quoting his own words back at him, 'that I've got rid of that "drink-sodden oaf" I won at dice? No.' I laughed. 'Authari is presently at home opening boxes. He remains my best and most trusted slave. If we must go to Constantinople, he goes too. This time, be assured, he'll be reminded of your station. Even you'd not deny, though, he can be very handy with a meat cleaver.'

I waited for the recollection of our escape from King Agilulf's torture garden to come fully back into his mind. For my current purpose, I needed Martin the terror-prone clerk: all this fatalism was no use to me at all. I looked again at the empty cup. Martin filled it to the brim.

I returned to the matter in hand. 'Look, Martin,' I said, 'I'm not asking for much this time. All I need is for you to stand for one meeting without your knees giving way while I talk our way out of this lunatic mission. Can I count on you?'

From the scared look now coming into his eyes, we might just about be in business.

'We need to make His Excellency aware', I said, 'that whatever debts we once variously owed him were discharged in full back in Pavia. I don't imagine he's asking for a repeat of Pavia – no snooping around this time, no waiting on moonless nights to pass information about warlike intentions. But I don't like this stuff about consulting libraries there. It smells like a priest's armpit.

'Have another look at these instructions. How much work do you really think they involve? Three days? Five?'

As he unrolled it again and looked down the sheet of tiny writing, I took up a handful of dried onion seeds and began crunching on them.

Martin looked up at length, confusion on his face. 'I'll swear most works on his list are here in Rome,' he said. 'This one, I know for a fact, is in the Papal Library. This one was condemned a hundred years ago. It may still exist in some private collection, but can't be anywhere on view in Constantinople. As for this one, Paul

34

of Halicarnassus never wrote on the Council of Nicaea. The work mentioned is mistitled, but is a book of sermons against the Aphthardocetic heresy – that's the one', he explained, noting my questioning look, 'about the incorruptibility of Christ's physical body after death.'

'So,' I asked, 'in your opinion, everything in these instructions can be done right here in Rome?'

'Yes,' he said. 'Here in Rome. At worst, there might be a trip to Ravenna.'

I'd already guessed as much. But Martin was the expert in this. The Dispensator could bully till he was black in the face. He could put whatever gloss took his fancy on why someone employed by the Emperor or by Heraclius or by someone else who didn't give a toss about heresy in Spain had wanted me dead here in Rome. But I knew he was no expert on the scholarship of heresy.

Yes – I'd have the man by both his tits.

'Then it's agreed', I said, 'we go to the Dispensator just before dinner-time and tell him to go jump. And when we celebrate in my house afterwards, we shall indeed be what he calls "an harmonious and lucky team"!'

And that did seem to be it. There'd be no trip to the East. The nearest I'd come to the civil war would be betting on whether Heraclius the son or Nicetas the nephew would race each other fairly to Constantinople, or if they'd turn on each other before either could get there.

I rolled the letter back into its case. Feeling peckish again, I was thinking how most delicately to ask if Martin had been able to afford to buy bread – the free-distribution stuff was fit only for pigs.

Just as I was about to speak, the monk who'd accosted me the day before was shown into the kitchen.

'I bring verbal orders from the Dispensator himself,' he said in a dramatic whisper that could probably have woken the now-sleeping child upstairs. 'They supplement or replace your written letter of instruction. Listen carefully, as I am required to give you these orders once only and then to forget them.'

35

He looked round to make sure no one else was listening, and recited:

'The citizens Alaric and Martin are hereby requested and required to proceed at once to Constantinople, there to receive such further instructions as may be transmitted from Rome. Each will be collected from his home tonight at the midnight hour and be conveyed thence to the river under armed guard and in a covered chair. The citizen Alaric will be conveyed home now by the same means. Each may take whatever he has time to pack. Anything he cannot pack shall be listed for His Excellency the Dispensator to have sent on by faster intercepting ship.

'Neither shall tell anyone that he is leaving Rome until he is beyond the city walls, when free communication may be re-established for all purposes. The citizen Alaric is exempted from this requirement so far as concerns his banker, the Jew Solomon ben Baruch, who has already been instructed to attend on the citizen Alaric at his house.

'The Lady Marcella has received separate instructions regarding the safe-keeping of her slave Gretel. The wife and household of the citizen Martin shall be conveyed at the same time and by the same means from his house to the fortified house of the Sisters of St Eugenia, there to remain as guests until such time as His Excellency the Lord Dispensator shall think appropriate.

'The citizen Alaric shall bear the whole cost of the stay in Constantinople and such other costs as may attend his stay. He shall, on his return to Rome, render an account of these to His Excellency the Lord Dispensator, who may see fit to order reasonable reimbursement.'

The monk finished his recitation in a blaze of self-congratulation. He sat down and fanned his shining face. He drank deep from the wine jug and wiped his lips after an appreciative smack. He pretended to ignore the chaos of screams and recriminations that had broken out around him.

Sveta had caught enough of the message to send her into a vicious frenzy. She'd lost command of her Latin, and I couldn't follow the rapid Slavonic of her nagging. But the repeated hissing of my name, and the nasty looks she threw me, told me it was best to sit still. No point trying to explain she'd misapprehended me again.

The slave woman had caught none of the message, but assumed it was a notice of eviction. She was beating her head against the kitchen wall, screaming to be struck dead for the shame of it all.

His voice muffled by his hands, Martin was calling out again and again: 'God forgive me my sins! God have mercy on my soul!'

Overhead and unregarded, the baby wailed piteously.

'I am not at liberty', the monk shouted happily above the noise, 'to take any question regarding your instructions. In any event, I am already forgetting them.' He took another long swig.

'If you don't wipe that fucking smirk off your face', I shouted back, 'I'll give you something you won't forget. Now pass me that jug.'

I fought to suppress the horror bubbling up within me. For all I sneered at Martin, he seemed right enough this time. Perhaps I had just heard a death sentence. Only a day earlier, I'd been rejoicing at the turn my life had taken. Now, I was caught like a rabbit in a snare.

I hadn't just been had by the Dispensator. I'd been really had.

I looked out through the now-open door to the street where I could already see my covered chair and a couple of armed enforcers standing by.

'Fuck the Church!' I muttered into the jug. 'And fuck the fucking Dispensator!'

And that's how I came to be standing on the Senatorial Dock a month or so later, with Martin for company, with a fat eunuch to bid me welcome, and with a whole row of stinking corpses swinging to and fro behind him.

So, let us now unfreeze everyone and thank them for their patience, and get on with the story.

5

'You will, of course, be staying in the residence of His Excellency the Permanent Legate,' Theophanes said as my chair drew level with his. After a blockage caused by some building works, the road had widened again to allow any amount of traffic side by side.

'You will find the Legation eminently suited to your station in the City. Besides, it is very close by the Patriarchal Library attached to the Great Church, and fairly close to the University. It would be a poor use of your valuable time to have to cross the City unattended every time you wanted to go about your duties.'

We reached a main junction, and he turned to nodding and smiling at other persons of quality as they were carried by. I saw that few people in Constantinople went about on horseback or in wheeled carriages. Most were in open chairs like our own, each carried by four strong slaves who sweated in the sun. Some rode in closed chairs. I took these to be women of quality.

While Theophanes exchanged his ritualised greetings, I turned my own attention to the sights of Constantinople.

When Constantine rebuilt the City, he tried to make it so far as possible a copy of Rome. His Senate House, for example, was a direct copy of the one in Rome. Indeed, his Covered Market exactly copied the jumble of styles that centuries of extension had given the one in Rome.

Now, Rome was fallen on evil days, but Constantinople had come through unharmed. Whether in shadow or still catching the beams of the afternoon sun, the painted stucco clearly marked one building from its neighbours. From the homes and businesses of the mercantile and professional classes to the garrets of the poor, the buildings rose in careful gradations from ground to topmost floors. Every dozen yards or so, the torch brackets were set up to light the streets when the sun had gone down. Smoothly paved, with drainage points unblocked, the streets were spotlessly clean – swept and washed several times a day. Carried by aqueduct or in underground pipes, water splashed from fountain after fountain, and in bronze pipes running down the walls carried waste from the larger buildings.

Looking up the hill to the approaching city centre, I could see the vast, glittering domes and arches of an unsacked capital. Around me, the bronze and marble and even gold statues looked down securely from their unbroken plinths. Some of these were of emperors and officials going back to the time of the Great Constantine. Others, I could see from their perfect beauty, had been carried there from the temples and cities of ancient times.

But I'm describing Constantinople by comparing it with Rome. And if you haven't been in a settlement larger than Canterbury or perhaps London, these are just vague words. Try then to imagine a city so vast, you can't see open countryside at the end of any of the streets: the only signs of Nature are cultivated trees and cascades of flowers falling from the window-boxes of the great houses. Try to imagine an endless succession of broad avenues connecting squares, each one as big as the centre of Canterbury and filled with public buildings and palaces every one as big as the new great church in Canterbury.

Try to imagine smaller streets leading off from the greater, all paved with stone or brick, or with regular flights of steps to join different levels, these little streets themselves all lined by houses so tall they often stop the sun from falling on the ground. Try to imagine little alleys leading off these smaller streets, connecting the whole like the strands of a web, so that you can wander for an entire day and not see all of it, let alone conceive its plan.

Try then to imagine all those people – some dressed finer than any bishop, some in rags that a churl would despise. And try to imagine all these in a continual bustle of activity.

Think of just of one incident I recall from that first afternoon. A slave was painting one of the houses in a main street. He hung by one arm from the sill of a high window, a brush in his free hand. Another slave leaned out of the window, paint-pot in hand. Others stood below, arranging a net in case the painter should fall. Around them the pedestrians flowed like water about a rock in a fast stream.

Imagine this, and you have Constantinople, the greatest city in the world.

Theophanes ignored everyone on foot as we passed through the crowds. He made sure, though, to greet anyone who passed in a chair. Sometimes he would introduce me with a flattering reference to my quality that seemed always to magnify his own importance. With a grave nod of his bearded and carefully groomed head, the stranger would acknowledge my presence and utter some exactly worded greeting. More often, I'd be ignored throughout an interminable exchange of courtesies.

In Rome, at this time of year, everyone who could afford to get out would have escaped to the better air of the country – that is, assuming the Lombards weren't on the prowl. In Constantinople, I soon gathered, everyone who hadn't actually run off to join Heraclius found it advisable to show loyalty by staying put, regardless of the heat.

On a blank wall by one of the road junctions, someone had written a long graffito in a language I couldn't then recognise, but that I now know was Coptic – Greek letters are used to express Egyptian sounds. I saw a recognisable version of the name *Heraclius* and I could make out the sign of the Cross. Some official-looking slaves were hard at work scrubbing it off.

I felt Martin plucking at my sleeve. I looked down at him as he padded along beside us.

'If you look over to your right in the square coming up, sir,' he said softly, 'you'll see the High Courts.'

Faced with many-coloured marble, topped by two giant symmetrical domes, each itself topped by a golden cross, the court building took up an entire side of the square. The Latin inscription above its central portico recorded its rebuilding by the Emperor Theodosius, the son of Arcadius. Above this, in a sheltered recess, was a giant mosaic of Christ sat in judgement. On each side of him,

40

in Latin and in Greek translation, was the legal maxim: *Fiat Iustitia Ruat Coelum* – 'Let Justice be Done, though the Heavens Fall'.

Almost like ants around a cottage door, the litigants and their slaves ran up and down the steps to the great building. The chairs of the great and the carts of the humble crowded the square, awaiting their owners. The dense mass of stalls clustered in the centre around a column topped by a golden statue – I think of Justinian – Martin told me, were selling legal forms and services to those unable to afford proper representation.

'Is that where the bankruptcy case was decided against your father?' I thought to ask. It would have been a redundant question. His face already answered. What was it like, I wondered, to be back here after such personal catastrophe?

The Papal Legation was housed in a small but imposing building on the far side of the square containing the Great Church. In its essentials an old palace, arranged around a set of gardens, it must have dated back to the early years of the City. At some point, its central front portico had been graced with an incongruously modern dome of a translucent green and blue, topping an entrance hall as large as a middling church.

It was here, bathed in the eerie light from the dome, that we were greeted by some decidedly secondary officials. One of these stood forward.

'I am Demetrius,' he said, 'Acting Head of the Legatorial Secretariat. I report directly to His Excellency.'

He went on to explain in a Latin so slipshod he might have been a tradesman that the Permanent Legate remained indisposed.

I looked at him. A small man in late middle age, with the movements of a startled bird and a face that had somehow escaped any touch of the sun, this official stood out from his colleagues partly on account of his greater age, and partly because, while their beards had the lush fullness of the Greeks, his own was either kept short or of recent growth.

It was evident he wasn't a Latin. Nor did he sound Greek. His Excellency doubtless would send for me when he was less indisposed, he added. In the meantime, I should settle into the little room he'd found for me beside the kitchens and rest myself from a journey that must have rivalled that of Ulysses himself from Troy. As the Legation slaves had other duties, it was my good fortune to have brought enough of my own to attend to my ordinary needs. They could be accommodated in the corridor outside my room.

I glanced at Theophanes. Was that a look of sour impatience? Hard to tell. It was there for a moment, then he was all charming smiles again.

'Demetrius is surely mistaken,' he said. 'I am sure that His Excellency the Permanent Legate had in mind for young Alaric and his party to be given the distinguished visitors' suite on the upper floors.'

Demetrius himself pulled a face that wasn't so fleeting. But it was obvious that no one argued with His Magnificence the Great Theophanes. He bowed and threw a look at one of the other officials, who promptly vanished.

'Most sadly, the work of the Great Augustus calls me away,' said Theophanes with a brief glance at Demetrius. He would leave me for now, he added, but would send for me after lunch the following day to discuss my schedule and attend to the necessary paperwork for my stay.

After more embracing and protestations of mutual regard, he was off with his little army, leaving us alone with the Legation officials. The hall seemed to grow duller by his leaving it. The officials there remained awed, though, and did their best to improvise a reception that anyone could have seen was not on their list of instructions.

42

6

I never did find out what Demetrius had intended for me. The suite Theophanes had ordered him to give me was a self-contained unit within the Legation. Branching off to the left from the back of the entrance hall, and covering two floors, it had its own access from the hall. It might have been an apartment in a residential block.

'Good for defence,' Authari whispered, for the moment forgetting he was no longer at the head of a Lombard raiding party. 'I'll guess the main building could hold off an army for days.'

I silenced him with a frown, and followed Demetrius up the stairs.

On the upper floor, there were about fifteen living and business rooms, some interconnected. All were approached by a corridor lit during the day by glass bricks set into the roof above. There could be no windows in the corridor, as they'd have looked out into the main square, and compromised the security of the Legation.

The doors that led off the other side into the rooms of my suite were all of solid wood with locks that turned from both sides. The rooms looked inward over the central gardens. The ground floor covered the same area, but the connecting corridor had no natural light except when the doors were open to the rooms leading off it. These were to be the quarters for my own slaves, and had a little kitchen that made me independent of the main household.

Right at the end of the corridor was a bathhouse and furnace that would be for my use.

Outside the main reception room and my own bedroom next door was a balcony. A bronze staircase led down from this to one of the central gardens, where trees and a fountain promised relief from the blazing summer heat. Looking out from the window of my office, I saw five monks shuffling about in a garden beyond this with watering cans and various garden implements.

Thinking back to Authari's comment, I wondered if this might be a weak point for defence. I put the thought from my mind. This was Constantinople, not Rome. On the whole journey up from the dockside, I hadn't seen a single fight, let alone a killing.

The upper rooms were placed to catch the morning sun, but had ceilings high enough to make the afternoons bearable. They were furnished with a taste and luxury that any self-respecting priest would have denounced as a mortal sin. But although it was Church property, the Legation was the place from where the Pope spoke through his representatives to the Emperor himself, and where, from time to time, the Emperor and the greater dignitaries would have to be entertained. For reasons of obvious prestige, its splendour could not fall below a certain level.

As we entered the suite, a few slaves and even officials were running frantically about with dusters and aired linen. Demetrius fawned around me, trying to divert my attention from the obvious change of accommodation.

'We trust the young citizen will not be overcome by the splendour of these rooms,' he said in his poor Latin. 'We is told that Old Rome has not a single working bath in these last days of the world. Here, the young citizen has his own all for himself.'

I sniffed, and asked to see the toilet. Very important things are toilets. Forget beds and chairs, which can always be found at short notice. The toilets tell you exactly how civilised a house is, and your own position within it. I had to admit these ones did me proud. The fittings were of marble with four seats of polished ebony. A channel ran under the seats, for water to carry away the waste. Another channel ran in front to give continual water for the wiping sponges that were set on sticks of elegant design.

The glazed tiles that covered the floor and the lower walls were of a variegated blue. The plaster that ran above these was a dark and luxurious red. There had once been a fresco on the wall opposite the window, but this was now painted over in the same red, and I was unable to see what images or designs it had once had. The only evidence for it was a few patches of colour that had leached through the red.

Demetrius had to grope about to find the handle that turned on the water. With a gurgle that sounded like a belch from the depths of the Legation building, and then a hiss that died to a gentle splashing, the water burst up in a slightly higher point of the latrine. At once, as the water flowed through its appointed channels, the room came to life. The little tiles of the channels turned from dull to various shades of sparkling blue. The glazed tiles of the lower walls bounced back the shimmering light thrown up from them.

Come the winter months, ducts set beneath the floor would carry heated air from a central boiler to keep the latrine warm. For the moment, the gentle but continuous trickling of the water would keep it cool on the hottest days. This was a room appointed both for practical use and for mental reflection. I felt I'd be spending a fair bit of time in here.

I smiled inwardly as I realised Demetrius had pulled a muscle by reaching about for the lever, and his hands were covered with dust. He stood facing me, a suppressed wince on his face and evidently resisting the urge to hop from one foot to the other in agitation. So I sent him off with orders that Martin's bed should also have clean linen and that the slave quarters should be provided with all that fitted my status as a halfway guest of the Emperor.

Walking backwards, he bowed out of my presence. I had a most gratifying sight of the confusion on his face as he bumped into Authari. Our kitchen cupboards might be bare. It was plain, though, Authari had found the wine store.

Back upstairs, while Martin supervised the unpacking and disposal of our baggage, I went into the main office and sat at a great ebony desk inlaid with gold and ivory. On this, a leather bag marked for my attention contained letters from Rome. Some were impressively recent. The roads hadn't been so impassable after all. At least the post was now getting through again.

There was something about the Cornish tin business. As it was in code, it would be interesting. But it could wait. I rummaged in the bag and pulled out a thick letter from the Dispensator. I went over by the window for a better look at the microscopic writing.

Apparently, the Bishop of Ravenna had found a whole nest of heresy under his own nose. His most senior deacons were dissenting from the true position on the Trinity anciently settled at the Council of Chalcedon. They accepted that there was but one Person in Christ, but further inferred that there was but one Will and one Operation – thereby denying the true position, that there were two Natures, Divine and Human, which were hypostatically united in Christ, not mingled . . .

My eyes glazed over as I read sentence after sentence of denunciation of this most horrid innovation. My job, I gathered, was to procure a formal refutation of all this in Greek – the longer the better. It would be the penance of the offending deacons, who knew only Latin, somehow to understand this and then to memorise it by heart, so they could preach against their heresy in every church in Ravenna.

As I looked down from the window, one of the monkish gardeners stared up at me from the main central courtyard, an oddly intelligent look on his face.

Back at my desk, I called for a jug of iced wine, and reached for another letter. This was from Gretel. The secretary who'd taken her dictation had faithfully copied her style of speech. She prattled on about her morning sickness and her longing to see me again, and her profound gratitude for all I was doing on her behalf. She was no longer confined to the house, though had no cause to go out. She emphasised that Marcella was now treating her as one of the guests.

In Rome, I'd always found Gretel's conversation something to be endured. Now, I felt tears coming to my eyes as I read about Marcella's vexation at the theft of linen by one of her less salubrious lodgers.

There were other letters – from an agent who was handling the sale of some land on the Aventine Hill, and reporting movements in prices that I could relay to traders here in Constantinople. There was another, dated last Easter from Canterbury, thanking me for a complete Virgil I'd sent over from Rome and asking for another *City of God*, the one I'd sent previously having been spoiled by the sea voyage.

I'd deal with all these in due course. The light was beginning to fade, and I didn't feel up to writing or dictating late into the evening. For the moment, I kept going back to the letter from Gretel. I kissed the mark she'd written at the foot of the papyrus sheet, telling myself I'd done right to announce marriage to her rather than concubinage.

Martin knocked and entered. The baggage we'd managed to bring with us was now arranged, he said, but there was no sign of our main luggage from Rome. Also, the lack of any food was now pressing. Should he try to rouse the Legation slaves? Or should he send out for a takeaway? Our own slaves were famished.

Now that I thought about it, so was I.

'Do arrange for a takeaway,' I said. 'I'll eat here alone. Do also try to get some better wine than this stuff. It smells of pine needles. Something red and rich, if you can get it.'

I reached across the desk. 'Here's a letter for you,' I added. 'I imagine it's from Sveta. Do send her my greetings in your reply.'

Martin's face paled as he looked at the scrawled writing on the outside.

'Do cheer up,' I said with an attempt at jollity. 'She can't go at you with a knife at this distance!'

Outside the room, I heard Martin try again at giving orders to Authari. It was only a matter of time before he made a right fool of himself. I took up the jug and went on to the balcony. For what seemed an age, I stood and watched the flowers turn pale against the gloom that gathered round them.

7

'Thank you, but I have washed already,' said Martin, peering dubiously into the water.

It was late the next morning, and a bath and quite a passable wank had done for my hangover.

'Besides,' he added, 'I thought you said there was a steam room and all.'

'Well, it's all bleedin' broke, innit?' Authari rasped at him from the other side of the lead tub he'd eventually managed to find enough hot water to fill. You could have opened a wine shop with the fumes from what else he'd managed to find. Another moment, and he'd forget who was slave and who freedman.

'Indeed,' I said, rising hastily from the water. 'Authari assures me that any attempt to light the furnace would cause an explosion. This will be a temporary arrangement. I have no doubt His Excellency will advise on how to proceed with engineers.'

Once he'd patted me dry, I sent Authari to sit on the other side of the bathhouse door.

'Oh, come on, Martin,' I urged, now we were alone. 'Those streets must be baking.'

I looked away as he undressed. It was hardly his fault he'd once been a slave. But it was his business if he didn't care to show off the white scars on his back.

'I didn't think to go far from the Legation,' he said, easing himself into the now cool water. 'Since we haven't any papers yet, I thought it was best to keep to the market before the Great Church. I managed to get nearly everything on your list.'

I sat down beside him and asked what he'd found out from the stallholders. As I pumiced at my legs, he spoke in a whispered and

48

very slow Celtic I could just understand from my days among the bandits on the Wessex borders.

He hadn't that much to say. No one in the streets had been inclined to pour out his innermost thoughts to strangers – not at a time like this. The mood out there, he said, was ugly beyond anything he'd ever known. All business was winding down, and the loss of Egypt to Heraclius meant questions over the free distribution of bread to the poor.

'Have you managed to pick up any information about our Most Noble Host?' I asked, stretching my legs.

Martin looked away from me and over to some mosaics of life in an Eastern city. He reached into the water to scrub his feet.

'I bumped into one of those officials as I came back into the Legation.'

'You mean Demetrius?' I asked.

'No,' said Martin. 'That's the Armenian – or so I think he must be. The one I met is called Antony. He at least is a Greek, though from Nicaea across the Straits. I believe he's some kind of lawyer. Even so, he was quite friendly.

'He told me that he and the entire household, slaves and all, were brought in last month after the regulars were sent off to Ephesus. The only one of the regulars the Permanent Legate kept on was Demetrius, and Demetrius is the only one he'll see. Absolutely everything goes through Demetrius.'

Martin swallowed and shifted to wipe some splashed water off his face. 'His Excellency, I am told, takes offence at the alleged need for an unordained barbarian too young for a beard to come all the way from Rome for a mission he believes himself quite capable of doing by himself.

'Besides, all correct procedure has been set aside in this case. The Dispensator has sent us over here without consulting with the Permanent Legate. The only formal notification, apparently, was a letter sent through the Master of the Offices.'

I stared at Martin. There was no point in trying to look surprised. The Dispensator never made mistakes. I doubted if he broke wind without a stratagem.

49

'The further instructions I've had from Rome', I said flatly, 'will keep us here a month at least. Whatever point we could have made about the Spanish stuff is now redundant.'

Martin's face sagged as I explained about the heresy in Ravenna. He looked down again at the water. Then, in a slow voice:

'My letter from home you gave me last night – the seal was lifted and replaced. There were scorch marks on the back. Had all your stuff been read and checked for secret writing?'

'Yes,' I said. We sat a while in silence.

'Tell me about the old eunuch,' I said. 'Who is Theophanes?' I spoke more to break the silence. I didn't want Martin to think I had no control at all over our circumstances.

He wiped what little remained of his fringe from his eyes and leaned forward, dropping his voice even lower.

'Since he's with the Master of the Offices, he may be head of the security services. For people of his rank, though, formal status is only a matter of convenience. If he doesn't report directly to the Emperor, I'll be surprised.'

Martin's voice took on a quoting tone: 'The only settled passions in the eunuch heart are avarice and revenge.' He paused, then in a more natural tone: 'Whatever he wants, we give him. But we don't fall for any of his charming ways.'

We fell silent again. Once dressed, I'd go through the motions of paying my respects to the Permanent Legate.

'All right,' I said at last. There was no point in pretending. 'It's Pavia all over again. And I suppose it's my fault, at least indirectly, for getting you here.'

'Forget Pavia!' said Martin with a failed attempt at lightness. 'We had clear instructions for that. This is wholly different. Your Spanish instructions were an obvious ruse. The Ravenna business came up after we'd left. We've been sent here for reasons unspecified. We are now stuck here as pieces in a diplomatic game played far above our heads. His Excellency has withdrawn from all official business so long as we remain in the city. The Emperor's messengers call every other day. They go back unreceived.'

'Then, I suppose we just wait on events,' I said. 'What the Dispensator actually wants of us will no doubt be revealed in time. For the moment, we carry on as if we hadn't noticed anything odd – and look around for means of a quick getaway if things turn horrid.'

'You can forget thoughts of escape,' Martin replied with flat bitterness. 'Getting back from Pavia to Papal territory was nothing compared with this. You can't get across the city without the right stamp on your permit – let alone get out of it. And you can bet that, long after there's no bread in the shops, the old eunuch and his police will be grinding away like a watermill.

'I don't like this place,' he whispered, now in Latin. 'I never asked to be sent back here. I know my duties, but I shan't rest easy until we see Naples again – if we see Naples again. Let us praise God that our families are safe.'

8

The chair that collected me put us down inside the main hall of the Ministry building. This was a squat, overblown cavern of a place, faced inside and out with carved granite and white limestone. Hundreds of offices on floor after floor faced inwards to that main hall. Except on the higher floors – and then above eye-level – I don't think there were any windows that faced outwards. Business was transacted there in a constant glow of lamps. The offices were places of unending gloom.

Light streamed down into the hall from a circle of windows set into the base of the dome. The floor was covered in a giant mosaic showing the sufferings of the damned in a Hell that seemed to owe more to the Old Faith than to anything in the teachings of Holy Mother Church.

Clerks hurried about bearing thick files. Some of them stood in corners in whispered consultations with men dressed in black. These were big, powerful men, with obvious body armour under the cloaks that covered them from head to foot. They moved with confident swaggers as they tapped at the sheets of papyrus offered them by the clerks.

A couple of the big men who stood together looked over at me and opened a conversation with one of the clerks that I was sure must relate to me.

Once he'd finished helping me from the chair, Martin stood quiet and very still beside me. His body almost radiated fear and depression.

There had been a change of plan. We were now invited to lunch with Theophanes. He himself had been waiting for us with only one clerical assistant for company. This was the man I'd seen yesterday, though I'd given him no attention. A little man with dark eyes and the hooked nose of the East, he looked like a younger, slimmer, unmutilated version of Theophanes. He spoke only in reply to his master, and then in a rapid and very correct Greek.

After another elaborate display of courtesy, and theatrical flourishes that nearly floored me with the wafts of rose and sandalwood perfume they sent in my direction, Theophanes led the way on foot to a restaurant in the square outside the Ministry.

On the way in, I hadn't noticed the little crowd gathered outside. All women and the elderly, they stood silently in the scorching glare of the sun. Some held up placards with names written on them. We attracted a few odd looks from these people, but most turned their faces away, refusing to acknowledge the grave but slightly mocking greeting Theophanes went out of his way to give them. They in turn were ignored by those who passed around them.

'They are the relatives of certain persons the Great Augustus has been compelled to regard as traitors,' Theophanes said, answering my unasked question. 'Their own evident age and poverty remove them from suspicion of wrongdoing. And the presence among them of several monks dissuades us from enforcing the laws against riotous assembly.'

I looked away from the gathering. Just across the road from the Ministry, on a patch of watered and neatly tended grass, was a small statue of the official who, back in the days when the Emperor Julian had tried to restore the Old Faith, had shut down the Ministry. He'd turned the clerks into the street and started burning their files.

Then Julian had been killed on his Persian campaign, and the next Emperor, Jovian, had re-established the Ministry. The official had apparently committed suicide while awaiting arrest and questioning. But his statue remained, though with much of the inscription on its base chiselled out.

Around the neck of this statue, someone had managed to tie a wooden placard. There were public slaves fussing about with ladders and knives to remove the thing. It was too far away to read the words. No one else was stopping to read them. Theophanes gave the placard a brief glance as we passed by, and added a mild comment about the need for greater vigilance in these days of tribulation.

Once in the restaurant, we were shown directly into a private room on the upper floor. Slaves there bowed silently to us, and waited on us with a deft and practised ease. It was a very decent lunch – fresh bread, light fish and uncooked vegetables, and a couple of pleasant wines.

'I have taken the liberty of drawing up your permit myself,' Theophanes said, putting down his goblet of crushed ice and fruit juice. He beckoned to his assistant, who came forward with a folded sheet of parchment. It bore a large seal. With it was a gold medallion that would save me the trouble of carrying the document about with me.

'As befits one of your status, it is an open permit with no restrictions, so long as you keep within the safely of the walls. I have decided that, as you may wish to visit an unknown number of libraries and other places of scholarly interest, there is no point in placing any limits on your movement within the City. You will doubtless find the streets of Constantinople far safer than those of Rome. Even so, I advise you to take reasonable care if you choose to go out at night. You should at least inform the doorman at the Legation of your probable movements. I will speak with him myself. I think you will find him a useful point of contact in my absence.'

'I have yet to meet the Permanent Legate,' I said, 'but I'm sure he will wish to thank you for your invaluable kindness in these matters.'

Theophanes looked at me. His face creased in a benevolent smile, his eyes seemed to look straight inside me. 'If His Excellency should decide to call you to his office,' he said, 'you will be in my debt for passing on my best wishes and my reminder that we have much routine business to transact.'

He changed the subject, asking me about England. He knew the Great Constantine had been declared Emperor there, back in the days before my people had gone in and smashed everything up. Since then, it had dropped out of the literature. The best information he'd been able to find was of a place without sunshine and inhabited by black dwarves and Germanic barbarians.

Could that be true? he asked in a voice that sounded just a little naïve.

'Your Magnificence will surely—'

'Do please call me Theophanes,' he broke in with a confidential smile. 'I would not have one of my dearest friends stand on ceremony in private.'

'Then Theophanes,' I took up, 'you will surely know that England is divided into a number of kingdoms, all with shifting frontiers. My own part, Kent, is presently blessed with King Ethelbert, who is a firm convert to the Faith of our Lord Jesus Christ. He rejoices in the friendship of the Church mission to his realm, and is untinged by the faintest trace of heresy.'

And untinged, I thought to myself, by the faintest tinge of anything else beyond a taste for other men's wives and generally for getting his own way. My strongest memory was of a drunken savage, leering up at me with a gelding knife in hand. It was only because dear old Maximin had turned up at the last moment that I had been packed off to Rome.

Doubtless, he found Bishop Lawrence and the other missionaries useful when it came to lording it over the other kings. Without that – and without Queen Berthe to nag him into church come Sunday – he'd have had the whole mission stuffed into the first ships out of Richborough.

But I continued with the sanitised version of the man's doings in Kent. Theophanes prodded me along with short supplementals that showed a far greater knowledge than he was willing to admit.

'Of course,' he said at length, 'we have never officially accepted the loss of the Western Provinces. With the extinction of the Imperial line in the West, sovereignty devolved in full upon our own Emperor in Constantinople. Whenever possible – as, most importantly, in the time of the Great Justinian – we have been eager to restore Imperial rule in the West. Our recent embarrassments in

55

Italy do not affect the solidity of the restored Empire in Africa. You will find this rebellion by the African Exarch a trifling matter set against what has been achieved there.

'We have plans to extend our rule from southern Spain. That the barbarian King who rules much of that Province has converted out of heresy will not prolong his sway over the many multitudes of the orthodox who sigh for their rightful allegiance.'

'So you're thinking of a reconquest of Britain?' I asked, trying to keep the derision from my voice. I'd have thought the Slavs running wild below the Danube, and the Persians marching in from the east, would have been more important items on the Imperial agenda.

'I am not sure if the present correlation of forces would permit a reconquest,' Theophanes said smoothly.

Too right there! I thought. My people took by the sword, and will hold by the sword. Given a choice between Ethelbert and a swarm of Greekling tax gatherers, even I'd go back and fight.

But Theophanes continued. It was as if he'd read my thoughts.

'A military intervention so far into the West would not be convenient at present,' he said. 'But it is most edifying to learn about the progress of civilisation in regions we had almost given up for lost. Do tell me, though,' he asked lightly, 'would it be fair to say that your King Ethelbert was a friend more of His Holiness in Rome than of the Lord Exarch in Ravenna?'

'If Ethelbert has even heard of Smaragdus, I'll be surprised,' I said emphatically. 'Given the present chaos among the Franks, and the state of the roads passing through their territories, a journey from Rome to Canterbury is at least three months. Missionaries can do it easily enough. To put the sort of pressure on Ethelbert you can put on the Goths in Spain would take another Julius Caesar, let alone another Justinian.'

Theophanes smiled. He now turned to Martin, with questions about the political and theological position of the Celts. Was there any chance their own Church would accept communion with Rome *via* Canterbury? Or was the national hatred between them and the English too great to allow of reconciliation?

Martin gave closed and cautious answers to the questions. He said he'd left Ireland when he was ten and hadn't been back since.

I couldn't see why he should so want to avoid discussions of Ireland. The place was of no importance to anyone. I just assumed it was that tooth troubling him again. He'd been sucking it and wincing ever since Corinth. I'd have a dentist to him once I could get my own bearings in the City.

Theophanes gave up on the questioning – but not without exacting his own price.

'I have no doubt', he said to Martin with a sympathetic smile, 'you will find Constantinople a more friendly place than you did when last here with your father.'

He stopped a moment to relish the sudden strain on Martin's face. 'You may not be aware', he added, 'that the Professor of Rhetoric Anthemius is no more.'

He smiled gently as Martin's face changed colour. 'It was found last month', he continued, 'that the Illustrious Professor way paying too little attention to his ancient books, and was circulating material that appeared to touch on criticisms of the Great and Ever Victorious Augustus. His *Sample Oration of Plato to Dionysius* was the seal of his doom. He was closed into a bread oven beside the University with a fire stoked very slow. His cries, I am told,' Theophanes added, 'were as musical as his declamations.

'The teaching assistant who denounced him has just received his share of the estate. This may include some of your own former property. Perhaps you would care for an introduction? We shall, I have no doubt, meet to discuss such things.'

'He accused my father of heresy,' said Martin in a dreamy voice, his eyes looking inward. 'When that failed, he bought up the debts of our academy, and forced us into bankruptcy. He put in a bid for me at the slave auction.

'But roasted alive – and for *that* oration?' Martin took a long draught of wine. 'He must have written that before I was born. It's the one where he doesn't use the letter *gamma* for the whole middle section. He used to deliver it every Easter.'

'It was the Will of Caesar,' said Theophanes smoothly. 'As such, the punishment was just.'

'Let His Will be done,' said Martin, pulling himself together. 'We are all one beneath His Benevolent Sway.'

He lapsed into silence. Called forward once more, the assistant produced a sheaf of letters of introduction from Theophanes to all the main libraries in the City that I'd be using. Coming from the Master of the Offices, these would prompt more ready co-operation than whatever I might have brought or might procure via the Roman Church.

There was also an introduction to the Professor of Theology at the University. His department, I was told, had been unaffected by the spending cuts recently applied to the main University. Theophanes understood that my mission might involve enquiries that could only be answered *viva voce* by the highest theological authorities. This letter of introduction would ensure immediate and full consideration of all points raised.

'I must inform you', Theophanes said, 'that His Excellency the Dispensator and my superiors have been in close contact ever since your mission was raised as a possibility. Both agree that nothing should stand in the way of its speedy completion.'

I sprayed back a stream of flattering gratitude. I was now horribly alarmed. What was Theophanes up to? Why such interest in our mission? What was the function of that nasty little assistant of his? He'd stood silent throughout the conversation, for all the world as if memorising every word for later transcription.

And what was the Dispensator up to?

'You will enjoy Constantinople, young Alaric,' Theophanes said at length with a smile of astonishing charm. 'The only pity is that you will have so little time here on your first visit. Your mission is of the highest importance, and must come before all else.'

He waved aside another helping of his fruit concoction. His assistant leaned forward to whisper something in his ear.

Lunch was over. I now had other business.

9

The banking house of ben Baruch lay at the extremity of a dead end that backed on to one of the larger churches. It was a building of windowless stone walls with a three-inch wooden door plated both sides in bronze. There were the usual armed guards inside and out.

No sun reached the paving stones of that narrow street. Aside from the thin slit of blue sky overhead, the only splash of colour came from a caged bird just outside the door. It sang and sang, and no one looked on.

Nothing unusual about this, I should say. Wise bankers don't go for the sort of frontage that allows easy access. Baruch in Rome always did his business from the basement cells of a converted prison.

The difference between this and its smaller equivalent in Rome was the seemingly recent absence of any Jewish symbolism. The Star of David had been hacked from above the entrance and the gap partly filled with an enamelled icon of the Risen Christ. Inside, the walls were covered with painted icons – most of them jewelled and gilded.

'Welcome, O Welcome, dear Brother in Christ!' said Baruch of Constantinople. He shuffled into view, a much larger and heavier version of his brother in Rome. Indeed, this Baruch had the same shape as my building contractor. Also unlike his brother, he had a gold cross embroidered on his shabby robe and a jewelled icon of the Virgin hung round his neck so large it had to be seen to be believed. He spoke loudly in Latin of the saints who must surely have watched over my journey to Constantinople. To this he added even louder praise of the divine care of the Emperor in

59

keeping the sea routes clear. Then he fell to a more reassuringly Jewish inspection of the draft I'd brought with me.

'That's a pretty sum you're expecting me to honour, isn't it, my dear Brother in Christ?' he rasped in Greek, hurriedly crossing himself at the mention of Our Saviour's name. 'A pretty sum indeed. What will you be doing with all this gold – buying a palace?' Without moving his nose from the parchment sheet, he looked up at me from the corners of his eyes.

'I must ask this, you know,' he explained, seeing my look of slight shock. 'There is a new ordinance limiting cash withdrawals without good reason. I can give you some gold, but the rest in promissory notes. You'll have no trouble passing these, I can assure you. The House of Baruch is the strongest in the city.'

'All the stronger now for your conversion?' I hazarded. He gave me a queer look, then darted a glance at one of his clerks, who'd been paying us much attention from the moment I came in.

'My poor brother in Rome,' he sighed. 'He may be close in the confidence of His Holiness, but he lacks the stern and loving command of the Great Augustus to abandon the error of our ancestors for the Word of Christ – as clarified, of course, at Nicaea and at Chalcedon and by all lesser Councils of Holy Mother Church.

'You must come to dinner on the next main feast day,' he said loudly, reaching under a blue scarf to scratch his head. 'There will be pork with every dish, you know, or shellfish. This is a good Christian house, be assured. We serve no *kocha* muck here.'

I thanked him. Trying to turn the conversation, I complimented him on the icon.

'Picked up at an auction of confiscated property,' he said proudly at the recollection. 'If you look closely, you'll see the bloody tears that run down her cheeks are picked out in rubies – genuine rubies too, I'll have you know, not glass. I paid a tenth of its true value. I . . .' He trailed off. Then, very loud: 'Of course, I'd have paid ten times more than its true value if I could thereby have shown my loyalty to the Lord Augustus who watches over all of us.'

'I am a true son of the Church,' he bellowed after me as we left. 'I pray twice a day at the Church of All the Saints!'

Turning out of the little street, I noticed another Jewish bank – this one closed, with the Imperial Seal on its door and a notice of auction above.

There followed the best spending spree I'd ever yet known.

You can forget Rome for shopping. If you have no taste, the shops there are good enough. If you search and nag, you can usually get the basics of a civilised existence. If you want something really special, though, you have to order it from Ravenna, and hope it won't get pilfered or spoiled on the way.

In Constantinople, you can get absolutely everything. Most of the shops are just stalls set up outside houses in the side streets, the owners calling out and catching at you as you pass in the street. You ignore these. They are for the lower classes. Those in the main streets are large establishments, with many rooms, all gorgeously furnished, where the staff behave like the best household slaves. Some even have glazed windows, so you can stop and gloat over the riches within. Mostly, the shutters block off any view by night. But a couple of the very grandest shops, where the city guards can be trusted to patrol, keep the windows exposed all night long, with lamps to give a clear view within.

Once you get used to the fact that the Greeks are the most shameless rip-off merchants, who'll try selling you moulded for carved work and silver plate for the real thing, you can have a glorious time in those shops. And it isn't just the shopping. The better shops are places of general resort. The upper floors have private dining rooms and even the occasional brothel. You can meet old friends there. You can make new ones.

It was turning out fortunate that all our main baggage from Rome had never arrived. The clothes I had brought with me, it seemed, were rather frumpy for Constantinople. Trousers were not at all the thing in the city. They showed you up as a provincial or even a barbarian. Tunics there were the fashion. You could have shortish ones, with close-fitting stockings right up above the hemline if you had legs to show off. But no trousers.

I passed an age at the most expensive tailor Martin could remember, inspecting bales of cotton and the finest silks to be had from the East. Rather pretty youths of about my own age sauntered around my chair, showing off the elegance that could be achieved for just a few of those Baruch notes. I must have assumed every conceivable pose while the assistants hurried round me pinning lengths of cloth into the most fashionable styles.

'If you'll pardon my liberty of comment,' Martin told me over dinner in a decidedly fancy restaurant opposite the Legation, 'you'll soon be needing more of those notes.'

The complete new wardrobe I'd forced on him now forgotten, he'd gone back to looking anxious. His idea of the evening had involved another takeaway in the Legation, and then making up a shopping list to send with our slaves to the Covered Market. I'd wanted something grander, so had chosen the restaurant on the basis of its evident expensiveness and the just as evident quality of the other diners I'd watched going in.

My attention had been drawn to it by the two blazing torches set up each side of its main door. The shops had been closing one after another with the onset of the dusk that comes late to Constantin- ople in summer, and I was feeling starved after walking what must have been five miles through the shops.

'I suppose I shall need eventually to go back to Baruch,' said I, dipping my bread into a glass bowl of some delicious yellow sauce. 'But rest assured – more wine, if you please, and unwatered this time,' I added to the owner of the restaurant, who'd come over to serve us with his own hands – 'rest assured, there can be plenty more notes where those came from.'

And there were. Cash, I'll grant, has its uses. It's good for small purchases. It's good in quite large sums for bribing officials. In a crisis, nothing can beat it: that is, after all, what got me to Jarrow after that pig Constantine had ordered all my accounts frozen. But it also has its limitations. You don't use it for big purchases. You certainly don't carry large amounts when you travel.

'Listen, Martin,' I said, with another attempt at introducing him to the ways of finance. 'The letter from Baruch in Rome creates a debt against him with his brother in Constantinople. This can be paid from Rome by a later shipment of gold. More likely, it can be offset by issuing a draft in Constantinople to someone who wants to buy goods – relics for illegal export, perhaps – in Rome. It may be bought by the Imperial authorities if they ever want to remit funds for Italian defence. Or it may be traded via third parties in Carthage or Alexandria.'

'And if the Roman Baruch has no money?' Martin asked with a glimmer of understanding.

'The web of trust is broken,' I replied, 'and everyone's in the shit. But that won't happen. Those brothers know which way the wind is blowing before others feel the draught. Besides, I have letters of credit from the Papal Bank. I don't want to use them, though, because of the discount.'

That lost him again. But never mind. It's enough that I wasn't short of money, and wasn't likely to be. In any event, if I wanted quick and ready service to get us out before Heraclius turned up to sound the political equivalent of the Last Trump, it wouldn't do to go about looking like some semi-barbarian from the outer fringes of the Italian Exarchate.

'Leave the money to me, Martin,' I said, giving up on explanation. 'That bag of clipped silver you had nicked off you in Corinth won't be missed here.

'Any further thoughts on the old eunuch?' I asked. I'd dropped my voice, but was speaking in a Latin that it seemed unlikely that anyone else in the restaurant could understand.

'He plainly knows everything about us, and took great pleasure in having us know that he knows.'

Martin opened his mouth to answer, but no sound issued.

IO

Instead, the whole restaurant fell suddenly quiet. It was as if a singer were about to begin a performance. There was that same feeling of hushed expectancy. The chattering and laughter of the diners had ceased. The serving slaves left off their darting around and clattering of dishes. All was suddenly fallen silent. All was still.

I looked round to my left. Over by the door, their set faces pale in the glimmer of the lamps, three men dressed in the black I'd earlier seen at the Ministry stood looking at the diners. They were as still and silent as everyone else in the room.

Then one of them stepped forward. Taller than the others, his wiry build partly compensated by the bulk of the armour under his cloak, he added to the impression of a performer about to begin. He looked from table to hushed, expectant table, dwelling on none. A smile on his thin lips, he seemed to bask in the terror his appearance had created. A slave was pushed forward to stand trembling beside him.

'Well?' the Tall Man asked in a voice of quiet but silky menace. 'Where is he this time?'

The slave pointed silently towards a table on the far side of the room from ours. A single diner sat there. I'd noticed him playing with some bread.

His assistants two paces behind him, the Tall Man approached the indicated table. As they passed each table, I could sense a slight sagging of the tension. But it was only a very slight sagging. Everyone remained still and silent.

The slave lightly touched the diner on his shoulder, and fell back. He squatted down on the floor, covering his face. His body

64

shook with suppressed sobs. I could see dark bruises on his arms and his bare legs.

'Justinus of Tyre,' the Tall Man opened now, still quiet but in a peremptory tone, 'do you know the reason why we stand before you?'

The face of the diner turned grey in the lamplight. He was short and balding, in early middle age, the fingers of his upraised hands heavy with gold rings. His appearance cried merchant of the richer sort. He muttered a few words I couldn't catch. Those at the next table looked down steadily at their wine.

I noticed that all the other diners in the restaurant were also looking away. One man at a table near mine was breathing heavily despite himself. With shaking hands he fingered what looked like a pagan charm. The other diners hardly seemed to be breathing. Mine was the only head turned in that direction.

Martin had drained his cup with a single gulp. He was looking carefully down at the table, his hands spread out before him. He kicked under the table at my foot, desperate to have me do likewise. I ignored him and continued watching the scene played out before me.

'There are questions to be put to you – *in the usual place*,' the Tall Man added with an ominous stress. 'You will come quietly.'

With a clatter of overturned cups, Justinus rose unsteadily to his feet. The vase of yellow flowers placed on his table went over, and, from a good fifteen feet away, I clearly heard the spattering of water on to the floor.

'Please—' he gasped in a deathly voice. His words were cut short with a heavy blow to the face from the Tall Man. Justinus fell back against a chair that broke under the shock. The two assistants reached down and pulled him to his feet. The neighbouring diners rose quickly and went over to stand with outspread arms and their faces pressed to the far wall. I could see one of them shaking as if in a mild epileptic fit.

'You will remain silent,' the Tall Man said in a soft voice. 'You will speak only in the place where you are questioned, and when you are questioned.'

As they moved away from the table, one of the serving slaves restrained himself from hurrying forward to pick up the broken vase from the floor. Instead, he remained squatting on his haunches with the others.

With a sudden convulsion, Justinus broke free from the grasp of the men in black and looked desperately round for escape. The door was blocked by another of those men in black who stood just outside the room. He looked menacing, though seemed not to be armed. The only window was shuttered against the evening draught.

A look of wild despair on his face, Justinus crashed heavily through the tables in my own direction. Crockery and knives clattered to the floor behind him.

Knowing he was trapped, the arresting officials stood watching to see what he might do.

I suppose, with my size and colouring, I stood out the most from the other diners. It didn't help that I was the only one not looking carefully away or down at the table.

Justinus made straight for me. 'You've got to help me,' he cried in a deathly voice, clutching at my robe. 'Tell them I can explain everything. Nothing is what it seems . . .'

Before I could so much as open my mouth, the two assistants in black were with us. They pulled Justinus back from me. He fell to the floor, his hands clamped round my left calf. They pulled harder, but nothing could break his grip on me. I tried to shake him loose but with no success. Big as I was, I was nearly pulled to the floor with him. But for the attendant circumstances, there was something faintly comic about the scene.

From his robe, the Tall Man pulled a heavy cosh. With two short and exact blows, face still without marked expression, he smashed hard on Justinus's wrists. I heard the dull crunching of lead on bone and felt the grip relax.

The Tall Man stood back to admire his work. He wiped a splash of blood off the cosh and balanced it in his right hand.

As the assistants pulled Justinus away from me, he curled into a ball, now screaming with pain and fear. They still couldn't get him to his feet. Each time they seemed about to get him up, he'd go limp on them, and his dead weight fell through their grip.

66

The two assistants now set about him with their coshes. They hardly seemed to move as, with careful and practised blows, they smashed his body to pulp. Blood oozed though his clothing as flesh burst and bones cracked. The screams gave way to an animalistic whimpering, and then to rattling gasps as blow after blow continued to fall on the more delicate and exposed areas of his body.

Trembling with excitement, the Tall Man directed his assistants to areas of the body that hadn't yet come under the cosh. In that silent restaurant, I could hear every blow and every rasping breath. Blood splashed my sleeve. There was a rich, high smell of shit as the man's bowels relaxed.

The other diners continued looking away.

Moving round to get a new position, one of the assistants knocked into me. My cup went over, spilling red wine into my lap.

'For God's sake,' I cried, disgust taking the place of alarm – 'for God's sake, is this really necessary?'

I stood up and faced the Tall Man. My cup hit the floor, shattering on its hard surface. Lacking my bulk, his height was deceptive. I stared him straight in the face. His assistants fell back before me, obviously unsure how to respond to this kind of challenge.

The Tall Man held his ground. His pale features again took on a thin smile. He stepped over the motionless body of Justinus. He put his face close to mine and I could smell some kind of spiced drug on his breath.

'Do you presume to interfere in the arrest of a convicted traitor?' His soft voice reverted to its silky, menacing tone.

'My Lord,' one of the assistants said. 'My Lord' – he bent to take up a letter that must have rolled out from that bloody robe.

The Tall Man ripped at the seal and scanned the contents. His face contracted into what looked like the beginnings of a seizure, but he gripped the back of a chair and fought to recover himself.

'You are aware of the treasons in this document?' It was both a question and a statement. His voice still smooth by effort, his hand was shaking.

67

'Of course not,' I snapped, suddenly aware that I was splashed all over with blood. I was wearing the clothes I had brought from Rome. It would be days yet before the new ones were ready.

'Please, Illustrious Sir,' Martin broke in, scrabbling in his satchel for our documents, 'please, but my colleague is a stranger to the City. He doesn't understand City ways. We are under the protection of—'

The Tall Man held up his arm for silence. 'Not another word,' he said with a grim pleasure. 'You are the known associates of a convicted traitor. I have no doubt you will come quietly.'

'Traitors?' I blurted out, incredulous. 'How about some charges?' I asked, remembering my law.

The smile expanded to reveal a row of stained teeth. The Tall Man waved at the other crouched, silent diners.

'These are the accused. They wait the call of the Emperor's Divine Justice. That offal on the floor' – he glanced down at Justinus – 'is the convicted one. And you are now his convicted associates.'

He turned to one of his assistants.

'Cuff them.'

Then he turned to the slave who had denounced Justinus. He was still grovelling hopelessly on the floor. I could now see that the fingers on his left hand were broken and already swollen black.

'Return to your master's house,' he said, his voice silkier than ever. 'I'll send for you again when I need you.'

As we left, the restaurant had all the still silence of an hermetic monastery. I looked briefly back. No one moved. No one so much as breathed heavily. On the bright ceramic tiles of the floor, a dark smear showed where the body of Justinus had been dragged along behind us.

The sky overhead was now black, and I felt a chill breeze on my face as we emerged from the restaurant. There was a small crowd in the street outside. Blank faces lit by the flickering of the torches, no one spoke. A few turned their backs to us as the Tall Man looked in their direction.

We were pushed into a black windowless carriage. The possibly still living body of Justinus was thrown in beside us.

II

I'd nearly vomited at my first smell of the place: it was like an unwashed abattoir – all stale blood and rotted offal which almost overpowered the smell of damp.

The creatures running this imitation of Hell kept up the resemblance to an abattoir. They wheeled silently about us in the stained leather aprons you normally see in a butcher's market. As one whispered with the Tall Man, another darted a hand inside my robe. He squeezed hard on a nipple, all the time looking up at me with the bright, panting smile of a mad dog.

'Tomorrow!' he whispered triumphantly – 'And tomorrow and tomorrow, and all for us!'

I cut him short with a smart head-butt to the face. 'Fuck you!' I snarled. The others danced back out of my reach.

I was in the Ministry where I'd earlier visited Theophanes. No – I was in the basement that ran far beneath the Ministry. Once unloaded from the carriage, we had been dragged in through a small side entrance, and then taken down worn steps that had twisted round and round and round on their course into a subterranean world of endless corridors lined every few yards with iron doors.

At first, all down there had seemed quiet. As my ears began to adjust, though, I could hear a chorus of low, despairing moans. They came from behind the closed doors of the cells. They came from all directions. They came from as far as the ears could reach, and from further than the eyes could see in the dim glow of the lamps hung at every junction in that labyrinth of horror.

As the one I'd butted lay grovelling on the floor, the Tall Man pushed his own face close to mine. 'Tomorrow, indeed, my fine young barbarian,' he crooned, 'but not for these trash. You belong to me.'

He stood back and took a deep breath to savour the endless despair of our surroundings before continuing in a tone of eager intensity: 'I will show you how pain is very like pleasure. It too has its rituals and instruments. It too has its orgasms. It too can be prolonged by those who have studied the responses of the body.'

'Fuck you!' I snarled again, though I'd not felt inclined to try anything physical with this living image of Satan. He was on his home territory, and had seemed to grow taller and more substantial with every breath of that foul air.

'We shall see how long your courage holds up under my personal ministrations,' he said, turning to rap a few orders to his minions. 'You will give me the answers to my questions, and much else before the end.'

Still cuffed, we were pushed into separate cells spaced far apart. I don't know how long I sat in darkness on that damp, stinking floor once the door had swung shut on me.

Few definite sounds now reached me through those stone walls and the heavy door. But I felt aware of continual movement outside, and perhaps the occasional low moan.

'I'm a guest of the Emperor,' I shouted in the darkness. 'I demand immediate release.'

No answer. Instead, the sound of my voice within the invisible walls of that blackness chilled me more than the dank air. The wine fumes that had so far buoyed me up were now dispersing like a morning fog, and I was beginning to realise the full horror of my situation.

Once I did hear voices. Though muffled by the close-fitting iron door, they'd come from just outside my cell.

'So is this one Justinus?' one had asked.

'Nah!' another had replied. 'That's the one back there. We'll see what we can get out of him come the morning. I don't think, though, there's much left for us to do. He's all smashed up now.'

'Shame,' had come the answer. 'I suppose it is the right Justinus this time. I said the other one was telling us the truth.'

The voices had drifted away, leaving me in a silence broken only by a steady dripping of water somewhere in the dark.

I've seen people go mad in prisons. Even a short stay is unnerving. The blackness and the silence are bad enough. Far worse is the uncertainty of how long the stay there will be. Will you be taken out and tortured or killed? Or will you just be left there to rot to death?

I kept my nerve in that cell by refusing to think about what might happen next, and by instead reciting in my head the whole of the Creed, first in Latin then in Greek. Yes, it may be a mass of words made up to torment the devout. But it can also at times have a certain anaesthetic value.

So, for what seemed an age, I sat huddled on the floor, every so often muttering like some novice monk, and willing my teeth not to chatter with fear and the sudden cold of that place.

Then, at last, with a jingling of keys and the creak of unoiled hinges, the door swung open, and I saw Theophanes standing in a pool of light.

'My dear young fellow, you cannot imagine how embarrassing this is to all of us.' Speaking in Latin, Theophanes sat behind the desk of his office in the Ministry. He still wore his bedgown under his cloak. The single lamp his assistant had lit for us showed the lines on his unpainted face.

'I came as soon as Alypius could inform me of the situation.' He waved with a feeble effort of cheerfulness at his assistant. 'Alypius', I thought. I filed the name carefully into my memory.

I took another mouthful of the wine Alypius had poured for me. I tried to think of something ornately suitable for the occasion, but I gave up on the effort, instead asking: 'Where is Martin?'

'I took the liberty', Theophanes said, now in a more businesslike tone, 'of having your secretary sent back directly to the Legation. Being a person of only middling status, he was given a roughness of treatment on his arrival that might not have been yours until morning.'

He raised his arm to silence me, continuing rapidly: 'Please be assured, he came to no harm. I was able to prevent that. But I

71

found him somewhat overcome. I thought it best to have a sedative administered and to send him straight off to the Legation.

'Now, Aelric,' he continued – he used my proper name. Was it a slip? Was it an intended slip? In any case, how could he have known it? I wanted to break in and ask, but didn't dare – 'Now, Aelric, it would not be an act of friendship or convenient to any of us if I were compelled to vary the terms of your residency permit. But I must urge you never again to interfere in the work of the Black Agents. It is of the highest importance to the Empire, and they do not report to me. Do I have your assurance?' he asked. 'Next time, I may not be so easily found to help you.'

For the first time since we'd met, he spoke naturally, a look of tired strain on his face. His lank, undressed hair fell around his eyes.

'Have I your assurance?'

'Yes,' I said. 'Thank you, Theophanes,' I repeated, avoiding all the usual circumlocutory courtesy.

He nodded.

Back in the Legation, I went straight to Martin's room. He was sleeping heavily. He looked unhurt. I asked to be called as soon as he woke. In the meantime, I fell into bed for some sleep of my own. I can't say it contributed to settling my nerves.

I dreamed of empty shops under empty colonnades and empty streets in the sunlight, and of a shadowy creature that flitted about me forever only in the corner of my eyes. Dressed in black, it smelt of death.

My first sight on drifting back into wakefulness was of the wine cup placed on my bedside table. I drained it with a single gulp, and called loudly to Authari to bring me more as I reached for my clothes.

Martin hadn't been tortured, he told me from his bed. He'd been tied to the rack, but Theophanes had appeared before any of the gears could be set in motion. Of course, he'd gone hysterical. Sedation was probably the only answer.

Now he was calm enough. The sun streamed into the room. Birds twittered on the balcony outside his room. Below in the courtyard garden, one of my slaves sang quietly to himself. This wasn't Rome, but it was pretty close to safe normality.

Once I'd sent the slave out of the room, Martin sat up in bed and clutched at my arm.

'Aelric,' he said firmly in Celtic, 'you must never do anything like that again. Even when I was last here, when Maurice was Emperor, the Black Agents frightened everyone, high or low. Now, they're out of control. You didn't see how Theophanes had to bargain with them to get me off that rack. If you see another arrest like last night, *you must look the other way*. Whoever they come to take is already one with the dead! He does not exist. Soon, he will never have existed.'

I patted his arm. 'I'm sorry, Martin,' I said. 'I will be more careful. Perhaps, in future, we might be a little quicker to produce that permit from Theophanes.'

Martin fixed me in the eye. 'Aelric,' he said, 'I want you to know that they tied me to the rack *after* they had seen the permit. And they were joking about what to do with you when the old eunuch arrived. He had to keep on and on repeating that, contrary to any other orders they might be issued, we were under the Highest Protection.'

I kept a look of renewed jitters off my face and told Martin he should get some more natural rest. As I turned to leave, he tugged gently at my sleeve.

'And please don't carry that knife with you,' he said. 'It's treason to go armed in the city without a permit.'

I did now make an attempt to see the Permanent Legate. His own rooms, I'd guessed, could be approached from a door in the main hall of the Legation opposite the entrance to my own suite.

My hand almost on the door to the Permanent Legate's suite, I was stopped by Demetrius.

'And where might Sir be going?' he asked in an obsequious but firm tone.

'Oh,' I said, trying to sound nonchalant, 'I'm just going to pay my respects to His Excellency.'

'I don't think, sir, that would be appropriate,' Demetrius answered, positioning himself between me and the door. 'His Excellency is a busy man, and will call those to him only such as is needed, and when they be needed.'

'I have messages from His Holiness in Rome,' I lied.

I got in response only a nasty squint. Demetrius then produced a key from his robe to pull back and forth in the door lock until a click told me that whatever lay beyond was off-limits.

'His Excellency,' he sniffed before walking off about his business, 'will call on such as he wants and when he wants.'

So much for that.

I sat behind my desk and looked at the icons of Saint Peter and Saint Andrew that hung on the wall opposite. I thought for a moment of writing to the Dispensator, but immediately decided otherwise. If all my incoming post was read, Theophanes – I supposed he was in charge of this – would be neglecting his duties if he allowed outgoing post not to be similarly inspected.

Instead, I began a long letter back to Gretel in Rome.

I told her about the shops and the crowds and the great buildings. She'd understand all this when it was read out to her. I could even see her in my mind's eye, clapping her hands and having the description of the shops read over and over again. She'd love the idea of glazed windows lit with lamps. She'd then dictate a long letter of her own that was little more than a shopping list.

I didn't think it a shame that I'd be on my way home before it arrived.

I said nothing about the arrest. As I finished, the sky outside was turning dull with the approach of evening, and a draught from the window gently rustled the sheets of papyrus. Made almost happy by their less than truthful content, I rolled them up and sealed them into a small leather bag that would protect them on whatever voyage they eventually took back to Rome. I made sure to mark the attached tag for the attention of Marcella.

'Authari,' I called loudly. 'Ah, there you are, Authari,' I said, pretending not to notice how close he'd been. 'Is everything in order for you and the other slaves to have a good dinner this evening?'

'Yes, Master,' he replied with a forced steadiness of voice. He looked away from me so I'd not smell his breath. Our kitchen had only been stocked with bread and cheese the night before. Now, there was goat stew on the boil.

'Excellent,' I said. 'Don't stint yourselves on the food. I want everyone to have good, solid chunks of meat every evening. We might as well make the best of things.'

Authari bowed. He'd nagged me earlier to the borders of respect about my having left him behind the day before. I'd ignored this and passed on Martin's advice that he should not go armed about the city. He'd scowled back at me and gone noisily about his duties. But he was evidently taking no chances in the Legation. He'd rigged up a long bar on the only door into our suite, and set up a rota of the other slaves to keep watch there.

So long as the door held, we were secure in our fortress.

As he left the room, I added: 'And please do see if Martin is recovered from his ordeal. I'll be dining out again this evening. He might care to accompany me.'

12

It was my ninth day in the City, and my fourth in the two libraries that were already becoming part of my life there. Afternoons I'd spend with Martin and the army of copying clerks assigned to us in the Patriarchal Library. This was not far from the Legation, and was very close by the Great Church. Mornings I'd spend in the University Library with just a few copying slaves we'd picked up. This was about a half-mile from the Legation, and fronted the Forum of Constantine.

I was there now, seated at my own table in the main reading room. It was proving every bit as splendid as I'd been told. The vast book stacks, I'd found at once from the catalogue, had just about everything you could ever want to read in Greek – and much in Latin. Most of the books were fat, heavy things in the modern style. Many, though, even today, are the older papyrus rolls that require an education in itself to handle and to read. You have to unroll them with great care, and then put up with the narrow columns and lack of page numbering.

I had everything I could have desired – everything, that is, except the company of my equals. I wasn't sure what genteel pursuits I'd find in Constantinople. But they involved drinking, whoring and gambling with better company than Authari, and the horrified tutting of Martin back in the Legation. Here I was, looking drop-dead gorgeous in the first of the new clothes I'd ordered, and I had no one to admire me in them.

The students sat around me at their own tables. Many of them there were rather low-born, but it was the custom back then for young men of the better classes to study awhile to qualify for places in the bureaucracies of the Empire or the Church. They mingled and chatted happily enough in the canteen and the square outside the University – that is, unless I were in range. I'd caught a few curious looks when I appeared to be deep in study, but no one saw fit to approach me or even acknowledge my presence with a wave. If I approached one of them, he'd respond at best with a distant politeness.

Well, I'd just come back from the mid-morning break in the canteen on day four when I decided it was time to make my introductions.

'Hello,' I'd said brightly, seating myself at the table where the best-dressed students were gathered. 'I'm Alaric, a citizen from Rome. I'm here to . . .'

There'd been a scraping of chairs as nearly everyone got up.

'Exams coming round, you know,' one of them had said with a sweaty glance around the canteen. 'Nice robe,' he'd added, with a nod at the thing I was wearing.

'What is the procedure of these examinations?' I'd asked of the one person left seated in the canteen. He sat alone at the next table with a plate of bread and cheese. Quite a bit older than the others, he'd smiled coldly and brushed the crumbs off his robe of severe but expensive cut with long and very white fingers.

'Somebody from the East once told me', he'd said in a quiet voice, 'a story about the Great Alexander that probably isn't true but is worth repeating. Apparently, he was let down into the Red Sea in a glass container, and passed a long while watching the fishes and other sea creatures swim about him. They could see each other, but never touch.

'If true, that was as it ought to be. Neither could be anything but dangerous to the other. The glass wall was to protect both.'

'Who are you?' I'd asked.

'My name is Sergius,' he'd answered with another cold smile. 'I am presently attached to the office of His Holiness the Patriarch.'

Now he mentioned it, I'd thought, he did have a rather clerical look about him. What was he doing here?

'Now, Alaric, "citizen" from the temporarily alienated British Provinces,' he'd continued, 'I hadn't expected to see you other

77

than in the Patriarchal Library. But I'm aware that you have much work to do in the City. If there is anything I can do to help expedite this, please feel free to approach me. Are the librarians less than attentive to your needs? Have they kept you waiting unreasonably for any of the somewhat unusual books you have been ordering?

'I think not. This being so, I suggest you finish your wine and return to your table, where work of what I have no doubt is the highest importance to Church and Empire awaits your doing.'

With that, he'd been off. Now, back at my table, I was trying to return to the vanished age of light and freedom that had earlier seemed to blaze from the lectures of Carneades on the unknowability of the truth.

'I'm going out for a walk,' I said, standing up. The copying slave opposite me stood too and bowed low. 'If you can have the third and fifth books of this copied by tomorrow morning, I shall be grateful,' I added.

I looked around the room. Every head was bent intently over whatever text was being read and memorised. There was an unbroken murmuring, as of prayers in church, of those who, in the ancient manner, sounded the words of what they were reading. No one looked up. No one seemed to notice as I walked out into the blistering sunshine.

As my eyes adjusted to the light, I looked about the crowded square. Naked children danced and squealed happily in the central fountain. Dressed in white, the humbler citizens went about their business in or outside the buildings of unsurpassable opulence that fronted the square. Persons of quality, of course, were carried about in open chairs. One of these, I was sure, had been among those I'd seen on my progress up from the Senatorial Dock. I gave him a hesitant smile. He looked straight through me as the slaves hurried him past.

I stood back to avoid a crowd of jabbering Syrians, and nearly fell under a closed chair.

'Do please forgive me, My Lady,' I said, pulling off my cap. I could see a dark shape behind the gossamer curtains and feel a long and intent glance that took in the whole of me. I stood more upright and smiled. An ebony stick reached through the curtains and tapped the largest slave on his back. In a moment, the chair had moved forward and was buried in the crowds.

I thought to do a spot of shopping before lunch. At least in Middle Street there were people who would talk to me, even if it was only about the quality and price of merchandise. Instead, as I wandered aimlessly through the wide but crowded streets of the city centre, I found myself before the dark Ministry building that I'd vaguely hoped I might never see again.

I can't say what I was doing there. Perhaps it was because one of the only two persons I knew in the City beyond my own household was hard at work in there. He'd been at his most courtly over lunch the day before. Would Theophanes welcome an unannounced visit now?

I swallowed. I made up my mind and stepped towards the open blackness of the gateway that led inside. Like everyone else, I ignored the permanent demonstration outside. Like everyone else, I paid no attention to the graffiti that were still being removed from the previous night.

'State your appointment, citizen,' said one of the two guards who suddenly barred my way. 'If you've a written denunciation to make, you place it in the urn outside the gate.'

'I have an appointment with His Magnificence Theophanes,' I lied.

Unimpressed, the guard said something to his colleague about foreigners. He pointed brusquely to a queue that stopped outside a curtained opening.

'When you get to the front of that,' he said, 'you take off your outer clothes. You put your shoes in the box provided. When you go in, have your papers ready. When you are stripped for the search, you stand with your legs apart and your arms spread. If you need an interpreter, tell the clerk. One will be provided.'

Shuffling forward in that queue was a depressing experience. No one spoke. No one looked at anyone else. I did think to turn and walk out again but a woman in front of me who tried that was stopped and pushed back to the end of the queue. By the time I got

79

to the front, I was in no mood to do other than meekly take off my coat and shoes and walk through the curtain.

'Strip and bend over,' one of the clerks said in a hoarse, gloating voice. I gritted my teeth and reached for the brooch that secured my inner tunic.

'Sir, sir,' another of the clerks said with a scared wave of the residency permit I'd given him. They huddled over the thing and looked up at me.

'If you come here in future without an appointment,' Alypius said as we reached the corridor where Theophanes had his office, 'you show your papers at the main gate. You will then be brought straight up. Otherwise, you will be taken to a private waiting room.

'You will say nothing to His Magnificence of what has happened. He has more important things to concern him. You will sit quietly until he has dealt with the matters in hand.'

Inside the office, Theophanes was hard at work. Three junior eunuchs stood before his desk pulling out letters from a basket. As I entered, one of the eunuchs broke a seal and scanned the contents. He read in a flat voice:

'His Eminence Michael of the Lucas family is denounced by his younger son for publishing treasons in his sleep. He is declared to have called out two nights ago that the Emperor Maurice of foul memory was unjustly deposed and murdered, and that the Great Augustus who rules in his place is possessed by a demon who has prompted him to deliver all the lands of the Empire to the Persians and barbarians.'

Theophanes took the letter and read it in full. 'The young man is ambitious to possess more of his father's goods than would come to him in the natural course of things,' he said in a bored voice. 'Have Michael taken in. He will be deprived of one-half of all he has and then flogged through the Circus. One-half of the fine will be handed to the son. Michael will otherwise be released to continue with supervising the repair of the city aqueducts. He is advised in future to consult an apothecary for the means of sleeping more soundly at night.'

The next denounced person wasn't so lucky. The accusation was more serious. He was to be taken in and committed to the care of the Caesar Priscus – that is, to the Emperor's son-in-law. The eunuch dealing with this case drew a black cross on the letter and dropped it into another basket that stood half full on the floor.

So they worked through the list. Wives were denouncing husbands, neighbours and business rivals each other. Some of the denounced were persons of great quality, others from the mercantile and intellectual classes. Sometimes with an explanatory comment, sometimes with none, Theophanes passed judgement on all. In two cases only were denunciations rejected as frivolous. In all others, at least a fine was imposed – more often, a fine and mutilation. Around half were remitted to the attention of Priscus, whom I'd been told by Martin was author and chief agent of the Terror. Some were to be sent to the Emperor himself.

At length, Theophanes looked in my direction. He composed his features into something that approximated a smile and waved me forward.

'That will be all,' he said to the eunuchs. 'We shall deal later with the Antioch business.

'Allow me, my dearest Alaric, to help you to some wine,' he said. 'I regret that I have not so far been all that could be desired of a host. But you will understand that the repression of treason is the highest duty of all who serve the Empire.

'The usurping traitor Heraclius has found his way to Cyprus. His followers here in the city have redoubled their efforts, and are recruiting fools and the disaffected of every condition.'

'Was that the case with Justinus of Tyre?' I asked, dropping my voice to a whisper. 'And is it so with all those lives I've just watched you smashing up?' I was aghast. I hadn't known exactly what Theophanes did when he wasn't entertaining me. But I hadn't imagined it was anything so gross as this.

Theophanes looked sharply at his assistant, Alypius, who went over to the door. He opened it and looked out to right and left. He looked back. Theophanes nodded. Then Alypius went back outside and stood there, leaving the door very slightly ajar.

'Alaric,' said Theophanes, speaking low, 'you must by now be aware that we do not do things here in Constantinople as they are done in Rome. This is not a small provincial city, surrounded by barbarians and left largely to the governance of the Church.

'You are here on business for His Holiness in Rome. As such, you are under the highest protection. His Holiness our own Patriarch is less safe in his palace than you are with the backing of the Lateran. But you must learn not to interfere in matters that do not concern you or your mission. And when I say not to interfere, I mean also not to notice that certain things may be happening around you.'

'Is that why everyone's been warned off me?' I asked. 'Is that why I'm to be treated as a leper by everyone else in the city?'

Theophanes looked hard at me. 'Alaric,' he sighed, 'the traitor Justinus was accused and convicted by wholly regular means – means that long predate the present emergency. He has disappeared from the face of the world. His goods have been confiscated. His wife and household have been turned into the street. All that remains to show that he ever lived at all is the number that you may have noticed on the bills of auction posted in the financial district – and I know that you were there the morning before last with the Jew Baruch.

'As for his body, it may have been left out in the streets for clearing away by the public slaves. Or it may be swinging from the City walls. Do not even ask me what has become of it. His treason was dealt with outside my jurisdiction. I do not make it my business to look outside that jurisdiction.

'So far as I can tell, the man was most inconsiderate in dragging you into his affairs. I will not waste time in asking if you really did know the contents of that now destroyed letter. I will only remind you of the pressing duties that lie among your books. His Excellency the Dispensator assures me that these duties should not detain you in the City beyond the end of this month. You will surely agree that nothing should be permitted to keep you from them.'

★   ★   ★

82

'So, who is this man Sergius?' I asked for the second time.

It was later, and I was back in the Legation with Martin. He rinsed his mouth again and spat more bloody wine into the bowl that a grinning Authari held under his chin. My promise that it wouldn't hurt had been optimistic. But the dentist had been and done his work, and Martin would soon get over the pain and trauma of the extraction. For the moment, though, he was out of sorts with me.

He put the cup down and looked at me through tear-filled eyes.

'I didn't say I knew him,' he said. 'I heard his name from one of the copying clerks. If he's the man who spoke to you in the University canteen, you've encountered someone really big in the Greek Church. He's the leading authority among the Patriarch's advisers on the Monophysite heresy. And I'm told he's leader of the party that doesn't want us here. They don't believe we were sent to clarify the meaning of the Creed. They think you are an envoy from the Pope to negotiate a deal on the Universal Bishop title.'

Martin spat again and looked back at me. 'But you say you only met him this morning,' he said. 'You seem to have been with him quite a while.'

'I went shopping afterwards,' I said hurriedly. 'I know you don't approve of opium pills. But the unrefined resin, heated over charcoal, can be most comforting . . .'

Martin wasn't interested in that either. He must by now have spat out enough of our best wine to pay his rent for a month in Rome. But the thought of something that might take the pain clean away seemed somehow to strike him as improper.

I looked out of the window. Perhaps I had been a fool to drift off to Theophanes like that. But it had been incidentally useful. Without trying, I had gathered up at least two facts in one day. The problem was to work out how everything fitted together.

The Dispensator was up to something, but hadn't thought it necessary to let me know what it was. That had been obvious back in Rome. Now it was clear that Theophanes was up to something, too. And whatever that thing was, it was important enough to justify diverting him from what was currently the most vital job in the Empire. For once, the Greek Church was refreshingly straightforward in its motivations – even if only because my own motivations had been misapprehended.

I looked back at Martin, who was glaring into a mirror. Since he never smiled, the gap in his front teeth would never show. The look on his face, even so, would have curdled milk.

'I'm having dinner with Theophanes again tomorrow night,' I said, now in Latin. For all he understood of our situation in any language, Authari was looking annoyed at being cut out of the conversation. 'It will be in that same restaurant by the Ministry. He wants a report from me on the political situation in Kent. He also asked me to remind you about the written account of affairs in Ireland and the Celtic areas of England.'

Martin put the mirror down. 'And you'll give him what he wants?' he asked. 'Don't you think it's all very suspicious? Haven't these people enough to worry about nearer home? Britain dropped out of their world two centuries ago. Ireland was never in it. Don't you wonder what is going on?'

'You know I'm eaten up with curiosity,' I said, now peevish. 'I will get to the bottom of this before we're finished here, but I'll also give Theophanes whatever he wants.

'You've been whining at me ever since we got here about not upsetting anyone. If the eunuch wants a map of Canterbury, I'll draw him one. If he wants one of London, I'll make something up. It's the same with diplomatic relations between the barbarian kings in the old Western Provinces, and the flux and reflux of heresy there.

'Whatever he wants, I'll give him. You'll do the same, whether you have any current information or not.'

And so we continued about our work. That open permit Theophanes had pulled out with such a flourish had been a sentence of solitary confinement. The main difference between it and prison was that my place of confinement followed me about. I had Martin. I had my slaves. I had formal dealings with all those assigned to assist in our mission. I had discussions with Baruch about making money without ever making any. And that was it.

It all, even so, had its convenient side. With nothing else to distract me by day, I had no choice but to throw myself heart and soul into the work of collecting materials.

Given this kind of consolation, you can get used to most things. Day followed day, and the sun grew hotter. Our work gave shape to our lives, and Martin and I soon barely noticed the Terror around us or the almost general shunning that insulated us from it.

13

Or so it continued until one morning late in August.

I was sat in the University Library. As ever, I sat alone. One of the books Epicurus had written on the good life had finally been located among the reserve stock. I was half into it when Theophanes came into the reading room.

He was announced by the collective intake of breath and the shuffling as several people stood for their formal bows. With a benign look around him, Theophanes waved everybody back to work.

'I came as soon as I heard the terrible news,' he said. 'No, my dear friend, please do not trouble yourself with rising in my presence. This is an informal visit.' He sat down at my reading table. The cane chair bowed under his weight, but held.

I looked at him and thought hard. My favourite writer on his favourite theme had taken me clean out of Constantinople. Had Antioch declared for Heraclius?

'Oh,' I said eventually, pulling myself back into the present, 'you mean the roof tiles. That could have been nasty. But I knew that warning slide overhead well enough to get away in plenty of time. Shame about the old woman, though.'

'Alaric,' he said with slow deliberation, 'whatever may be the case in Rome, roofs here in Constantinople do not shed their tiles on passers-by. I am informed that every pin had been removed.'

'Oh!' I said again. I tried to add something to break the resulting silence, but nothing came.

'What can you tell me about the man who engaged you in conversation at that very point in the street?' Theophanes asked.

'Not much,' I said. 'He was in early middle age. He might have been balding – though the hood made that hard to tell. He was well-spoken, but I think his accent was from the East. He wanted me to interpret a new law set up on the wall.'

'And you think nothing out of the ordinary that a stranger should stop you and ask for a Latin translation?'

'Not at all,' I replied. 'Latin may be the official language of the Empire, but it's gone decidedly out of fashion in the Imperial capital. I often wonder why you don't just publish everything in Greek and have done with it.'

In support, I looked down at the uncluttered areas of my table. Generations of students had worn it to a dull gloss. What were obviously the older comments carved into the wood were all in Latin. The more recent ones were invariably in Greek. You could write a book about change in the City on the basis of that table. But I won't.

Theophanes gave a mirthless smile. He turned to Alypius – as ever by his side – and spoke rapidly in a guttural language I'd never before heard. With a curt answer in the same tongue, Alypius was off. Theophanes turned back to me, now with one of his most charming smiles.

Of course, I'd been suspicious at the time. That stranger had jumped back before the noise overhead, and had been off very sharp. But whatever Theophanes might care to say, roofs did give way, even in the City.

So, at least, I tried forcing myself to believe. A murder attempt in Rome was one matter. I was at home. I had friends. I understood my surroundings. I was in control of my life. If someone tried to end that life, I knew exactly how to respond. In the street, I could carry weapons. My home was fortified.

Murder attempts in Constantinople were different. They rubbed in just how dependent I was on one man whose interests were as beyond calculation now as they had been at the Senatorial Dock.

I smiled weakly back at Theophanes. I tried again to place his accent, but couldn't. His Greek was admirable. For all his

courtliness, he always avoided the diffuse pomposity of the educated. But I'd never imagined he might be a native speaker. He
didn't sound Syrian or Egyptian, but was undoubtedly from the
East.

'Your stay in the city', he said with an abrupt return to a
ceremonious manner, 'has been prolonged somewhat beyond
our expectations. While your presence is a source of infinite
pleasure to us all, and to me in particular, I have for some while
now been looking forward to discussing when and how you intend
to go back to Rome. A sea journey might present certain difficulties
at the moment. But an armed guard along the whole length of the
Egnatian Way is yours for the asking.

'We could get you to Ravenna within twenty days. His Excellency the Dispensator could then use his known relationship
with the Lombards to ensure a safe journey from there to Rome.'

'Look, Theophanes,' I said, growing impatient, 'it was you and
the Dispensator who arranged for my visit. I have every personal
need to be out of here by the middle of September at the very latest.
If I could go tomorrow, I'd run to the Legation now and pack. It's
hardly my fault if every post from Rome brings letters of further
instruction.'

I looked over at the most recent. Martin had wept with horror
when it was opened. The Dispensator's requirements seemed to
expand every time he took up a pen. From a straightforward
collection of materials against the Arian heresy, I was being pushed
into a general defence of Orthodoxy. Was he storing up favours
from every Church in the West? I was beginning to wonder.

Theophanes ignored the letter. Why not, after all? He'd probably seen it well before it got anywhere near the Legation.

'What is the book you are reading at the moment?' he asked.

'It is a work of technical philosophy from before the Triumph of
the Faith,' I answered cautiously. 'Such works are often useful for
the light they shed on the terminology of the Fathers.'

Theophanes gave a brief upside-down glance at the unrolled
part of the papyrus. He sighed.

'I am aware, my young Alaric, that you and Martin are a pair of the most wondrously fast scholars. I have been informed of the packets and whole boxes of copies of translations and of original commentaries and glosses you are sending with every post back to His Excellency in Rome. Your diligence, indeed, is the talk of Constantinople.

'My correspondence with His Excellency, however, did not assume such productivity or such prolongation of stay. You are an honoured guest of the Great Augustus himself. It is my duty to see that your stay is without mishap. But half of every day in this place and only half in the Patriarchal Library may not be the full straining of effort needed to get you home for the birth of your child.'

I was sufficiently used to Theophanes by now not to stare at this latest revealing of knowledge.

'I am aware, Your Magnificence,' I said as smoothly as I could, 'that His Excellency the Permanent Legate is displeased at my presence, and that his displeasure is not wholly to your advantage.'

Theophanes frowned. He looked about at the hushed, bent heads of the students. He dropped his voice, though not by much.

'When the traitor Heraclius does finally arrive in the City,' he said, 'it will be minus his body, and what remains will be put on display in the Circus according to the traditional etiquette. Until then, he remains stranded in Cyprus, his forces dwindling by the day as his means fall short of his need to keep them in good spirits.

'However, because of the love he bears us all – those who remain loyal and those who through weakness or folly have strayed from their proper loyalty – the Great Augustus is eager to see how this almost insignificant revolt can be brought sooner rather than later to its end. There are certain services His Holiness in Rome can render. In return, there is something that we can give.

'The longer you stay in Constantinople, the more our discussions with His Excellency the Permanent Legate are disrupted.'

I looked back at him, the whole tangled knot of the previous few months seeming to unravel around us.

'I am indebted to His Magnificence for such clarification and advice,' I said. I leaned forward and dropped my own voice to a whisper. 'Though surely you might have told me all this over dinner.'

'I regret that I am unable to enjoy the pleasure of your company this evening,' came the reply. 'You cannot imagine how I shall miss our little repast in the usual place. But urgent business elsewhere in the City calls me away.' He stood up. 'You will appreciate, however, that my concern for your safety is ever uppermost in my thoughts, and you will forgive my disturbing you in work that is, I cannot but suppose, of the highest value to the Faith.

'You may suppose yourself a little old to be advised not to speak to strangers who accost you in the street. It may, nevertheless, be advice worth considering.'

'We can be sure, then,' I said later on to Martin, 'we were sent here to freeze negotiations. I'm ready to believe His Excellency in Rome does want materials for his Spanish council. And he probably is annoyed about the heresy in Ravenna. But all that is really just a cover. Our true purpose here is to put a brake on the diplomatic wheels. That explains why we weren't told anything. We aren't here to act, but to provide others with an excuse not to act.'

We were walking alone on the City walls. A strong breeze cooled us and carried our hushed voices out over the narrow sea beyond. For additional safety, we spoke in Celtic, replacing names and untranslatable titles with circumlocutions.

'Right from the start,' I added, 'I knew it was all connected with the Universal Bishop business. The Dispensator wants it sorted – but not if the price is calling down anathema on the rebels. I imagine the Permanent Legate was under pressure here to make a deal. Then we turned up, and gave him cause to shut himself away.

'I did think it was the rebels who'd tried to murder me in Rome. I now see it was the Emperor.'

Martin turned and looked straight at me. Oh dear – I hadn't meant to tell him about that. As I filled him in, it mixed with the roof-tile incident and got him into a right panic.

'For God's sake, Martin,' I had to hiss, 'can't you keep a stiff upper lip, at least in public? Gibbering away like this, and in a foreign language, is the quickest way into one of those cages.' I nodded at a cluster of freshly gibbeted corpses further along the wall.

It didn't help that I could feel my own legs starting to shake.

But Martin controlled himself. 'Might there be anything else you've neglected to tell me about this sojourn in Hell?' he asked, a dash of bitterness now in his voice. 'You may be the primary target. But you have nearly got me killed once already; and our families have been in protective custody on and off since we left Rome. You surely have some duty of openness with me.'

My apology and reassurance fell oddly flat. We looked awhile in silence out to the boundless freedom of the waters. If there had been a sensible falling off in numbers, the wind still brought ships from every trading port of the world.

'So what if His Excellency has locked himself into his rooms?' Martin asked with a return to the original subject. 'There's not a door in this city the Emperor can't kick open.'

'Oh yes there is.' I smiled. 'The Permanent Legate represents the Pope in the fullest possible sense. An attack on him is an attack on His Holiness. If he refuses to see anyone, he must be cajoled. If he won't continue negotiations, they come to a halt.'

'So why are we still alive?' Martin asked again. 'If we disappeared, the Dispensator might not even bother with a letter of formal complaint. And if it were an accident . . .'

'Good question,' I said, trying to sound less queasy than I felt. 'It may be what Epicurus called a "rescue hypothesis" ' – I ignored the look on Martin's face – 'but let us suppose that the Imperial Government is not a monolithic structure. Let us suppose it is a group of more or less ordinary people, riven by faction. One faction might want us dead. That would explain Rome and what happened here today. It might also explain what nearly happened under the Ministry.

'Another faction seems to want us alive. That would be led by the old eunuch. He certainly wants us gone – but his preferred means of getting his way seems to involve playing the Dispensator's game. This means keeping us hard at work and ransacking every library in the loyal parts of the Empire to give me whatever I ask for.'

'And you find that convincing?' Martin asked, his voice incredulous.

'Every hypothesis stands or falls according to the facts it is supposed to explain,' I said with a shrug. This one didn't explain everything, but sounded likely otherwise.

'Can you conceive how it feels to be forsaken by God?' Martin asked suddenly.

'Er, not really,' I said without thinking. I'd been watching some sea birds as they flew out from the walls to dive for rubbish tossed from the ships. It was a good moment before I realised Martin was going into one of his funny turns.

I thought about some heart-warming sermon culled from the Book of Job. But it was too late for that. In any event, Martin was now calm again. We'd come up level with the corpses and could see they were still fresh enough for the birds not to have had the eyes. Martin stood awhile in silence, looking into the dead faces. 'In the midst of life, we are in death,' he said mournfully.

'No, Martin,' I said, trying to pull him back to the present. 'In the midst of death, we try to keep our wits about us and stay alive.'

'How long do you suppose this will continue?' Martin asked. 'How long must we linger at these Gates of Death?'

'Search me,' I answered. 'It could be right to the time when Heraclius is sitting in the Imperial Box in the Circus – or being looked at from there.'

'Until then, we stay?' Martin asked. He was staring again into the dead faces, a look of horrified fascination on his own. 'We stay and do whatever duty may be required of us?'

'I'm afraid so, Martin,' I said, putting my arm in his as we continued our stroll along the walls.

'And is waiting to be murdered among those duties?' he asked.

'I wish I had a more comforting answer than I have,' I said. 'So far as possible, we don't go out of the Legation. When we do go to the libraries, we stick to the main routes where we shall be watched and reasonably protected.'

'Why did the eunuch tell you all this in public?' he asked with a change of tone, turning back on the conversation. 'It will be all over the place by now.'

That was the one fact my hypothesis didn't explain. I'd been chewing it over ever since Theophanes had left me. Was he trying to persuade some other faction to leave me to him? That didn't sound likely.

'I can't answer that one,' I said, abandoning all attempt at reassurance. 'The man has a reason for everything he does. Sadly, it's hardly ever apparent to people like us.'

'God have mercy! God have mercy!' Martin cried softly, crossing himself.

14

It was late evening of the same day. I was back in the Legation. His afternoon terrors settled by a light dinner and extended prayers, Martin had gone out for another of his walks. Authari had then come back from the brothel empty-handed – some problem of licensing had closed it without warning.

I was alone in my office. My eyes were beginning to hurt from reading by lamplight. I could swallow some opium. I could drink myself silly. I could have a slow wank. Any of those, and I'd fall asleep. But I fancied none of them tonight. The light aside, I didn't even fancy a book.

I was thinking again about the roof tiles. I nearly had been got this time. Martin was right – an 'accident' wouldn't have raised an official eyebrow back in Rome. It was down to luck alone that I was still alive. Who could tell if there would be a next time? Or, if there were, how that would turn out?

I got up from my desk and went out to the balcony and stood in the evening air. Distant, I could hear the sounds of Constantinople. There was a murmur of crowded streets. A dog barked. Below me, in the dark gardens, the night insects chirruped and a light breeze stirred the bushes. There was the ever-present smell of aromatic shrubs. A moon was rising.

From the slave quarters directly below, I could hear a drinking party in subdued but determined swing. Snatches of song and the occasional burst of laughter drifted upwards. I thought of the Permanent Legate and what news I'd just picked up. There could be no doubt he was sticking to his own rooms on the other side of the main hall. All access was blocked by Demetrius. Our slaves could find out nothing from the household beyond what Martin had discovered on our second day. The messages I sent him were never answered.

I looked at the sky about the risen moon. It was black. Looking down, I could see neither the little garden at the foot of the steps down from my balcony nor the larger, central gardens. I turned and looked along the blank shuttered windows beyond my own suite. No movement. No sign of life.

The Legation, I must remind you, was built around a central square divided into a jumble of enclosed gardens. Its four sides were on two storeys of very high rooms. Seen from the square outside – not that anything could be seen through those blank, marbled walls – my suite was on the top floor to the left of the main entrance hall. It took up half of the front elevation. All its windows, remember, were at the back, facing on to the gardens.

I looked left along the upper storey of windows in the Legation. Next door was my bedroom, with its own door to the balcony. Beyond that were a few guest and reception rooms. From the far end of my suite, the Legation continued at a right angle, reaching down in a long enclosing arm to join the other buildings opposite my balcony. The far side was mostly hidden by trees but I was sure I could have seen lights over there, had there been any lit.

With Martin, I had found a way into that enclosing arm from the garden. Its rooms hadn't been used in years and were falling into ruin. The only signs of maintenance had been on the street side of the building, to preserve the symmetry of the Legation and to protect it against intruders.

I looked to my right. The line of windows continued until it reached the back end of the main hall and its dome. All of these were mine. Martin's bedroom was the fifth window along. Next to that was his office. After that were another four windows of rooms that were mostly unused.

Though he'd made some attempt at the front of the building, the architect employed to add the dome to the main structure had done nothing at the back to hide its incongruity. The brickwork of the dome broke all the harmony of the rear elevation. The parapet wall that hid the roof tiles from an observer below had been demolished in part, and its jagged edge shone white in the pale moonshine.

Beyond that must lie the rooms of the Permanent Legate. Seen from the square outside, the front of the Legation was symmetrical about the dome. Seen by day from my window, the right enclosing arm of the Legation looked in much better order than the left. I couldn't gain access to it but I supposed here was where the Legation did its work.

An elongated square of light played on this right arm. I couldn't see its source because of the dome. But there was a lit room on the other side of the dome from where I was standing.

The idea was one of those things that pops fully formed into the consciousness. Without realising it, I must have been going over it as I stood there. But all I can say is that one moment I was thinking nothing whatever, and the next moment I had the plan complete in my mind.

If the Permanent Legate wouldn't call for me, I'd go calling in my own way.

About eight feet above me, the balcony was part shaded by a ledge that jutted out from the base of the parapet wall. It was covered in lead sheeting, so far as I could tell, and ran along that whole line of windows. I could see that it sloped very gently down away from the wall, so rainwater could be collected in a gutter along the edge and carried off to downpipes.

There was an abrupt narrowing and increased sloping as the original parapet was broken by the dome. But a ledge seemed to extend all round the dome. Though I couldn't see what lay on the far side, I could see it continuing along the right arm of the Legation.

When I had finished the jug of wine, I stripped off and laid my clothes carefully on the little couch against my office wall. Then I went back on to the balcony and looked up.

Making sure nothing was likely to give way under me, I climbed on to the balcony rail. This got me up about chest height to the ledge. The slope was noticeable and I'd need to take care not to fall off. But bare, slightly moist feet on eighteen inches of heavily weathered lead give a reasonable grip.

I hauled myself up and, facing towards the dome, lay on the lead sheeting. Though the sun was long down, it still gave off a faint warmth. I could now see that the sheeting was covered in places with raised layers of shit where birds had gathered. For the most part, however, the lead shone white and smooth in the moonlight.

It didn't matter how hard I pressed the right side of my body against the parapet wall, still my left shoulder and my left arm hung over the edge. I kept myself stable by resting my left arm very lightly on the lead guttering.

Lying flat on the ledge, I twisted my upper body out over the balcony. I gripped the outer wall of the gutter with both hands, and carefully lowered my head and shoulders. So long as I kept enough body area in contact, the sloping was no cause for instability. The lead of the guttering was thickly folded, and held my weight without buckling. Without any risk of sliding forward, I was able to look through the top part of the window and into my office. Bathed in the pool of light thrown out by a single lamp, my desk and the papers on it were clearly in view.

I got up and, keeping the front of my body close against the wall, edged sideways along the ledge all the way to the dome. I had a slightly queasy feeling as I left the safety of my balcony. There was nothing now beyond that eighteen inches of lead but a thirty-foot drop to the gardens. But those eighteen inches seemed fully sufficient to keep me safe.

Passing along the ledge around the dome was harder. It narrowed to about nine inches here and sloped rather more. Far worse, the moonlight showed me that the lead was rippled in places, the underlying material having crumbled.

As I stepped up on to the ledge I told myself not to look down into the darkness where the moonlight didn't reach. Arms spread wide, my body pressed forward against the lower convexity of the dome, I slowly and very carefully continued edging to my left.

Once or twice, I stretched my left foot down into nothingness. The ledge had crumbled, and the lead had sagged downwards. This explained the damp patches on the inside of the dome. It probably also explained the musty smell in some of my unused rooms.

The moon was now rising higher and I could see by twisting my head that the breakage in any one place was no more than a foot or so. I could step over it and be on a firm surface again. The lead was raised here and there, and my weight pressing down flattened it with a gentle creaking. Again, the lower walls of the dome were thick enough to prevent the noise from carrying inward.

The arc of the dome must have been only two or three times the straight length from my balcony, but the distance must have taken five or six times longer to cover.

At last I was through. Panting from the careful effort, and slightly shaky from all the risk, I stood still for a while on the firm and wide ledge that, as I'd expected, ran along the other side of the Legation.

I'd never have got this far from my suite inside the building.

Taking care not to make any additional noise, I got down on my hands and knees and inched along the ledge. Seeing a dim light within the first window beneath me I lay flat and took hold of the lead guttering. Making sure not to bend what was here fairly soft metal, I pulled myself over and down and looked briefly in through the lit window.

15

It was a smallish room – about half the size of my office – and fitted up as a chapel. There was a silver crucifix on the altar and icons of Saint Peter and of the Virgin covered the plain walls. At first I thought the man praying by the altar was Demetrius. He was about the same age and had the same bald patch.

It was hard to tell in that light whether the man was naked or partly clothed. The wide circle of darkness on his back might have been a piece of cloth, or it might have been some peculiarity of the skin. His outer clothes lay beside him in a crumpled heap. He knelt on the plain wooden boards, his arms raised in a prayer of intense devotion.

The man held himself so still that he might have been a statue. I watched him awhile, then grew bored. I hadn't risked my life to see someone saying his prayers. And the withered flesh of his back and buttocks was about as diverting as an empty wineskin.

Just as I was about to pull myself back on the ledge, the man groaned. 'O sweet and merciful Mother of God,' he cried softly, 'take this cup of bitterness away from Thy servant.'

He repeated the prayer, and again. Then, still on his knees, he twisted round to his left. It was now that I saw his huge erection. Throbbing, foreskin retracted from the swollen glans, it jutted upwards from the dark tangle of his crotch.

It was Antony, the legal official. But for the fact that he would tell us bugger all about the set-up in the rest of the Legation, he'd been about the friendliest of the officials. Now, I could see a wild gleam in his eyes.

I resisted the urge to pull myself out of sight. Unless he was looking, it was doubtful if he'd see me. He'd more likely notice the sudden movement. For the moment, I held still.

Antony stretched over to his clothes and took out a pouch of polished but very soft leather. It was about the size of a small correspondence bag. He kissed it reverently and turned back to the altar. He held it up before the crucifix and prayed again.

'Lead me not, O Lord, into temptation,' he said over and over, an edgy, fanatical note coming into his voice.

At last, he untied the bag. From it he produced a small corded whip. He held this up for Divine Inspection. It was one of those nasty things with sharpened iron triangles that you use as a last resort on your slaves. He kissed the handle and, with a melodramatic flourish, pulled himself upright on his bended knees.

'Sweet Virgin, give me strength to resist and endure,' he snarled through clenched teeth. With a sudden hiss of leather, and the staggered *smack!* of iron on flesh, he took the whip to himself. With wild force, bearing in mind his awkward position, and obviously much practice, he struck again and again. His prayers rose to a loud babble as he tore lumps out of himself and the blood ran freely down his back.

It was now that I realised the dark patch on his back was the scabbed-over effect of previous devotions. Those vicious bits of iron had the scabs off in an instant, and were ripping into already raw flesh.

Well, this had made the trip worth the effort! I'd not be telling Martin about it for fear of imitation, but I watched in fascination.

Indeed, as I watched that frenzied performance, I felt myself coming up in sympathy. For all he was no looker, the man was putting on a fine performance. You'll pay through the nose to see anything half so good in a brothel.

I unclamped my left hand from the gutter and pushed it under my belly, down towards my crotch. With a horrid fright, I found myself sliding forward. One moment, I was as stable as if back in my bed. Another, and I was in free movement. I tightened my right grip on the gutter, trying to stabilise myself with brute strength. That stopped the sliding. Instead, I began to roll on to my left side. With my head and shoulders already hanging over the ledge, I was barely an inch short of rolling straight into the darkness. If the lead guttering held, I might be able to swing myself into the chapel.

Otherwise, it was the darkness.

Just in time, I got my left hand back on the gutter. My body pitched to the right. I was stable again.

I pulled myself up and lay flat along the ledge. What had looked wide and solid from my balcony now felt like a tightrope. The hundred or so yards back to the balcony stretched into as many miles as I lay shaking and sweating. For the first time, I wondered how I'd get back. Crawling on hands and knees had been easy enough. How to stand up again and turn with nothing but a blank wall to steady myself?

But I forced the thought from my mind. So long as I kept my nerves steady, I'd find my way back. I'd just have to be more careful.

Looking back into the room, I could see that Antony had given up on the scourging. He was now lying on his back, scrubbing the boards with his tattered flesh. A real enthusiast, I can tell you, would have had a dish of salt handy. As it was, those boards must have hurt like dry buggery.

Gasping with passion and at the terrible pain, he smashed hard with the whip handle on his balls and his continuously throbbing erection. It was all to no effect – or it was to none he might have admitted. With a despairing but subdued wail, he went off like an enema syringe. It was an impressive sight. Then, with a convulsive heave, he was over on his front. He buried his head in his clothes and sobbed disconsolately.

'Oh, filthy, filth of filthiness,' he mumbled into his clothes. 'How shall I ever look back from the Jaws of Hell?'

Still erect and throbbing, his cock poked out from beneath his body.

'Yes,' I thought to whisper into the room – 'Get out more often!' But I resisted the urge. In his present mood, he'd probably think it was the Virgin herself giving him advice, and there was no telling what mischief I'd inflict on the streets.

I could have stayed to watch more of the tears and broken prayers. But I was still getting over my fright, and Antony had turned to slobbering over some relics. It was plain I'd seen the best he had to offer. Time to move on.

I continued along the ledge. The other rooms I passed below me were dark and silent. It was beginning to look as if that singular wank was all I'd see tonight.

But no – from the very last room before the right-angle turn to the left, I could see a flood of light. That was surely what I'd seen from my balcony. I positioned myself above and prepared to look down.

Before I could get my head down to look in, I pulled sharply back.

16

'My dear Silas, if I can't bring you to sympathise, you might at least take into account the problems we face.'

It was Theophanes, though it took me a moment to recognise the voice. His Latin had none of the ceremonious courtesy that it usually had with me. Instead, it was rapid and colloquial. He was standing by the window directly beneath me. He was so close, I could have reached down and touched his elaborately styled hair.

Another voice spoke indistinctly from deep inside the room. I couldn't catch the words, but the voice was one of those affected noble drawls you still occasionally heard in Rome when I was young.

This was His Excellency Silas, the Permanent Legate to the Emperor of His Holiness in Rome. I badly wanted to twist down and get a look at him, but with Theophanes walking about the room, it was best to stay fully on the ledge and listen as well as I could to the conversation.

'Can you imagine what it's like to collect taxes when there are no taxpayers? To direct armies and ships that have their only existence on a sheet of papyrus? To govern cities that are for the most part become heaps of stinking ruins?

'The revolt got up by the Exarch of Africa has brought on a crisis. Even if it can be handled, it has forced us to an awareness that we cannot continue indefinitely to act on the assumption that the plague of seventy years ago was a problem no worse than the barbarian invasions of the West.

'We now have a solution to the problem. For the first time since we deposed Silverius, it is a solution that involves the Roman Church. You will soon not be tacking in your usual manner between increasingly ludicrous definitions of the Creed that only involve us in endless difficulties.'

There was more mumbling from inside the room. I could catch something like one word in three. But it brought an explosion of rage from Theophanes that left its meaning as plain as if I'd heard it all.

'In private, Silas, let us be plain. Heresy is whatever your man in Rome declares it to be when the Greek and Eastern Churches disagree. And you support one side or the other exactly as suits your temporal interests. At least when there was an Emperor in the West, he only intervened in our affairs with some regard for the Empire as a whole. I increasingly think you people will only be happy when there is no Empire at all, and you can lay down your law among the successor kingdoms of the East as you are doing in the West.

'But' – his voice fell – 'we now have an agreement that gives you what you want and safeguards every legitimate interest of our own.'

His voice rose suddenly to a strangled shout from deeper in the room: 'So why are you doing your personal best to ruin everything? Aren't we giving you enough?'

Delivered in a faint whine, there was more from Silas.

'There is nothing more to discuss,' Theophanes snapped. 'The matter is fully agreed.'

Another reply, then Theophanes spoke again:

'So far as they can be, the Lombards are squared. The Franks will not intervene. I have done what I can here to ease matters. For the rest, I look to you and yours.'

Outside on that ledge, I fought to control my breathing. There was no doubt I'd stumbled across something important. The question was what?

But that's the problem with eavesdropping. If you don't hear the beginning, you probably won't understand all of it. What I did hear, though, knocked out every theory based on what I'd been told earlier. That was a lie for public consumption. Theophanes wanted people to think there was some difficulty with the Permanent Legate, and that I was its cause. So far as I could now tell, there was an underlying agreement. The two of them, plus the Dispensator, were all in this together.

But what was this? If I'd been able to catch more than the occasional word in reply, it might all have made more sense. But the Permanent Legate was stationary on the far side of the room, and mumbling away like an adulterer at confession.

Why was he pretending to have withdrawn? Why had he let Theophanes in to lecture him? What was this deal? And where did I come into it? If I wasn't needed to negotiate anything or to be an excuse for others not to negotiate, why had I been sent here? Why was I in so much danger?

I checked my thoughts. Did I now hear a mention of my name?

'You will leave him also in my hands,' Theophanes replied, a very hard tone in his voice.

Something now from Silas in a nasty voice, and an affected laugh.

'I don't care if he is!' Theophanes said. I could almost hear the impatient wave. He moved back to the window. 'Like most others of his sort, he was brought up a beer drinker, and he still drinks wine as if it were beer. As for what you call orgies, I have no doubt this Legation has seen worse.

'Whatever the case, he's no fool. I saw straight through your Dispensator on that point, and I've now had over a month of personal observation. If he is to be of any use at all, he will need careful management – and that must come entirely from me.'

Theophanes moved deep inside the room. I think he stood opposite the Permanent Legate, but his voice came up to me clear though faint.

'I grow tired of the repetition,' he said, impatience now mingling with contempt. 'Justinus told him nothing. The boy didn't even touch the letter. As for Justinus, he was in a coma when he arrived at the Ministry. I left him dead in his cell. Had he spoken, it would be different. But his letter said nothing to the uninitiated.

'So long as you stay locked in here, Silas,' Theophanes said with finality, 'your safety is guaranteed. But withdrawal means total seclusion. You will not receive anyone but me. You will not receive the Master of the Offices. You will not receive Phocas himself, should he come calling. You will certainly have no dealings with that lunatic Priscus. If *he* comes knocking, you will send at once for me.

'You will remain out of sight. You will also ensure that Demetrius does not leave the Legation. If I see him in public, I will have him taken in and flogged.'

'You'll do no such bloody thing!' The Permanent Legate's outburst came clearly through the window. Theophanes brushed him aside.

'I do not want any repetition of the game you tried with such idiocy to play in Ephesus,' he said flatly. 'If the report of the investigating magistrates hadn't landed first on my desk, you and I might have found ourselves swinging side by side from the City walls.'

Theophanes must now have been standing opposite the Permanent Legate. Whatever the case, his voice was low and fast, and I couldn't hear the burst of conversation that followed. The next thing I clearly heard was about the younger Heraclius.

'He's stuck in Cyprus,' Theophanes said with a laugh. 'Remember the deal brokered by old Heraclius in Carthage between son and nephew – whichever gets here first to depose Phocas and become Emperor? That is a weakness in the whole scheme. Heraclius and Nicetas have been racing each other from the West like drunken charioteers.

'Nicetas has Egypt, and virtually the whole Army of the East is now in his hands. But he can't get here soon without ships, and Heraclius can't easily move from Cyprus without military support. If either of them does arrive between now and Christmas, everything will be in place.'

Theophanes began another sentence that might have gone some way towards explaining things. But he broke off suddenly.

'Did you hear that noise?' he hissed, his voice a mixture of malevolence and alarm.

It was me. I'd lain so long in one place, you see, that sweat had dissolved the bird shit under my body. At first, it had been as hard and rough as concrete. Then, without warning, it had turned into a rather gritty lubricant. I'd slid forward and to the left. My left leg was trailing over with no support.

Again, I'd looked into the darkness. Then my hands had closed over the edges of the gutter. This time, though, it wasn't a matter of restoring equilibrium. I had to hold myself continually in position. If I relaxed, I'd slide again. With a loud creak, the lead of the guttering bent outward. I'd moved my hands sharply left, to grab at it. The gutter held, but I couldn't say how much noise I'd made.

Theophanes was back at the window. He pushed his head out, looking furiously to right and left. He ignored the dog that had started barking again in the distance. It was obvious he was looking for something much closer.

Thank God he didn't look up. He'd have seen straight into my terrified face!

By the time he did think to look upwards – and I could hear his panicky breathing barely inches away – I'd managed to pull my head back. My fingers were still clamped hard on the outer edge of the gutter. But although Theophanes must have been too dazzled by the lamps inside the room to see those two tight lumps, he knew there was someone above.

'I want you over here, Silas,' he said softly. 'I'm going for Alypius. If you see or hear anything, call out at once.'

I heard the quiet turning of a key in its lock. In a moment, Theophanes would be making his way along the right arm of the Legation, to see what he could from one of the far windows. And I could then expect Alypius underneath me, poking up with a sword as his master directed him.

I'd learned little enough from listening in to the conversation. But the fact that I knew of it must have made it worth putting me out of the way. A soft heart doesn't get you far if you want to run an Empire.

It was lucky for me there was no balcony on this side of the dome. The only windows I could see from my position on the ledge were at the end of the right arm. By standing, of course, I'd see more, but I would be equally visible to anyone able to look in my direction. But if keys were needed – and there was always the need for secrecy – discovery was still some way off.

I slithered back along the ledge until I was on dry lead again. Too frightened of discovery even to think about falling, I got up as carelessly as if the drop had been only a few inches. In the same way, I turned and walked quickly back to the dome. There was a momentary rush of fear as I felt my heels projecting over the narrower ledge. But, body arched forward, I was shuffling quickly to the right.

The moon was now fully up. Unlike on my way out, I didn't continually stop to feel my way, but kept moving further and further to the right – that is, increasingly out of view. As I moved, the patterns of light and shadow on the brickwork of the dome seemed to race past an inch from my nose.

As the furthermost windows of the Legation's right arm disappeared behind the bulk of the dome, I heard the outward swing of shutters and a hissed command in the language Theophanes had spoken in the library.

If I jumped straight down to the balcony at the first safe point and dodged inside, I might not be seen.

17

'And where the fuck have you been?'

His face making up for any lack of volume, Authari stood on the balcony. He must have been watching me all the way back from the dome.

Normally, you expect a certain dignity where exchanges with slaves are concerned. But these weren't normal circumstances, and Authari wasn't a normal slave.

'Let's get inside,' I whispered. 'I think we can be seen out here.'

As we stepped into the dim light of my office, I looked back once. Far over, in one of the last rooms of the Legation right arm, there was still a light burning.

Was that a face looking back at me? It might have been a trick of the moonlight.

'You're back early, Martin,' I said, trying to sound nonchalant. I glanced at the wine jug to see if it had been refilled. No such luck!

'I'm back late, Aelric – very late,' Martin said. His face was ghastly in the moonlight that streamed into the room. Was that his blue robe he was wearing? I wondered vaguely to myself. I thought he'd gone out in the yellow one.

But he continued: 'We've been hunting the place down for you. If I hadn't seen you staggering round like a drunk on that ledge, we'd have raised the alarm. We were terrified for you up there. Please don't do this again.'

I ignored the slight on my balancing abilities. Before I could think of a reply, Martin spoke again: 'Did you see the Permanent Legate?'

'No,' I said. I thought briefly whether to say more and I decided not to. There had been a thawing of relations lately between

Martin and Authari. On the one hand, it had saved me the endless trouble of mediating their spats. On the other, I was beginning to appreciate the value of 'divide and rule'.

Besides, I needed time to sit down and think all this through. I was like a fisherman who'd set out to catch a meal and had pulled up a feast.

'Do you know how dirty you are, Master?' Authari asked, his temper back under control.

I looked down at my naked body. I was black with filth. Aside from the general rubbing off of lead on me, the bird shit clung like an oily gel. A trickle of sweat that started from my chest was carrying bits of it on to the floorboards.

'We can't get a silent bath arranged,' Martin said. 'Authari, I'll help you with cold water and sponges.'

They looked at each other. It was as if they were taking up a conversation I'd interrupted.

'No,' I said, suddenly cold with the ebbing of the excitement. 'There's plenty of water running through the latrine. I'll scrub up in there.'

I heard a subdued wailing from some other room in the suite.

'What in God's name is that?' I asked weakly. I was suddenly too exhausted to feel the alarm I felt I ought.

'Let's get you clean first,' Martin replied edgily.

I looked down at the baby boy. He couldn't have been more than a day old.

With infinite tenderness, Martin wrapped him in the sheet and laid him back on his bed. Authari took up the sponge again and was squeezing milk into the little open mouth.

'He was lying all alone in the porch of the Mary Magdalene Church,' Martin explained again. 'There were some dogs sniffing at him. I couldn't leave him.'

It was impossible to know who'd dumped him there. The mother would never come forward to say.

'Well, you can't keep him here,' I said firmly. 'You'll have to take him back to St Mary's. Let someone else take him. There's always someone out there trawling for boys.'

'Oh please,' Martin gabbled, 'please don't say that.'

'He was dumped too late already, Master,' Authari broke in. 'He'll have to survive the dogs before he's any chance of a foundling hospital.'

A foundling hospital? With beggars dying in the streets, the most likely outcome was that some priest would baptise the boy to save him from the fires of Hell, and then clap a hand over his nose and mouth.

'What is to become of him?' Martin asked.

What answer was there to that? I looked down at the boy again. I thought of my pregnant Gretel. I thought of Edwina and my living child. I swallowed and looked away.

'We'll look after him, Master,' Authari added. 'He'll be no trouble to you. He can stay in the slave quarters below. You won't know he's down there.'

'Then we'll need a wet nurse,' I said. 'He'll need to be fed.'

Those weren't the words I'd intended. What I had intended was to order the child to be put back early the next evening and was astonished even as I uttered them. It was like watching a close friend say something unexpected.

Having said these words, though, there was no going back.

'Martin,' I added after a pause, 'go to the slave market tomorrow. I'm sure you'll pick up someone. You know where the key is to my strongbox. Take what you need from there. Do make sure to buy someone in good health.'

I cut off their excited babble and continued: 'I take it you will adopt the child as your own. That, or you'll rear him as a slave.'

Silence.

Martin's wife would never allow him to adopt – not with their own child. He was plainly thinking of Sveta's scolding voice. As for enslavement:

'Such is against the laws of the Empire,' Martin said with sudden pedantry. 'If you pick up a foundling, its status is automatically freeborn.'

I gave a cynical laugh. 'That's what the lawyers say. Didn't they also tell you and your father that enslavement for debt had been abolished? You really should ask the brothel keepers where they get their stock.'

If Martin wanted a boy slave, he had one here for the taking. But he still wasn't interested.

I looked hard at the child. No longer crying, it lay calm before me, eyes still squeezed shut. It was very, very small.

'Your next act of goodness', I said slowly, 'will have rather more thought about the practicalities than this one.'

I paused for silence. Then: 'I will adopt the child myself. I don't know if I'm of age yet to do that sort of thing within the law. But the Law of Persons can be flexible if approached in the proper way.'

I bent down and scooped the child into my arms. 'I accept this child as my own,' I said, speaking loud. It really was like watching someone else. 'I name him' – I thought quickly – 'I name him Maximin after the dear man who saved my own life as an act of charity.'

Yes – that was right. I thought back two years to that time in Kent, when Maximin had walked all day through the rain to snatch me back from King Ethelbert. But for him, I'd be dead by now. And that was if I were lucky.

It was right that I should rescue someone equally helpless, and that I should call him Maximin.

I brought the child's head up to my lips. After so much cold scrubbing downstairs, I was more than usually sensitive to the sudden warmth. A strange lump came into my throat as I breathed in the babyish smell. I wanted to add some formal-sounding declaration of paternity. But I found I couldn't speak.

I put the bundle down again and walked quickly from the room. As I went back down the corridor to my own bedroom, I could hear Martin and Authari fussing over my Maximin. He would need a room on the upper floor now, Authari said. Martin replied in a dreamy voice that was part relief and part something else.

Had I lost face? I asked myself as I undressed for what remained of the night. Had I shown weakness? Perhaps I had. But I didn't feel that it mattered.

I was woken by the sound of banging outside my window. The sun was still low in the sky, and there were long shadows that kept the gardens overcast.

Standing on the balcony, I looked along the line of windows towards the dome. There was a long ladder going all the way up to where the ledge above the windows joined the dome. Slaves were hard at work, fixing an elaborate contraption of spiked railings.

How the thing had been put together in such a short time was beyond me. But there would be no more night wanderings around the outside of the Legation.

One of the slaves noticed me. Holding the ladder carefully with one hand, he touched the other to his head and bowed as best he could.

I nodded and looked away. In the enclosed garden just below the balcony, those five monks were at work again. They seemed to be under a vow of perpetual silence. When I'd spoken to the one I had seen looking up at me on the first day, he'd drawn his hood closer over his face and turned away from me. Was he watching me now, as I stood observing the slow and rather haphazard tending of the flower-beds?

I stepped back inside. I needed to think all this through. Why had Theophanes killed Justinus of Tyre? What had been in that letter? Above all, what was the nature of this agreement between him and the Church? If it involved suppressing the African revolt, why be so frightened of the Emperor? What was that stuff about bribing the Lombards?

And where did I fit into this scheme of things? Theophanes had confirmed I was useful, and so worth keeping alive. But for what purpose and for how long?

My thoughts were interrupted by the sound of Maximin crying in the room next but one to mine. With a jumble of recollection, I realised it hadn't been a dream never mind what had happened in Kent nor what might in Rome: I really was a father.

'God's tits!' I muttered. I looked round for something to drink, but found only lemon water. I threw on a dressing gown and stepped out of the room.

Authari was folding a fresh napkin for the child. There was a bright shitty smell all around. Martin was making a proper mess with the milk and sponge. Every so often, he was getting a drop into the child's mouth and the cries turned to an odd gurgling.

As I entered the baby's room, Martin stood. I motioned him to continue. One way or another, my son had to be fed.

I looked at Maximin in the light of day. Babies by nature are never beautiful, and he was gasping and choking as if in a fit. Even so, he seemed to be shining slightly.

I forced my eyes away. I might be his father, but I also had a position to maintain.

'When you're ready,' I said, 'we'll go off to market together. I feel I ought to choose the nurse. I want one who doesn't know any civilised language. I don't think you need ask for my reasons.'

'Indeed, sir,' said Martin. 'Would you allow me to buy your son a rattle?'

'Of course,' I said – 'though he'll not be in need of that for a while.'

As we were leaving, a messenger arrived from the Ministry.

'Do tell His Magnificence,' I said, fighting to keep my voice steady, 'that I expire with joy to receive his invitation. I will join him tonight for dinner at the usual place.'

I settled on a fattish, rather plain woman who spoke Lombardic but came from somewhere more remote. Her own child, the dealer said, had 'died' on the journey to market. She'd be the ideal nurse.

Ideal she was. I wanted a nurse for my son, and only that. If I wanted sex, I'd continue to send out for it. I did have certain duties to Gretel, you'll understand.

As I finished paying up and giving the delivery address to the dealer, I felt another nervous twinge about Gretel. She'd go off like a volcano when she heard the brief message I'd dropped earlier into the collection bin.

The problem with women is that, unless you beat them all the time – and I've tended to neglect that side of my duties – they always get ideas above their station.

But what was done couldn't now be undone. Indeed, I'd just allowed Martin to arrange the baptism for the day after next.

It's surprising how much you need for a child of the higher classes, and how much it all costs. It's all silk and linen and things of horn and lead, and polished wooden boxes for storing it.

I made sure to pick up another nice present for Gretel – a rope of black pearls I was assured had come from England. They might calm her down. Or they might not. Still, I told myself, I'd not have to face her until the autumn. Perhaps, I could ask the Dispensator to get us married in front of the Pope . . .

After my bath, as he dressed my hair, Authari hummed a cradle song of his people. I'd laughed several times in the bath and splashed water over the side.

The other slaves smiled as they went about their business. Even one of the Legation officials gave me a less than usually sour look as I passed him on my way to the chair Theophanes had sent from the Ministry.

Martin had retired to his room to pray. It was nice to know that, after yesterday's wobbly, he was back on praying terms with God. Doubtless, I thought, he'd be asking God to overlook my numerous sins in return for one act of charity.

Perhaps He would.

18

Theophanes got to his feet as one of his eunuch clerks burst into the private dining room. He'd just reached the really interesting part of his lecture on the correct application of gold leaf to the face. Now, he was all official coldness.

Puffing slightly, the clerk dropped a message on to the table and stood back.

Theophanes broke the seal and read in silence. There was a hard, impassive look on his face. My stomach turned to ice. Had I after all outlived my usefulness? I put my cup down and put my hands under the table to hide their tremor.

'Alaric,' he asked in a voice that hovered ambiguously between the friendly and the official, 'are you aware of last night's murder?'

I shook my head. I'd seen how everyone in the slave market was passing the official news bulletin around with greater than usual interest, but had been too involved in my own affairs to get a copy for myself.

'I am surprised you have heard nothing. This was perhaps the most horrid crime the City has known all year. The Court Poet to His Late Imperial Majesty Maurice was found this morning in the St Antonia Park. His neck had been broken in a struggle with some person or persons unknown. We believe this happened around the midnight hour.'

He handed the message to Alypius, then turned back to regard me with the same cold expression. I shifted uncomfortably in my chair. A moment before, Theophanes had been at his charming best. Now, was he trying to fit me up for murder? It would get me out of the way for what I might have overheard the night before.

Should I just confess everything? Should I tell him all I'd overheard and assure him I knew nothing more? I could promise silence. I could plead for expulsion from the City.

Yes, I could certainly plead for that!

If my throat hadn't been so dry of a sudden, I'd have opened my mouth there and then and started babbling. That stare was terrifying in its blankness.

Just then, it shifted back to eunuchy softness.

'But my dearest Alaric,' he said, 'you have nothing to fear. The poor man was quite elderly and much given to seeking the friendship of strangers in the quiet places of our great City. I cannot imagine that you would ever find yourself in such danger. And we do now have a suspect. That message' – he nodded towards the sheet Alypius was still holding – 'is notice of the arrest.'

'Your efficiency is surely an inspiration to the whole universe,' I said, trying to keep my voice from a croak. Had I been able to trust my hands, I'd have grabbed at my wine cup.

'But you flatter me,' said Theophanes with one of his most benevolent smiles. 'It was my intention to make my apologies and to leave you to finish dinner with none but the serving slaves for company. However, your kind words, and the recollection of an interest you have more than once expressed in my work for the common good of the Empire, suggest you might welcome an invitation to come with me, even at this late hour, to the Ministry, where the suspect awaits my interrogation.'

If I'd been able to think of a polite way of saying 'No thank you', I'd have come out with it on the spot. Go with him to the Ministry? And what on earth was someone of his seniority doing in charge of some petty murder investigation? The victim had been a retired minor functionary of a dead and disgraced Emperor.

Besides, I wanted to go home and join Martin and Authari in looking at Maximin. I wanted to send them to bed so I could continue looking at him by myself.

I realised Theophanes was staring at me again. To people like him you refuse nothing.

'I'd be honoured,' I said, now finishing my wine.

Was that a smile I saw as Alypius coughed into his sleeve?

As we rounded the corner into the Ministry square, I could hear a chatter of voices. The demonstrators were praying together before breaking up and going home for the night. The voices fell silent as we came into view. The sight of Theophanes and a police guard appeared to subdue even these desperate souls. One old woman, however, still came forward. She clutched at Theophanes, catching his right sleeve.

'Where is he?' she pleaded in the cracked voice of the very old or slightly mad. 'When will he come home?'

Theophanes gently prised her hand loose and patted it.

'Go home, my poor woman,' he said gently. 'Your son is not inside. You have no son. You never had a son. Please accept my deepest sympathies. Go home before you take chill. The evenings are not as they were.'

She fell back with a deathly look. Her mouth opened to speak again, but no words issued. We turned from her and walked into the Ministry.

Though all was quiet outside but for the demonstrators, the clerks in the Ministry were still hard at work. There was the same rush of activity in the main hall that I'd seen on my first visit. One of the clerks was waiting for us. He bowed low before Theophanes.

'The young man is with me,' Theophanes said in answer to the unspoken question.

We passed by the staircase leading up to his office. Instead, Theophanes led me to the far end of the main hall and into a corridor of closed doors. Carefully dimmed lamps were fixed beside each door. On each was screwed a small brass plate, giving one or more names, though no functions. At the far end, bright light streamed from an open door.

The first thing I noticed as I walked into the windowless room was an icon, high on the wall, of Christ in His most forbidding Majesty. Otherwise, the walls were of bare plaster. The only furniture in the room was a small table with three chairs. The light came from a tight array of lamps hanging from the ceiling.

Theophanes had motioned me in before him while he spoke to one of the hushed attendants outside. Alypius settled me into one of the chairs and then sat himself across the table from me.

So when, and of whom, was this interrogation to be? I tried not to ask myself. Because I could think of no reason for subterfuge from Theophanes, I willed myself not to speculate on what I was doing in this room.

Alypius looking fixedly at nothing in particular behind my left shoulder, we sat for what seemed an age without speaking. At last, the door widened and Theophanes came into the room.

'My dear young friend,' he began with easy charm, 'I do so regret having brought you here for nothing. But I am now in no doubt that the interrogation would be distressing to one of your youth and sensitivity. It is sad how much moral, and even physical, harshness these matters often require.'

So it wasn't just the basement they used for torturing people.

In a fair imitation of his own manner, I thanked Theophanes for his great consideration and assured him of how comfortably I was seated.

'I would release you now from my invitation,' he said with a smile, 'and allow you to go home to your bed. But the streets are less safe at night than I might wish. And it will take me a few moments to deal with outstanding business before I can arrange for an armed guard to escort you back to the Legation.'

'I wouldn't hear of it!' he said, in reply to my suggestion that I could make my own way back. 'While you remain my personal guest, you must accept my personal concern for your safety. I really do not think I shall be more than a few beats of the heart about my business. I am sure you will find Alypius excellent company.'

How long we sat there in stony silence was beyond my reckoning. It may have been half the night. It may not have been so long at all. But with no diversion, nor any means of marking time, I sat there in a kind of numb apprehension.

Once, and only once, there was a sound. It was a gentle scraping that came from behind me, as if a mouse were running along the top of the icon.

And was that a muffled gasp?

I wanted to look round but Alypius had shifted his glance and now stared me straight in the face. Whatever it had been, the noise was over in a moment. All was silent again until, eventually, the door opened again and Theophanes was back in the room.

'You cannot conceive how embarrassed I am to have wasted your evening,' he said, trying to suppress a look of the most immense self-satisfaction. 'You must come to dinner with me again tomorrow. Then, I promise, things will go more as you have the right to expect.'

I got up. I could have asked what the Devil had been going on – why had I been brought here for nothing at all? But you don't ask a spider's business in the middle of its web. And whatever had happened, it was over. The tension falling sweetly away, I turned on the charm myself.

'For me, and for the good of the Empire, yes,' he said, answering my question, 'it was a most productive interview, and I guarantee that you can go about your business in renewed safety. Such are the fruits of civilisation.'

'Can I go home now?' I asked. I just wanted to get away.

'But of course, young Alaric.' Theophanes beamed at me. 'Only we who are of full years can bear the strains of governing this great Empire. At your age, lateness to bed must ever be attended by dangers that may shorten life itself.'

I lurched forward into his outstretched arms.

19

'This isn't the way to the Legation,' I said to Alypius.

We were alone in the dark, silent streets. Now the nights would be so much safer, Theophanes had said, I'd have no need of the armed escort he'd had in mind. It would be enough to have Alypius with me. He was armed, and that would be sufficient protection.

'It is the way I am instructed to take you,' he said coldly as we turned into the street that was one of the approaches to the square containing the University.

Light or dark, I'd never seen the streets of Constantinople so empty. The sound of our feet on the pavements echoed from the blank walls or shuttered façades of the buildings. I knew them well enough by day but they were very different at this late hour.

Alypius led me into a side street, and then into a clearing that was neither a square nor a park. We stopped by a low brick building. He stepped forward and stroked the polished wood of the little door.

'Do you know what this is?' he asked.

'No,' I said. It was about the size and shape of a rich man's tomb from the days of the Old Faith.

'Behind this door', he explained, 'lies a flight of steps. They lead up from the basements that run beneath the Ministry.'

Dear God! Theophanes had kissed me goodbye in the main hall a quarter of a mile back. And every step I'd been taking since had still been just feet above that vaulted labyrinth of horror. How big was the place?

I looked at Alypius. If he was armed, it was at best a small sword he was keeping out of sight. Even unarmed, I might be able. . . .

I dropped the thought. Behind Alypius stood the whole power of the Empire. I was as much in its power now as if tied to one of the racks under the Ministry.

He smiled, no doubt appreciating the look of dull fear I couldn't be bothered to keep off my face. 'I did say', he added, 'that the stairs lead *up* from the basements. You have already seen the place that invariable custom has made the entrance. At the first light of dawn, the heavy bolts that secure this door on the inside will be drawn and the door will swing outward. Twenty-three bodies will then be carried out. It will be neither more nor fewer than twenty-three. I checked the release forms that His Magnificence signed before dinner.

'According to their station, some will be put into gibbets for display from the City walls. Some will be scattered in the main streets, there to be stepped over and shunned by shopkeepers and by those who toil in the manufactories. They will be reclaimed or cleared away before people like you are accustomed to fall out of bed.'

'Why are you telling me this?' I asked. Alypius was evidently trying to keep me scared. But for all he strained to imitate his master, he was no equal of Theophanes. Whatever else happened tonight, I was realising, the Empire would not be disposing of twenty-four corpses.

'Why did you bring me here?' I asked again. 'No – since your sort never act but on orders, why did Theophanes have me brought here?'

'Why do you suppose we do this, day after day?' he asked in return.

'The official answer', I said, my nerve returning, 'is that they are traitors. Really, of course, none may be guilty of anything at all. It's really a matter of keeping control, isn't it?'

If I'd annoyed Alypius by draining the surprise out of his answer, his face said nothing.

'Back in the days when Maurice was Emperor,' he continued, 'we were victorious on all fronts, or holding our own. It was nothing to the scum who inhabit this City. Once when he returned from a victory over the Slavs, he was screamed at in the street because he'd put up taxes. The Ministers and even His Magnificence were mobbed in their chairs.

'The function of Terror is to break up all the guilds and clubs and professional groupings of the City into an agglomeration of individuals, each looking over his shoulder to see what the others might be saying about him. If no one speaks his mind, no one joins forces. This means Heraclius can come here whenever he likes, and he'll beat his head against the city gates until pestilence and famine have thinned the ranks of his followers.

'How anyone gets on our death-lists is left to chance. The use of those lists, though, is wholly deliberate. Kill enough people and you can announce that the sun rises at dusk and wait for the applause. It also helps compensate for the falling off of tax revenue.'

'I'll ask again,' I said. 'Why are you telling me this? Why has Theophanes sent you here with me?'

Alypius moved away from the door and reached within his cloak. He pulled out his leather satchel.

'While you were at dinner,' he said, 'there should have been a small riot in the Jewish quarter. A priest who was active in policing the conversion of the Jews will have been seriously injured. In view of this, His Magnificence will suggest to the Most Noble Caesar Priscus the need for making an example. A number of prominent persons will be arrested. Among these will be your banker, Solomon ben Baruch.'

This was the last thing I'd expected to hear. All thought of the Ministry dungeons was swept aside by the realisation that I was holding at least a dozen notes from Baruch. If he were taken in for treason or whatever, they'd be worthless.

But Alypius was continuing: 'As you know, the Great Augustus has seen fit to command all the Jews of the Empire to embrace the True Faith of Jesus Christ.'

'Yes,' I said jeeringly, 'and it's set off wild rioting in every Eastern city still controlled by him. Haven't the Jews of Antioch lynched the Patriarch there? Certainly, you'll find no business with the Syrian traders.'

'They have indeed murdered His Holiness of Antioch,' came the stiff reply, 'and the Jews will be punished just as soon as we have any spare forces in Syria. The word of Phocas is law, and he has been assured by a monk of the highest orthodoxy that the Empire will only fall to a circumcised race. He has therefore seen fit to accomplish what Saint Paul on his various missions failed to do.'

Well, that was an interesting prophecy – and it was made before the event. A shame, I suppose, the drunken fool hit on the wrong circumcised race.

Still Alypius hadn't finished. 'The Jew Baruch will be allowed', he said, 'to pay off some of the Caesar's more embarrassing debts. In return for this, he will be released unharmed at nightfall. He will be free to give thanks the day after tomorrow in whatever Sunday service takes his fancy.'

'I see,' I sneered. 'I suppose you'll want paying for this information.'

Without bothering to reply, Alypius pushed his satchel into my hands.

'This contains a number of drafts on a bank run by two Saracen brothers,' he said. 'You will pass these on the Exchange at whatever time and in whatever manner you see fit. The drafts are made out in your name. When you eventually see the Jew Baruch, the proceeds will be made payable to bearer. You will hand the new drafts to His Magnificence when you see him in a sealed packet. You will not discuss them with him.'

The moon came out from behind a cloud and lit up the space in which we were standing.

'I don't think', I said to Alypius, 'I need detain you any longer. I can probably make my own way safely back to the Legation. And, let's face it, whoever tried to murder me yesterday will be snoring like a dog this time of night.'

'There is one more matter,' he said. 'Though he has not yet had an opportunity to offer his congratulations, His Magnificence is aware that you became a father last night.

'Of course, now you have been blessed with fatherhood, you will need to be still more prudent in your conduct. You have seen that Constantinople can be a dangerous place for those who do not look at all times to their safety. It can be dangerous for them – and, I feel it worth saying, *for those around them.*'

'Martin?' I asked next day over breakfast.

He looked up from his beer, bleary and unshaven. He should have been glad he was awake at all. I'd got back to my suite, only to find him and Authari huddled together on my office floor, knocked out on wine and opium. I'd thought at first that Martin had killed himself with the so far untasted fruits of the poppy. But he'd still been breathing, a look of rapture on his face I'll bet he'd never got from praying.

Now he was paying for it.

I smiled brightly, pretending not to notice what a wreck he looked. If I said I was cheerful, I'd be exaggerating. Nevertheless, if I was stuck in Constantinople, still without a guess of why and for how long, I'd got myself out of what might have been a thoroughly nasty scrape. All I had to do was rip off the Jews and I was back in favour with Theophanes – or so it appeared.

'Yes, Martin,' I said, 'you realise we shall have to invite Theophanes to the baptism.'

He looked down again and grunted. He began another of his unflattering comments about eunuchs.

'I don't think there's any question of not inviting him,' I said, cutting him off. I looked again at the note of elaborate congratulation I'd found on bouncing out of bed. Theophanes was promising – I read – 'a cot of polished ebony, trimmed, of course, with ivory and with gold'.

Not bad, that, and at short notice. With Martin, I'd combed every shop in Middle Street the day before looking for almost the same thing. We'd been told in five establishments that ebony was out of the question for at least a month. Theophanes, it seemed, had far greater powers of persuasion than I with a mere purse full of gold. He was assuring me he could have it made ready in a day.

'I'll leave it to you', I went on, 'to draft the invite. I have urgent business coming up that will keep me busy all day. But I'd like something in the most pompous and flowery Greek style.'

Martin scowled and went back to his beer. Then he switched into a Celtic that he appeared suddenly to know less well than I did myself.

'I've heard the rumour from Antony', he said, 'that the Emperor has offered the Persians all of Syria east of Jerusalem and the Avars all they've already taken south of the Danube, if only they'll leave him a free hand with the revolt.'

'None of our business now, Martin,' I said briskly in Latin. 'We obey whatever instructions come from Rome. We accept whatever protection Theophanes sees fit to give. In short, we wait on events.'

I called him back as he reached for the door handle.

'Can you remind me what happened with Pope Silverius?' I asked.

'Why,' said Martin, 'wasn't he the one who was deposed by Justinian for being in the pay of the Goths?'

'That's the one,' I said. 'I think we can agree that politics can be dangerous.

'By the way, if you bump into Gutrune, do remind her to clean her nipples before she feeds Maximin. I once read that the seeds of pestilence can gather in those little folds of skin.'

Though I'd told him nothing, Authari now doubled his precautions. He found another, heavier bar for the door of my suite. He also took to locking every room not immediately in use. He put all the keys on an iron ring and carried it about on his waist. No other slave was now allowed to leave without his permission.

He even took to searching the copying secretaries when they came to work in my suite. He confined them to one room, and had them followed as they went off to the slave latrines. Crabbed little creatures who knew only how to wield a pen, they were no danger. But Authari was taking no chances now we had Maximin.

He took the wet nurse, Gutrune, into his own charge. To be honest, he took her into his own bed. Both facts were a relief to me. I had excellent reason, beside her looks, to keep my hands off her. And I didn't have to worry about giving directions for the care of Maximin.

I still found myself strangely drawn to the child. After those first couple of days, the fascination grew even stronger. I'd spend as much time as I could working in the nursery. Sometimes, when alone with him, I'd put my things aside and pull my chair over to the cot. There I'd sit talking endlessly to the child in English.

I didn't fail to notice that time was passing. I knew that Marcella would, in her usual way, be haggling with the midwives and doctors in preparation for Gretel's confinement and that I had, sooner rather than later, to be away. But now we were settled in and its rules were accepted, the Legation had become our home. Once Authari had barred the door to my suite, we were inside our own world. It was as if we were again on the ship that had brought us here. I passed through the world outside the Legation as often as I travelled to the libraries but I was never part of it.

So day followed day. The endless chatter in those baking-hot streets of high summer often reminded me of the sound of bees as they swarm together and begin to turn angry, but the people never did turn constructively angry; they were held in check by the Terror. The flow of events was smooth and predictable on the surface and I made no further efforts to look beneath it.

20

'Such is the Word of God and of the Universal Church,' the Professor of Theology intoned for the third time that afternoon. Martin scratched madly on his waxed tablet, his shorthand barely keeping pace with the complexity of the answer.

'In the name of His Holiness the Universal Bishop in Rome, I thank you,' I said, recalled from a reverie on nothing at all. It beat the exposition on some polemicist who'd found a way of reading one word in different ways, depending on the orthodoxy of the writer.

But I'd slipped up there. I'd used the hated title. With a barely suppressed intake of breath, the Professor and half his panel of experts glared pure hatred at me. Leaving aside that I hadn't been paying attention, the slip was pardonable. I'd been baptised six months in Canterbury before I discovered the title everyone around me used was of dubious propriety.

Still, even if I'd got up and begun a defence of the Arian heresy, I'd not have given so much offence to the conclave of hunched, bearded clerics gathered there to answer my questions. I thought for a moment that the Professor would get up and set about me with his stick.

It was the last Saturday in September. We were well past any time for leaving that would get us back to Rome in time for the baby's arrival, and there was still no end in sight. Every time the posts came in, there would be another letter from the Dispensator. It always began with curt thanks for work already done, before getting down to an immense list of briefs for new research.

I'd sit with Martin, telling him to get a grip on himself and fighting back my own despair. It swept over me in black waves. I wanted to be in Rome. I *needed* to be in Rome. I was sick of these meetings. I was sick of Constantinople and my regular dinners with Theophanes. I was even sick of the libraries. I wanted to go home.

Under different circumstances, of course, I'd have loved the place. I've spoken already of the University Library. The Patriarchal Library, where most of our research was done, was less exciting in its contents. But there was the same convenience and even luxury of accommodation. Even so, we were exhausting its resources in technical theology. We were finding that – as with the heresy uncovered in Ravenna, which was turning out more serious than expected – there were no comprehensive refutations from the past. It was then that I had to approach the Professor of Theology at the University. I'd send over written summaries of the points to be covered. A day later, I'd go in person with Martin to take down authoritative answers culled or interpreted from the Church Fathers.

What the Dispensator chose to make of all this I left to him. Now I knew my presence in the city was a cover for something else, I'd given up on much more than a token effort. We were there for a particular period of time, and the amount of work required would expand to fill that time. So, while Martin still worked himself and the copyists at breakneck speed – and it did seem to keep his mind from giving way entirely – I'd gone back to spending every morning in the University Library. I might as well get something out of this visit. And it kept me from that dreadful counting of days and from moping over the stream of optimistic chatter Gretel was issuing from Rome.

At last the conference was over and I could go out into the courtyard of the Theology Department for a breath of air and to stretch my legs. Behind me, I could hear Martin fussing with the slaves to get everything back to the copyists.

Turning a corner, I nearly bumped into Sergius, the man who had so mysteriously and in so sinister a fashion warned me off the students back when all had been so new in the City.

'Hello,' he said, in a manner as close to friendly as I'd ever seen in these people. We had, you see, struck up an odd sort of friendship during the regular conferences in the previous month. It didn't run to things like dinner and sharing of confidences. It was more an implicit agreement on the stupidity of every other party in our discussions.

'I thought you'd be straight out of here – back to the sinful books of the ancients.'

That had been my intention. But you don't snub people like Sergius. I still hadn't been able to work out his position. He didn't sit in on every conference. When he did, he'd sit quiet beside the Professor. If he did have advice or questions, he'd whisper them to the professors. No one presumed ever to whisper back.

We walked together down the long colonnade, keeping to the inner wall to avoid the sun, still powerful when full in the sky. We spoke in a desultory way about the difficulty of finding exact Latin equivalents for some of the terms of Greek theology. As I found myself defending *Pater Omnipotens* as the translation of 'Father the Ruler of All' I noticed his attention was wandering just as mine had earlier.

I waited for what I suspected was coming.

'I feel I should apologise,' he said, 'for a certain coldness you may have noted in some of my colleagues. But you are beginning to raise questions that many do not at present find welcome.'

'If I am taking up your time,' I answered, trying for an apologetic tone, 'with repetitions of what you find obvious—'

'But they are not obvious at all, Alaric,' he broke in. 'And they do open issues the practical implications of which you Westerners might not fully understand.'

'How so?' I asked. I'd managed to hit the note I wanted of respectful ignorance.

He looked at me. 'You will understand', came a reply of sorts, 'that I am speaking entirely for myself here. If you want authoritative statements for sending back to Rome, the Illustrious Professor must be consulted. But I meet so few persons of ability from the West that I cannot resist the temptation to exchange a few random thoughts with you – always, of course, in a spirit of brotherly love.'

'I suppose the withdrawal of His Excellency the Permanent Legate', I replied, smiling, 'has been a great loss to you.'

'Not such a loss as we at first thought,' came the reply. Sergius looked up at the coffered plaster of the ceiling. 'Tell me what is meant by the Trinity,' he suddenly asked.

That was easy. I opened my mouth and recited:

'"And the Catholick Faith is this: that we worship one God in Trinity and Trinity in Unity; neither confounding the Persons nor dividing the Substance . . . The Father is made of none: neither created, nor begotten. The Son is of the Father alone: not made, nor created, but begotten. The Holy Ghost is of the Father: neither made, nor created, nor begotten, but proceeding . . . And in this Trinity none is afore, or after another: none is greater or less than another; but the whole three Persons are co-eternal together: and co-equal . . ."'

'Good,' said Sergius, 'and you will agree that nothing could be more obvious or more simply expressed.'

I nodded. Of course, it all makes sense. You only have to believe that there is a God, and that He has a sick sense of humour, and that He has chosen to make understanding this mass of nonsense one of the requirements for not burning in Hell. Believe all that, and one is three and three is one. Equally, the seventh inch on a ruler is followed by the fourth, and lustful thoughts are wrong.

But I kept this to myself, and followed the nodding with what I hoped was a look of devoutness.

Sergius continued: 'This follows by necessary implication from the words of Saint John. Moreover, the True Faith is impossible without it. If, as Arius claimed, Christ were just a Creature of God – no matter how superior to other created beings – where does that leave the Faith? What difference would remain with the Platonists who tried to sustain the Old Faith? Christ becomes indistinguishable from the pagan gods, which are said also to be emanations of the One True God. What then would it matter if we directed our prayers to Christ or to Apollo? The difference between our Faith and any other cult might be of no more consequence than the difference between one house painted white and another painted blue.

131

'We must, therefore, assert that Christ was God. At the same time, though, we cannot agree, with Eutyches and the Monophysites, that He has but a single Nature, which is God. Christ could not be a mere projection of God, as He suffered in ways that are inconsistent with the notion of Godhood.

'Therefore, again, Christ must be *both* God and man. The notion that His Human Nature is subsumed in His Divine Nature, as a drop of honey is dissolved in the sea, is a most damnable heresy, and was rightly declared such at the Council of Chalcedon.'

'Absolutely,' I said, breaking in. I had no wish for a basic lecture on matters I'd been studying for the better part of three months. But Sergius was coming to the point.

'We have been discussing', he said, with a downward glance, 'your proposal made in writing that the Creed might usefully be clarified by adding the words "and of the Son" to the phrase "the Holy Ghost is of the Father".'

I looked closely at Sergius. We'd stopped on our round of the colonnade and were standing by a large plaque on the wall that recorded a gift in the old days from a Roman benefactress. Still avoiding my eye, he continued:

'This is unacceptable. The words may do no more than clarify. But the Creed cannot be altered except by a General Council of the Churches. And we do not think, bearing in mind their continued slide into the Monophysite heresy, that the Churches of Alexandria and Antioch would accept any wording that might imply more than One Nature.

'We continue to hope for a settlement of differences between all the Churches in the East. We cannot risk this by helping you to proceed against a heresy that has been dead everywhere but in the West for hundreds of years.'

Oh, I thought – just like in Rome, it was politics. The Syrians and Egyptians had to be kept happy. Because of that, we could look to ourselves.

'This being said' – Sergius was walking again: I kept pace with him – 'This being said, we might think more favourably of certain incidental changes that did not require a General Council.

'For some while now, the various Churches of the Empire have taken what we regard as an unsatisfactory approach to the use of language. The Gospels, the Letters of Saint Paul, and all the Fathers of any note, are in Greek. It is obvious that Greek is the language most acceptable to God. However, claims have been made by His Holiness in Rome for Latin to be regarded as a co-ordinate language. For historical reasons, these claims could not until recently be challenged. At the same time, Coptic and Syriac liturgies have been tolerated in Egypt and Syria. With the decay of Greek in those regions during the past hundred years, the vulgar languages have risen in importance.

'We might be willing to consider a regularisation of linguistic use. Greek would be regarded as the one authoritative language of the Church – as the language in which God has most recently spoken to man. All would look to Constantinople for final author-ity on any matter of doctrine. Other languages, though, would be formally accepted for those unfortunate peoples unable to receive the Word of God in its original. Such languages might be Coptic, Syriac and Latin. These would all be equal in status, below Greek.

'Once this was agreed, new liturgical translations could be prepared. Being regarded as secondary statements of the Truth, these could contain such additions as might render them com-prehensible to the people. Rome could then make what glosses it pleased on a new translation of the Creed. The Syrians and Egyptians could also gloss other texts so that what may be verbal differences rather than points of fundamental difference might be removed from dispute.'

'A "new translation" of the Creed?' I asked. I knew what was coming but wanted it spelled.

'Oh, indeed,' Sergius said airily, 'a new translation. We have already agreed that *Pater Omnipotens* is not a precise translation. My Latin is not all that it might be, but would not *Pater Omniregens* be more precise? There are many other words and phrases that might bear a second look.

'It would be an honour for us to help in these translations. We accept that our brethren in Rome are less able in Greek scholarship than we remain in Latin. We could very quickly supply new Latin translations of greater accuracy than those undertaken in the past by Westerners.'

'That is unacceptable to us,' I said flatly. I was competent to reject this purely on my own initiative. 'Latin is the official language of the Empire. We could never consent to a settlement that degraded it to the same level as Syriac – or, given time, Lombardic or even English. Whether or not you accept him as Universal Bishop, His Holiness is the senior Patriarch. The language in which He addresses the faithful is to be respected by Greeks and barbarians alike.'

And so we passed the remainder of the afternoon, wrangling over words – and, behind the words, over whether Rome or Constantinople should rule the Churches. I couldn't care less about the relative status of the Father and the Son. But I was a Westerner, and I wasn't having our priests and bishops put in leading strings by a pack of shifty Greeks – being doled out a new set of translations every time we went begging for support.

Not even the dangled promise of no objection to the Universal Bishop title could shake me. It wouldn't have shaken the Dispensator, I could be sure. What point in settling words when the facts they described had been altered?

Our voices rose occasionally as Sergius and I walked up and down the colonnade. We switched back and forth between citations from Scripture and the Fathers and arguments over historic meanings. Martin, who'd sat himself at the far end with a book, was mostly out of hearing. A few Greeks from the conference lounged inside one of the doorways. Again, they were mostly excluded from this exchange of 'random thoughts'.

'Well, Alaric,' Sergius said at last, 'I think this has been a most interesting afternoon. We must repeat it. Something I'd like to discuss in more detail is this heresy uncovered in Ravenna. As you know, some of us regard much heresy as stemming from a misunderstanding of words. The difference between us and the Monophysites is that we regard Christ as One Person with Two Natures, and they regard Him as One Person with One Nature.

'It may be that the Monophysites can be brought to agree that Christ has Two Natures if He has but a Single Will. We might also agree that He has but a Single Will but Two Natures. We need to think about this. I am sure you will make a note of these discussions. All things considered, though, it may be best not to commit anything to the posts, but to wait until you are personally in Rome.'

It was my intention to write all this down. I might as well go through the motions for the Dispensator. But when I got back to the Legation I found myself in another of those acrimonious disputes with Demetrius. Unlike the other officials, he hadn't warmed at all to the presence of a child in the Legation and was lodging endless complaints about the crying at night. He claimed that it was disturbing the sleep of the Permanent Legate. I found this unlikely, bearing in mind the size of the building, but usually found an apology was enough to shut the man up.

Now he'd been complaining to Authari, and had received a mild kicking for his impertinence. It was nothing much – just a scrape and a few bruises – but he was demanding that I have the man hung up and flogged.

'No wine for the rest of today,' I said to Authari, 'and you'll give Master Demetrius the respect in future that becomes a man of his station.'

To Demetrius: 'I will, of course, apologise in person to His Excellency – just as soon as he sees fit to receive me.'

That stopped him short. With a scowl and a mutter about letters to Theophanes, he was off back to his part of the Legation.

21

The bells were still sounding the call to prayer. For all my connection with the Church, I've never been a frequenter of Sunday services. I'd been alone since dawn at my desk in the University Library. Sergius had broken my routine and, day of rest or not, I had work to do.

The Chief Librarian had finally made good on his promise to dig out the complete letters of Epicurus on government. This was a glorious find. Written over eight hundred years ago, the letters were as fresh today as when first dictated.

I'd guessed right about his political opinions. A wise man, he said, is one who wants to be left alone, who wants to leave others alone, and who wants others to be left alone. Therefore, the sole functions of government are to secure individuals in the possession of life and property.

'Most unlike our own dear world of universal love and justice,' I muttered, looking up at the frescoes of the Creation and Fall that adorned the ceiling.

I looked down again. The book rolls must have been four hundred years old. From the *protocol* still attached to one of them, the papyrus dated from before the reorganisation of the Egyptian factories. The last time I'd seen anything that old with proper attribution, it dated from the reign of Caracalla.

How they'd reached the Library was clear. The tag on one of the rolls recorded a confiscation about a century earlier. Less obvious was how they had survived for so long and in such an indifferent climate. A whole line of owners must have treasured them. Perhaps they too had been borne up by the knowledge of death as the end of things.

Half into the third volume, I decided to vary the pleasure of this find by taking a shit. The public latrines of Constantinople are best avoided unless the call of nature is particularly imperious. But the University Library had a nice, clean one that I didn't scruple to use. It was scrubbed and polished three times a day, and gave off very little smell.

I took off my outer robe, hitched up my tunic, and sat on the common bench. Just as I was preparing to finish off, someone else sidled in and sat beside me.

Small, balding, he had the look of a Syrian or Egyptian. He wore good but nondescript clothing. He was rather old for a student, but might have been one of the Sunday lecturers. As I sat there with open bowels, I thought with vague interest that I might have seen him before.

There were five other places on the common bench, and I took a little more interest when the man chose to sit right beside me. Did he fancy me? I wondered, as I unfolded some of the linen scraps I carried for such purposes and leaned forward to dip one in the water channel. I didn't fancy him at all, with his hairy legs and pallid skin.

But I was thinking most about what I'd been reading. Perceiving the truth and having a good shit are both pleasures, so far as they lead to peace of mind. But how to compare them? If they produce the same end, they do so by very different means. There had been nothing in Epicurus to suggest any answer. An idea was floating through my head about comparing not whole experiences, but small increments of each . . .

I got no further. The man next to me cleared his throat and shifted his position slightly.

'That's a good practice, young man,' he said, with an approving look at the wet cloth in my hand. 'I normally carry my own sponge with me. You never can tell what contagion may lurk in these places.'

In the Greek of an educated Syrian, he described various modes of cleansing he had observed on his travels through the East.

I grunted and set about wiping myself. Since he evidently had no sponge with him, I wondered if it might invite more familiarity if I were to offer him one of my private bum-wipes. I decided it would.

'But you are', he continued, 'rather a fastidious young man in all respects. Isn't that so, Alaric of Britain?'

'What business have you with me?' I asked, keeping my voice neutral. This wasn't an attempted pick-up. More likely, I was being approached by some agent of provocation. If he was fishing for treasonable words, he'd get none out of me.

'Why have you followed me here?' I varied my question.

'Partly because getting hold of you in any other way was proving difficult,' he said in a voice so quiet I had to lean towards him even in that little room. 'It was pure luck that I saw you coming into the University on a morning when we'd be alone.

'I believe you tried to save Justinus of Tyre.'

'Your belief is mistaken,' I said flatly.

'You may not yet be aware,' he continued, his voice still low, 'that Heraclius has moved from Cyprus. I was with him just before he set out. He'll be at the Straits within the next few days, and Abydos will open its gate to him without a fight. With a secure base there, he'll move forward to the City. The gates will then open without any need for violence.'

I wondered if I should just grab my clothes and bolt for the Legation. Instead, I leaned forward to wash off the shit I'd smeared over my shaking hands.

'I'm a stranger to the city,' I said at length. 'I've no interest in politics. If you are as you seem, I ask you to understand that I cannot and will not get involved in your affairs. If I see you again, I'll denounce you.'

As I got up to leave, he said in the same level tone: 'I'm not here to recruit you to our band. I only wanted to make your acquaintance, and to commend you for your brave attempt to see right done by poor Justinus. But it was foolish of you to interfere. The work you have been sent here to do is too important to be risked for the life of any one man.'

I looked hard at the man again. I did know him.

'You've changed your mind', I sneered, 'since you tried to kill me with those roof tiles.'

He looked back at me and grinned. He'd given up on his air of mystery.

'Call that a mistake,' he said lightly. 'I follow my orders as given. Let's say that they weren't so clear last month as they have become since. I won't ask if Justinus did tell you anything before the eunuch cut his throat.'

I got up again.

'Keep to your work, Alaric,' he said. 'And remember – God is on our side. What Heraclius is doing, he does not for himself, but for the Greater Glory of God.

'God is with us,' he continued, as if telling the way to the spice market. 'God is before us. When the Blessed Heraclius rules the world as His Universal Exarch, Justice and Peace and Glory will be restored.'

He gave up on trying to sound committed to his cause, continuing in his normal voice: 'But if you want to see something remarkable, that will explain the exact importance of your work, be at the Great Church this afternoon. I can't say more, but the Patriarch himself will be there, and perhaps the Emperor. The service will end before you normally go back to the Legation for your evening entertainments.'

He smiled at the stony look I gave him.

'You will see me again, Alaric, and when you do, it will, I assure you, be to your advantage. In the meantime, you are under our quiet protection.'

Back at the Legation, I called for a jug of wine. And then I called for another.

'Where's Authari?' I grunted at Martin, who had come in with the wine.

'I thought it best to ask him to stay with Gutrune,' he said.

I grunted at no one in particular. At least someone was having a good time in Constantinople.

'Another altercation with Demetrius, I'm afraid,' Martin added.

'Not again?' I sighed. Perhaps I really should beat Authari this time. I was frightened. Much more, though, I was angry. For

139

months, we'd had no more trouble. I had chosen not to ask further questions. Seemingly, in return, whatever was truly going on had retreated from direct view, or did so far above my head or behind my back. I had just learned that I was under the 'protection' of people who had already tried once to murder me.

The last thing I wanted was another whining complaint from Demetrius.

'He told me he'd expect to see you in his office the moment you got back,' Martin said. He flinched as I sat back and opened my mouth.

But I controlled myself. 'If you see Demetrius as you go about your duties,' I said with icy calm, 'you will ask him to attend on *me* in *my* office. You will remind him that my status as a guest of the Emperor is considerably higher than his. If he has a complaint, therefore, he must bring it to me, and at my convenience.

'Before then, you will ask Authari to unhook himself from Gutrune and come to me at once. I will do such things . . .'

I trailed off. I would, of course, do nothing. I hadn't laid violent hands on a slave since leaving Rome. I'd not start now – not on the say-so of bloody Demetrius, and certainly not with Authari.

I looked at the empty jug. If I asked politely, would Martin bring me another?

I pulled myself together. I'd show what I thought of that spy and his advice, and I'd put off any contact with Demetrius until I was less likely to knock his teeth out.

'Martin,' I said. 'The dispatch we were intending to write this afternoon can wait. Today is the Feast of Saint Victorinus. I believe that means a holiday outside the City walls, and no need of any special permit. Let's get changed. If Authari is sober enough to stand, he can come with us.'

22

It seemed the whole City had had the same idea. It took an age to get along the wide Middle Street to the Charisian Gate and then out into the ruined suburbs. Old and young, rich and poor, all wearing their best, the people of Constantinople were streaming as one out of the City. We had to push our way through crowds of the semi-washed, and thread our way through the chairs of the great.

The Terror forgotten for the moment as we passed through that massive gate, everyone chattered brightly. I even heard natural laughter, as children ran about playing with balls and little sticks.

With the coming of bad times, the city had reacted like an alarmed snail and withdrawn behind the impenetrable fastness of its walls. But if the houses and gardens that had once stretched deep into Thrace were now largely abandoned, the churches and religious houses were still kept up.

The Church of St Victorinus was one of these places. It was far too small for the thousands who'd come out for the festival, but was an elegant place – built in the shape of a cross, and painted a tasteful red. About fifty yards distant, some hermit had taken up residence at the top of a column that still stood over the building it had once helped to support. With lunatic eyes bulging from his dishevelled face, he stared down at the crowds from the edge of the wooden platform his followers had put up for him. He was uttering benedictions and prophecies for anyone who could take his attention from Saint Victorinus and provide him with morsels of bread and wine.

According to the interminable sermon a young priest delivered to us while we stood in a dense mass outside the church, Victorinus was a fuller from Adrianople who had been clubbed to death here after having delivered to the heretical Emperor Constantius a long oration in the best theological Greek on the equal substance of Father and Son. Afterwards, flowers of unearthly beauty had sprung up on the spot – flowers that sang the Creed of Athanasius to everyone whose life so far had been exceptionally blameless.

Of course, multitudes were soon claiming to hear these singing flowers, and there had been the usual cures of the lame and the blind. So a church had been built there, and the anniversary of the martyrdom was a standing excuse for a good time outside the walls.

Now we were there to say hello to the man, and to see if his flowers could be persuaded back into tune.

'I must be going deaf in my old age,' I whispered to Martin as, during a pause in the sermon, we all stood looking up to a raised patch of ground close by the church on which a shrivelled rose bush was shedding its petals.

'Shut up, dolt!' someone next to me hissed. 'I can barely hear the singing of the Creed for your barbarian ribaldry.'

Barbarian, indeed! Anywhere else, he'd have got my fist in his mouth and my knee hard in his groin. But I held my peace. There would be food and drink soon enough. From the preparations I'd seen in hand when we arrived, there would be acrobats and jugglers too. The whores who flitted discreetly round the edges of the crowd were already taking bookings for later.

I looked over the heads of those gathered outside the church, bowed in reverence. There was a bit of shuffling and coughing, and a few groans that I took to be outpourings of rapture. No bird sang in that hot September air. Even the various bugs had been intimidated into silence.

It would be jolly enough later. For the moment, though, boredom and the late-afternoon sun were making the time drag. Was there anyone in that crowd worth looking at? Was there any face there I could bring to mind for a good wank later?

'How sweetly the flowers sing of the True Faith,' a voice behind me whispered. 'Do you not hear the delicacy of phrasing?'

'But of course I do, Theophanes,' said I, turning. 'I hear them as well as you do.'

Did I see the man's face twitch for just a moment? It was hard to say. He stood a few feet back from me in a small parting of the crowd. For once, Alypius wasn't in attendance. Instead, Theophanes was accompanied by two black slaves who fanned him gently with ostrich feathers. There was enough paint on his face to cover the prow of a warship, and enough jewellery on his bloated neck and arms to stock one of the finer shops in Middle Street. Certainly, the robe he wore must have kept the silkworms busy for a year.

'It is so restful to breathe the pure air of the country, do you not think, young Alaric?' he said in a more conversational tone. 'I regret that my duties prevent me from leaving the City as often as I might wish.'

He turned to Martin. 'And you too, my little Martin, how unexpected to see you outside the City.'

Martin gave a rather shifty downward look. Before he could be expected to answer, Theophanes was continuing:

'But why not join me? I have a private tent beyond the crowd, where food and wine await your attention.'

I suppose the country has its charms. But refreshments have a charm of their own, and lunch was a distant memory.

'Did you not hear the singing flowers?' I asked Martin as we pushed our way out of the crowd.

'No, sir,' said he in a mournful voice. 'I don't think my life has been sufficiently holy.'

'Never mind,' I consoled him. 'You did see that miracle in Lesbos that I said was a trick of the light.'

I decided to leave Authari to stand out the rest of the sermon. He'd not have approved its anti-Arianism if he had been up to following the Greek. We had taken up a position convenient for the wine stalls, because I didn't fancy risking an evening of fruit juice.

I needn't have worried. Theophanes' refreshment tent was about the size of a small house and was all of yellow silk. It was furnished with an opulence I will not try to describe except to say that, gleaming in the suffused yellow light, there was some of the finest silverware I'd ever seen, and piled high on this was a quantity and variety of delicacies an epic poet might have struggled to enumerate.

'I am ashamed to bring you before so miserable a *collage*,' Theophanes began. 'Had I known I should be blessed by such worthy company as your own—'

He was cut short by a scream outside.

One scream we might have ignored. Perhaps a woman was giving birth. Perhaps someone had trodden on her toes. Women can't keep their mouths shut at the best of times. But that first scream was taken up by others in the crowd. What had been an enlarged gathering of the reverent was breaking up into a shouting, terrified commotion.

Fast-moving shadows flitted at random across the walls of the tent. Someone now tripped over and broke one of the retaining cords. The corner it had held taut went limp and began gently to sag.

I wrenched open the tent flap and looked out. All was breaking up in chaos. People ran about, some shouting and waving their arms, others with firm determination as they dashed for the road leading back into the city.

I saw a man climb into his chair, which fell abruptly to earth as the slaves dropped the supporting poles and raced off in the same direction. He struggled to his feet waving his arms despairingly at them. Then he was off himself on foot, following the slaves as fast as his tangling robe would allow.

'The barbarians,' a man turned to shout at me, 'the barbarians are upon us!'

And they were!

I saw them about half a mile away coming down a little incline behind the church. Mounted on short ponies, they approached slowly in a wide crescent. There must have been a few dozen of them, spaced apart. I could see their chainmail glittering in the late sun, and the glint of their drawn swords. I could see their squat, beardless faces, and could feel their anticipatory smiles as they looked on the harvest of wealth and human flesh spread out before them.

The road back to Constantinople was already a seething mass of bodies. The ground about was crowded with derelict buildings and bare rocks and bushes.

The Stylite hermit had pulled up his folding ladder and withdrawn to cower unseen in the middle of his platform.

People ran about, crashing into each other, as if they were terrified hens whose coop had been broken into by a fox.

I turned to Theophanes, who looked like death. He leaned heavily on the back of an ebony couch.

'Where are your guards?' I asked.

He waved vaguely at the jostling multitude. His blacks had no weapons. Authari was God knows where in the crowd, and was himself unarmed. The soldiers who'd come out with us to keep order were nowhere to be seen. I later heard they'd been the first to mount up and ride for the walls, followed by the priests and then by anyone who had brought or could procure some animal of burden.

We were on our own. Our only available weapon was a jewelled fruit knife. I'd not have trusted the thing for spreading olive paste. I thought of making a dash for it, but Martin and I would have trouble forcing our way to the head of the crowd. No – we'd never get through. We were too far behind.

And what of Theophanes? It didn't cross my mind to dump him. But how to make our escape with him?

The raiders broke into a gentle gallop as they closed the distance. A great, collective wail of terror went up and rippled forward as they crashed into the back of the fleeing crowd.

Now they were close enough for me to see the evil grins on their faces, the flash of steel as swords were raised. I heard the bubbling screams of the stricken. I saw blood spurt from a man dressed in the formal robes of a senator. His hands went up to the red gash where his face had been, then he went down. I saw a child skewered like game on one of the barbarian lances. Screaming and twisting, it was raised aloft, then shaken loose into the crowd.

Like an arsonist's fire among ripe corn, the raiders cut their way into the crowd. If they were looking for prisoners, they hadn't yet taken any. For the moment, they were giving way to the sheer joy of killing the defenceless citizens of the great City.

'Cover yourself with this,' I shouted to Theophanes, throwing him a cloth I'd ripped from the table. Dishes of food crashed heavily to the ground. 'Get this on and come with us.

'Martin – get the fuck from under that table! There's no safety here.'

To the blacks, who'd taken to jabbering and clutching at each other: 'Get hold of your master. Pull him along behind us.'

Even if we managed to reach the City, the gates might well be shut on us and we'd huddle under the outer wall, hoping the artillery was sufficiently in order to cover us. By now there must have been a thousand bodies between us and those mounted savages but that dense buffer of flesh might be enough to protect us. Sooner or later, the raiders would slow their approach and start taking prisoners and booty. In the meantime, we might find somewhere to hide in one of the ruined buildings.

Once he was over the initial shock, Theophanes moved with surprising speed over that broken ground. The main difficulty, I found, was to keep Martin with us. Once or twice, I thought of knocking him down and then carrying him.

We dodged out of main view into a side street. There was no shortage of hiding places. It all depended on how long the barbarians wanted to hang about the city. Even Phocas might send out a brigade to chase them off. At the least, it would soon be dark. That meant we needed to look for a reasonable bolt hole.

The problem was that others had had the same idea. When you're trying to vanish, there's no safety in numbers. Squeezing into an already crowded cellar is just an invitation to trouble. It can be worse than hanging about in the open. You might get paving slabs thrown down on you. Or you might have the building set alight over your head.

We had to put some distance between us and the others.

'Out of my way, shitbags,' I snarled, shoving a couple of monks back from the breach in a ruined wall we needed to climb over.

We darted round the corner into what had once been a narrow shopping street. From here, those mingled wails and shouts came from a comforting distance. I could hear the birds singing and the wind rustling through the dry grass of late summer. It was a matter of finding the right hole to disappear into.

Then: 'Oh, Sweet and Merciful Jesus!' Martin cried in a high falsetto.

At the far end of the street, a barbarian sat on a tall horse. He was of a different race from the others. Lank, blond hair fell over his shoulders. A yellow moustache covered his lower face. He gave us a predatory smile as he raised his drawn sword.

23

When attacked, there is a time to fight and a time to give quietly in. There's no shame in the latter when you have no means of the former. I did think of picking up a fallen roof spar and using it as a lance. But there was more than one of those Germanics, and Theophanes was urging me to let him do the talking.

The introduction he made in basic Latin didn't get us as far as he might have wished. The three of us were tightly bound and roped together for dragging along behind one of the horses. So far, we were unharmed, but, for all they wailed so piteously, the blacks were butchered on the spot – throats cut, hands hacked off to get at their gold bangles.

We were dumped with about seventy other prisoners inside the walls of a ruined guardhouse. The gate had fallen off and the roof had long since rotted. This was on the extreme edge of the old suburbs and, except for patches of scrub about a yard high, was surrounded by open ground.

We were a select bunch. The raiders had killed or released everyone who didn't look fit for a ransom. We were untied, stripped of our cash and jewellery, and then given to feed from bowls of miscellaneous refreshments gathered from the festival preparations.

I looked around. Everyone just sat quietly eating. I turned to Theophanes, who had taken off his silk slippers to nurse his bruised feet.

'What chance of a rescue?'

'Not much,' he said flatly, pulling a slipper back on. 'There are few enough of these creatures, but overcoming them would require a force I don't think Phocas will want to spare from keeping the City quiet.'

'Very well,' I said, moving on to the next obvious point, 'we must outnumber these animals five to one. A concerted rush, and—'

Theophanes stopped me. 'Please, Alaric,' he said, 'this is not Rome. Here in the Imperial capital, there is an order to these things. Even in more settled times than now, I cannot say how often I have seen fires burning outside the City walls. The appropriate response is to chase the raiders away, or to bribe them to go away. If there are too many of them for that, some other nomadic race can be persuaded to attack them in the rear.

'A counterattack being out of the question, the gates will open in due course and the priests will come out to begin ransom discussions. The Yellow Barbarians are from a race we seldom encounter. They drift in now and again from the lands far beyond even Scythia. But the Germanics are reasonably close to the Lombards.'

'And have you seen what the Lombards can do?' I asked, breaking into the lecture.

Theophanes waved me to silence. 'They are doubtless here for the money,' he said reassuringly. 'They can be trusted to know the rules. They are probably Christians of a sort. You will notice there has been no more killing without good reason, and no rapes of the better looking. We each have a financial value that will be set by the appearance of our clothing and then by detailed negotiation with our friends and loved ones inside the city.'

I snorted in disgust. 'So this is your civilisation,' I said. 'You disarm the people. Then, when it proves impossible to defend them, they can be shoved around like farm animals.

'Back in Rome, I can tell you, the priests alone would have been able to fight off this pissy little raid. Given that everyone, ordained or lay, carries arms, we'd have them back inside the walls before dark. Then it would be a matter of exchanging them for anyone who'd fallen into their hands. Failing that, we'd hand them over to the surgeons for live dissection outside the Prefect's Basilica.

'Get there early enough for a seat at the front,' I said with strong approval, 'and you can learn a lot about anatomy as well as the workings of justice.'

'Be that as it may,' Theophanes said with slight amusement, 'we do things differently here.' He patted my arm with his fat and now unjewelled fingers. 'Your best chance of getting out of here alive is to wait for the ransom negotiations. I imagine they'll start tomorrow afternoon.'

Martin looked suddenly up from his inspection of the robe of blue linen I'd made him put on for the occasion.

'Shut up,' I rasped at him before he could ask his question. 'I'm thinking about other matters. It goes without saying I'll pay any ransom. You came here with me. You'll get out with me.'

Handing over an ounce of clipped silver to these swine would stick in my gullet for a year of Sundays. But if it came to that, I'd send the necessary instructions to Baruch.

Theophanes went placidly back to rubbing the weal on one of his arms where a bracelet had been ripped off with exceptional force.

But no priest or Imperial official came to us the following day, or the day after that. We sat in huddled groups, stiff from the night cold and the hard ground where we slept, and sore from the hot sun of the days. Though unbound, we weren't allowed to go outside the place where we were held captive. The dozen or so guards set over us kept order by the liberal use of beatings. This meant that we shat and pissed where we lived and slept. I did suggest some basic sanitary arrangements but no one listened to me and I soon shut up. I was surprised how many people soon gave up on removing their clothes first.

For the first time since my arrival in the City, I heard people speaking their minds.

'The drunken fucker won't allow negotiations,' one man said bitterly, pulling his soiled robe over his head. 'They'd puncture his claims to be in control of events.'

'Do you suppose we'll be killed?' another asked.

'Well, there aren't many of these raiders, and they'll hardly want to be slowed by a train of slaves when they do finally make off. Of course we'll be killed.'

'But surely Saint Victorinus will keep watch over us?' an old woman cried, clutching a wooden crucifix to herself.

'As he did all the others?'

The discussion trailed off.

Early on the third evening of our captivity, Theophanes opened a new line of conversation with me. So far, he'd kept up his insistence that ransom talks were imminent. But there comes a time when optimism blends into stupidity. And Theophanes was never stupid.

'Aelric,' he said softly, having checked that Martin was asleep, 'I must beg of you the favour of a swift death before morning.'

'Those are not words', I replied, 'I ever expected of Theophanes the Magnificent.'

Nor had I expected him to start using my real name.

'They are my words now, dear boy,' he said. 'I have saved your life once, to your knowledge. I have saved it on other occasions unknown to you. I ask you now to return the favour by ending mine.'

I looked him steadily in the face. It was days since his last *toilette*. Since then, he'd neither scraped off the painted mask nor been able to maintain it. Rain and sweat had washed the dye out of his hair, and dried rivulets of black stained his forehead and cheeks. The effect was like the wall of a ruined building, where courses of brick show through the cracked and discoloured stucco. But there was an ordered resolution about Theophanes that banished any trace of eunuch effeminacy.

'Do you see this?' He held up a stone about the size of a small melon. 'I want you to knock my brains out as I sleep. You and Martin must then keep away from my body. These animals are not sober enough to have noticed who is with whom. Nor will they make proper enquiries. If I wake tomorrow morning, I shall have to consider it a grave breach of our friendship.'

I took the stone into my hand. It was smooth and cool, and it balanced nicely. It was just the thing for bashing heads in.

The man had a point. If they hadn't even started yet, there would be no ransom negotiations. It really did seem to be a matter of waiting for these savages to run out of patience and start dispatching us in the manner of their doubtless very brutal choice.

I'd got that much in the afternoon I overheard two of the Germanics speaking together. 'I say kill them and fuck off,' one said, spitting to emphasise his words. 'We can't stick around here under the walls of the city itself. There'll be soldiers come out sooner or later, or brung in from the sea behind us. We've got a nice stash of movables from this raid. Let's be off, I say, while we've still got hands to carry it.'

'Not yet,' the other had said. 'I heard that slit-eyed yellow fucker – the one what knows Latin. He said the Big Man has something going on. We wait until tomorrow.'

'I dunno,' had come the reply. 'I seed him yesterday talking to the King Phocas people. Those priests was back again. He sent them off with a flea in the ear. "No deal," he said. Whatever happens, there won't be no ransoming. We've got our share of the gold. Let's take it and be off. Hermann had the right idea – and you know he never sticks round when there's real danger.

'I've got a woman with kids back home. She don't like these Imperial raids. We're going in deeper each time. She'd have boiling water all over me feet if she knowed we was outside the City. Let's kill them.'

They'd drifted out of earshot. Nothing had happened since, but it could only be a matter of time before the general nerve snapped.

I hadn't realised Theophanes could understand any of the Germanic languages. But there seemed no limit to his abilities. It was after listening quietly to the raiders that his mood shifted.

Martin had also understood. He'd spent the rest of the afternoon and early evening praying in five languages. He was for all the world like a man trying different keys in a lock. But none had fitted. No Saint Victorinus had come down with his now armed singing flowers to save us. So Martin had left his stale bread untouched and started on the beer that remained abundant.

'Come now, Martin,' I'd whispered, 'we must set an example for these Greeks. These people won't kill us. We're all far too valuable.

We'll surely be sold into slavery at worst. Then we can be bought back out. Directly or indirectly, we'll be ransomed.'

'No, Aelric,' he'd said flatly, giving me a look somewhere between pity at my own naïvety and offence at my transparent attempt to deceive him. 'You know we'll not be sold. In any event,' he'd added, 'I'd rather be dead than a slave again.'

'I can't agree,' I'd replied, trying to keep the conversation going. 'Slavery must usually be better than death – especially if we can arrange to be bought back out of it.'

'Bought back, you say?' he'd replied with a sour laugh. 'I dare say in Kent, just like in Rome, you can find anyone if you look hard enough for a few days. But do you know just how big the East is? Do you know how long it can take to get messages back even from Ephesus? Can you begin to imagine the distances involved if you get sold into Persia or one of the barbarian realms? And that's just in settled times. In this world of armed chaos, you'd never get ransomed. Never!'

For a while, we'd sat in grumpy silence. Then Martin had begun again. 'Do you realise', he'd asked, 'what it means to be a slave? You own slaves. I know you've read up on the law governing slavery. But you have no conception of what is really meant by all those legal phrases about abolition of personality and the like.'

Another pause, and he'd continued: 'The first thing they do when you become a slave is break you. When I was sold for the first time, it was like a descent into Hell. We were beaten – beaten if we looked at the dealer when he spoke; beaten if we didn't. We were stripped naked and made to walk around in the open. We were made to draw lots. On that basis, we were assigned to have sex with each other – in front of everyone.

'I was made to have sex with a dying old woman, who barely knew what was happening around her. One of the dealers squatted in front of me, and I had to use his shit as a lubricant. Whenever I showed unwilling, I was flogged back into action.

'One of the others I was with was made to have sex with a dog. When he couldn't, they beat him to death. It was like with Justinus

153

in that restaurant. I saw someone else have his legs broken for no particular reason. Then he was drowned in a vat of piss.

'They do this' – Martin was now speaking fast – 'they do this partly because they enjoy the sight of so much humiliation. But they do it also to break you into your new status of absolute, unquestioning obedience to whatever orders you are given. Nobody wants to buy an uppity slave. You have to learn that, and learn it fast. You have to forget anything you might have been before your civil death.

'Don't tell me slavery is better than death. Rather than go through that again, I'll choose death any day. But there isn't any choice,' he'd finished. 'We're to be killed tomorrow. Because there are so many of us, it will be a quick death. I don't believe they'll be wanting to spend much time over us. I suppose I'll squeal like a pig when the first knife goes into me. You know I'm a coward, and I know you despise me for it. But I'm ready for death tomorrow. It won't be long. If you have any sense, you won't try making a fuss. Do that, and you'll get personal attention.'

With that, he'd drained his pitcher of beer and settled down for a siesta. Soon, he'd been snoring away with his mouth open.

24

But let me return to Theophanes and the notion of having me brain him while he slept.

'Now, Theophanes,' I said, putting the stone down, 'if I kill you, who will see to me? You don't suppose I can trust Martin.'

He smiled so suddenly and broadly that some flakes of paint dropped from his face on to his breasts and belly.

'I don't think you have anything to fear, Aelric,' he said. 'You and your secretary are safe enough. And the less you know, the safer you will be. If I am right, however – and I am sure that I am right – I have much to fear. I'm surprised I have still not been identified. My end will not be swift or dignified if you refuse this favour that you should know enough to realise you owe me.'

He fell silent for a while, looking towards the fire that burned outside the doorway. The raiders had lit this for keeping an eye on it by night and for their own comfort.

'Well, Theophanes,' I said, 'before I even consider taking that stone to you, I think there are certain things to be discussed. Can you explain, for example, why the ransom negotiators were turned back? Might it be because this is not an ordinary raid? Is there some unseen principal who might not be well-disposed to Your Magnificence once it is known you are among the captives?'

'You are most perceptive, my dear Aelric,' came the answer. 'But I repeat – your own safety is in proportion to your ignorance.'

I ignored that. 'So, let us think this through,' I went on. 'Heraclius is now a short voyage from the City. He hasn't the forces for a regular siege. Even if he had, it would fail. He must, therefore, rely on disaffection within for the gates to be opened.

Phocas keeps a tight grip on the city and people are frightened to move against him.

'What might a man like you advise in this case? Surely, you'd tell Heraclius to hire some barbarians to stage a raid. You make sure the Imperial envoys are turned discreetly away. You then arrange yourself for the release of captives. You show up your devotion to the public good at the same time as you reveal how little Phocas cares.

'Of course, you make an exception for certain people whom luck has put into your hands. Their death can be blamed on the barbarians. But so long as the other prisoners return unharmed, no tears will be shed over that.

'You will agree, Theophanes, this seems to fit very well with our own apparent circumstances – even down to your assurance that Martin and I have nothing to fear.'

Theophanes shrugged. 'If you are right, dearest boy, nothing changes. You are safe. And it remains that I seek a favour of the greatest value to my peace of mind.'

I wanted to jump in here and continue the questioning. This was my chance – perhaps my last chance – to find out what had been going on above my head. But Theophanes had almost forgotten I was his audience. He spoke now in a slow, dreamy voice, his eyes half closed.

'It was in the year before the first visitation of plague that I was snatched from herding my father's goats. The raiders came from out of the desert – the great, burning desert, as wide and illimitable as the seas that lie to the west of your islands. They came in daylight. They killed my father and his brothers. They carried me off, together with my mother and my sisters.

'My mother was left to die where she fell down on the long trek through the desert. My sisters and I were separated from each other at the slave auction outside Bostra. That is where I was castrated.

'For a while, I was a dancing boy ministering to a rich Syrian in Antioch. Then I was sold to a brothel in Beirut. There, I was bought by a lecturer in the School of Law . . .'

He drifted into silence again and reached for the stone. He cupped it in his hand. 'I know I can make myself sleep tonight. I can will myself to anything.'

'But you came at last into the Imperial Service?' I broke in. I'd get back to the main question shortly. For the moment, I'd learn what else I could.

'The plague that destroyed so much of the old world', he said, taking up the thread, 'gave unlimited opportunities to those of us who lived and knew how to survive. I achieved my present eminence under His Late Majesty the Emperor Maurice. You know, I signed his death warrant, and the warrants against his five sons. I watched the deaths, and then signed the release forms for the archive.'

He paused, doubtless reflecting on the enormity of what he'd done – breaking a peaceful continuity of centuries. Then he continued: 'I'll not deny that what I did greatly advanced my position. But I also insist that I acted in what I truly thought at the time was in the best interests of the Empire as a whole. We were beginning to face pressures within and without that Maurice had repeatedly shown himself unable to handle with the necessary resolution.

'I did try explaining this to the poor man as we took him from the cell. He simply bowed, quoting the old verse:

"One who does evil, then is caught,
I hate to hear insist he ought." '

Theophanes laughed gently. 'My real life began with a capture. Now it will so end. I have done many wicked things in the time between but I am not ashamed to ask that a final – and perhaps justified – wickedness against me shall be frustrated.'

Well, that was Theophanes – still secretive and still trying to be a slippery Oriental right to the end.

'What is it to be, then,' he asked, with a return to practicalities – 'mercy at your hands, or a roughness of handling that I am surprised has been so long delayed?'

'Neither,' I said, speaking softly but urgently. 'Even if Heraclius is trying some clever trick, I don't trust these savages. Their nerves are fraying, and I know what they're capable of doing once the

157

drink has gone round a few times. I've seen the Lombards at work any number of times on their prisoners. I've – er – seen much unpleasantness among my own people.

'Your death, when it comes, Theophanes, will not be at my hands. Nor am I planning to sit here in the hope that orders will come from Abydos or wherever before it's too late. I'm getting out of here,' I added. 'Come with me if you want to stay alive.'

Theophanes leaned forward and looked hard at me. He brushed some creases from the front of his tunic and leaned still closer.

'I do believe, my dear and beautiful boy,' he said, 'you have a plan. Would you do me the honour of sharing it with me?'

Speaking fast and in my quietist whisper, I explained the plan. At first sceptical, Theophanes, I could see, was brightening. He raised objections I hadn't considered. He made suggestions that I incorporated. By the time we were finished, the plan was settled.

We agreed that it had a slender chance of success, but was worth trying. At worst, it might bring us faster or at least more dignified deaths.

All that remained was to put it to Martin. Theophanes and I looked at each other.

'I think it will be best coming from you,' he said.

I put my hand over Martin's mouth and my knee in his stomach to wake him as quickly and silently as I could. We didn't want to alert any of the other captives, who'd gone placidly to sleep around us like good little citizens of the Empire. And we wanted no attention from our captors.

In the end, it took us both to convince him. Only when Theophanes spread his legs and hitched up his robe and belly to show his castration scar shining silver in the dim light from the dying moon, and spoke about the blood and pain involved even for a small boy, did Martin come to a semblance of his senses.

'But if it fails . . .' he said, his eyes rolling with terror at the thought of actually taking matters into our own hands.

'It won't fail,' Theophanes said in a tone that crushed dissent. 'Have you seen Aelric fail in any of his ventures? I can assure you, I have never once failed in mine.

'Do you see this stone in my hand? If you don't say "yes", now, this very moment, I swear I'll use it to provide a real corpse – your own.'

That was it. For what little he might be worth, Martin was in.

We waited until what was left of the moon was high in the night sky. The other captives had drifted as deep as they ever would into sleep on the damp, stinking ground. The Yellow Barbarians had all disappeared to wherever they went by night. The Germanics were left in charge of us.

Around us were the snores of the sleeping. From over by the fire came the shouted laughter and guttural calls on Lady Fortune of about a dozen barbarians having fun. I heard the steady rattle and fall of dice from a cup.

At last, one of them got up to do the rounds. On the first and second evenings, they'd taken care to go about in pairs, one standing outside the doorway, torch in hand, while the other came in with drawn sword to count us. But keeping watch over these Greeks really was less trouble than herding sheep. Tonight, they'd given up on what they'd found to be unnecessary precautions. The inspections were still frequent, and still armed and watchful. But they came now only one man at a time, and relied on the moonlight.

It was now or never.

'Oh, sir, do please come over,' I cried softly and pathetically in Latin.

A massive barbarian stood over me. He blotted out what little light still came from the moon.

'Well?' he said in a rough yet ominous voice. From the voice, I realised he was the one I'd heard earlier calling for our deaths.

'I think the fat eunuch has died, sir,' I replied. 'He made a funny noise a little while back, and jerked around. He hasn't moved since. I don't think he's breathing. It might have been a stroke.'

'So, what the fuck is that to me if he's dead?' came the reply. 'For all I care, it just saves a bit of time.'

He turned to go back out to the fire.

'But, please, kind sir,' I said, now speaking urgently, 'I can tell you something about him that I promise you'll want to hear.'

The barbarian turned back to me. 'And what might that be?'

'If I tell you, sir, will you promise not to kill me tomorrow?'

I could hear a smile spreading over his face. 'Well, my pretty young Greekling, that depends on what you tell me, doesn't it?'

He was evidently enjoying the power, taking every ounce of pleasure from the terrified grovelling of his betters.

I counted silently to five, then continued. 'I saw him stuff a purse filled with gold up his arse when we were taken. After every shit, he was putting it up again. I tell you, it's a big purse. He said to me you people would be too thick to look there. He did say that, didn't he?' I said, turning round to face Martin.

'Oh, yes!' said Martin, playing along. 'He told me he'd give the gold to the Church of the Double God to use against what he called the damnable heresy of Arius.'

'And', I added, 'he's still got huge nipple rings with sapphires on them – sapphires the size of grapes. They were making his dugs hang down like an old woman's.'

It was the nipple rings that tipped the balance. The gold coins up the arse would simply have led to my being made to do a necrophiliac fisting job on Theophanes. The nipple rings might have worked by themselves. But together, they worked a treat.

The barbarian was half cut. In any event, experience had given him no reason to be scared of us. With a predatory grunt, he stooped over the motionless body of Theophanes. He pulled at the robe. But it was wound too tightly about the lower parts. He had to get down on his knees.

'Get over there where I can see you together,' he snarled softly. With a quick look over his shoulder to make sure the others hadn't heard anything, he set to work. He rammed his sword into the ground on the side of Theophanes farthest from us and knelt to get a better purchase on the robe.

With both hands, he tried ripping the robe open. But it was cut from the heaviest weave of silk, stitched with a double hem. That sort of tailoring doesn't rend easily. He tried pulling the robe loose. But three hundred pounds of still flesh don't move easily either.

'Fat fucking bastard!' the barbarian grunted in his own language. He reached clumsily for the knife at his belt.

Crack!

Theophanes had got him straight on the head with that stone. The creature went down like a stunned ox.

Straightaway, Theophanes was on top of him, drowning any cries he might still be able to make under a mountain of blubber. I saw his legs jerking wildly, and could hear the muffled gasps. But strong as he was, he was wounded and sprawled in the wrong position to be able to lift even half that immense weight of eunuch off his chest.

Theophanes raised his elephantine arm for a moment, exposing the barbarian's head. With another stone, I finished the work.

I struck hard, and then again and again. On the fourth blow, the skull caved in like ice over a winter's river, and I felt the slime of blood and brains splashing on my hand. The legs stopped their jerking. It was over.

'Dear me!' said Theophanes, puffing as he rolled into a sitting position. 'I thought the beast would never die. For a moment, I thought he might even lift me off him.'

But the man was dead. Our first efforts had gone to plan.

'Hey, Ratburger,' came a cry from over by the fire, 'where in fuck's name have you got to? Come back over and lose some more.'

'I need a good shit first,' I replied, mimicking as best I could the voice of the late Ratburger. 'I'll be back, and then it's double or quits.'

As I'd hoped, they were too dazzled by the fire to see anything outside its pool of light. From where they sat, the entrance to the guardhouse must have been a patch of blackness.

'Ooh, isn't he a bold one!' came the cracked voice of an old man.

Another added: 'Double or quits? You won't have double nothing after that!'

There was a chorus of laughter, and attention returned to the game.

That gave us a while, but nothing more. Martin wrapped a cloth round the dead man's head to stop blood getting on to the clothes he was wearing. Then Theophanes and I stripped the body. The man's clothes stank beyond belief. I hadn't washed in days, and had been rolling in stale shit and piss, but nothing had prepared me for that awful rankness. My flesh crawled as I pulled the clothes on. For a moment I thought I'd vomit at the greasy touch of the things, but it had to be done.

Alaric, the golden 'light from the north', had become what, but for a stroke of good fortune in Kent, he might always have been – Aelric the filthy, bloodstained desperado.

When he'd finished turning up the trousers and pulling the upper garments tight by tucking the extra into my waistband, Theophanes stood back to admire me.

'Most fetching,' he said drily. 'You'd surely turn the head of every barbarian lass back in those forests.'

He tugged the sword free and passed it over. He took the knife for himself. We left the body where it lay, covering it with my own clothing and an outer garment of Theophanes so that it would easily pass in darkness for a sleeping captive. So long as the dogs didn't find it too soon, it would stay hidden as long as we needed.

We waited until a great shout of laughter and argument showed that all around the fire were more than usually intent on the game they were playing. Then we slipped quickly out of the guardhouse and dodged round the back of the place.

Keeping the remains of the guardhouse between us and the fire, we moved as fast as we could without making any sound until the ruins became denser and we could vanish into the still silence of the old suburbs.

25

The plan now was to get back to the road leading to the city. The Germanics were all hard at play. The Yellows, if they were still about, probably wouldn't know one Germanic from another, especially in the darkness. I was sure I could bluff my way past them.

Well before dawn, we'd be banging on the gates of the City. And these would surely open for someone like Theophanes.

The problem was, the moon had clouded over, and a light mist had fallen. We weren't in total blackness – there was a break in the clouds now and then – but it was darker than I had expected. More importantly, with the moon out of sight, we had nothing by which to guide our movements.

We'd struck out along a narrow street, guessing from our last sighting of the moon it would eventually lead to the main road. But after the first few dozen yards, we found it so choked with rubble that we couldn't tell road from general ruins. We turned left into another street – then, finding that also blocked, right into another. This soon twisted round to the right, before coming to a dead end.

What I mean to say is we got lost.

We stumbled for an age in what we thought was a generally straight line, the mist growing thicker and thicker about us. It was accompanied by a light drizzle.

We still weren't in total darkness, but the light we had was of little use for navigating through a sea of broken walls and fallen masonry. The old suburbs had once been half as big as the City itself. Now, spread around us, were occasional streets running between lines of semi-ruined buildings and otherwise vast expanses of quarried rubble. It was like being by night in one of the less frequented districts of Rome.

We must, I was sure, come eventually to the great clearing that separated the outworks and defensive wall of the city from its old suburbs. But that might easily be long after the sun had burned off both mist and cloud and left us exposed to view like thieves caught in sudden lamplight.

'I think we should be going that way,' said Martin, pointing left.

'On the contrary,' said Theophanes, pointing right, '*I* think we should be going that way.'

It didn't help that I had my own idea of the direction.

We stopped, uncertain.

'I think', Theophanes said flatly, 'we might have passed by this pedestal once already. Those legs, snapped off at the knee, look familiar.'

Possibly they were But one broken statue, in the darkness, is very like another – and they must, in this stretch of the old suburbs, have been as common as drainage grilles in the road.

'Perhaps', said Martin, 'we could go into one of the ruined houses. We can hide there until the barbarians go away.'

'No,' said Theophanes. 'Wherever we hid, they'd have us out come dawn like snails from a shell. With their dead friend Rat-burger to answer for, I'd not care to be in their charge again.'

I agreed. The old suburbs were not wholly deserted, but those who lived in them knew exactly how and where to hide when danger threatened. We had no such advantage. We had to keep moving even though we might have been going in a circle. We kept expecting to hear the dreadful clatter of nailed boots on crunchy brick but the only sound was our own soft voices, and the careful picking of our feet through the rubble. So long as we could somehow keep to a straight course, it would be rotten luck if we found our way back to the barbarians. More likely, we'd put a good distance between us and them, and could dodge back to the City when first light showed us where we actually were.

We didn't need a gate. We needed only to get within a hundred yards of the City walls to be under at least potential cover of the artillery. No one would follow us within that radius.

I stepped forward and let the others follow.

'Halt! Who goes there?' a voice called firmly in Germanic.

'Oh, fuck!' I said inwardly. What could he be doing this far out? Or were we really so far out?

'I am Aelric, born in Pavia,' I replied in Lombardic. I knew I couldn't manage a conversation in his language, but Lombardic would do for basics. 'I was told to get these prisoners to the Big Man in the Yellow Camp.'

No such luck.

'I don't know any Aelric. there ain't no Lombards detached with us. So who the fuck are you?'

He went for his sword. In a moment, he'd find enough breath to call out for help.

I was younger and bigger. I could probably have taken him out – but that wasn't anything like certain with a sword I'd only handled to put into its scabbard. And what if he managed to call for help?

I never had to find out.

How he got round me and behind that man – in perfect silence and in full cover of the mist – I couldn't at the time imagine. But Theophanes was there. With a single knife-thrust, delivered with tremendous force, straight through a seam in the leather jacket, he had the man in the back.

As the man went down on all fours, gasping with the pain and shock, the sound of blood frothing on his lips, I saw Theophanes emerge through the mist, a pleased smile on his face. For all the difference in expression, he might have been back in that restaurant, about to hug himself after some particularly apt repartee.

The man tried to reach back to get at the knife. It hadn't by itself been an immediately killing blow, but it gave me the chance for a sword-thrust just below the collar bone.

And that was the end of him.

Theophanes stood forward to admire his work. He leaned over the body, dabbing playfully at the knife hilt. It bobbed around under his hands like a very stiff erection. As he stood back up, I took his hand and embraced him.

Whatever happened next, we'd done well together this night.

When Martin had finished retching the fear out of his guts, we fell to a hurried conference on where we might be. We agreed that the man probably wasn't part of any search party. He'd been too surprised to come upon me, and then too straightforwardly suspicious of who I was. He must have been on some other mission, and alone.

We decided not to waste any time on hiding the body. Instead, we just recovered the knife – getting it back out, slippery with blood, took all my effort – and helped ourselves to the one from the dead man's belt. There was no point taking the sword for Martin. Its weight would only slow him down and he might even cut his leg open by tripping over the thing. But he might be some use with a knife. At least, he could turn it on himself if things grew desperate enough.

We pressed on. The buildings now were growing larger and less ruinous. Martin felt sure we were coming out of the old suburbs. The clearance between them and the outer defences couldn't now be far away. It might even be round the next bend in the overgrown street we'd been following.

Certainly, I had less feeling of confinement. We must be coming out of the old suburbs.

Then, just as we rounded the bend, came another voice, this one in a high, accented Latin:

'You have taken your time. The Great One doesn't appreciate delay.'

'Oh, fuck!' I thought again.

Looming out of the mist were a good half-dozen of the Yellow Barbarians.

'You'd better come quickly. The Great One will be impatient.'

26

Of course, having found our way into the old suburbs, we'd somehow managed a quarter-turn in our wanderings and had since been moving away from the City. The clearing I could sense ahead was the outskirts.

It was here that the Yellow Barbarians had pitched their own camp. Either they were uncomfortable with even ruined buildings around them, or they just wanted to be able to make the quickest escape if the City gates opened.

All that mattered to me until then was that we'd lost direction and would be horribly exposed when the Germanics turned up to report the loss of three captives.

It was all so bloody unfair! I hadn't anticipated having to stumble around half the night in those stinking clothes from one shock to another. The idea, let me repeat, had been a straight dash back to the City, with me in disguise to get us past any tipsy inspectors. Now, if anything, we might be in a worse position here than back with the Germanics.

But there was no escaping. There could be no fighting to get away from these Yellows. I had no choice but to go along for the moment with a pretence the nature of which I couldn't guess.

The Yellow Camp was disgusting in ways you can't imagine if you've only seen barbarians like the less enlightened cousins of my own people. There was a filthiness that by comparison made common dirt appear clean. Even that guardhouse with the other captives was more salubrious.

To be fair, these people were pure nomads. When you aren't accustomed to spending more than one night in the same spot, you tend not to observe the usual decencies of life. My assumption of a few dozen was based on those I'd seen on horseback, and then on the small number of Germanics. But this was an entire tribe on the move from God knows where.

The leather tents were huddled within a ring of high bonfires that hissed and crackled in the gentle rain, the gaps between them filled with piles of shit and rotting carcasses. Outside each tent, a pony was tethered. These at least looked clean and glossy.

Either these people were late sitters or early risers. No one seemed to be asleep. The men clumped around in quilted jackets, stiff and uncomfortable without their ponies. The women fussed over cooking pots. I could smell their food as soon as we were within the ring of fires. As a tenor voice stands out from a choir in church, it added its own texture to the general stink of the place.

Children ran about everywhere, shouting gibberish and throwing what looked like balls of shit at each other. About a dozen of them stood in a circle poking at a cowering figure with sharp sticks. I tried not to look too closely at what had been done to him as he staggered about to avoid the well-aimed blows.

And I thought the Germanics had been hard on us!

I turned from the horrid sight, restraining an urge to vomit. Even so, my legs were beginning to shake at the thought of what might be in store for us.

'Wait here,' the Yellow Linguist said as we reached the largest of the tents. 'When I call you in, you will kiss the dust of the Great One's floor.'

After seeing what passed for entertainment in his camp, I'd have licked the man's feet and painted his toenails. I nodded.

'I'm going to kill myself here and now,' Martin whispered in Celtic, with the settled composure of one who has lost too much hope to remain afraid. 'I will thank you, Aelric, for all your efforts to save us. I wish I had been brave enough to tell you certain things you have a right to know. Instead, I will say goodbye, and hope to see you again in a better world.'

'You'll do no such fucking thing,' I hissed back. 'We haven't got this far to lose now. Besides,' I added, 'we aren't here to be murdered. Just follow my lead, and we'll see Constantinople yet.

'And keep that knife out of sight,' I finished, with a faint enjoyment of the irony that almost removed my own terror. 'Captives aren't supposed to be armed.'

Theophanes must have guessed something of the exchange. He put a hand on my arm. 'I wish I could give active help in this dealing,' he whispered in Greek. 'But I must now rely wholly on your diplomatic skills. For what it may be worth, I suspect you are here to receive orders rather than give information. But how you explain having the pair of us with you I can't presently think.'

That made two of us. A drink and a brisk walk round the camp-fires, and I was sure I could think of some half-credible story. As it was, the tent flap opened and the Yellow Linguist beckoned us inside.

The tent was about fifteen feet square and about the same height. There were two heavily armed men standing just within, one each side of the flap. On a raised platform at the far end, with curtains on three sides and tended by two rather pert young girls, the Great One reclined amid a mass of stained silk cushions.

He was a mountain of flesh. Because he was shorter, he might only have been the same weight as Theophanes, but he looked half as fat again. Slitty eyes sunk deep into his bloated face, a lank moustache breaking through ritual scars and tattoos, he smiled evilly as we stepped into the light from the smoking tapers placed around what passed as his throne.

A runtish servant dressed in yellow struck once on a little brass gong. As its sound faded, the three of us were face down on the floor and licking its beaten, foul-tasting earth. We grovelled there for what seemed an age, until I felt a discreet kick in my side and got back to my feet.

We stood in silence before the Great One, looking respectfully down. At length, he spoke. The language he used sounded vaguely human – if you can imagine something spoken backwards on an indrawn breath. It was all wheezy trills and spat emphases. Just the sound of it chilled the blood.

'You are here to receive your instructions for tomorrow,' the Yellow Linguist interpreted in the basic Latin that is common among mixed groups of barbarians. 'But where is the usual white dog who comes among us for such purposes?'

I was prepared for this one.

'I am Aelric, his kinsman,' I replied, trying hard to think in English and speak as if Latin was an unfamiliar tongue. 'He sends his respects, but has a flux from drinking sour beer. He is not fit to be received in so Glorious a Presence. He sends me in his place.'

There was more of that sinister trilling back and forth. Then: 'Why do you presume to bring these captives before the Great One? Your instructions were to keep them together.'

'O Great One,' I said, 'these are objects of considerable value. They escaped our first attack. My brother and I found them wandering lost among the houses as we came before you. I sent my brother back with their gold, but thought it best to keep watch over them myself.'

As this was interpreted, I saw a gentle twitching of the curtain directly behind the Great One. I suddenly noticed a little rend in this at about head level. There was someone else in the tent, and he was watching us.

The Yellow Linguist saw this too. He broke off his interpreting and stepped forward, going respectfully round the Great One.

There was a muttered three-way conversation, the Great One listening intently and replying in monosyllables. I was too far away to hear any of it. But as it finished, the Great One smiled broadly. He leaned forward, beckoning me towards him.

I steeled myself and approached. There was a rancid smell of sweaty, unwashed fat and I could see the filed and blackened teeth as his lips were drawn back in a grin.

For the first time, I noticed a neat pile of about a dozen human heads just out of his reach to the left of the pillows. I hadn't taken them in straight away because they were a uniform dark brown and had been shrunk somehow into balls about the size of a cabbage.

All considered, it was rather like standing before Satan. The Great One took one of my hands between his paws and brushed it against the roughened, greasy flab of his cheeks.

'Such smooth and elegant hands for a man of the forests,' the Yellow Linguist interpreted. 'You are dressed as the Others. You have their colour and their language. Yet in all the time since we were called together, the Great One has been denied the sight of such beauty and daintiness of manner.'

There is a limit to what three days of roughing it can do to a manicure like mine. As I looked wordlessly back into that fat, grinning face, I wished I'd taken Martin's hint and put an end to myself outside the tent.

I thought of the shambling wretch at the mercy of those children and wondered if, even now, I'd have time to go for my knife. My sword had been taken as we entered the tent.

Instead, though, I repeated my story, adding something about the number and importance of my kinsmen. As I did so, I looked the Great One straight in the eye, trying desperately to ignore the freezing and unfreezing of my guts.

It got me nothing more than a curiously indulgent smile and a gentle squeeze of my hand.

One of those young girls suddenly looked up at me, an expression of cold mockery on her flat, delicately yellow face. I wondered what she might be like, knife in hand, with a bound prisoner. I put the thought from my mind.

'Did we not hear', the Yellow Linguist continued interpreting, 'how the Others shouted in their own camp after cloud had covered the sky? Was not the one summoned before the Great One to be questioned on the shouting?

'Yet all we have now is silence among the Others, and so much unexpected perfection of beauty set before us.

'Do the spirits mislead when they inform the Great One that those you bring with you are companions, not captives? Can it be that the one summoned wanders now beyond the protective fires, unseen by those who breathe?'

I've seen tax gatherers take longer to get at the essential point of a matter. But I was, you'll understand, in no mood for considering the relative balance in his mind of direct revelation and intuitive leaps.

He'd rumbled us good and proper, was the best I could think as I stood there, my hand still in his. All that remained was the question of what would happen next.

As usual, it was a surprise.

27

I heard a determined shuffling behind me. The Great One broke eye contact with me and looked over my shoulder. His face took on a look of slightly annoyed bafflement.

I looked round. Theophanes and Martin had moved apart and now stood facing each other at each side of the tent.

'We are honoured,' cried Martin in a bright voice, 'after hearing so many stories of his might and nobility, to be called at last into the presence of the Great One. We wish to perform for him as we have so often performed in the presence of Caesar himself.'

With that, the pair of them launched into song. It was a lyric popular at the time – 'Watchman at the Gates of Love', it was called. They sang together while Martin clapped his hands to keep time.

As they moved from one verse of cloying sentimentality to another, Martin sang in a pleasant light baritone. But the obvious star was Theophanes. Powerful, yet clear, the eunuch voice can carry every note from higher bass to soprano.

Theophanes was somewhat past his best for singing, and his voice cracked on some of the higher notes. But he covered this with a superb artistry, moving the more daring trills into a lower register.

During one note that he seemed to hold for ever without wavering, I glanced back to the Great One. He sat entranced. The two girls looked on, their mouths open with astonishment.

As they moved into the final long refrain, Theophanes broke off and began to dance about the tent, stamping his feet rhythmically and waving his arms in time to the music. Keeping his shoulders still, its angle never changing, he moved his head from side to side.

When, at last, the song ended, he took up three of those shrunken heads and, still dancing, started to juggle them. As he did so, Martin began one of those crooning, throbbing songs you hear in the better class of brothel. It's the sort that begins slowly and builds gradually to a clashing of metres that, handled properly, can imitate the sexual act.

Keeping time with the huge, undulating mass of his body, Theophanes threw the heads higher and higher, so I thought they would hit the roof of the tent and he'd lose them all. Yet, even at the climax of the song, when the dance movements must grow increasingly rapid and abandoned, he dropped not one. He began with three. He ended with three.

It was, all considered, a most remarkable performance. Perhaps, on balance, the world had been the poorer when Theophanes progressed from dancing boy to police state functionary.

As it finished, Theophanes and Martin threw themselves down in a perfectly timed and most elegant prostration.

The Great One squealed with joy, bobbing up and down as he clapped. He hauled himself up and lurched forward to pull Theophanes to his feet. He stretched up to plant a slobbering kiss on the eunuch's cheek. Then he reached into his robe and pulled out a red amulet to hang round Theophanes' neck. After a momentary hesitation, he added one of the shrunken heads. The Yellow Linguist interpreted the stream of appreciation that followed.

Puffing very slightly from the exertion, Theophanes acknowledged all this with a respectful bow. He added something about treasuring the gifts all the days of his life. If this was a discreet enquiry as to how many days this might be allowed to be, he got no definite answer.

But he had gained for the moment at least high praise where it seemed to matter.

Then it was back to business as usual. Rearranging himself on those nasty cushions, the Great One settled into place, and the audience continued.

'The one without stones in his pouch will go outside to recover

173

himself in the dawn air,' said the Yellow Linguist. 'You' – he pointed at me – 'will also perform for the Great One.'

I wondered what on earth I could do to match what had just been offered. I thought of some of the more tuneful ballads I'd used to bawl in taverns on the Wessex borders.

But it wasn't my voice the Great One had in mind. As Theophanes went out of the tent and half a dozen of the other Yellow Barbarians filed in, he kicked at one of the girls who sat at his feet. Toying with one of his shrunken heads, he hissed a stream of orders. When she remained squatting at his feet, with no apparent inclination to obey, he kicked her again. She landed about a yard before me and looked up into my face with a cold fury that made me want to sit down and fan myself.

At last, she got silently to her feet and began tugging at the laces that held the tunic to her body. In an instant, she stood before me stark naked, a closed, sullen look on her yellow face.

The servant who'd sounded the gong pulled out some more of those cushions and began scattering them on the ground.

I didn't need that poke in the back to tell me what kind of performance was expected of me. Clothes off and folded neatly beside the cushions, I was soon hard at work with the girl, making the beast with two backs while everyone else looked on.

You may ask how I was up to anything in that dreadful place. My answer is that I was young. I was also quite aware that this was not an occasion for polite excuses. And if I was about to die, I might as well take the chance of a good last fuck.

And if you've never tried it for yourself, I'll assure you that fear can be a tremendous aphrodisiac.

I might add that the girl was remarkably fetching. She stank like a dead fox – but I was no scented flower myself. And though very young, she was no virgin. After a few moments of hesitancy, she threw herself into the task appointed. She knew what she wanted, and I made very sure to give it to her – heart and soul, and all the usual graces.

After a while, it quite escaped me that everyone around me was cheering and wanking as I slowly brought the girl to a huge, shuddering orgasm. As she slid from underneath me and reached for her clothes, she looked decidedly more cheerful. Then her fingers probed her black hair and she pulled something out which she offered me in a closed fist. She opened it close to my face. The mass of crawling blackness on her palm was lice. With a gesture I took as intended to be friendly, she popped the things straight into her mouth and crunched. As she drew her lips back for a smile, I could see the still moving black specks all over her filed teeth.

Wheezing and drooling, the Great One lay back on his mountain of cushions. I stole a look at the curtain behind him. It hung still.

'You have obliged the curiosity of the Great One with his eldest daughter,' the Yellow Linguist explained in a halting voice. 'It is an honour that few are permitted.'

His daughter! Well, some of these more distant barbarians can have odd ways. But who was I to judge of these?

I glanced at the other daughter. Scared as I was, it was mildly flattering to see the jealous look on her face. It wouldn't be all sisterly love when they finally retired to the privacy of their tent.

That was the end of my part in the entertainment. Sitting up again, the Great One clapped his hands. Our audience filed out and Theophanes was brought back in.

No particular surprise on his face, he gave me an abstracted look before turning his attention to another long prostration.

As Martin helped me back into my clothes, I could feel a certain reserve in his manner. But it was only for a moment. It was prostration time again all round.

'You may leave us,' the Yellow Linguist said once we were back on our feet. 'We will accompany you to the place from where you may find your own way back to the camp of the Others. If the Great One desires your presence again, He will send for you.'

Cheering words! Two good fucks that night – and another chance to bolt for the City walls.

Outside, the drizzle had stopped. The sun was coming up and the mist had retreated to a chill whiteness around our feet. The fires had burned down to smoking embers.

Those children were still hard at play with their victim. But the wretch had now fallen down. Not even poking him with hot embers could raise more than an exhausted groan.

'He brought tidings from Caesar,' the Yellow Linguist explained, following my glance. 'They showed insufficient respect for the Great One.'

So that was the reason. I'd thought this was the Stylite hermit – getting his crown of martyrdom somewhat earlier than he'd had in mind. Instead, he was one of the envoys from Phocas that I'd heard the Germanics discussing.

As we passed out of the camp, I looked far over to my left. A dog had caught a rabbit which he carried in his mouth, his tail up, eyes shining. For us, too, it looked set to be a glorious day. I eased the stiffness from my back and took in a breath of the fresh morning air.

The Yellow Linguist walked in front. Behind us walked two armed guards. At the far end of the street we had entered, the only unruined building was a fortified church. Its heavy door had been scorched in a recent attempt on the place, but was unbreached.

Was that a movement I'd seen from the window of its tower? Hard to say.

I suddenly remembered my sword back in the camp. I hadn't thought to ask for its return. Nor had it been offered. No point in suggesting I should go back for it.

Then I heard Theophanes beside me. He spoke in a bright conversational Greek, pointing at the dog.

'Aelric,' he said, 'I must regret to inform you of a change in our circumstances. Do not plague me with questions – now or ever – about my sources of information. But it seems that our positions are reversed. I am safe. It is now you who are in danger.

'Ten paces after I finish talking to you, I will cry out and fall to the ground. I shall give every appearance of having had a stroke. Because my life has become of considerable value to them, these barbarians will turn all their attention on me.

'When that happens, you and Martin will run. The City must be to your left – perhaps only a half-mile away. You will outrun our

176

guards because they are more accustomed to riding. Do not stop, do not look round. Do you understand?' he asked.

'Yes,' I said with a cheerful wave.

'Yes,' said Martin, his nerve surprisingly steady.

Would I ever learn what these 'sources of information' had been? I looked down at my heavy, ill-fitting boots that had been made for everything but speed.

But we'd underestimated the Yellow Linguist. It wasn't only Latin he understood. He turned and barked an order at which he and the two guards drew their swords with a menacing rasp of steel, glinting in the early sunlight.

Having passed the church, we were now in a narrow street, one sword in front of us, two behind. All three were too close to be tackled one at a time.

I pushed Theophanes back against a broken wall and felt for my knife. Martin stood like a man turned to stone.

I might get one of them if I were lucky.

'Take this, you yellow fuckers,' a harsh voice cried out from above in Latin.

I think I shall be forgiven if I say I was long since past any degree of surprise. If it had been Saint Victorinus himself dropping down from that wall, his flowers tumbling behind him, I'd not have raised an eyebrow.

But it was Authari. Like me, he was dressed in the clothing of one of those Germanics. His sword glinted dull in the morning light.

So that's what had become of Hermann, I thought as I lunged at the Yellow Linguist while he was still in shock. But he recovered too fast. It was only the leather tunic that saved me from his raking sword-blow. I danced back, wrapping my cloak around my left arm and lashing out again with the knife.

No luck with that. Though largely useless for fighting on foot, a sword was still better than a knife.

I glanced round. My eyes lit on a spar that might be useful as a club. Before going for it, I threw the knife at his face. I was in luck this time. I got him straight in one of his eye-sockets. The knife

177

went in and dropped out again as he fell down squealing and writhing on the broken cobbles like a worm that has just had salt poured over it. Through hands clamped tight over his eye came a stream of black fluid. It was the sort of wound that doesn't kill at once, but can fester for days in an agony that doesn't abate.

Feeling a surge of joy I hadn't felt in months – not, indeed, since I'd skewered that killer outside the Lateran – I left the knife where it lay and bent down for his sword. Then, hearing a loud clashing behind me, I turned round to join in the action.

No need. Authari had made short work of the Yellows. He'd had that massive Germanic sword and had taken them too much by surprise. They lay at his feet in two crumpled heaps.

I saw Theophanes relax his grip on the knife in his hand. No more killing for him at the moment. The work was already done.

My legs went from under me in a sudden fit of the shakes. I flopped to the ground beside the Yellow Linguist. Everything about me went dark, with little flashes of light at the corners of my eyes.

'Not this one,' I whispered to Authari as he raised his sword in both hands above the Yellow Linguist. 'I want to finish him myself – with the knife.'

The beast had another eye, and much else that he might do before drawing his last breath.

But Authari ignored me. With a crunch, that heavy sword had smashed through quilted tunic and ribs, and the Yellow Linguist lay as silent as the other two.

He stood over me, breathing heavily. He put his hand down to me as I struggled to regain control over my little nervous fit.

'Get up, my Golden Aelric,' said Theophanes. 'Get up. Just one more effort before we can be safe.'

'Come along, Master,' Authari added, pulling me up with one arm. 'I want meat for my breakfast.'

28

'I think a touch more oil on your back, sir,' the slave said, flask in hand.

I could feel the heat baking though my sandals as I stood looking down at the brown sweat that oozed from every pore of my body in that room. Another slave knelt before me on a leather mat, scraping at my legs with his strigil.

'With all respect, sir,' he said, looking up, 'we'll surely cook before we can get all that dirt out of you.'

On the far side of the hot room, Martin was trying to insist that he could scrape himself. For all the notice his own ministering slaves took of him, he might have been speaking Celtic.

Theophanes had been right. The City was to our left, but some of the Germanics had been over on our right – four of them. I don't know if they'd been waiting for us on orders carried from the Great One, or if they'd still been looking for us.

All that mattered was that they'd almost caught us. We'd run like lunatics over that broken ground towards the defensive clearing. Martin and Theophanes had run hand in hand. Authari and I had followed, turning every so often to throw bricks at the exhausted pursuers. They'd been hardly six feet behind us, swords in hand, as we came within range of the City artillery. Only then had they given up the chase, standing out of probable range and shouting obscenities as we made for the nearest gate.

The negotiations required of Theophanes had seemed endless before the gate had been swung open by its quaking sentries and we were able to pass back into the City. But once inside, with nine inches of iron-clad gate between us and the rest of the world, I'd realised it was all over. We'd sat quietly drinking the dark, powerful

179

wine the soldiers gave us, listening vaguely to the stream of peremptory orders and explanations Theophanes had snapped at the officer in charge, the creaking of the iron gibbets overhead, and the muffled shouts that drifted underneath the gate.

Authari explained that he had become separated from us in the attack and by the time he'd caught up with us the Germanics had taken us. He had followed us back to the guardhouse, and hidden out in an old hen coop from where he could see all that passed. He'd waited there for a chance to to rescue us. On the second day, he'd come upon Hermann and broken his neck, taking his clothes and hiding the body. His plan had been to kill another guard early in the morning of the fourth day and take the dead man's place for an inspection.

'But I missed your escape, sir,' he said guiltily. 'I wetted my lips with a little beer I'd found, and then fell asleep for just a few moments. I woke to the sound of shouting. I knew it must have been you who'd got away.'

He'd wandered through the old suburbs all the remaining night, hoping to find us and lead us back to the city. He'd finally caught up with us as we left the Yellow Camp.

Now, a piece of advice for you, dear reader – advice you may be in a position one day to take. Always show gratitude to slaves. Thank and reward them for small services. Free them for great services.

Still in those stinking clothes, I'd hurried Authari straight off to the Church of St Peter and freed him before the priest and the whole congregation.

As Authari knelt before me for the last time as a slave, I'd bent down and kissed him, and promised him as much gold as he could carry on his journey back to the Lombards.

'With your permission, sir,' he'd replied, 'I'll stay on as your freedman. You were a good master and I do think you have need of my protection.'

The priest had nodded his approval as he laid his hands on us both. The congregation had shouted the traditional words. Before dusk, the news would be all over the city – to add to the other stories of our daring heroism that were already circulating.

Now Martin and I were making free with the bathhouse of Theophanes' palace. In his usual style, he'd called the place his 'miserable apartment'. But if not on the same scale as the Legation, it was undoubtedly a palace. Close by the Senatorial Dock, in one of the side roads, it was a modest affair of painted brick on the outside. Inside, the array of marbles and elaborate mosaics and frescoes dazzled the senses. No extreme of luxury had been overlooked for comfort or display.

Filthy as he was, Theophanes couldn't join us yet in the bath. As we'd come in from the street, he'd been accosted by a messenger bearing letters in a bag of purple leather.

'Do please proceed straight to the bathhouse,' he'd said, breaking the seal. 'I will join you when I have dictated the necessary replies.'

'Oh, sir, what have you been about?' The slave looked up from my crotch, disgust on his face fighting politeness. He called for a pair of tweezers and reached into the short hair above my balls. With a deft tug, he had the creature out and held it up black and twisting for my inspection. In the shimmering light of the hot room, it looked more like a spider than an ordinary pubic louse. Search me where I'd picked the thing up. It might have been from those sluts. It might just as easily have been from those beastly clothes that I hoped were, even now, feeding the bathhouse furnace. You wouldn't want those things clamped all over you, scattering brown dust into your clothes and raising a continual scabby itch.

The slave dropped the thing on to a spare linen cloth, then threw off his bathrobe to avoid catching anything himself. He then gave a renewed and closer inspection to the other hairy parts of my body. From the horrified tutting, more of the creatures came to light.

'Malik,' he called, 'prepare the depilation room. And bring the freedman as well. We'll deal with the Master when he's ready for us.'

Since I'll bet you've never been depilated, I think I'll pause here to tell you what it involves.

First, you go into a hot tub. This isn't the usual heated pool, which can be large enough for swimming but is never that hot.

What I mean is a small bathtub filled with water as hot as you can tolerate. From here, you're taken out, rubbed all over with oil and roughly shaved. The purpose of this is to reduce the body hairs to no more than an eighth of an inch, while making them softer and looser. Then you lie on a couch while slaves plaster you in strips with a special melted pitch called, in Latin, *dropax*. When this is set but not fully cooled, the strips are ripped off.

The operation is repeated as often as required until, from the neck down, your body is as smooth as a new-born baby's. And that includes toes and fingers.

The delicate areas of your body need a specially refined wax. Even so, this hurts. But you soon get used to the discomfort. Approached in the right frame of mind, it can be quite arousing. You'll not believe the inches it can seem to add to even the proudest manhood – nor the continued, sensuous kissing of the flesh it brings out in silk undergarments. So long as you maintain the underlying muscle tone, it can give your body an adolescent look and feel well into your sixties.

If Martin hadn't been there, wailing and thrashing about at every stripping of the pitch, I'd have given myself up heart and mind to those gloriously pretty boy slaves who were rubbing their bodies so provocatively against mine as they did their work.

Such was my first ever bath in the full ancient style. You can rest assured it was not my last.

Afterwards, I sat naked in a shaft of sunlight that came through the roof of the final room in the bathhouse. Here, in subdued contentment, I gave myself up to the ministrations of the barber and the manicurist. Those awful days outside the city walls were already fading to a distant nightmare.

'What do you think might be for lunch?' I asked Martin as he glowered into a set of mirrors that revealed the full extent of his bald patch.

'Something special, my dear boy – something very special,' Theophanes called as he entered the room on a wheeled couch. He lay on his back, a white cloth covering his bulk from neck to knees.

'Can you bear it if I ask to deprive you of your sunbeam?' he continued. 'My cosmetician will need all the light God can provide before I am ready to face the world again.'

Lunch *was* special, though we were all three now so wilting under the strain of that long, sleepless night that we were barely up to registering the succession of dishes.

I was happy in the fresh clothes brought over from the Legation. Even Martin was less dour than usual, wearing the best linen robe I'd bought for him and reaching up every so often to reassure himself that the elaborate styling that had brought a lock of hair over his crown still held in place.

We sat in a peristyle that ran all the way along the inside front wall of the palace. Through the limestone pillars we looked on to the central courtyard, in the middle of which a large fountain was cascading loud jets into a surrounding basin of blue granite.

For the first time, Alypius joined us at the table. He gave his master endless loving glances as he helped him break up his bread. He even threw me the occasional look that came close to being friendly.

Throughout the meal Theophanes continued to deal with his backlog of correspondence. The Imperial messages having been dealt with in private, he now turned to the ordinary petitions. He would listen to an abstract of each, then give a simple yes or no. A few times, he specified the fraction of the share of an estate. His comments would be scratched into the margins of each papyrus sheet and then all would be carried off for putting into the correct official form for stamping and delivery.

During an iced fruit course, the papers that confirmed Authari's freedom were brought in for me to sign. Having lost my signet ring to the barbarians, I signed my name at the bottom of each copy – one for the Registry, another for each of the parties. Theophanes and Martin signed as witnesses.

As the dishes were being cleared away, another messenger entered. He whispered awhile to Theophanes, who listened intently.

'Alaric,' he said in his most official voice, and using my common name to emphasise the return to formality. 'Alaric, I must bring two connected facts to your attention.

'The usurper Heraclius has intervened with the barbarians to secure the release of the remaining captives. For reasons of state security, these will not be readmitted to the city but will be ferried across to the Asiatic suburbs. At the same time, advance forces from the usurper have arrived outside the city walls. All contact with the Provinces has been cut. We are now under siege.'

29

I was alone with Theophanes.

He'd taken me across the courtyard and right inside the fountain. We'd used little parasols to keep the water off us as we passed through into a small dry space. Under the marble roof were a table and two chairs. A tray of drinks and various nibbles were already set out for us.

All around us, like a circular window of rippled glass, the water splashed and gurgled loudly into the basin. Through it, we had an unbroken if distorted view of the whole courtyard, which was now empty.

'I find this place so cooling in the hot weather,' Theophanes explained as we took our seats, 'and often so private.'

His voice lingered over the word 'private'.

He took up a silver pot with a long spout. 'Do please let us share this most refreshing drink.'

He poured two generous helpings of a black, steaming liquid. I'd seen him drink this at the end of some of our dinners in the restaurant. Knowing his abstemious habits, I'd stuck to the wine. Now, I took up my cup and sipped carefully.

'It is a custom I brought from my own country,' said Theophanes. 'It is an infusion of berries called *kava* that both settles the stomach and refreshes the mind. I have never made any converts to it among the Greeks. But it is used widely by those Eastern races that cannot or will not trust themselves with even watered wine. If, after your long ordeal, it does not wholly revive you, I recommend these other dried berries from Africa. Chewed in moderation, they are still more stimulating.'

I took up a handful of the things and crunched them. They tasted foul, but I washed them down with more of the *kava* juice.

Even as I doubted its efficacy, the combination set up a warming feeling in my stomach. This spread upwards and around, taking the heavy weariness from my body and giving a renewed sharp edge to my wits.

'Theophanes,' I said, putting my cup down, 'you will agree that we have much to discuss in the time available to us.'

'Much indeed, my dearest Aelric,' he replied. 'I hope, by the way, you will not object if, when we are truly *in private*, I use your proper name?'

'I want to know many things,' I said, ignoring the request. 'In the first place, I want to know what happened outside that tent while I was entertaining the Great One and his daughter.'

'You will recall,' said Theophanes through the steam from his cup, 'that I was sent out to refresh myself after those exertions that Martin had so usefully suggested during your attempts at diplomacy. Doubtless, your own exertions would in some manner have been polluted by the presence of one so sadly incomplete as I.'

I silenced him with an impatient wave. Those berries were making me testy.

'I'll have none of that official old toss, if you please,' I snapped. 'The day we were taken prisoner, I was approached by the man who tried to kill me last month. He said he was an agent.'

'I was told of the meeting,' Theophanes said as I finished my account. 'And no – please be aware that he really is working at the moment for Heraclius. I have used Agathius myself in the past. But I regard him as a person of little intelligence and therefore of limited usefulness. Only think of that crude and self-defeating stratagem of his to keep you inside the city walls. I would never tolerate such incompetence. Had *I* wanted to keep you away from the barbarian raid – and you are right in assuming it was arranged by, or for, Heraclius – you can be sure it would have been a *perfect* stratagem.

'I made the mistake of assuming that he and his associates would understand your apparent position here and act accordingly. It was most galling when they ignored what I hoped was the clearest evidence and believed you had been sent from Rome to arrange a deal between Pope and Emperor. That is why they tried to kill you with those roof tiles.

'I had no choice but to approach you that day in the University Library, and make it clear to everyone that your presence here had the effect of blocking any such deal. Plainly, they understood me then, but were too stupid to leave matters alone.'

'Of course,' I said, 'this was a lie. I wasn't sent – or brought – here to block anything. There are no differences between you and the Permanent Legate. You and he are in this together. If Silas has withdrawn to his quarters, it's only to keep him from being murdered by Heraclius.

'A dead Permanent Legate cannot agree to anything with the Emperor. Or if it has been agreed, it may be harder to put into effect. So, tell me now – what is this agreement you have reached?'

'My dear Aelric,' came the reply, 'I knew at once it was you above me in the Legation that night. I certainly got full sight of you as you swayed horribly round that dome. Please be assured that I prayed for your safe return to your own quarters.'

Theophanes gave me a close look. 'What did you learn that evening?' he asked.

'That you finished off that poor sod Justinus,' I said.

He shrugged. 'Anything else?' he asked.

I gathered my thoughts. 'I could say you are plotting with the Lombards for an attack on Rome,' I said. 'If you can depose Boniface and replace him with – with, er – Silas, you could get your excommunication of Heraclius and forget all about the Universal Bishop stuff.'

Theophanes smiled. There seemed a slight easing of tension in his shoulders.

'There would be a certain economy in what you suggest,' he said. 'Heraclius set out from Carthage last year with a shipload of bishops, all singing his praises as the New Apostle of Christ, come to redeem Empire and world alike. When he does eventually arrive outside the City walls, it will be with part of the True Cross that he lifted from the Sepulchre on his recent capture of Jerusalem.

187

'If only the Pope would say the right words, the theological wheels would drop straight off the chariot that Heraclius has made for himself. Bearing in mind how short he is of money, that could mean the end of him.

'But' – Theophanes held up a finger – 'but His Holiness will not say those words until after he has had everything that he wants from Phocas.

'I know that His Holiness is described in Canterbury as Universal Bishop. However, the title has never been mentioned by the Emperor in other than private correspondence. The phrases taught to a race of illiterate barbarians do not necessarily describe the laws of the Empire . . . Therefore, the Roman Church is insistent on a formal decree that admits of no ambiguity.'

'And you won't give it', I broke in, 'because it would upset the Greek and other Eastern Churches.'

Now grave, Theophanes nodded. 'The Church ruled by His Holiness of Constantinople might give way to an express command,' he said. 'But the Syrian and Egyptian Churches would never accept Western primacy. Greeks and Latins may hate each other for petty trifles, but this is as nothing to the hatred they share jointly in the East.

'Since the conquests of the Great Alexander a thousand years ago, you Westerners – Greek or Latin or barbarian is unimportant – have viewed the East as naturally subject. But this is not to be regarded as a natural or a permanent state of affairs. If the Great Constantine thought the Christian Faith would be the glue to hold this Empire together, he was wrong.'

Theophanes stood. 'You will forgive me if I must urinate in front of you. The latrines are inside, and I find my bladder grows weak with age.'

He looked up from the silver chamber pot. 'Do you really believe', he asked, 'that such a plot could be hatched between me and the Permanent Legate without knowledge of the Dispensator? Or can you believe His Excellency would ever join such a plot?'

'Of course not.' I smiled. It fitted more of the facts than anything else I'd been able to think of. It was a rotten hypothesis, even so.

'Then you do not fall in my estimation,' he said. 'And luck was truly with you that night you went spying in the Legation.'

I watched as Theophanes rearranged himself.

'There is also the matter', I said, beginning again, 'of your defection from Phocas. Any chance you might tell me what happened outside the Great One's tent? Who was that man behind the curtain? What did you agree with him?

'What is it that made me surplus to requirements – even an embarrassment, to be removed as soon as decently possible? And how did you persuade him not to have Martin and me killed on the spot? It's your business if you want to dump Phocas as you dumped Maurice. I don't blame you an inch. I'll even thank you for the limited favour. But I want to know how this affects me.'

I poured myself yet another cup of that hot infusion. Having drained it in a gulp, I sat back glowering. I also found myself trembling very slightly.

Cup in hand, Theophanes sat watching me. His face had no need of the white lead that covered it. There was no expression to conceal.

'The man', he said, 'was another of the fools who serve Her-aclius. Instead of realising that my death or extended captivity was in the best interests of his master, he let himself be persuaded that he had found a valuable ally.

'You are wrong, however, if you believe I have changed sides. The plan, as you know, was for the raid to build sympathy for Heraclius. The implementation was a disgrace. Those savages slaughtered two hundred people before they could be called to order. They atrociously murdered a senior diplomat who counted three Emperors among his ancestors.

'Thousands of the best people in Constantinople would turn on Heraclius if word got out that he was somehow behind all this. That alone was enough for his people to want you dead.'

'And I suppose your friend Agathius will now be after me again,' I said bitterly.

'No,' said Theophanes. 'I now control Heraclius to some limited degree. And you remain under my protection. You are safe as

189

things stand. Indeed, once this siege is lifted – however that may happen – you may go back to Rome. Your role in these proceedings is at an end. Any further instructions you receive from the Dispensator will be redundant.

'It is no longer necessary for the Permanent Legate to have any excuse for keeping himself out of circulation.'

I turned again to the overall agreement involving the Church.

'That I will not explain,' Theophanes said flatly. 'If there were the slightest suspicion that you knew anything, your safety would be at an end. All sides would want you dead or would take you in for questioning under torture. I have no faith in even your ability to know such a secret and consistently appear not to know it. And, if you will pardon my lapse into official mode, it might frustrate a settlement on which the welfare of millions depends.'

I pushed hard. Theophanes was like flint. I tried an indirect approach.

'If you haven't switched over to Heraclius, you must still be loyal to Phocas. But surely he's finished? Surely, he'll not be Emperor come Christmas?'

Theophanes sighed. 'You assume, my dear boy, that I must be on the side of either. My informants tell me Heraclius is a dreamy, idle creature. Without firm advice, he is indecisive. And he cannot judge the value of the advice he is given. The further away he travels from his father in Carthage, the less effective his actions appear to be.'

'Quite unlike the bloodthirsty drunkard you serve,' I said with a sneer. Would this draw him out? I wondered.

Theophanes smiled indulgently, and took his time to suck on one of the softer berries in the dish. The wind had dropped, but clouds were now darkening the skies outside our bubble.

'Let me be specific, Aelric. My ultimate loyalty is not to any specific Emperor. It is to the Empire itself.'

He paused at my look of incredulity. He ignored my faintly sarcastic wave at the glories that were visible, if distorted, beyond the sheet of water.

'For all his merits,' he said, 'Maurice clung to an order of things that was dead. He wouldn't let go of what we cannot much longer hold. His only solution was more taxes and a squeeze on military pay, and to hope against hope that his next military victory would sort everything out.

'Phocas was different. He came in without grandiose expectations. He cut non-military spending. He reformed abuses. He even quietly took the view that, so long as they paid on time, what the taxpayers said in church was their business. Before the African revolt, he was fighting the Persians at minimal cost.'

'But now he's a drunken killer?' I pressed.

Theophanes shook his head. 'With his responsibilities, who wouldn't turn to drink?' he asked. 'As for the Terror, that was begun by his son-in-law, Priscus – a brute whose eagerness to meet you must be satisfied in the next few evenings.

'Phocas may have grown to like the taste of blood. But it was not he who first raised the cup. If I administer the incidental details of the Terror, it is only because some order of killing must be maintained.

'All that matters ultimately is that Heraclius, if he becomes Emperor, will have all the faults of Maurice and none of his virtues. Phocas is useful to the Empire in ways that will outlast his reign.

'But I begin to feel very tired, my dearest boy,' Theophanes said after another long pause. 'Before I begin to wander in my thoughts, let me inform you of what officially happened last night. It is enough for everyone to know that you were the hero. You conceived and executed a daring plan of escape that got the three of us back to the City walls with a barbarian army on our heels. You may elaborate as you please on that theme. But our meeting with the Great One never took place. We were never close to his tent. We neither did nor observed any things there.

'As for the other captives, we are putting the word about that their release was secured by the timely intervention of Saint Victorinus. He worked a miracle with the Great One, who has returned to his own benighted land with a handful of missionaries provided by Phocas.

'People will more readily believe this story than that Heraclius secured the release. It saves us the fruitless task of trying to prove that Phocas really did all he could to achieve the same. Neither side really gains from the story we are circulating. Neither side loses.

'From what I know of the man, Heraclius will soon himself believe the official story.'

And that was the end of what Theophanes had to say. I could have asked more. I might have explored the advantages he had secured for himself. Because he'd escaped with me, Phocas had accepted him back inside the walls, his position unshaken. Because our escape had taken us to the Yellow Camp, he'd opened a line of communication with Heraclius that might be useful when or if there was a change of Emperor.

I knew I'd got as much as I would get out of the old greaser. Some of what Theophanes had said was undoubtedly true. Some was probably lies. Much else lay in the grey zone that separates truth from falsehood. I'd have to sort out what was what for myself.

Theophanes rose unsteadily to his feet. He looked down at me. The weariness on his face seeped through the lead gloss.

'I know, my dearest boy, you still think me an unscrupulous Oriental eunuch, practised in every form of deceit – including perhaps self-deceit. But let me assure you, I cannot forget what has happened during the past few days. You will have no better friend in the City than I. Should it ever be necessary, I will die for you.'

With that, and his parasol up, he stepped through the curtain of water.

I wanted to run after him. But as I emerged from the fountain, I saw the messengers waiting under the peristyle, more of those purple bags in hand.

The heat was gone from the afternoon. It was coming on to rain.

30

I was set down outside the Legation to a ragged cheer from the crowd that had gathered there. Word had already got round of Alaric the Hero. I had no illusions about what had happened. Some diversion was needed from the apparent shambles Phocas had made of handling the barbarians. I was the best on offer. I'd made a bloody and triumphant escape. If I'd also brought Theophanes back to the City, that didn't seem – even maybe in private – to diminish my glory.

I made a short speech of thanks, dwelling on how Saint Victorinus had guided my steps. That avoided my having to make reference to any human agency and saved giving offence to either party.

It went down well. As I finished, a woman held up a child before me. I pinched its cheek and told her he would grow into a fine young man.

Inside the entrance hall, Martin and Authari had gathered our slaves. These all stood with the skeleton staff of the Legation. No Demetrius, of course. But even the silent monks had left off their tending of the garden.

More congratulations, and another speech.

At last, back in my suite, I made sure Maximin was sleeping peacefully. Martin said in his delicate way that Authari had worn himself and Gutrune out in celebration of his freedom. Both were still groggy in bed.

Crashed out in my office, I sat alone with Martin. I finished the wine he'd offered and glanced at the letters that had piled up in my absence. There was the usual thick packet from the Dispensator. I threw this unopened to the far side of the desk. I'd see what Gretel had to say when I was truly alone. The time was approaching for some comment from her on the adoption of Maximin.

There was a gleeful letter in code from my partner in the Cornish business. So far as I could tell without the key at hand, all had gone to plan. The tin shipment had been unloaded and sold in Cadiz, then replaced with an equal weight of rubble packed in the same crates, together with a consignment of what was described as Spanish lead. Now overloaded, the ships had gone down with nearly all hands off Malta. The other shareholders not in the know were stuffed.

I was already richer by a straight three hundred pounds of gold. More would follow. I could now endow that monastery outside Canterbury to produce multiple copies in parchment of the papyrus books I was sending over.

'God be praised!' said Martin dreamily when I told him about the use of the money. 'He is surely with you.'

I looked at him. From his contracted pupils, I could see he'd been at my opium again. Well, if it kept him calm and busy after all the thrills of the past few days, I wasn't one to comment.

'Aelric,' said Martin as I threw the last of the correspondence aside, 'the slaves have approached me to ask if you would honour them with a visit to their quarters for dinner this evening. They are immensely proud of what you did outside the walls. We could combine this with a final dinner for Authari with the slaves. He will take his meals with me in future.'

Martin steadied himself and gave another of his little coughs. 'I wish also to say, speaking personally, how grateful I am for what you did. Once again, I owe you my life. This is a debt of which I shall ever be conscious.'

'Think nothing of it, Martin,' I said. I ignored his delicate reminder of the time when I'd freed him instead of racking him to death. 'Think nothing at all,' I repeated, now in Celtic. 'It turns out that we had only to stay put another night and we'd now be swanning about in the Asiatic suburbs with the other freed captives, awaiting the outcome of the struggle between Phocas and Heraclius – safely out of reach of both.

'Theophanes is back in the city under circumstances tending much to his own credit – at least with the Emperor. Authari earned his freedom. All you get is another set of horrid memories and more time in the city. I should apologise to you.'

I stopped Martin's protest.

'However,' I said, 'the news isn't all bad.' I explained that we could now go home.

It Saint Victorinus had cured him of his bald patch, Martin wouldn't have rejoiced more. Not even opium could dull that response. When he was calm again, I asked how he and Theophanes had co-ordinated their singing and dancing without prior arrangement.

'I whispered a suggestion to Theophanes,' he explained, 'when the Great One looked disinclined to believe your subterfuge. He took it up and elaborated while I merely followed.'

I made a weak attempt at a joke. 'Watching the pair of you together,' I said, 'anyone would have thought you were old friends rather than distant acquaintances.'

But the happy outburst was over, and all I got was a cough.

What I wanted now was to fall into a clean bed, and writhe around with my smooth body in the silk sheets before sleep claimed me. Still, I had my duties to attend to. And a dinner with the slaves might be a jolly affair – all solid food and unwatered wine.

Before we went down, I gave Martin the official line on our escape. Fortunately, he'd guessed the truth might not be convenient, and had told the slaves to wait for my own account.

I woke next morning with a sore head from all the wine and beer and those earlier drugs. But I was cheered by the sound of works in the bathhouse. Theophanes had sent over a detachment of his own slaves to get the furnace in working order.

Better still, an Imperial messenger was shown in as I finished my late breakfast. I was invited as a guest of honour to the races in the Circus the day after next – a Saturday, this – when the intervention of Saint Victorinus would be celebrated in full style.

'Can you look out the red and white?' I asked Martin once we were alone again. 'It looks vaguely senatorial, and it sets off my hair. Besides, I want the crowd not to lose sight of me. How about the yellow and red for you?

'Oh, yes – and please do take Authari to the tailor. He can't follow us about in slave clothes. Take advice, but I fancy him in plain white.'

Martin looked as displeased as I gradually realised I should have felt at the invitation. The world was coming apart at its seams, and we were being dragged in sudden and irresistible jerks towards its most unstable point. He'd much rather have been packing for Rome.

I cut the conversation short by dodging into the nursery, where Gutrune was offering Maximin one of her titties. She rocked back and forth with him singing some cradle song that reminded me of Kent. Tears ran down her face and she barely noticed my presence.

As I walked to the University Library to continue with Epicurus, it was still pleasingly obvious how my status had changed. For the first time, people stopped to greet me in the street. The bubble was suddenly burst. The crowds still separated as they streamed around me, but now it was with an acknowledgement of my presence. I was accepted as a part of the City life.

One man from the higher classes even got out of his chair and had his slave give me a strip of ivory bearing his name and status. I was invited to call on him at my leisure. I'd given up on carrying my own ivory cards. But there was no need of them now. Everyone seemed to know me. Everyone wanted to be seen taking my hand.

In the library, too, things were changed.

'Please, Alaric – do come and share our table,' one of the students called out as I entered the canteen. He was one of the finely dressed young men who'd scattered on my first approach, leaving me with Sergius. Now, they were all mighty welcoming. I was Alaric the Hero for everyone.

His name was Philip, he told me. Without giving it in so many words, he added that he was from one of the oldest families in the

City. His people had migrated from Rome when Constantine was eager for a lick of senatorial polish for his new capital, and they'd been big there ever since.

What he and his friends were learning at the University was nothing very impressive. They'd memorised some of the standard classics. For the rest, they were reading commentaries and abridgements. However well born, they had to be able to express themselves in the proper Greek of the ancients if they wanted preferment within the Administration.

We sat chatting well past the time when I'd wanted to be at my desk. Then again, there was so much catching up to do.

'You see,' one of Philip's younger friends said when the matter came up, 'we were told you were *ever* so busy. We didn't think it right to disturb you before.'

I let that pass and accepted an invitation to go hunting the following day. I could borrow a horse and everything, I was assured.

Still formal, there was an obvious unbending of manner among the staff. Someone had placed a bowl of yellow flowers and a jug of honeyed lime juice on my table.

I was soon yawning over Plato – you have to read him once, even if he was a prize bore and one of the great corrupters of reason. But I was aware every so often of a warm contentment at the back of my mind.

Next dawn found me hunting outside the city walls with my new friends. It was Friday the 25th of September. Autumn comes later to Constantinople than to Jarrow, but come it finally does. With the morning mist of autumn still on the ground, we rode far out, through the old suburbs, into the Thracian countryside. My leggings were soon soaked by the dew. My mind was quickened by the now chilly air, my eyes gladdened by the sombre reds and browns of a declining Nature. Though there would still be fine days, summer was definitely over.

No wild pigs, nor any sight of the Heraclians, whose siege was still mostly a formality.

As hoped, however, we did crash into a party of barbarians. The Great One and company were long gone but the smell and general mess of their camp were still there to remind us of their coming. By now they must have been at least fifty miles across country towards the Danube. The tide of devastation that had swept down to lap against the very walls of the City had for the moment receded.

Some of the Germanics were still about too. We came upon them as they fussed over their booty, trying to cram it into a wagon the wheels of which kept sticking in the mud. I picked up a slight graze to one of my shins from a sword-thrust, and got splashed all over with blood when I dismounted to finish someone off who'd backed me into some bushes. It was a raking blow along the lower belly. He had no armour and I sliced straight through the woollen tunic. He roared like a slaughtered ox as his entrails spooled about him. The dogs were over him in an instant, tearing happily at the dying flesh.

But the sad bastards weren't up to much of a fight. Most of them made straight off on horseback, leaving their booty to us. One of my companions managed to trample an old man before he could get to his horse, then broke his neck with a neat downward crunch of the knees. Another of the creatures was cut to death as he tried to stand and fight.

Authari hacked the left hand off yet another as he tried to pass on horseback. With a howl and a spraying of blood, the man dropped his sword to clutch at the reins. As he rode off, I called Authari back from the pursuit. Though victorious, it made sense to keep together.

We took no prisoners. The dogs ripped at the bodies till they resembled bloody offal in rags.

It was another glorious re-entry to the city. The dozen of us rode along Middle Street, waving our bloody swords at the cheering crowds. Slaves dragged the loaded wagon along behind us. Hung round the neck of my borrowed horse was the severed head of my latest victim.

'Hosanna! Hosanna!' the mob cried rapturously at me. 'All hail to the New Achilles!'

Half the booty we gave to the Emperor as a present. There wasn't much choice in this. The Black Agent who made sure our weapons were stowed away also made it pretty plain what was expected. The clumsy good humour he put on in our presence didn't for a moment detract from what he represented. The other half we dedicated to Saint Victorinus who had been sighted a hundred times the previous night pacing up and down the walls.

Then to a tavern, where we celebrated our victory in style. We arranged a night of gambling and whoring in further celebration. But, considering the races next day, we agreed to settle the time by further discussion.

I was shopping all afternoon. I felt the need for more clothes. Since we were to be off home before long, now might be my last chance. And the cosmetic box I'd thought so fine on my first shopping trip now looked mean and tatty.

I still had to prove identity with every purchase. But there was still that change in manner that made everything easier and more pleasant. Phocas needed a hero to divert attention from his own failure to do anything about the raid. Theophanes had thrust that role upon me. Now I had added to it. Everyone had seen or heard about my bloody sword and the severed head.

I was for the moment the 'Lord Alaric, Champion of the Faith'. Now there were crude images of me alongside the graffiti. In one of these, I held a cross in my left hand while I sliced off an impressive number of barbarian heads with my sword in my right.

'Shall I start packing our own stuff?' Martin asked eagerly before dinner. He was perking up after an earlier moroseness. 'I can order the additional crates for after the races. I was down in the harbour earlier. There's no end of shipping penned in by the siege. I couldn't get the Captain to speak to me, but one is certainly bound for Rome. If he won't take us, I'm sure we can get something else going that way.'

'Keep looking for transport,' I said. 'But we'll be here a few days yet. There may be trouble before we leave. Get Authari to arm the other slaves. If things do turn nasty within the City, we'll bar the gates of the Legation. But he and I need to agree a reserve plan.'

Martin turned thoughtful again. But I went happily to bed where I dreamed of home and Gretel. I even found time for a vision of the Dispensator's face when I told him of all that had happened.

Even Martin would not have denied that things had turned out better than they might have done.

31

The Great Circus is about a quarter of a mile from the Legation, and is set amid the main public buildings of the city. To its north is the Great Church. To the west, connected by Middle Street, is the Forum of Constantine and the legal district. To the east is the main Imperial Palace, with which it is joined.

Indeed, the Imperial Box is a branch of the palace, joining the main structure by a spiral staircase that can be shut off in emergencies. Though called a 'box', it is in fact more than a raised viewing platform. It has an audience hall, a dining room, and even a small office for use between races. A staircase leads down to a covered terrace where the Senators and other dignitaries of the Empire sit within sight of the Emperor.

Seen from the southern, semicircular extremity of the Circus, the Box is on the right-hand side, and sits about two-thirds of the way towards the flattened northern extremity. It is built over the stalls for the horses and chariots and the storehouses for all the machinery of the races and spectacles. Because of the sloping ground, the southern extremity is suspended on massive brick vaults. These ensure a perfect level for the Circus and provide additional accommodation for the officials of the various financial ministries.

The Circus itself is about six hundred feet long by about three hundred feet wide. The racecourse is divided by a long low wall – the *spina* – at the ends of which are the points round which the chariots have to turn. At one of these points are seven golden dolphins, at the other seven golden eggs. The normal length of a race is seven circuits, and dolphins and eggs are removed at the appropriate moments to remind spectators how far advanced the races are.

Between these points are various works of ancient art. At the exact centre of the *spina* is an Egyptian obelisk of the most incredible antiquity. Someone told me once that this dates from before the Flood. Since no one can read the picture writing that covers the thing, and since there was probably no Flood – where, after all, could the waters come from to cover the whole world? – I take this as one of those fanciful guesses by which people cover their ignorance. But the obelisk must be old.

I am on firmer ground with other works. For me, the most illustrious of these is the serpentine column of bronze erected in ancient days at Delphi to commemorate the final defeat of the Persians. This came to the city when the Great Constantine ransacked the world for monuments to adorn his new capital. You can read on it the names of the city states that took part in this unquestionably miraculous deliverance.

Martin and I arrived with Authari soon after dawn, and joined a long queue of chattering citizens dressed in their finest to gain admittance. As we filed in through the Great Entrance, I saw that slaves were stretching canopies high over the seating areas in the Circus to keep off the drizzle that had continued through the night. With successive, rippling cracks that reminded me of the sails on a ship, the slaves had the canopies neatly unfurled. They were stretched from poles set into the perimeter walls, reminding me of the teeth of a comb. The racecourse itself was uncovered, but the retaining cords of the covering connected to each other far above the course. The whole was then steadied with a network of other cords that held it rigid in the shifting winds and kept off both sun and rain.

We were met inside by Alypius. He led us through the gathering crowds to the semicircular end of the Circus. Our seats were right at the front on the lowest row. On our left, stretching all the way up to the highest row of seats, was a line of armed guards. A few yards before us, blocked by more armed guards, was a staircase leading down to the racecourse.

From here, we had a fine view of the whole Circus. I noticed the Senators filling up their terrace. On the plainer robes I could make out the bordering flashes of purple. Conspicuous in his black was what I guessed to be the Greek Patriarch. Among the men, I saw a few veiled ladies.

Most remarkable, however, were the humbler spectators. Around us were seated crowds in no particular style of clothing. These were the unaffiliated citizens. But on my right – that is, on the side of the Imperial Box – sat the Green Faction. On the other side of the Circus sat the Blue Faction.

There are, you see, two teams in every race – one blue, one green – and these have their fans among the spectators. These two factions are separately seated because of the riots that often attend races. They have always had some official recognition, their leaders being held responsible to the Urban Prefect. They have their own social life, providing insurance and support for their members. Since the first big siege by the Persians, they have been armed and drilled, and now form part of the regular City defences.

The Factions flocked together in their accustomed seas of blue and green robes, each facing the other across the racecourse. As the Circus filled up, and the rain left off and the sun began to peep from behind the grey clouds, the unofficial festivities got under way.

By custom, the first insults traded between the two Factions are generally accusations of heresy or treason, and curses that go back to before the establishment of the Faith. This is the only place left where you can hear public venerations of Isis and Serapis and others of the dethroned Ancient Gods. Often, the phrases used are so old and garbled that most are unaware of the blasphemy.

Then, as the teams enter and go one lap about the Circus, the abuse becomes more tailored to the alleged faults of the charioteers. The first team that day to enter was the Green. Through the internal gateway beneath the Imperial Box the team entered to thunderous cheers and groans, the charioteers in green robes, the two horses to each chariot also dressed in green. As they passed by the Green section, the charioteers dismounted and took the plaudits of their faction.

With neatly trimmed beards and gravely impassive faces, they stood by their chariots – these stripped back to the absolute minimum needed for a riding platform. They stood beneath a shower of rose petals, and were treated to an elaborate choral ode in their honour.

Then, from across the Circus, came the first sustained mass of abuse. Directed at the team leader, Paul, and in a rolling chant, carried by perhaps ten thousand voices, it went something like this:

> Ye Nymphs lament, Ye Cupids too,
> And every man of feelings true
> And decent. For, such her meanness,
> Fate has robbed Paul of his penis –
> His penis that he loved so well;
> His penis that could often swell
> From one to maybe two or more
> Full inches, if not quite to four.
> It never felt the warm embrace
> Of any vulva, nor in place
> The firm grasp – by law denied us –
> Of a playful young cinaedus.
> But his left hand as well it knew
> As a foot its favourite shoe.
> And limp now, nor more to present,
> There will it rest, all passion spent.
> Ah Savage Fate – cruel to devour
> His solace of a silent hour –
> Behold the product of thy power:
> Tucked in bed, lies Paul unsleeping,
> Ever red his eyes from weeping.

As the last measure ended, the chanting dissolved into screams of laughter and individual abuse. There was a volley of green dildoes from the Blue Faction, and a less organised repetition of the final lines.

His face creasing into a smile, Paul took the assault in good spirit. Indeed, it was hard not to. Someone among the Blues had a good ear for the Latin classics and had done a fine job of parodying Catullus in the fixed syllabic lines of modern Greek. Paul took up one of the dildoes and waved it derisively back at the crowd. Then he pulled up his robe to show the whole Circus what the truth was regarding his manhood.

I was too far away to see the details, but they pleased the Greens. The approving roar must have been heard outside the City walls.

Matthias, leader of the Blue team, got the same treatment. His epigram went as follows:

> Beside Matthias, have no fear,
> Your wives and daughters may sit near;
> And lustful glances, if he cast,
> Can bring to them no harm at last.
> Nor for your sons you need take fright:
> Matthias is no sodomite –
> Or, much as he'd love to insert
> Himself, he'd never dare assert
> Himself sufficient to succeed:
> A timid little man indeed!
> And he, to complete your data,
> Is neither a lewd fellator,
> Nor some other fornicator.
> You'll find his pleasures are very,
> Very, very solitary:
> For every other vice unfit,
> Matt eats and masturbates in shit!

Well, that got everyone going nicely. I thought the chaotic shouting that followed this recitation would never end. So far, though, it was all good-humoured fun. Even Matthias had to smother a laugh at the inventiveness of the epigram someone had taken the trouble to compose against him. He knew that if the verse made it into one of the anthologies, it might be good advertising throughout the Empire.

Martin sat beside me like a frozen block of his lemon water. He was never one for big crowds, except at a good church service. Authari was impressed by the spectacle, without understanding much of it. But I joined in the cheering and laughing as if I'd been going to the Circus all my life.

Rome had nothing to match this.

At a burst of louder cheering and catcalls, I turned round to see Philip and some of the other students. Dressed in wonderful clothes – Philip himself was wearing shoes all of woven gold thread – and sprawled along one of the higher rows, they had a fine view of the racecourse and over the Imperial Box to the palace and the City beyond. They had brought food and drink and were sharing a jolly breakfast. Philip beckoned me up to join them but Alypius pounced before I could move.

'You stay in your allotted place,' he breathed from beside me.

Even so, they did send down a jug of reasonably unwatered wine to keep me going through the remainder of the festivities. Alypius brought it, concealed in the folds of his robe. Most welcome, this. Martin for some reason had got Authari to pack only fruit juice in our hamper.

The Factions now burst again into chanting – yet more celebration of the qualities of their champions. So long as they don't turn ugly, proceedings in the Circus follow a ritual as set in its essentials as in a church.

At last, however, the teams began to move towards the far end of the racecourse and the shouting diminished in volume. There was a flurry of movement on the Senatorial Terrace. Everyone there was on his feet and facing away from the racecourse, looking up. Even the Patriarch was standing.

On each side of the Imperial Box above them, seven men in golden robes had appeared. They stood looking around and waiting for reasonable silence. Then they raised their golden trumpets. A peal of bright sound rang out across the Circus.

There was silence.

A herald stood forward in the Imperial Box. He raised his arms to maintain the silence.

'We unite', he cried in a slow, clear voice that reached to the topmost rows behind me, pausing at each phrase to draw breath, 'in greeting our Lord and Master, the Most Holy and Orthodox and Ever-Victorious Flavius Phocas – Caesar Augustus, Autocrator, *Dominus et Imperator*, appointed by God Almighty Himself, Ruler of the Universe.'

32

I'd seen representations of Phocas any number of times. There was a crude image of his face on all the coins. There was an icon of him in every public building throughout the Empire. And, of course, there was the golden statue of him atop its column in Rome. His presence was evident in all things.

Although I'd been living in his shadow ever since my arrival in the City, this was the first time I'd seen the Emperor in person. At a distance of three hundred yards, I can't say I was able to make out that much of him. It was a small, dumpy figure who shuffled into view at the front of the Imperial Box. Dressed in shimmering purple, a band of gold on his dark head, he stood with set features to receive the acclamations of the Senators and of the whole crowd.

On the Terrace below him, the Senators stretched out as one in the formal prostration, or Adoration of His Majesty. The Patriarch, of course, was exempt from the full prostration, but he bowed low before the Living Symbol of Divine and Earthly Power that was currently Phocas. The rest of us stood with bowed heads in reverent silence. Far off, on the racecourse below the Imperial Box, a choir was singing praises of Christ and the Virgin. As we raised our heads again, the Patriarch was getting ready to bless the teams.

At last, with an elaborate sign of the Cross that could be seen from every point of the Circus, the Emperor took his seat far above us. There, he sat as dignified and impassive as a painted statue.

Another blast of the trumpets, and the herald stood forward again. 'To God the Father and Son', he cried, 'be Glory in the Highest.'

'Be Glory and Honour ever in the Highest,' came the response of the whole Circus.

The herald: 'And to the Empire, be victory and glory on all frontiers.'

The crowd: 'Victory and glory on all frontiers.'

And so the litany continued. Peace and plenty in all the Provinces. Plague and famine to be banished from the earth. Solidity to the foundation of the Churches. Anathema to the variously described heresies. Anathema to the Great King of the Persians and his heathen armies, and to all the barbarians who had violated the frontiers of the Empire. And so on and so forth as if in some huge service in church.

Then from the herald: 'And to Heraclius, renegade Exarch of Africa, and to Heraclius, the usurping son, anathema and oblivion.'

Silence throughout the main Circus. On the Senatorial Terrace, hard under the watchful Eye of Power, the response sounded in grim unison. From the rest of the Circus came a scattering of shouts that died at the realisation of its own thinness of volume. From all other places there was a tense and ominous silence, as of a landscape that darkens under gathering stormclouds.

The herald looked round. Though I couldn't make out his features, I could sense the consternation from the movements of his body. Then I saw Theophanes step forward beside him. Dressed with a splendour that eclipsed all previous appearances I'd seen, his face shining with white lead and gold leaf, he began a rapid conversation with the herald. Their voices didn't carry outside the Box. But I could tell from their furtive glances that their conversation involved Phocas, who continued looking steadily forward at no one in particular.

It was obvious they were in a bind about how to continue. The litany should have culminated in a long set of praises of the Emperor but if these went ahead, there was every chance of humiliation from the crowd. They had expected at least one of the Factions to take up the responses but instead they were facing a citizenry united in hostility. It might even provoke rioting that, given the siege, could be fanned into revolution.

But dropping the culmination risked hardly worse. I saw Theophanes look up at the sky. The clouds were lifting to leave the day

208

cool but bright – ideal rioting weather. Perhaps he was thinking of his deal with Heraclius – whatever that might be.

You see, there's nothing much to be done when people are gathered together in the Circus. Whereas, as individuals, they can be terrorised into obedience, together in the Circus they can make their feelings known with impunity. An Emperor secure on his throne can set the army on the crowd. There's nothing like an indiscriminate massacre for restoring order.

But Phocas wasn't at all secure. I never could make out why the races had been allowed to go ahead in these circumstances. I suppose it was in the hope that a pretence of normality would bring on its reality. They had begun badly and might easily turn catastrophic.

Then came salvation. Instead of waiting for events to move in their direction as inexorably as water runs down a gully, whoever was behind all this tried hurrying them forward. Someone in the Blue Faction began reciting from a chorus of Sophocles. It opened with the lines:

> Wasted thus by death on death
> All our city perisheth.
> Corpses spread infection round;
> None to tend or mourn is found.

One voice became two, and then a dozen, and then hundreds. Almost at once, in a rolling blaze of sound that united all parts of the Circus beyond the Senatorial Terrace, the words continued to their conclusion:

> Golden child of Zeus, O hear
> Let thine angel face appear!

There is no public theatre in Constantinople. Even so, the old plays do get a regular airing in the Circus. They're put on in afternoon sessions during the hot summer months, when it's too hot for racing, or there are no executions left over from the morning.

This, by the way, comes from *Oedipus the King*, and is part of the long opening cry of the Chorus for salvation from the curse that is destroying Thebes. Bearing in mind how circuitously both Thebes and Constantinople were saved, these lines had a new irony that I don't think was lost on the crowd.

And they saved Phocas.

As the recital ended, the crowd sat back and broke out into a chatter of mutual compliments on how educated everyone was. The embarrassment wasn't forgotten. There might yet be another crisis but for the moment the tension was broken. The stormclouds had wafted away on a gust of hot breath and pedantic self-praise.

I saw Theophanes turn to the herald.

The herald stood forward again. 'O Most Excellent and Erudite People of the City,' he cried, 'we have suffered grievously from the barbarians.'

He quoted further from *Oedipus*:

> Our city reeks with the smoke of burning incense,
> Rings with cries for the Healer and wailing for the dead.

'Be it known that our Lord Phocas is aware of duplicity upon duplicity that brought the dark host of barbarism to our gates, more savage than the Assyrians that of old did smite the Children of Israel. And be it known that he will, when evidence clear enough for all to agree shall be available, make the authors of this duplicity answer for their crimes.'

A clever touch, this. Direct accusations against Heraclius from the Emperor would have done much to check the progress of the rumours put into circulation. A delicate allusion, on the other hand, could do much to hasten their progress.

Phocas was not yet out of trouble. But the prospect of wild rioting was for the moment in retreat.

There was a ripple of muttering sweeping back through the Green Faction from its leaders. This was followed by a burst of chanting – taken up by the Blues – this time about the disappearance of olive oil.

The herald made the emollient reply that bread and wine remained plentiful.

This was answered by the Blues with a complaint about the low quality of the grain in the public warehouses.

So the conversation continued a while. As said, proceedings in the Circus follow a ritual not unlike that in church. The crowd expresses itself in phrases and whole sentences that can be adapted to any purpose – you need only hear the first few words to take up the rest. The herald responds in the same fashion, demonstrating both the strength of his lungs and his ability to turn the mono-syllabic whispers of the Emperor or his Ministers into persuasive responses.

That the people had now been persuaded into one of these conversations meant that the crisis was past.

The herald changed the subject. 'For the moment,' he cried, 'let those who did abandon our loved ones, even as they prayed beyond the walls at the Most Holy Shrine of Saint Victorinus, be subject to the Divine Justice of our Lord and Master, Phocas, Most Holy Ruler of the Universe.'

At this, the gate beneath the Imperial Box opened again. Through it now came a troop of the Palace Guard, dressed in their finest uniforms of red and silver. Their hollow square en-closed seven men, stripped naked and tightly bound. The captives looked desperately round the immense, silent crowd, jerking at the chains that held them together.

'Behold the malefactors and authors of our woe, dear and cultivated people of the City,' the herald continued. 'Behold these woeful seven, chosen by lot from those whose duty it was to stand and fight in defence of our loved ones, but whose inclination was to flee for the safety of the gates. Let them now suffer the punishment of cowardice.'

The administration of the Circus is nothing if not professional. It can bring on and set up a display with wondrous speed. It can clear the wreckage and bodies of a racing accident almost before the cheers are ended.

Now slaves brought out seven great bronze vessels. Each was about four feet deep and three across. Covered with a domed iron cage, each stood on three legs about three feet off the ground. The slaves set these at points about the racecourse so that each was no more than a hundred yards from the spectators. Under them the slaves heaped piles of faggots and charcoal.

As the chains holding the prisoners together were unlocked, and each was dragged towards one of the vessels, the men let out a terrified wail. Lamentations and pleas for mercy mingled with sounds of pure animal fear. One fell down on the packed sand and, still tightly bound, tried to wriggle like a worm back towards the now closed gate. But he might as well have tried to hold back the progress of the seasons. He was dragged to his fate, leaving a trail of excrement behind him. A slave followed behind, thoughtfully cleaning the mess away.

The domed cages swung open on their hinges and each prisoner was put into one of the vessels. Then the cages were locked down.

Even before pitchers of water were rushed in for filling the vessels, I knew what was coming. My hunting companions of the previous day pushed their way down to the front and stood beside me. One stretched himself over the barrier to get as close as possible to the domed vessel placed at the apex of the Circus bend. He was pulled back by one of the guards and made to stand at the same distance as everyone else.

Apart from the continuous horrified wailing of the prisoners, silence descended over the Circus. The upper rows were now deserted. The front rows were blocked with a scrimmage of people who, in their bright robes, reminded me of the surf on Dover Beach where, of a late summer evening, the white is mingled with blue and red and green.

Not a man so much as coughed as the kindling was set alight.

To narrate the full detail of these executions would be artistically wearisome. It is enough to say that, if you are boiled alive slowly enough from cold, you cook before you die, and you remain conscious well into the cooking.

But this wasn't the end of the proceedings. As the last body splashed silent into the bubbling waters, the herald spoke again.

'Be it ever such with those who dare betray the Sacred Trust of Our Gracious Lord Phocas, anointed with the Holy Oil of our Blessed Mother Church. Let oblivion be their lot in this world, and eternal perdition in the next.'

And now the crowd was back to the expected responses. With the thundering fervour of these words, I could feel the general mood brightening. The people still weren't happy with Phocas. His alleged bungling of the barbarian raid was a cover for all the other grievances against him. But everyone seemed to agree that he had done well to make an example of those guards. It had been their duty to stand and fight. If they had done that, they might even have driven the savages off. There was no doubt they had some punishment coming.

And the Circus crowd in Constantinople does enjoy a good public execution. For all his other derelictions, Phocas certainly knew how to jolly the Circus along in that respect. A few years earlier, he'd had one of his best generals burned to death in the Circus. That hadn't gone down well with the armies of the East, which had downed weapons in protest, but it had delighted the crowd.

The herald still wasn't finished. I saw Theophanes raise one of his arms. I felt Alypius touch me from behind.

'Get ready,' he whispered. 'They need you sooner than expected. When I push you, get up and go down to the racecourse. Walk slowly across to the Imperial Box. Go to Caesar. Don't stop, whatever happens. Don't speak to anyone but Caesar, and wait till he speaks to you. Do you understand?'

'But' – the herald's voice now took on a brighter tone – 'let us now behold how graciously Caesar receives those who in his service have acquitted themselves nobly.'

I felt a pressure on my lower back.

'Go,' Alypius hissed. 'Remember what I told you.'

As I stood up, Martin reached for my hand. His was cold and trembling. 'Go with God,' he said in Latin.

Authari mumbled a blessing in Lombardic, his other languages swept away by all the brutal mysteries of the Circus.

I patted them both on the shoulder, trying to look more nonchalant than I felt. I was beginning to shake, my head curiously light.

The guards by the staircase parted and I walked down to the racecourse.

'We stand for Alaric of Britain,' the herald shrilled, 'Champion of the Empire, witness to the Miracles of Saint Victorinus.'

I heard the collective rustling of cloth as thirty thousand people rose together. From every direction around me came the roared acclamations. They seemed to go on for ever as I walked alone across the racecourse. From the corner of my eye, I could see the puffy white flesh of an arm that still broke the surface of the water in one of those vessels. It left me impassive.

Then I was walking with the *spina* on my left as I approached the Imperial Box.

As I reached the charioteers – who were still waiting for their races to begin – they touched their foreheads in a simultaneous gesture of respect.

The guards parted again to let me up the staircase to the Senatorial Terrace. The Patriarch scowled at me through his beard as I passed. The Senators stretched out their arms to me, shouting the same acclamations as the crowd. I paid no attention to them, but continued past, up the final staircase into the August Presence.

As I arrived there, I was met by Theophanes. He gave me his most inscrutable look. 'You know the ritual?' he said, speaking softly.

I did. I now performed it for Caesar – down on the knees in one slow movement, then down again, arms forward, palms upward, face on the ground, in the gesture of complete submission to power that the ancient Emperors had made a point of not demanding. It had come in with Diocletian, had been kept on by the Great Constantine and used by every Christian Emperor since.

As a matter of course, it had also been claimed by the popes as soon as there was no Western Emperor to make a fuss.

As I was grovelling elegantly before Phocas, and wondering what else might be expected of me, I heard a voice above me – rough and strangely cheerful. I could smell the wine fumes from a good six feet away.

'Well, come on, my lad, get up. I can't have my champion taking cold on that marble.'

33

As I got up, Phocas stood forward to help me to my feet. Holding my hand in his aloft, he faced the crowd. As planned, the roaring started again – but this time for Phocas as well as for me.

'Many years and good fortune to Phocas, our Great Emperor,' the chanting began. 'Many years to the Orthodox Augustus and Autocrator. Many years to the New Constantine, the New Justinian. Glory and Honour to His Mighty Name.'

The chanting switched to Latin, which was – and still is – used in moments of great public solemnity.

'*Bene, bene, Auguste,*' it began. '*Conseruet Deus imperium tuum. Uictor sis semper. Deus te praestet . . .*'

And so it continued in great waves of adulation. The Empire is no sort of democracy. But you need to know how to manage the crowd in the Circus if you want to last on the Imperial Throne. And Phocas had, against all the odds, pulled that off again.

His Empire might be confined to the City. The Persians and barbarians and Heraclius might be dividing the rest among themselves. But Phocas was Emperor in the only place that mattered. The barbarians could be bribed eventually into leaving. The Persians could be expected eventually to suffer some reverse. And Heraclius was stuck in Abydos, short of cash – his forces outside the City in the rain waiting for the first whiff of pestilence.

Phocas, on the other hand, was still in Constantinople, still holding court in the Circus.

Standing there beside him was not, perhaps, the safest place to be. But I was going home soon. This would be the culminating point of my stay in the city and would serve me well in the wine shops of Rome so long as I could remember any anecdotes at all.

For the moment, I soaked up the adoration of more people than could be found in the whole of Rome, and bowed to receive the embraces of an emperor who seemed not unmindful of my usefulness in getting him out of trouble.

There is something wonderful about these acclamations. To stand in their blast is like having an orgasm in bright sunshine. In the street, you wouldn't give a second glance to those cheering trash. You might even have one of them set upon if he didn't keep his distance. But the collective adoration of the Circus can do wonders for your self-respect. You might plan a *coup* to get it all for yourself.

Many have tried. Phocas did. He would, within six days, be a corpse floating headless in the Golden Horn. But no one at the time could have guessed that.

Now so close to them, I nearly jumped out of my skin when the trumpets sounded again for quiet in the Circus. That drew an approving belly laugh from the crowd, and even a smile from Phocas.

When silence was restored, the herald gave a tastefully sanitised official account of my doings. Among much else, apparently, I'd brought with me to the City news that the arms of Phocas had prevailed in Kent, and had won the whole province of Britain back to the Empire. No one in the crowd thought to question the inherent improbability of this event.

So the narrative continued through my visions of Saint Victorinus and His Saving Miracles, and my dispatching of a most flattering number of barbarians with my own hands.

More cheering and shouted acclamations. And a full service of thanks to Saint Victorinus. The Patriarch officiated, and even managed to utter my name without spitting.

Fortunately I wasn't expected to take any further part in the proceedings. I'd been turning over some words that might not be held against me now or later. But one of the officials attending Phocas turned to me.

'Sit over there,' he said curtly, indicating a chair set into the white marble of the steps that led up to the throne. 'Look ahead – neither words nor motion.'

I gratefully took my place. If lower than Phocas, I still had a fine view over the Circus. Now the proper games got under way.

When Constantine built his new capital, he decreed that there should be neither temples to the Old Faith nor gladiatorial combats. Constantinople was to be the City of God, and the bishops were adamant that its entertainments were to be unstained by human blood. The gladiatorial combats had grown out of the Old Faith, and remained too closely identified with it, so they were left behind with the old order in Rome. In this New Rome, there would be no amphitheatre to match the Coliseum.

For a while, there had been displays and hunts of wild beasts in the Circus. But these also had sacrificial undertones, and the bishops had nagged the Emperors about then until they, too, were banned.

This left only chariot racing, which soon became all that it had ever been in Rome and much more.

As with the executions, I won't burden you with a close description of the races. But there is no public spectacle more exciting. As those chariots speed round the course, you almost feel yourself there beside the charioteer. Usually, the races seem to be over almost as soon as begun. Sometimes, though – as the fourth lap is passed – you feel that time has stopped. The chariots seem to slow down. The roars of the crowd seem to come from a great distance. Clouds of dust hang in the air. It's now that wise men lay their bets in a quiet voice.

As the front-runners come to a halt before the Imperial Box, the crowd goes wild. You see the rippling wave of green or blue as the victorious Faction stand briefly, row by row, and seat themselves again. There are the various kinds of applause – clapping with cupped hands for a victory on points, flat handed for a victory based on pure skill and so on. There is the presentation from the Imperial Box and the roars as the victor stands beside the Emperor.

All personal troubles are forgotten in the excitement of a close race. All political differences are put aside in the greeting of the victors. Whatever might go on in the streets outside late into the evening, the mood inside the Circus is one of total identification with the incredibly rapid thunder of hoofs and wheels on the racecourse.

The morning session came to an end. The races had gone well. All victories had been decisive – with no need for the Emperor to upset either Faction by having to adjudicate on a hung race.

Slaves appeared pulling great carts and began distributing bread and very thin wine to the crowds. Many had brought their own hampers. But the poorer classes needed to be fed if the afternoon session was to go well. And what is a circus without bread?

The Senators and other persons of quality filed up from their terrace to the Imperial Box and then joined the Emperor for a buffet lunch in the dining room beyond.

A nice room, this. Its great windows faced away from the Circus and gave a good view over the palace down towards the sea. The room itself was of chastely white marble that contrasted with the variegated colours within the Circus. The only permanent splash of colour there was the double row of busts of all the emperors since Constantine. These were placed equidistant between the columns that ran down each side of the room.

The earlier busts – the anti-Christian Julian in particular – are in the realistic style of the ancients. Starting with the Great Theodosius, though, the features become more sharply etched, the eyes turning inward. From Anastasius on, the departure from realism becomes increasingly confident. The bust of Phocas himself was a lump of purple barely recognisable were it not for the shape of his beard and the slightly odd look in the eyes.

As everyone joined the queue for food, I found myself beside the Emperor at the wine table. He took up what looked like a small gold bucket and drained it without drawing breath. Then he directed one of the slaves to hand me a cup nearly small enough for Maximin to have held. Over in a corner, I could hear Theophanes discoursing to a group of very deferential officials on the merits of his *kava* juice. As ever, he found no takers for the stuff.

'So, my little Briton,' Phocas rasped in Latin, 'how was our handling of the mob?'

What do you say when an Emperor throws that sort of question at you? You could try gross flattery. That works in most circumstances. But this was a casual opening and didn't seem to admit of a formal response. So I tried the truth.

'I thought for a moment you were in trouble,' I said, gulping at my wine. 'But all looks set fair now.'

'Yes,' he said, 'I thought it went rather well. If I can find the traitor who started reciting from that old play, I might even reward him!'

He gave me a searching look, then: 'Come over and eat something.'

He took me by the arm and led me to the front of the queue, which jumped back three paces at the approach. Phocas pointed silently at the dishes and waited as slaves piled golden plates high with delicacies. Then, we moved away again, our plates held before us by slaves dressed in long robes of green and blue stripes.

Back in Rome, Lucius had told me that Phocas didn't know any Greek. He was wrong. The Emperor was from Thrace, where a common sort of Greek is the main language above the barbarian dialects. But he'd spent much of his career in a Latin regiment and was happier in military Latin than in the educated Greek of the City.

Anyone who believes that Phocas was a mere brute, devoid of all sociable qualities, has swallowed the line put out by his enemies. He had his faults, and I'll not deny them. But he was neither stupid nor without the rougher social graces. So long as he wasn't verging on the paralytic, or in fear of yet another plot against him, he knew how to put subjects at their ease. How else do you think he managed to depose poor old Maurice? How else did he arrange that rapturous entry into Constantinople after his *coup*? How else did he get Pope Gregory on his side?

Though now past sixty, he still had a good head of dark hair and a jauntiness about his manner that put you in mind of a much younger man. He soon discovered that I was new to the races, and he spent some time explaining rules that I hadn't been able to pick up for myself. He even made me laugh a few times. This isn't normally something you should do in front of an emperor, except the politest, most strangled titter. But he seemed to be in the mood for uncourtly behaviour. So I downgraded my own Latin to match his, and we chatted away like two outsiders in this most rarefied society of the Empire.

After a rough start, I was feeling remarkably full of myself, but I was also beginning to feel distinctly odd. I had to steady myself once or twice to stay on my feet.

'But even an Emperor can't monopolise his hero,' said Phocas at length. 'Let me introduce you to some of the Divinely Fortunate who are able to share My Exalted Company.'

With this, he had everyone in the room lined up for a presentation. As he walked beside me, looking deeply into their faces, a slave called out the names and titles of the assembled grandees. Those who survived the last purge of Phocas and the first of Heraclius I got to know rather well later on. For the moment, they were mostly simpering yet scared faces, sweaty through the paint.

They were, that is, except one.

'And this', said Phocas with a flourish, 'is my supremely talented and loyal son-in-law, Priscus – Count of the Palace Guard, who will succeed me as Emperor as soon as I am called away from this world.'

I found myself looking straight into the face of the Tall Man – that is, of the Black Agent who'd supervised the arrest of Justinus.

34

'You will scarce credit', said Priscus in his smoothest voice, 'how delighted I am to make your acquaintance. I have heard so much about you. All Constantinople sings your praises. And now I am doubly blessed. I bask in the Divine Presence itself, and I meet the one who has for so long been in my thoughts.

'Accept, O Alaric of Britain, my heartiest greeting,' he called in a raised voice. 'Unless the Augustus has need of you, I must demand the honour of your company at dinner this evening.'

I took the clammy hand and looked into the coldly mocking eyes that stripped all pleasantness from the smile with which he greeted me. Is this how he'd have looked at me had we met again in those stinking cells under the Ministry? Was it with the same impassive gloat on his face that he'd have brought me to his 'orgasms of pain'?

'My Lord Priscus,' I said, fighting to keep a semblance of outward composure, 'your name is already familiar to me – your name and the tales of your devoted service to the Empire. I also have looked forward to this meeting. Unless I must bow to a command still higher than your own, I shall feel myself honoured to accept your invitation.'

'Then I must count myself very fortunate,' said Priscus. 'Isn't that so, my dearest colleague and friend?' he added to Theophanes, who'd just arrived beside us.

It was like watching two very hostile but well-behaved cats face each other. They smiled. Theophanes made a little bow. Priscus took him by the arm and helped him back up.

'My Lord Caesar is too kind,' Theophanes said, brushing his lips against the hand that raised him. As Priscus pulled away, I could see a smear of scarlet lip paint on his wrist.

'Darling Theophanes,' Priscus smiled back, 'you will, as a matter of course, be joining us tonight?'

'You will pardon me', came the smooth reply, 'if I must remind you that the Great Augustus has need of our services tonight.'

'Too right!' the Emperor broke in, still in his good mood. 'Until we've laid hands on that fucker Heraclius, these races are all the entertainment we'll get. That means no official banquets.'

Priscus opened his mouth as if to protest, then thought better of it. In any event, Phocas ignored him.

'Now' – he dropped his voice to a confidential tone – 'I need to make a decision pretty sharpish on the punishment. We haven't had an *unsuccessful* attempt on the Purple in three hundred years. We'll need to put on something really memorable for the mob. Something lingering goes without dispute. But should it involve boiling oil or melted lead?

'Hey, Nicias,' he called, catching hold of a short flabby creature who was so shocked at the sudden attention that his false teeth fell out on to the floor. 'Which would you prefer – boiling oil or melted lead?'

'As the Lord Augustus wishes,' the man mumbled, hand covering his mouth, 'so let it be.' He scooped up his teeth then scuttled sideways, rather like a crab. Phocas laughed. Priscus and I joined in.

'You'll have fun with Priscus soon enough,' said Phocas. 'He assures me you have so much in common.'

With that and a very queer look, he was off. I saw him take up with some leading members of the Green and Blue Factions who'd somehow been invited to the Imperial Box. Shifty-looking, low-born, they'd looked conspicuously uncomfortable so far, and had formed their own gaggle over in a corner. Now Phocas was among them, dispensing charm and good humour.

Theophanes looked at my tiny cup. Since meeting Priscus, I'd been knocking back cup after cup of the nearly pure water some slave was dishing out every time I caught his eye. Other than to reinforce that feeling of oddness, they seemed to have no effect.

After the buffet lunch I returned to my place at the foot of the Imperial Throne. I should have paid more attention to the races. They were every bit as exciting as in the morning. Indeed, there was a big smash in the final lap of one of them, and one of the lesser charioteers had his arm torn off right at the shoulder. The crowd went wild at this and it gave rise to a rhythmical grunting that rippled up and down the rows.

But the sun was shining in my eyes, and my mind wandered over everything but the events on the racecourse. I almost nodded off a few times.

As the Patriarch gave his final benediction of the day and Authari kicked and punched our way through the crowd into the street outside, Martin confessed that this was only his second visit to the Circus. His father had always regarded the games as sinful, and they'd normally spent Circus days at home in quiet prayer.

'Well,' I said, 'you'll surely make a point of going in future. Just think what you've been missing.'

'You forget, sir,' came the obvious reply, 'there are no games in Rome nowadays – not since Pope Gregory cut off funding for the Circus there. This will be our last view of the races.' Martin caught hold of my sleeve, as if I were about to lose my footing.

He was right. It was homeward bound for us – back to boring but safe Rome. There, under the rule of those old womanly clerics, all we had to fear was the Lombards and the occasional fleck of gutter scum that didn't know its place.

I gave him the basic details of lunch in the Imperial Box. Martin didn't seem impressed by the stuff about Priscus.

'The first meeting was accidental,' he said, 'the second unavoidable. Let us pray there will be no third. When I was last here, he was permanently away at the front. In those days, he was only a general with a good background. Even then, though, his name stank.'

Back at the Legation, Demetrius was preparing a surprise dinner.

'We hear the young citizen is not much more to be with us,' he leered as I walked through the main hall. 'In celebration of which we shall kill a pig and feast our full this night.'

Well, this was a better mood than I'd seen from the man in months. We never had got round to the meeting he'd demanded over Maximin's crying, instead of which he had received a soft kicking from Authari and threats of worse if he didn't piss off. Now he was inviting me as guest of honour – even if that did mean sitting beside him.

'We regret that the citizen Alaric is indisposed,' Martin surprised me by saying. Before I could protest, he and Authari had shoved me through the door into my suite. Even more surprisingly, while Authari propelled me up the stairs Martin turned back and accepted the invitation for himself and the rest of my household.

'You're going to bed, Master,' said Authari as he pulled me out of my fine clothes. 'You look awful.'

I tried to disagree but was overcome by a fit of the shivers as my sweat-soaked undergarments fell to the floor.

'I'll sleep until the dinner starts,' I said as Martin drew the bedclothes over me. 'Make sure to get me up.'

That's the last I recall before crashing out. I hadn't done much all day. But the adulation I had received at the Circus had taken its toll. I was shattered. I sank backwards into a bottomless slumber. Was that Alypius, I thought as the blackness closed over me, talking in a low but urgent voice? If it was, it would have to wait.

After some unmeasurable period of mist, it was night-time. I was standing somewhere in the outer suburbs of Rome outside a small public park, which now doubled as a churchyard. I must have been there earlier in the day for I had left my bag on one of the benches that surrounded a monument in the centre. I'm not sure what the bag was supposed to contain, but it was plainly of some value to me.

There was no moonlight in the street where I was standing, and the high terraced houses behind me were also dark. Like most buildings on the edge of Rome, they must have been abandoned. In daylight, I'd have seen them in ruins.

There was, however, a brightness in the clouded sky, and I could see the monument about a hundred yards beyond the locked entry gate. It stood out oddly white in the surrounding gloom. My bag, I felt, should still be there.

I could also see that the park was not empty. I can't recall how many of the creatures stood looking back at me, but I do recall their appearance. Smooth and covered with scales that glinted in a light that shone from nowhere, each was about the size and shape of a ten-year-old child. They had about them the strange stillness combined with rapid, darting motions that one sees in certain reptiles. Most striking about their appearance, though, was the eyes. These glowed a bright green. It was a strange brightness, having great intensity but no power.

The creatures looked at me over the top of the gate, pointing and whispering to each other in a low, sinister gibberish.

I was frightened, but I wanted my bag, so I climbed the gate and jumped down among them. They scattered from me as if frightened, but as I moved deeper into the park towards the monument, they seemed to recover their nerve and clustered round me, plucking at my clothes and whispering excitedly.

By now I was terrified. My heart was beating wildly and I could feel my hair standing on end. My mouth was dry and I bit my tongue in an effort to control my chattering teeth. I wanted desperately to turn and run, but I also wanted my bag so I forced myself to carry on.

When I reached the bench by the monument, all I could find was a white cloth bag filled with scraps of papyrus. I grabbed it and turned to run back to the safety of the street.

But the street had vanished. I found myself no longer in an enclosed park but at the top of a low hill. As far as I could see in the now bright moonlight, there was only neatly cut grass, and in the distance a copse of trees that cast shadows of indescribable blackness. Though I could see for miles, there were no lights or any other sign of human habitation.

The low whispering took on a triumphant note, and the creatures moved closer, now wholly surrounding me. I could feel their sharp little hands brushing cold against mine as they tried to pull me to the ground . . .

*   *   *

226

I woke with a start. I was still in my bedroom. Outside, the light had long since faded and stars were shining through the window. On the beside table, a lamp was turned down low.

I reached for the jug of melon pulp Martin had thoughtfully left for me in place of the usual wine. A bad dream, I told myself – just the sort of thing to round off a day of repeated excitements.

'Authari?' I croaked. Then I remembered the dinner. Everyone would be with Demetrius. Straining, I could just hear the sound of merriment. It must have been coming from the public areas of the Legation. These were beyond the dome, just under or close by the Permanent Legate's quarters.

Good luck to the old sod, I thought, wondering how His Excellency was taking the noise from dinner. If his hearing was sensitive enough to be upset by Maximin's crying, this must be driving him out of his wits.

Laid neatly out over by the door, my clothes were ready for the morning.

Could I tie the leggings on for myself? I wondered.

35

In the central districts, Constantinople by night is lit up almost like the day. Here, the function of dusk is only to mark the tipping point of activity between business and pleasure.

I had thought of visiting the usual brothel. But the excitements of the Circus had filled these places already to bursting, and I wasn't in the mood for being some whore's second or third helpings. Indeed, I wasn't in much of a mood for sex. As I pushed my way through those chill, crowded streets, I found myself shuddering with a nervous energy that made me game for anything – except whatever I turned my mind to.

Why had I gone out? I'd gone out because I could, and because I had no wish to show myself in any company led by Demetrius. Back to bed was out of the question so I paced the streets, unfocused and discontented.

Beggars huddled together for warmth under the flaring torches. Someone must have been busy with paint during the Circus performances. The street walls were covered in graffiti – most of it for Heraclius. No one had bothered yet to clean it off.

For the first time, I saw men stop to read the competing libels. Stood in little groups, not looking at each other, they blocked the colonnades outside the Covered Market as they followed the crudities of the debate. Taking all this in, my eyes had the super-sharp focus you normally get only in the bitter cold – or in certain kinds of dream.

I was stopped as I tried to enter the Senatorial Dock. There was a wine shop just inside where Baruch transacted his evening business. He hadn't really blamed me for my part in the shakedown. And there was a refinement on the tin business that I wanted to put his way.

'Halt and show your papers,' I was told. 'You are entering a controlled military zone.'

I looked at the guard. A pile of lard squeezed into a semblance of order by armour that, even so, only fitted because of leather gussets down both sides. He might have been seventy, but wrinkles never show properly on fat.

'I am Alaric,' I said. 'You might have seen me earlier today with the Emperor.'

The Aged Guard grinned back at me. 'Of course I know who you are,' he said. 'But orders are orders. If you don't have no papers, I must arrest you on suspicion of treason.'

'I don't think that will be necessary,' a voice drawled behind me. The Aged Guard stood stiffly to attention, his arm raised in a good military salute.

I turned. It was Priscus, got up in some very fine golden armour.

'My dear young friend!' he said, taking me by the shoulder. 'I really did think I had been deprived of your company for tonight. Now, it seems Saint Victorinus smiles on us both.'

I looked at him. In a huge place like Constantinople, how could I have run almost at once into Priscus? Could I still be dreaming after all?

'Think nothing of it, my sweet and dearest Alaric,' he replied, brushing aside my thanks. 'I might wish you hadn't been there once. Very few go twice under the Ministry.'

Phocas, he told me, had armed the Circus Factions and called up everyone in the city who had ever done military service. Priscus had been put at their head and told to come up with a plan of defence, should Heraclius get through the gates.

'Do you suppose there will be an attack?' I asked at length to break the long silence of our walk. I wondered if he, too, had seen Alypius behind us. I'd spotted him earlier when inspecting myself in the reflection from a shop window. Now he was following us, dodging round corners or into the crowds whenever I looked round.

'There can be no doubt of an attack,' said Priscus. 'Do you see that?'

He waved his hand over the battlements of the sea wall. The moon was not yet bright enough to reveal the flotilla that was ferrying in the main part of the rebel army. But there was no need of illumination. The ships were as brightly lit as the better class of shops in Middle Street. They were guided by further lights on the Asiatic and Galatan shores.

'No one can get through these walls,' he added. 'Even if the Persians and every barbarian race known to man joined forces with Heraclius, they still couldn't get in. But no one believes the gates will stay closed. Heraclius has his people all over the city. My job is to go through the motions of leading an army of trash into battle against some of the best fighting units in the provincial armies.'

Priscus paused and lowered his voice. 'Fat lot of good to give me any command now,' he spat. 'If Our All-Wise and All-Conquering Augustus had trusted me with an army two years ago, we'd by now be laying siege to Ctesiphon, or at least be dictating terms to the Persians. As for Heraclius and his father' – he broke off. Then: 'Instead, he gave me his daughter and a few promises.'

I looked nervously over my shoulder. There was a respectful void around us. But probably tens of thousands of people were lining the sea walls to watch in silence as the siege preparations were completed.

Priscus laughed. 'You'll not need to worry about spies in my company,' he said. 'Everyone else you saw at lunch may be wondering when and how to change sides. It's like the last days of Maurice. All things considered, though, my loyalty is above suspicion. And, I might add, all the spies in the street report to me. When it comes to snooping indoors and lifting seals, your friend of the third sex reigns supreme. But the streets are mine.'

Priscus had now crouched down for shelter against the breeze. He reached inside his cloak and pulled out a leather pouch. Opening it, he carefully shook about a spoonful of powder on to the blade of his dagger.

'Can I possibly tempt you, my dear boy?' he asked, motioning the pouch in my direction. 'It comes from the regions beyond the outermost East and has the most glorious effect on the faculties.'

'If you please, My Lord,' I said, 'I must for the moment refuse your kind offer.'

The sea beyond the walls was crowded with vessels but I knew I was seeing double the real number of lights and that they couldn't be dancing as my eyes told me they were. I pressed clammy hands into my cloak and willed myself not to sway.

'As you will,' said Priscus. He carefully lifted the blade to his nose and sniffed in sharply. Then he leaned against the battlements, waiting for the drug to take effect.

It did, with a contorting of features and a rush of darkness into his normally sallow cheeks. With the gagging and the bulging eyes, I thought at first he had brought on some kind of seizure. But his knees didn't buckle and his hands didn't lose their grip on the mortared stone.

I took the chance to give Priscus a close examination. Months before, as the Tall Man in the restaurant, he'd been an instrument of state, more interesting for what he represented and was doing than for the kind of person he might be. It had been almost the same earlier in the day.

He must have been about fifty. But he had the sort of wiry build that doesn't change much between youth and old age. His hair was carefully dyed, his face painted – we stood beside one of the lighted torches – with a careful understatement that Theophanes might have done well to study.

Most striking about him, I suppose, was the sharp glitter of his eyes and the almost continual twitching of his facial muscles. Even without his drug he was a man driven hard by internal demons, the power of which was evident in his every movement and utterance.

The seizure over, the ecstatic look fading from his face, Priscus leaned forward with renewed concentration. 'I do think, my sweetest boy,' he said, 'you were one of the last people to see Justinus alive.'

My eyes suddenly gave up on their tendency to see Priscus as two people. I looked hard at his now unified face.

'You will appreciate, My Lord Priscus,' I said, choosing my words carefully, 'that I had other things on my mind while we travelled to the Ministry. In any event, I suspect he was dead on arrival.'

'You suspect wrongly,' said Priscus with a smile. 'But I was unable to question him as I wanted.'

'But you have his letter,' I said, cold sweat running down my back – 'his sealed letter that you took up?'

'I have it still,' he said. 'Unfortunately, it seems to be nothing more than a statement of account from a bank in Syracuse. That is no more than I'd expect of a shipowner handling trade with the West.'

'With all respect to My Lord Caesar,' a voice trilled behind me, 'your presence is urgently desired by the Great Augustus.'

I looked round. It was another of the eunuch clerks I'd seen around Theophanes. He stood overshadowed by two armed guards.

'The clerk Alaric is to be escorted back to his bed,' he added.

Priscus scowled. I was sufficiently alert myself to glower at being called a mere clerk.

'I suppose I'm expected to report on how many bricks I've made without straw,' Priscus said, speaking loud. 'Still' – he dropped his voice – 'you can give my best wishes to His Excellency the Permanent Legate. Do tell him how greatly I miss his company.'

He smiled. 'But please, don't say I miss him that greatly.

'Now, you run along home like the good little boy you surely are. I'll get your nice Uncle Theophanes to come and tuck you in.'

36

Once more in the Legation, I managed to light the portable stove in my room. It wasn't yet cold enough to justify firing up the main heating. I dragged it to stand between my bed and the unshuttered window.

Now somewhat muted, the sounds of merriment still floated through the window. I dropped my clothes on to the floor and climbed back into bed. With an effort of will, I drifted into a gentle doze. I should have gone looking for the opium pills, I thought, but finally decided it was too much trouble.

Despite the chilly air that drifted over from the window, I felt too hot in bed so I threw back the covers. I tossed from side to side, rolling the undercovers into a ball. I was glad of the draught from the open window. Closed in with that stove, I'd have felt stifled.

I finally found some comfort lying naked on the cool, polished boards of the floor beside my bed. There was no moon visible. Instead, there was a dim light from the sea of glittering stars that shone through the window from a clear autumnal sky. Another month, and the sky would be overcast by the smoke of a hundred thousand charcoal burners. For the moment, the stars glittered beyond the window like diamonds on black silk.

Looking deep into the square of starry blackness, I thought of those beautiful lines written so long ago by Sappho, the only woman poet of any genius:

> The moon has set. The many stars
> Have passed beyond the midnight hour.
> And, here in bed, I lie alone.

It must have been twelve hundred years since those words were first uttered. Since then, nearly fifty generations had come and gone. Empires had risen, had blazed at their zenith as bright and apparently permanent as the stars in that sky, but had eventually fallen into decline.

The Old Faith that had so comforted Sappho had also grown decadent and passed away. The New Faith of the Jewish carpenter had taken its place. It was impossible to know how these words had sounded amid the fountains and perfect buildings of ancient Mytilene when they were first written. But they could still be appreciated by those prepared to make the effort.

And beyond the words, the stars on which she had looked remained. They were the same stars on which the first rational being of all had looked in some remote past. They were the stars on which the last rational being would, in some perhaps still more remote future, choke out his final breath.

They had shone for Sappho. They shone for me.

I thought of Gretel in far-off Rome. I suddenly missed the living warmth of her body and I wondered about the progress of my unborn child. It, too, would see those stars. It, too, would come to know the words of Sappho.

Sleep came at last. But it still wasn't the sleep of rest. Still, it was a night for dreaming.

I dreamed that my Gretel was standing over me. She reached out to me with arms white as if bathed in moonshine. Her white-blonde hair gleamed in the bun she had taken to wearing in imitation of the better classes when it became clear that she was about to join them.

I tried calling to her, but my voice had no sound. She smiled and looked away. Our hands touched for a moment and I fell back weak with delight and a feeling of exaltation I can't describe.

Gretel pointed her arm one last time at the open window. Her lips moved noiselessly. I thought she was trying to say the word 'Beware!' Then she left the room through a door that had appeared where none was before. She didn't look back.

As if a lamp were turned down, the room dissolved into blackness and I drifted deeper into sleep. Every so often, as I came towards waking, I noted how the sweat on my body had dried. But

I was still sufficiently comfortable on the floor not to bother with movement.

I thought I dreamed that a face was looking into the room. It made itself apparent as a greater blackness that obscured the sky beyond. Someone stood on the balcony outside the room, looking in through the upper part of the door. There was a click of the lower door, and I could sense the presence of someone actually inside the room.

My nipples went stiff in the sudden chill of the draught from the open door and I was now fully awake. I hadn't been dreaming. There *was* someone in the room. I could hear the gentle rise and fall of his breath.

I lay still. As yet, the intruder could see nothing. Even I could see only his body framed by the window. Then, as he moved, I saw the dull glitter of steel in the starlight.

'Die, fucker,' he snarled softly, throwing himself on to the bed. I saw him stab again and again at the rolled-up bedclothes. As he stabbed and sliced like a man possessed by some drug, he switched into a language that I think was Syriac.

Then, another snarl – this time of frustration, as he realised the bed was empty. There was a moment of silence before the intruder was back on his feet and casting around for his bearings.

I thought I might try sliding under the bed but he'd surely see the movement now that his eyes were adjusting to the darkness. Another moment, and he'd see me on the floor.

There are times – travelling, for instance – when you'd be mad to do other than keep weapons by you at night. At home, it's never been my habit. It's far more likely that you'll do yourself or some un-fortunate slave an injury than save yourself from nocturnal assault.

Naked and unarmed, I leapt silently to my feet. I snatched at one of the sheets and draped it round myself, then danced back against the wall opposite the door. The window was on my right.

'Authari,' I cried, 'come quickly. Murder, murder!' I added, raising my voice to a shout.

'What the fuck?' I heard the intruder snarl. He sounded puzzled and alarmed. But, after just a momentary pause, he was at me, raking forward with his knife. He must have been able to see as little of me as I could of him. Except for the glitter of his knife in the starlight, I might have been fighting with a shadow.

I dodged along the wall closer to the window. I grabbed at a vase of flowers and threw it at his head. It missed, making a dull thud on the floorboards, followed by a spattering of water. I picked up the little table on which the vase had stood and jumped forward, waving it like a club. He came at me again, parrying the table with his left hand.

I thought with a momentary surge of joy that I'd managed to knock the knife from his hand but the intruder recovered his balance and clung on to it. He now snatched at the bedcover and wound it round his left arm as a buffer against the blows I was raining on him with the table.

He came forward again. I fell back.

No help from Authari. We must have been making enough noise to wake the Permanent Legate beyond the dome. But the door remained closed and I couldn't risk the distraction or the effort of another cry for help. I'd have to handle this by myself.

With a sudden lunge forward, I got the intruder on his left shoulder with a sharp corner of the table top. He swung back again to keep his balance. Now I closed with him. Before he could recover himself for another stab at me, I was upon him. I clamped my left hand tight on the wrist of his knife arm, thrust my arm upwards, drawing the intruder towards me, and I tripped him up with my right leg. He fell backwards, with me on top of him. I could smell his stinking breath as our faces came close.

I had advantages of weight and strength, but he was a slippery sod. As we struggled on the floor, he got his right arm free and stabbed at my back. I felt nothing at the time except for blood trickling from the wound he opened.

I head-butted him repeatedly in the face. At last, I regained control of his knife arm, clamping his wrist to the floor. With my free right hand, I closed on his windpipe and squeezed hard. I squeezed until his breath came in ragged gasps and the strength ebbed from his right arm.

Or so it appeared. As I moved again to take control of his arm, I felt him slithering out from under me. This time, I felt the knife-point jar against my collar bone. The pain came with a sudden burst that I thought would paralyse my upper body.

My object had been to disable him and then question him at leisure. You can do a lot with a hot knife and a variable gag. But it now looked as if I'd run out of energy before he had. If he could get control of the knife at such close quarters and in darkness, it might easily be all over for me. It was time to finish matters while I still had some degree of advantage.

The intruder was bald, so there was nothing to take hold of to smash his head on to the boards. Instead I managed to get his head in my hands and twist it hard upwards to my left.

I felt the sharp click as his neck went limp. There was an arching spasm that threw me sideways off the body, then a momentary twitching.

And it was over. I was alone with a corpse.

I sat a while to gather my thoughts. I could feel a continual trickle of blood down my back and the pain was getting worse.

Still no Authari. Had he been killed in a concerted attack?

I got up and took the lamp from the bedside table. At first I thought I'd drop it but I took a deep breath and brought my fit of shaking under enough control to open the stove and pour a few drops of oil on to the glowing charcoal. In the gentle flame that leapt up, I lit the lamp, then went over to the still body.

Now I nearly did drop the lamp in alarm. The face was understandably battered and contorted. But I could see at once who it was.

It was Agathius – that agent of Heraclius I'd met in the latrine.

37

Outside in the corridor, Authari was snoring like an old pig. He sagged in his chair in a cloud of farty and wine-sodden belchy smells. Sword still clutched in his hand, he would have been just as much use tucked up in bed as in his self-appointed mission as guard.

Otherwise, all within the Legation was still. All was dark. All was quiet.

No point waking him yet.

I checked the nursery. Maximin was sleeping peacefully, Gutrune was also emitting drunken snores.

In Martin's room, I knelt beside the low bed and put my hand over his mouth. 'Martin,' I called gently, 'wake up – it's me.'

'Oh my God!' he whispered when I felt sure enough of his reaction to take my hand away. 'Are you all right, Aelric?'

He sat up. I noticed he was fully clothed.

'Just about,' I said. 'But I've just killed a man in my room. He was sent by Heraclius to kill me.'

Martin stood beside me looking down at the body. It lay as I'd left it, the dead eyes staring up at the ceiling, the knife close to the right hand.

'Let me see your back,' he said.

'What?' I said, looking at him.

'Your back,' he said. 'It's covered in blood.'

I winced as I pulled away the sheet I'd draped over myself. The blood had dried in the cold night air and the thin silk had stuck to me.

'Not a pretty sight,' said Martin, holding the lamp so close I could feel its heat, 'but a little water will rid you of that.'

238

The hangover was doing him good. Except that he staggered when he moved, and kept putting a hand up to his obviously throbbing head, he was on better form than I'd expected – not a panic attack in sight. When I filled him in properly on that latrine encounter, he simply furrowed his brows and looked away. It was as if he had given up being alarmed at anything more I could do or say.

'What do you suppose we should do?' he asked.

I sat on my bed and looked across at the body.

'Search me,' I said at length. 'I suppose we could raise the alarm. Or perhaps not,' I added, dropping into Celtic.

Martin got up and shut the door, then came and sat beside me. Together we studied the body.

'God knows what the Emperor will do,' he said, 'if you say anything about what happened in those latrines. You know that not reporting treason at once is treason in itself. And how much do you think he needs you now? You were useful in the Circus. That may have been it.'

He went over to the body again and began searching through the clothes. It was something I had been intending to do myself. He pulled out a small leather satchel that had been fastened to an inner garment and handed it to me.

I took it and opened it. Inside was a sheet of papyrus folded in four. I smoothed it open on my bed, taking care not to crack the fragile document. With Martin holding the lamp very close, we pored over the small characters. As we read, his composure slipped to the point where he had to sit down on the floor and rock back and forth to fight off an attack of sobs. My own hand trembled as I took the lamp from him.

It was a letter to me from the Dispensator. It instructed me to give all possible assistance to the Permanent Legate in anathematising both Phocas and Heraclius and in declaring for an alleged son of Maurice, who was said by the Persian King to be the legitimate Emperor.

'It's a forgery,' I said weakly. 'The shitbag is up to many things, but he'd never put that in writing. Look' – I turned the sheet over.

239

There was no scorching on the back – none of the usual signs of checking for secret writing. 'It was brought here to plant near my body.'

'It can't be a forgery,' Martin said with quiet despair. He insisted that the letter was in the correct Lateran style and bore the correct seal. He should have known. Drafting stuff like that had been his job for five years. The rhythmical clauses and contracted script screamed Papal Chancery. There wasn't a giveaway Greek letter in sight. It even had a signed subscript thanking me for confirming the Emperor's unorthodoxy regarding the Creed.

There was a sudden pain low in my belly. I groaned and pointed at the piss pot. Martin got it under my chin just in time. I thought my head would burst as the black and red waves swept over me, and I puked again and again.

'Drink this,' said Martin, pushing more water between my lips. He dabbed his sleeve in the cup and wiped at the sweat on my face.

'What the fuck have I been eating?' I gasped as I flopped on to the bed.

'Cabbage by the look of things,' Martin said, glancing up from an inspection of the pot. 'I don't know about the other stuff.'

I leaned forward. I'd managed to fill the thing almost to the brim. Still, aside from the raw pain in my throat and all points down-ward, I was beginning to feel better. I wasn't at all sleepy.

I looked again at the body. Martin had pulled the bedcover over it but the head was still visible. With mouth and eyes wide open, it was twisted at an angle that I was beginning to find distasteful.

What was it the dead man had told me in the latrine?

'You will see me again, Alaric, and when you do, it will, I assure you, be to your advantage.'

I laughed. Before I could draw breath again, I felt a wet sleeve slapping my face. 'I'm not hysterical,' I wanted to say primly. But Martin had the letter in his hand.

'We say nothing,' he said flatly. 'Even a suspicion that this letter existed, and that we'd seen it, would have us under the Ministry. I say we burn it and get the body out of here. Then we come back and don't go out again until we leave for home.'

A thought crossed his mind. 'You say Heraclius was behind this?' he asked. 'Why are you so certain? I thought you said they were protecting you.'

Not a good time for answering that one. But Martin's thoughts had moved on.

'You do suppose Heraclius will let us go once he's inside the gates?' he asked with rising concern. Would he recognise our immunity? His people didn't.

'That could be days and days away,' I said. 'I'll think of something by then. For the moment, we'll stay indoors. If anyone in the Legation asks why we're not going out to Sunday service, we'll plead indisposition from too much drink. The day after tomorrow can take care for itself.'

I needed to sit down and think all this through. But that would have to wait. Now was the time for action.

I took the letter from Martin and staggered over to the stove. I held it over the charcoals for a moment. Though I could smell the scorching of reasonably new papyrus, no secret writing emerged on either side. I let go of the sheet. As it fell into the fire it buckled upwards in the heat, the tightly pressed strips of papyrus reed coming apart as the glue melted. Then, with a sudden flare of light, it turned to ashes.

Now there was no letter. There had been no letter.

'Where do you suppose we can dump a body in this city?' I asked. This wasn't Rome. People had a habit of asking about stray bodies in the street. There'd be more to this, if noticed, than paperwork and a few clerking fees.

38

After an age of shaking and slapping at his face, I eventually managed to wake Authari. To be on the safe side, Martin had moved his sword out of reach.

No, I wasn't angry that he'd nodded off for a moment. No, I didn't think he'd been bribed into looking the other way. Yes, I would want the duplicate key to the wine store, though not until morning. No, I didn't think he'd been drugged – though I was beginning to wonder about that wine Alypius had brought down to me in the Circus.

I simply wanted his help in disposing of the body.

'Cut the thing up,' he said, looking ferocious. 'Cut it up in the lead bathtub. Wrap the body parts in old cloth and dump them one at a time into the rubbish bins placed at the main street junctions.' Authari spat on the body and gave it a hard kick.

Inventive advice, but easier given than followed. Hacking off limbs in a fight was nothing to either of us. But we weren't butchers, and dissecting a body neatly into its component parts takes a skill we hadn't acquired. Besides, there was the blood to consider. Even if the three of us could lift that lead bath, the chances were that we'd give ourselves away carrying it down to the bathhouse.

Then there was the matter of disposing of the body parts. The streets might not be so crowded with armed pickets as earlier, but it was still too risky to go about dumping suspiciously shaped packages into the public bins.

No. We'd have to get the whole body out of the Legation, and then out of the city centre. Just inside the walls, it would be more like Rome. There'd be plenty of room for dumped bodies.

242

But how to get from here to there?

'What about a public chair?' Martin suggested. 'Get it here in the morning, while most people are at Sunday service. Take the body in that.'

That wouldn't work either. Public carriers will do most things for cash, and usually keep their mouths shut afterwards. But smuggling corpses out of the Papal Legation might not be among these things.

Besides, I wanted that body out of the way now. The longer it remained here, the more chance that it would need explaining.

We discussed dumping it in the sea. But how to get it past the guards on the shore? Even if we found a boat, it would only take us into the Golden Horn, which no tides ever washed clean. Even if we weighted the body, it would break loose and float to the surface.

The course of action we finally decided on was still risky, but it was the best we could manage at short notice.

Getting out of the Legation was easier than we'd expected. No longer just drunk, the doorkeepers were all asleep. From their stillness and shallow breathing, they had clearly been drugged. That removed all need for lies or concealment.

On the other hand, it raised the problem of how to get back in. Before leaving my suite, we'd decided to close and bolt all the window shutters. If one killer had got in, who was to say another wouldn't? The door to my suite would have to be left unbarred as everyone else was asleep, but we took the precaution of locking the door to the nursery.

Leaving the main gate of the Legation unbarred wasn't an option, now that all the doorkeepers were out cold. I needed someone to stay behind and look after things, so we spent more time slapping some life into Radogast, who was now the most senior of my Lombard slaves. He had all the strength and loyalty of Authari but none of his resourcefulness. Still, he would easily be able to lift the heavy bar into place behind us, and then to let us in again.

'Sit over there,' I said, motioning him to a bench against the wall. It was midway between the gate and the doorway to my suite. 'If you see anyone strange, kill him.'

He nodded. There was no point giving him more detailed instructions.

At last, we set out. It was still blackest night and while the streets were brightly lit, there were fewer people about than when I'd been carried back from the Imperial Palace. Mostly drunk, the Circus Faction bands took no interest in us. No one asked us for identification.

We'd dressed the body in a long hooded cloak. Similarly clad, Authari and I walked on either side of it. The leather thongs about its wrists that we clutched tight to our chests made it look as if the dead man had his arms around our necks for support. The hood was of a stiff enough fabric to hide how the head flopped low on the chest, and the length of the cloak to some extent concealed the fact that the feet weren't stumbling beside us, but trailing along the ground.

Authari and I swayed gently from side to side as we dragged the body along, giving our best appearance of a trio of drunks – one being helped along by the others.

Also hooded, Martin walked a few yards ahead, keeping an eye out for Black Agents or anyone else who might be inclined to give us more than a passing glance.

We dumped the body in the cellar beneath a derelict wine shop where the stench of decayed human shit and other filth was already overpowering. Martin struck steel on flint to get our lamp going and, as in Rome with any dead burglar, we stripped the body. He slid a ring off the signet finger for later dropping through a drain cover.

As a final precaution, Authari took out the short sword he'd brought along and cut the head off the corpse. Then we heaped rubble over the body, and hoped the rats would find it before anyone else did.

'Murderous fucking Greek!' he snarled, spitting on to the mashed-up brains.

'I'll see you in Hell!' Martin added with uncharacteristic passion.

'Mustn't the Last Trump sound first?' I asked with a deliberate lack of relevance. My own head was coming on to ache again.

After disposing of what remained of the head in a neighbouring cellar we crept back to the Legation by a different and very circuitous route, arriving there just as dawn was preparing to fringe the eastern sky with rosy fingers.

I couldn't speak for Authari. He was now in impassive freedman mode, carrying out his duties without question. But I know Martin and I were feeling rather better for having got rid of the body. So I was surprised by the argument that broke out between him and Authari as we approached the Legation.

'I told you,' Martin whispered, 'not to leave him alone.'

'Don't moan at me,' came the reply. 'I left the dinner earlier than you. I only nodded off for a moment.'

I turned and shut them up. This was not the time or the place for discussing anything – not even what Alypius might have been doing in my bedroom earlier.

'We'll sleep,' I said firmly as I knocked at the Legation gate and Radogast raised the bar. 'We'll sleep until the sun is well up. Then we'll decide with clear heads what to do next.'

Inside the main hall I helped to lower the bar on the gate, then I led the way towards my suite.

Just at that moment Demetrius burst through the door to our right.

'There you are, sir!' he cried, his eyes wide with terror. Other officials milled around him, silent in their panic. 'Oh, sir – we've been looking for you everywhere. Do come at once and help. I fear His Excellency the Permanent Legate has come to grief.'

39

The Permanent Legate had his private rooms arranged almost as a mirror image of my own suite. Where mine were to the left of the main hall, his were to the right. For the first time since my arrival, the door leading in was unlocked and open.

With an involuntary but brief pause at the doorway, I stepped through into the corridor and made for the staircase, which was in the same relative position as my own. I hadn't before realised how my suite had come to differ from other parts of the Legation because we'd improved it by a series of incremental touches over the past few months – a rug here, an ornament there, and so on. We'd made it into a home.

Over on this side, there had been no improvements. The change of season had combined with the dilapidated externals to produce a damp smell on this side of the dome. Paint was flaking off the plastered walls to reveal brown stains beneath.

At the top of the stairs I encountered the legal official, Antony. He was dancing from side to side with agitation. Behind him, a slave was pushing in vain at what I took to be the door of the Permanent Legate's bedroom.

'Oh, sir,' Antony cried, 'the door is locked and bolted from the inside. We fear the worst.'

'What are you talking about?' I shouted above the wailing of the slaves.

'Shut those fucking slaves up,' I added with a snarl, 'or I'll have them flogged.'

There was silence. Then Demetrius embarked on a babbling explanation in his wretched Greek. Just before dawn, he'd been woken by a scream coming from the Permanent Legate's room.

'Where do you sleep?' I broke in. He indicated quarters beyond those of the Permanent Legate, in the right arm of the Legation. I wondered if he'd managed to hear any of the disturbances in my suite much earlier in the night. Perhap he'd been drunk in any event.

Demetrius explained that he'd got the key to the Permanent Legate's rooms – they were normally locked, he added – and had gone up to knock on the door.

'All I heard,' he said in a sepulchral whisper, 'was a shuffling, and then nothingness.'

'Well,' I said, 'you have the key. Get the door open, and we can see for ourselves.'

'I tried opening the door,' he replied. 'The key pushes and pulls from the outside but the door is bolted on the inside. Look—' He pushed the key in and out again, and rattled the door handle, to make his point. He fumbled again with the key.

'Let me,' I said, pushing him out of the way. I wanted my bed and I wanted to see the Permanent Legate. I'd achieve neither unless I took matters into my own hands.

I banged hard on the door. 'Your Excellency,' I shouted, 'please unbolt the door. We need to speak with you urgently.'

Nothing.

'Please, Your Excellency,' I tried again, 'we fear you are in some trouble. Please open the door, or at least reply. Otherwise, we must force the door.'

Still nothing.

The officials were looking agitated again. Martin's face was a blank of tired confusion.

I turned to Authari. 'Go back with Radogast,' I said, nodding towards our own suite. 'Find something we can use as a battering ram. We'll get in there soon enough.'

It didn't help that the narrowness of the corridor gave us very little room for battering the door down, or that it was tougher than expected. While Martin kept the officials out of the way, the three of us – big strong Northerners all – smashed again and again at what was as unyielding as a brick wall. By the time we'd loosened the door in its frame, the oak bench from our own kitchen would never see service again except as fuel for the ovens.

With a massive splintering of wood, the door was at last off its hinges. We'd damaged most of the frame and part of the wall in our assault. Once the dust had settled, and it was clear that no one in the room was moving, I was first through the doorway. With the window shuttered, the room was as dark as night.

'Give me one of those lamps,' I called to the Legation slaves as I gently prevented Authari from going past me into the room.

'Whatever we find,' I explained, 'mustn't be disturbed.'

The lamp only allowed my eyes to confirm what my nose had told me. There was a pool of blood on the floor. It was perhaps six foot across. It began just short of where I'd stopped on first entering the room. Another few inches, and I'd have been sliding on the stuff.

I cautiously made my way round the edge of the room and drew the bolts that held the shutters in place. The cold silver of dawn streamed in.

A body in a dark robe lay face down in the middle of the blood pool. A few feet away from it, a chair was overturned. So far as I could tell from its fast-congealing edges, the pool of blood was undisturbed.

'No!' I said sharply as others stepped in behind me. 'No one comes into this room. No one touches anything. I want you all out now!'

I took hold of Demetrius and slapped him hard across the face. He choked back his growing howl of terror. I glared the others into silence.

'Martin,' I said, 'please get a message sent off to Theophanes. Then do come straight back. I need your assistance.'

'His Excellency has committed the ultimate sin against God,' Demetrius struck up again in a melodramatic whisper.

Antony joined in: 'We are all polluted by the enormity of his sin.'

'Shut up!' I snarled at the pair of them. 'Shut up if you don't want to be shitting teeth tomorrow. Whatever you think, whatever you think you've seen, doesn't constitute a fact until it's been verified. You will all go and sit together at the end of the corridor. You will say nothing to each other. You will wait until I speak with each of you.'

It seemed an age before Martin came hurrying back up the stairs. He'd brought a book of waxed tablets and some of our silver pens. If I hadn't known him better, I'd have complimented him on his forethought. As it was, I marvelled that he hadn't gone to pieces on the spot and joined in the lamentations around me. Instead he gave me a calm glance that called for instructions and looked into the room. He added that he'd checked the nursery. Except Gutrune was returning to her previous grumpy self, all was unchanged there.

Like me, Martin was coming to terms with this new horror by following a procedure that, since our first investigation together in Rome, had become a familiar routine.

Unless Demetrius was lying or mistaken about times, the man I'd killed couldn't also have murdered the Permanent Legate. The chance that two unconnected killers had broken into the Legation on the same night was equally unlikely.

That attempt on my life might not be the last. This being so, it made sense to get as much information as I could from the crime scene before the usual duffers arrived to remove any possible clues. It would also help to take my mind off the growing chaos of my own life by focusing on the last moments of another person's.

'It is dawn on Sunday the 27th of September,' I dictated, walking carefully back into the room. Martin followed, making silent strokes of his shorthand on the soft wax surface of his boards, while Authari kept the doorway barred to anyone who might be inclined to ignore my instructions.

'We arrived to find the door locked and apparently bolted from the inside. Having broken the door down, we found the window bolted from the inside.

'There is a body lying on the floor. It seems to be of a man in late middle age. Without turning the body over and looking for a wound, it seems fair to say that death was violent and from a slash to the throat.'

249

I looked around. The only real difference between this room and my own was the lack of any balcony with stairs down to the garden.

'There are no other obvious means of entry to the room,' I said, again looking around me. I went to the window and looked down. It was a sheer drop of some thirty feet as I knew from experience. I'd have the ledge above the window checked later. If there was a ladder long enough to get someone up here, it would surely have left some traces.

I turned back to the room and stood over the body. I could see that Martin was sketching its position unbidden.

'The body,' I added to my description, 'is wholly unstained by blood behind. It is dressed in outgoing clothes. There is no evidence that it was approached once the blood had spread around it. There is no evidence that the bed has been slept in.'

I learned over the body. The left arm was outstretched, the hand empty. The right arm was underneath.

I took hold of the right shoulder and lifted the body over. It flopped stiffly on to its back. Eyes open, face contorted with some final terror, it stared lifelessly up at me. A dark gash across the throat, stretching from one ear to the other, confirmed the most likely cause of death.

The right hand was empty too, with traces of congealed blood on the wrist where it had touched the floor. The index finger and thumb had the sooty blackness of a hand more accustomed to pen and ink than to water. It was only then that I noticed the body had a rather clerical smell about it of unchanged undergarments.

The lack of hygiene aside, was that how I might have been found, had I gone to bed as usual? You may think the question would depress me. In fact, it rather cheered me. I hadn't gone to bed as usual. Because of that, I wasn't lying in a pool of my own blood.

My luck – so far as you can call it that – was holding.

'Martin,' I asked after another round of dictation, 'can you see any razor in the room, or other weapon that might have produced this wound?'

He swallowed hard, fighting back an obvious urge to vomit. But he edged round the blood pool and looked under the bed. I looked in and behind the cupboards. We went carefully through the bedclothes together.

No weapon.

'Well,' I said, dropping my voice to a soft mutter, 'whatever can be said about the locked door and window, this isn't looking much like suicide.'

I leaned over the body again and gently pulled the head backward. That slash across the throat had severed not only blood vessels but also the windpipe.

'My understanding of suicide', I said, 'is that the culprit starts with light strokes across the throat, getting up courage for something more radical. Whoever did this almost took the head off with a single stroke.'

'I'm not sure a man would have the strength to do this to himself,' Martin added.

'I agree,' I said. 'And where's the weapon? If this isn't murder, I don't know what is.'

We looked again at the locked window and smashed-in door, and back at each other.

'But how?' Martin asked.

'It was the Dark One himself,' someone called out from behind Authari. It was Antony. He'd crept forward to poke his head through the doorway. The Dark One has been among us. Let God bear witness—'

He would have said more but Authari had seized him from behind, his sword against Antony's throat. The sudden pressure on the scabbing of his back choked off his words to a gasp of pain.

'Get back to where I sent you, scum,' I reminded him, pushing my face close to his. 'Or you'll be joining your boss on the floor.'

I stopped. Since I'd taken on the preliminary investigation, I might as well do it properly.

'No,' I said to Authari, 'release him. You' – I pointed to the man – 'come over here.'

Antony shuffled reluctantly forward, keeping his eyes off the body.

'Is this the Permanent Legate?' I asked.

'I don't know,' he said. 'Only Demetrius ever dealt with His Excellency.'

I had Demetrius brought in and repeated the question.

'Who else could it be?' he muttered, looking away from the body.

'I didn't ask who it must be,' I said, resisting an urge to grab at the man. 'I will ask yet again – is this the body of the Permanent Legate?'

Demetrius looked down at the body. Yes, he said quietly, this was the Permanent Legate.

I asked if anyone else could identify the body and he confirmed that there was no one. He was the only official who'd not been sent out of the city before I arrived. Since then, he'd been the only one to deal with the Permanent Legate. He'd been with him every day – most recently the evening before, when they'd been going over the accounts of a charitable foundation in Ephesus.

I stopped him at the mention of Ephesus. Hadn't Theophanes discussed the place with the Permanent Legate? I'd investigate this later.

Alone again, Martin and I searched the room more thoroughly. We kicked at the boards to see if any were loose. We stripped the bed. We tapped carefully along the walls. We pulled the bookcase and the wardrobe away from the wall to make sure there wasn't any hidden doorway or other point of access.

As I finished dictating my notes, Theophanes arrived.

'This is a terrible thing,' he announced in a sonorous voice. 'A suicide – and of one so high in Holy Mother Church!'

He looked at me, plainly taking in my outdoor clothes. His eyes flickered to Martin and Authari.

'Not suicide,' I said, choosing to ignore how quickly he had got here. I gave him the facts we'd gathered. His eyes darted rapidly about the room, taking in the scene.

'Alypius,' he rapped in his official tone, 'I want the Legation sealed at once. No one enters. No one leaves. And I want this room and the whole corridor sealed off.'

'Theophanes,' I suggested, taking him aside, 'you should station someone here in the room – someone you can trust not to mess

252

everything up behind your back. There might be someone hidden in the room. You need to make sure he doesn't slip away before the room can be taken apart.'

Theophanes nodded. He suggested Authari should stay and keep watch. It would take a while for any of his trusted investigators to get over from the Ministry. For the moment, the Legation officials had to be watched as well as the body.

He gave my outdoor cloak another hard stare and seemed about to remark on it. Instead he arranged his features into their official blandness.

'I'm afraid the pair of you will need to give the story in person to the Emperor,' he said. 'This is a matter of state importance.'

40

After a long wait outside his office, we were ushered into the Imperial Presence. Phocas sat at his desk, giving responses to a mass of letters and petitions. Secretaries surrounded him, taking down his brief words for the usual writing up into more ceremonious utterances.

Theophanes had made sure to tell us that there was no need for the usual prostrations in a matter of utilitarian business. We nodded respectfully at Phocas as he looked towards us. He pointed at two chairs against a wall as he continued work with his secretaries.

Theophanes went and stood beside him.

'Have the man torn apart by hyenas in the Circus,' Phocas said in a low monotone, discussing someone presumably accused of treason.

The secretary scribbled a note in the margin of the papyrus sheet. He added the sheet to a pile on a wheeled table beside him, then reached into a bag for another.

Phocas stopped him. 'Correction,' he said, taking hold of the anonymous denunciation. 'Have that done to his wife and children. Make him watch. Then have him blinded and put in the Monastery of St Placidius. There he can await our further pleasure.' He paused, taking one final look at the denunciation. 'Total confiscation of goods,' he added. 'Refuse any Petition of Share if the informant comes forward.'

He raised a hand to indicate that the matter was closed and moved on to the next one. Should the Army of the Euphrates be ordered to Constantinople? It could be used here against Heraclius, who was now sending further contingents over from Abydos to complete the encirclement.

Phocas got up and walked over to a mosaic map of the Empire that covered the far wall away from the windows. This was an old map that showed the Empire as it had been in ancient times, including the Western Provinces and even Britain. He put up a hand to trace the length of the Euphrates frontier with Persia.

'Leave the army where it is,' he said at length. 'It can't arrive here in time to serve any useful purpose. In any event, it's all we have left to cover Syria. Whoever is Emperor come the next moon, he'll need something there to stand against Chosroes.'

He laughed unpleasantly as he turned to face me.

'You stay,' he said, raising his voice. 'Everyone else – out!'

He pointed at Theophanes. 'That includes you.'

Theophanes opened his mouth to speak but thought better of the idea. He bowed low and followed the secretaries out, closing the door softly as he went.

Before it closed, Martin turned back and stared at me, a frightened look on his face. I tried a smile of reassurance. I don't think it worked very well.

Phocas returned to his desk. He motioned me forward. He looked at the wine jug beside him, sighed and looked away.

This wasn't the jolly creature who'd charmed me during lunch at the Circus. It wasn't the hieratic image who'd presided over the races. It was the bureaucratic, supremely powerful Ruler of the World – or whatever of it still paid attention to His Word.

Phocas took up a sheet of parchment. On it was a list of names, all with black marks against them.

'Do you see these names?' he asked in a smooth voice. 'Every one of these is of someone who wants to be Emperor in my place. Do you want to be Emperor?'

'No, Your Majesty,' I said, trying to keep my voice level. 'I'm just a barbarian, here on business for Holy Mother Church.'

'Perhaps I believe you,' came the reply. 'I didn't want to be Emperor when I was your age. Fate can play strange tricks on a man if he lives long enough. But I do believe you. People like you don't want to be Emperor. All you ever want to do is to feast on the rotting entrails of the Empire.'

Phocas took up another sheet of parchment. It was covered on one side in a tiny Latin script.

'Alaric of Britain,' he began, speaking Greek in a voice of quiet menace, 'I have in my hand a signed request from the Exarch in Ravenna for your immediate removal to his presence. You are accused of a fraud on the Sacred Treasury.'

He pushed the sheet towards me. I read it with freezing insides. My knees shook with the unexpected shock. My idiotic associates had sold half the shares in that Cornish tin shipment to a consortium of Jews and Armenians backed by the Exarch. His agents in Cadiz had got wind of our scheme. It was they who had bought the shipment. They had then observed the reloading of the ships.

The Ravenna contract had been voided. The tin was forfeit. My associates had decamped from Rome to take shelter in Pavia with the Lombards. I was wanted for questioning and trial in Ravenna.

'You do realise, I think,' Phocas continued in a more conversational tone, 'that you are in the technical sense a traitor. I could have you flayed alive in the Circus for this. And that's without dragging up another matter from outside Ravenna that I may still regard as pending.'

He got up again and went over to a cupboard. He took out a golden key from his robe and opened the ivory doors. Inside was what looked like a golden birdcage. This he pulled out on a sliding shelf.

It was a cage. But instead of real birds, it contained three golden and ivory figurines of birds. He pulled at a wheel and pushed a lever. As he stood back, there was a whirring of little gears, and the room was filled with the sharp, artificial singing of birds.

It was an odd accompaniment to a death sentence. Oh, if you set aside the bathing and more frequent changing of clothes, the main difference between Phocas and the Great One was that the second had to rule somewhat more by persuasion than the first. This man could, if he pleased, do the most awful things to me.

But the chances were that it didn't please him. If he'd managed a shock just as great as I'd had in the Great One's tent, I was recovering much faster. I was angry at how those duffers back in

Rome had, despite my urging, overreached themselves. I was vaguely apprehensive of a crushing fine. But I didn't really expect I'd be used any time soon as a warm-up for the chariot races.

'Come over here,' said Phocas, speaking softly. He beckoned me close. 'Come and stand by this little miracle of workmanship. Beautiful, isn't it?' he said, pointing through an opening under the cage at a spinning wheel. 'It was made for Justinian whose grand design was to reconquer all the lost Western Empire.

'Do you know that, following the reconquest of Italy, he even had plans drawn up for an assault on Britain?'

We looked a while at the little birds. I watched in fascination as they opened and shut their mouths and fluttered their golden feathers.

Phocas spoke again, now in Latin. 'I want to know what really happened in the Great One's camp.'

So that was what he wanted. I stepped back to gather my thoughts – those artificial squeaks and trills were beginning to annoy after their first surprise.

'No, Alaric,' said Phocas, pulling me gently forward. 'You will watch these birds as you answer. Speak into their sound. And you'll speak softly. I'm not deaf yet.'

I thought quickly. What to do? On the one hand, repeating the lies Theophanes had imposed on the world would probably put us both straight under the Ministry. On the other hand, the truth wasn't much to his advantage. And disclosing it might not be much to mine, if Theophanes should survive to hear about it.

That was if Phocas chose not to take against me on account of it.

'You were observed, you know,' Phocas prompted me. 'You were seen from the Monastery of St Euthemius as the three of you came away from the Great One.

'An ant doesn't fart in this Empire but I don't get some wind of it. Don't you imagine otherwise. I want to know what happened with the Great One,' he said, dropping his voice still lower. 'I want the full truth. I know when people are lying to me. Give me the truth if you rightly understand your interest.'

I swallowed and took what seemed the least risky option.

257

'I will tell you everything as it happened, Caesar,' I began. 'But I want your promise that you will not act against anyone who may emerge from my story without full credit.'

Phocas creased his face into a nasty smile. 'You presume to ask an Emperor for his word?'

'No, sir,' I said, 'I ask for your word as an officer in the Danubian Army.'

As a rule, one doesn't bandy words with a creature like Phocas. You give him what he wants and when he wants it. If you think that it may not show you in the most favourable light, you still give it to him – but do so while licking the man's instep and begging for mercy.

But, you see, I didn't think that approach was likely to work. The previous day, however, he'd been willing to play the part of one simple man talking to another, to the exclusion of the sophisticates and yes-men who generally surrounded him. That might still take his fancy.

There is a time for abasement, and a time for playing along. I had no choice but to keep my nerve and take a chance on the latter.

'Your word as a soldier,' I added, 'will be quite enough for me.'

Phocas turned back to his artificial birds. He spoke slowly, as if recalling distant thoughts and feelings.

'I've not been asked for that in over eight years in this den of lunacy they call an Empire. And fuck-all good my word as a soldier did poor Maurice,' he added bitterly. 'I broke my military oath when I raised the Danubian Army against him. I broke my word when I promised him his life, and the lives of his sons. I broke my word when I promised his widow and daughters that I'd spare them.

'And now, as my enemies gather to destroy me, you expect me to give you a word of honour that has any meaning?'

'I want your word, even so,' I persisted.

He looked hard at those pretty birds. 'Very well,' he said at last. 'You have my word that neither you and your secretary nor my ever faithful accomplice-in-crime Theophanes will come to harm as a result of what you tell me. But I want the truth – and only the truth.'

I gave it to him. I left absolutely nothing out.

'So you fucked her, and with her father looking on?' he asked with a suddenly admiring grin as I finished. 'I'd like to have seen that. My darling son-in-law Priscus would have had trouble keeping his hands off you afterwards. You can be sure of that!'

He fell silent. I was still alive.

The wheel began to run down, and the birds now wheezed and trilled in falling notes.

'Would you like to go back to Canterbury?' Phocas asked suddenly. I couldn't keep the look of astonishment off my face as I stared back at him.

'I know all about Canterbury,' he added. 'Your penis may have saved you with the Great One. It nearly got you killed with Ethelbert when you got that daughter of his chief man up the duff.

'I could write to Ethelbert, you know. I'm told he's started calling himself an Emperor, doubtless egged on by those Roman priests. If I wrote to him as my Brother in Purple, he'd have you back with open arms. Would you have me do that?'

I opened and closed my mouth. I swallowed, wondering what on earth I was supposed to reply to this. If he'd asked about the geography of India, I'd not have been more completely astonished.

But Phocas stood silent, his eyes burning into my face, looking for something I couldn't imagine was required. Then he whispered so gently I had to bend forward to catch the words: 'This conversation did not take place.'

As the birds fell finally silent, he changed back to Greek and said in a louder voice:

'I understand that His Excellency the Permanent Legate has been murdered, and in his own bedroom. Am I correct in believing that you found the body and established that it was murder?'

'Yes, sir,' I answered.

'Well, this,' said Phocas, '– and I put it mildly – is an embarrassment. I had need of His Excellency at least to stay alive, and preferably to be on speaking terms with me. Now he's dead, we'll have to find the killer. I'll not have any difficulties with Rome.'

259

Phocas returned to his desk and took up a sheet of parchment. He held it away from me.

'I am told you have some ability in these matters. That is more than I seem able to say for my Semi-Divine son-in-law. I therefore appoint you Investigator of the Death. You will work together with Priscus. However, you will be in sole charge of the investigation. Any advice or resources he cares to give you may be taken or rejected as you see fit. You will report directly to me as often as I call for you.

'I want the case solved within a reasonable time. I'll not ask more than that for the moment – but I want someone I can put on public trial and then execute.'

He paused, looking again at the parchment sheet.

'I also have need of a new Permanent Legate. There is no time for sending to Rome. The most eligible local candidates for an Acting Legateship are all out of the city. Therefore' – he pushed the parchment sheet towards me – 'I appoint you, Alaric of Britain, Acting Legate until such time as a replacement can be obtained from Rome.'

'But Caesar,' I cried – I hadn't expected this – 'I'm not ordained. I'm not even of age to be ordained. How can I accept your commission?'

'You'll accept my commission,' he said, now cheerful again, 'because I'm the Emperor. My word is law. If I wanted, I could hang the present incumbent and make you Patriarch of Constantinople. I could very easily make you Patriarch of Antioch, now there's a vacancy.

'If His Holiness in Rome has any objections, they can be handled when communications are reopened. And bearing in mind the lack of any other candidates, I can't see how he will object. It's either you or some slimy Greek cleric who really would raise eyebrows in the Lateran.'

I looked at the commission. Its ink barely dry, it looked chillingly formal.

'He shall be regarded', it read, 'as the Representative and Plenary Agent in all matters, both spiritual and temporal, of His Most Sacred Excellency the Patriarch of Rome.'

No mention, I noted, in all the surrounding verbiage, of a 'Universal Bishop'. I wondered if I'd be expected to raise that issue before this whole ghastly comedy was played out.

There is a limit to how far you can argue with any emperor. I'd already pushed Phocas further than anyone else had dared in years. I bowed my acceptance of the commission.

'So, Your Excellency,' Phocas laughed softly, 'I'll not trouble you yet with any request for your benediction. But I'm sure you'll have much to discuss over your brotherly kiss with His Holiness of Constantinople.'

He went over and pulled the door open. Theophanes almost fell into the room. He steadied himself and entered. Martin followed at some distance behind him with the other secretaries.

Phocas handed the commission to one of them, who read it to us in a loud flat voice.

Theophanes stiffened slightly, then made a grave bow in my direction.

Martin almost fainted with shock, clean forgetting his own duty to bow.

As we shuffled out into the sunlight of a cold autumn morning and made towards our chairs, I turned to Martin.

'The Permanent Legate was rather small,' I said. 'We'll need to get those robes altered in a hurry if I'm to attend evening service at the Great Church.'

41

'But it's blasphemy!' Martin whispered in Celtic over his fourth cup of wine. Back in the Legation, he'd at last fallen apart.

'Be that as it may,' I said, jug in hand, 'it is the Will of Caesar.'

I refilled his cup and slopped more wine into my own.

'There are things even he can't do,' Martin snapped. 'At least it was your duty to refuse.'

'Refuse Phocas?' I laughed gently. 'I don't fancy another trip to the Circus. And, don't forget – you're my secretary. You'd be in the next pot.'

'Men have accepted martyrdom rather than participate in lesser blasphemies,' he replied primly. 'Whatever can be done to us on earth is nothing compared with the fires of Hell!'

'Oh, shut up, Martin,' I explained. Go and see if those bloody tailors have arrived yet. I need something good for the funeral service. All else aside, I've been granted senatorial status. I *must* have something with a splash of purple.

'And do get me that stupid little official, Demetrius. I want to know what's become of the Legatorial seals.

'No, Martin, I don't have any other plan,' I said between gritted teeth, cutting off his renewed protests. 'You may have noticed that every time I do something in this city, everything else gets worse. When and how we can leave is beyond me. Just be grateful we're still alive, and let's see what turns up. Now, go and find me Demetrius.'

Alone, I refilled my cup and drank deep. I crunched up another of the dried berries I'd earlier begged from Theophanes. I needed a clear head for when Priscus finally put in an appearance. At the same time, I was feeling decidedly less ebullient than I'd appeared to Martin.

Seven days earlier, I'd been placidly wiping my bum in the University Library. Now I was barely one down from Pope Boniface himself, and was lined up for a course of private meetings with a man you'd not have wanted in your nightmares, let alone in the same room.

Did I mean, by that, Phocas or his equally dreadful son-in-law? It was a hard one to answer.

An afternoon of quiet reflection was essential for trying to take all this in. I needed to establish in my head what had been a dream and what was real. Then there was the murder investigation that didn't seem to admit of any answer but was under some obligation to provide one.

Facts are everything. But a fact isn't a fact until it's been verified, and I had almost nothing that could be classified as such. Late in the night, Agathius breaks into my room to kill me. Or was it to kill me? He'd been as much confused as angered by our fight. Whatever the case, I kill him. While we're out dumping the body, the Permanent Legate appears to have been murdered, and in a locked room with no other known access.

By treating these events as related, was I confusing two separate chains of causation? Possibly, but hardly very likely. That would require two separate killers, both deciding to act on the same night, and both gaining access to a normally secure Legation.

It would have been useful to suppose that Agathius murdered the Permanent Legate and then came for me. I'd been told he was working for Heraclius. That gave him some motive for wanting to kill Silas: whatever the deal was that Theophanes wouldn't tell me about, it might not be effective with His Excellency out of the way.

And since at least one of the Heraclius people had wanted me dead outside the city walls, there was a credible motive for killing me as well.

The problem here was that the timings seemed all wrong. Agathius must have been dead by the time of the Permanent Legate's murder. There seemed little room for doubt on that point. Forget Demetrius. This much had already been confirmed by the other officials and slaves in the Legation.

Perhaps there had been two killers with one mission? But that brought me back to the question of how murder could be committed in a sealed room.

No – I needed facts. Without those, speculation was worthless and even a barrier to the truth.

I'd slipped into the Permanent Legate's office on getting back from the Imperial Palace. While Martin was trying to compose himself, I'd gone through all the drawers and cupboards in the room. I'd also got the main filing room opened and had given myself a brief tour of the Permanent Legate's files. There were gaps all over the filing racks that I'd need Martin to help explain.

I needed facts. I needed facts and more facts. My experience of investigations so far had given me some grasp of basic principles. You dig and dig without preconceptions, and see what turns up. Until then, you avoid hypotheses. When you are able to form one, you test it against whatever new facts emerge.

That approach had always worked for me in the past. If this case looked insoluble, it was only because I hadn't got far enough with gathering the relevant facts.

A hangover adding to his other exertions, Authari had himself been wilting when, after the filing tour, I'd dropped in on the Permanent Legate's room for another look at the body. But I'd told him to stay put. Now I was in charge of the investigation, it was necessary to keep my own watch on things. If this meant Authari had to fight sleep in the presence of a butchered corpse, that was tough on him. But I needed Martin for other things, and there was no one else I could implicitly trust.

The body had looked horrid. Even half a day hadn't been kind to the thing. The face was now as ghastly as an ancient theatrical mask I'd found on sale in a relic shop in Rome. The body had stiffened further, its right arm raised in a sort of greeting. Black patches were spreading over the legs.

I'd ordered a medical inspection. I doubted if this would reveal more than I'd been able to gather from my own inspection, but it was worth doing just in case. Doctors are occasionally good for something.

In any event, time was against us. Alypius had turned up when I was with Authari, carrying orders from Theophanes for the body to be removed for a service that night in the Great Church.

This was, you'll agree, an irregular proceeding. A funeral on the same day as a death – and coinciding with Sunday evening service? You'd not have got away with half of it in Rome.

But Constantinople wasn't Rome. The Church here did as it was told.

I put my cup down, and settled back for a nap. In spite of the berries, I was out in perhaps five beats of the heart. It was like snuffing a lamp last thing at night.

Without knocking, Martin rattled the door open. I jerked myself awake. It was early afternoon so far as I could tell from the now overcast sky outside the window. Those cuts on my back were now hurting so much, even Antony might have sympathised.

'His Most Serene and Imperial Excellency, the Caesar Priscus, begs the honour of an audience,' he called in a voice that might have been satirical had he possessed any sense of humour.

As he finished, Priscus walked in past him. Dressed now in black, he made every show of beginning a prostration.

'I don't think, My Lord Priscus,' I said, standing and patting my clothes into a semblance of order, 'we need bother with such formalities in private.'

'But, Your Most Sacred Excellency,' he crooned, rising from his knees, 'I've always wanted to meet the Pope. And you are now, in the legal sense, his very projection from Rome.'

With a flash of his riddled teeth that I took as an attempt at charm, he sat in Martin's place and reached for the wine.

'So, my brave and golden – and now Most Holy – Alaric,' he said with a flourish of cup and jug, 'it seems my wish is to be granted. Did I hear a child crying as I came in?' he asked with a change of subject.

'I have no doubt', said I, 'you've heard many children cry on your entry.'

Perhaps it didn't do to treat the man with the contempt he deserved. But unless he happened to be standing over you in one of his dungeons, it was a hard reaction to avoid. And I was for the moment at least his equal in status.

Priscus looked into the various compartments of his pouch. He took out a spoonful of green powder and dropped it into his cup.

'This has a far more soothing effect than wine,' he assured me as I waved him away from my cup.

There was a long moment of silence.

'Now,' he said finally with a drugged brightness, 'I've had the main facts from my Divine and Ever-Sagacious Father-in-Law. It all sounds utterly intriguing.

'I know it's Sunday, but would you mind awfully if I had the whole household taken in for questioning? I promise not to have any of them on the rack until tomorrow morning.'

'My Lord Priscus,' I said, looking coldly at him, 'I am in charge of this investigation. It will proceed by my rules, not those of the Black Agents. There will be no use of torture until we have a definite suspect.'

Priscus smiled and poured himself more wine. 'Oh, come now, Alaric – none of this softie philosophising,' he said with a dismissive wave at my bookshelves. 'If you'd been in charge of things, Justinus would still be running about to spread his poison. The surest road to truth runs through the rack.'

I thought of a jeering question about how many other people he'd arrested in place of Justinus, before tracking the man down to a public table in one of the city's most expensive restaurants.

But it didn't do to push things too far. I went back to the business in hand.

'We proceed by my rules,' I said, 'or you can explain yourself to His Majesty when I back out of the investigation. What you do with the criminal when I've produced him is for you to decide. Investigation is my business.'

As I rose to my feet, a sound of distant cheering drifted through the window.

'What's that?' I asked with involuntary interest.

'That', said Priscus, 'will be my Divine and Ever-Victorious Father-in-Law declaring an amnesty for all offences but treason. He really needs the crowd on his side, now that Heraclius is moving over in person to handle the siege.'

Fat lot of difference that would make, I grunted to myself. During my entire stay in the City, I'd not seen a single offence – from murder all the way down to cutting purses – that hadn't been twisted into some variety of treason.

Still, Phocas seemed to have pleased the crowd again.

I frowned and returned to the original subject. 'I think, My Lord, you can be spared for the important work of defending the City. I am myself under some pressure of time – I must ready myself for the funeral service in the Great Church. The investigation will move faster if I am able by myself to interview the key witnesses between now and this evening.'

'Then, my darling Alaric, we shall begin tomorrow morning.'

No, I thought to myself. Not only did I want to interview every actual and potential witness without Priscus beside me to put them off. I also needed to do it now. The longer matters were left unresolved, the more people would start forgetting important facts. Continual repetition to others would blur and distort re-collections that even now were still reliable.

Before I could think of some emollient lie to send Priscus on his way, the door opened again. It was Martin.

'Aelric,' he said, ignoring Priscus and the need to use my public name, 'you'd better come quickly.'

His voice shook. I saw tears glistening on his deathly pale face.

'It's Authari,' he said.

42

In his last convulsion, Authari had pitched forward out of his seat. When I arrived in the Permanent Legate's bedroom, he lay face down in the pool of now congealed blood.

Martin had found him after he'd finished gathering all the papers he could lay hands on into one of our document crates, ready for inspection in my own office. He'd gone into the room to see if Authari wanted something to eat.

At first he'd supposed that Authari had got himself some wine and drunk himself into a heap. Now, weeping softly, he stood back while Priscus and I inspected the body.

'My darling boy,' Priscus drawled, 'would it alter me in your estimation if I observed that this doesn't look at all like the Permanent Legate?'

Yes – where was the other body? Nothing else in the room had been disturbed. The window shutters still lay open as I'd left them. There, now in sunlight, was the blood patch still on the floor. But where the Permanent Legate's body had lain was now only an expanse of less bloody floorboards.

Two sets of footprints led away to a rug on which bloody footwear had evidently been cleaned before the body was taken off to God knew where.

Now, in place of that corpse, lay Authari.

I swallowed and made no reply.

Priscus took up the wooden cup that had lain in a corner of the room. He ran a finger round the moist inside of the cup and licked his finger. He spat vigorously and rinsed his mouth from a wine flask he carried in his robe.

'It's one of the metallic poisons,' he said, rinsing his finger. 'This

268

isn't the low-grade muck women buy in the shops to use on their husbands. You need a licence to buy it, and use is confined to the Imperial Service.

'I've used it myself many times,' he added thoughtfully. 'When I was operating against the Persians in Mesopotamia, I once had a pair of gloves steeped in the stuff, and presented them to a barbarian ally I thought was dealing both ways. Everyone believed he died of a heart attack while wiping his arse.'

Priscus gave me a complacent smirk, then looked down at the twisted, blackened face as I rolled the body over.

'Taken as a liquid, and in that concentration,' he added, 'I'd say your man was dead before the first mouthful reached his stomach. The tongue would have swollen like that just after death.'

He turned to the blood patch on the floor.

'I imagine he was killed so the body could be removed,' he said. 'My normal preference is for something a little slower. But I can see this was an emergency.'

'That seems to follow,' Martin broke in, still agitated. Ignoring Priscus, he looked at me. 'My suspicion is that the Permanent Legate's killer was hiding somewhere in this room. Just because we didn't find the hiding place on first inspection doesn't mean there isn't one.'

Priscus gave Martin an unpleasant look, then turned back to an inspection of the body.

'Whoever poisoned Authari must have had his trust,' I said. 'That wouldn't be someone who'd just crawled out of a wall space. More likely, someone he knew came in, put him out of the way, then rescued the hidden killer and helped him lift the body.'

It made sense that a hidden killer would need Authari out of the way. But why bother taking the Permanent Legate's body? It wouldn't have been an easy thing to carry. And where had it gone? The Legation was sealed.

Perhaps there was something about the body I hadn't noticed, but that the medical inspection I'd ordered might reveal. But this was more speculation.

'My Lord Priscus,' I said, turning back to the matter in hand, 'if, back in my office, I gave any impression of not welcoming your involvement in this case, I apologise.'

I steeled myself, and followed with the inevitable: 'Can I call on you for immediate assistance?'

Priscus smiled. He knew that everything had changed. Finding the Permanent Legate's killer was a duty that I had to discharge sooner or later. Now I also had Authari to avenge. Unlike Martin, I wouldn't give way to emotion in front of Priscus. I forced myself to remain calm. But I could feel the grief and the outrage clawing away deep inside me. It was dulled only by the immense weariness that was beginning to sweep over me in waves.

Authari was dead. He'd taken hold of that cup with perfect trust. He'd drained it in front of some smiling face, blessing the man who'd thought to bring him refreshments.

I'd catch whoever had done this. I'd have him in those dungeons under the Ministry, and I'd gladly turn the rack while Priscus played with his branding irons and hooked gloves.

'Of course you have my fullest co-operation,' Priscus said in his most slimy drawl. 'Whatever you want is yours. Just say the word. Only one thing I'd ask in return.' He paused and took a swig from his flask. 'I'd be most terribly grateful if you could drop the "My Lord". All my friends call me Priscus.'

'Thank you, Priscus,' I said. They were difficult words to force out. But I had no choice. I'd have said more, but he was over by the door. He clapped his hands smartly. One of the Black Agents appeared immediately. He must have followed us over, though I hadn't noticed.

'Alaric,' said Priscus, 'do say what you want.'

The Black Agent produced a book of waxed tablets and a stylus.

'I want this room taken apart,' I said. 'I want the boards taken up. I want the plaster off the walls. I want the ceiling pulled down. I want this room broken up atom by atom. If there is any hiding place here, I want it found.'

I bent and carefully lifted the wine cup from where Priscus had left it.

'I want this matched with any other set in the Legation. The building is still sealed. No one can get in or out. Whoever poisoned Authari was known to him. If we can find where the cup came from, we may be closer to discovering who filled it with poisoned wine.

'And I want the entire Legation household lined up outside my office for questioning. That includes secretaries, officials, slaves – and those monks who look after the gardens.'

The Black Agent scratched laboriously away with his stylus. I could see he was operating at the limits of his ability. I only hoped that he and his people were up to following my instructions.

Priscus looked at him and then back to me. 'It will all be as you wish,' he said quietly.

'There is more,' I added. 'The Permanent Legate's body can't have gone far. With your people blocking the entrance, I can't see how it's left the Legation. I want a room-by-room search of the entire building – excepting only my suite, where I will arrange a search of my own. I want that body or any remains of it.'

'Martin,' I said softly, patting his shoulder, 'please have Authari taken back to our quarters. Have him washed and dressed for burial the day after tomorrow. Can you book the church where I freed him the other day?'

Martin got up and silently left the room. For all that it had once seemed unlikely, his friendship with Authari had become an established fact. Now, just a few days into his new and better life as a freedman, Authari lay dead. Martin was disconsolate.

Another of the Black Agents entered the room. He handed a message to Priscus.

'Just as I expected!' he snarled. 'Those fuckers in the Blue Faction have taken offence at the defensive role I gave the Greens. They say it's less exposed than theirs and more glorious. I'm needed urgently to stop a battle from starting in the streets.'

With a dramatic swirl of his cloak, he was off.

'You will find the killer,' Martin said later when we were alone. 'You always get to the truth. You never fail.'

He spoke like a child looking up at his father, expecting all to be put right with a few words.

'Whatever can be done', I said gently, 'will be done. The world may be coming apart around us. But I'll have the killer if it means arresting Phocas himself.'

It sounded a brave promise. In truth, though, I did have an idea. It had been forming for a while without my active participation. It would continue forming until I could see its proper shape. It might not be a complete answer. In the nature of things, it would probably lead to further mystery. But I was no longer so utterly baffled as when I'd first drawn those window bolts to let in the morning light.

I sank into a chair and looked over at Martin. The afternoon light streamed in from the garden outside my office. I sipped indifferently at the fruit squash he'd arranged in place of the wine I'd ordered.

Martin needed a shave, I could see. There were ginger bristles all over his face. They, plus the haggard eyes, made him look like a much older man. Bad posture didn't help. I never had persuaded him to join me in regular exercise. Now, all the compulsive gorging on honeyed things was beginning to tell. If he ever got out of here alive, Sveta would have something else to nag him about.

I reached up to feel my own face. No need of a razor for those boyish cheeks, I decided. I rather thought my eyebrows might need plucking though, until I could replace Authari, I'd probably have to live with them as they were.

I checked myself. Authari was dead. If my eyebrows were growing out, that was of no present consequence.

'Before we have everyone in for interview,' I said, 'do please send a message to Theophanes. Ask him to get me written instructions on what I'm supposed to do at this evening's service. Am I expected to officiate in some way? Or do I just watch the proceedings?

'And do arrange a search party for Demetrius. He was the last person to see the Permanent Legate alive. He'll be skulking somewhere in the building. If not, I'll have to get Priscus to make enquiries.'

More like his old self at the resumption of work, Martin pointed at one of our document crates.

'These are all the papers I could find in the Permanent Legate's office,' he said. 'I haven't been able to go through them in detail. But you are right that they've been carefully sifted.'

Martin swallowed. 'There are, even so, many writings of a licentious nature. You may wish to commit them to the flames once we've checked for secret writing.'

I tried to think of a cynical comment. Instead, I found myself wondering if I should have taken advantage of the drug Priscus had offered me. I was aching for my bed, and those berries Theophanes had given me were losing their effect.

I changed the subject. 'Martin, is everyone, excepting Demetrius, lined up outside?' I asked.

He nodded, adding that he'd made sure they were sitting far enough apart to prevent any conferring.

'Good,' I said briskly. 'We'll have Antony in first. He's a lawyer, which means he might understand the difference between fact and supposition. Are you ready to take notes?'

He nodded again.

'Well,' I said, 'we're almost ready to start. Before we do, Martin, I'd be grateful if you could run down and see if those bastard tailors have arrived yet. I can't be seen at the Great Church with four inches of leg showing below my robe.'

43

'Brother Thomas,' I cried, 'I bring you all the love and regard of His Holiness the Universal Bishop.'

I planted as brief a kiss as decency allowed on the hairy, lice-ridden cheek of the Greek Patriarch. Several thousand pairs of eyes turned in our direction. Thomas ignored the provocation.

'This is supposed to be a Christian burial,' he hissed without moving his lips. 'You may not be aware of it but the body comes uncovered into church.'

'You haven't seen the face,' I whispered back. 'It would give even the Black Agents a turn.'

It had given me a turn, I can tell you, when Theophanes had insisted we should substitute Authari for the Permanent Legate.

'No!' Martin had sobbed – 'In the name of God, no!' Authari should rest in a grave under his own name, he'd insisted.

I'd joined in the protests. The dead can feel nothing one way or the other. But that doesn't relieve the living of their duties. I'd agreed with Martin, adding some very strong words of my own.

But Theophanes had been adamant. Murder was one thing. A stolen body violated all the decencies of life in the city.

It wasn't safe to try smuggling in another body through the dense crowds now surrounding the Legation. Nor would a sealed coffin do. We could get away with a cloth covering, but, one way or another, there had to be a body.

So Authari it had to be. He had died a freedman and glad of his status. Now, in death, he wore the white-and-purple-bordered robe of full senatorial status.

For a moment I thought the Patriarch would step past me and pull the cloth away. But, with the Emperor glowering down from his throne, he backed off, taking this as just one more irregularity to add to all the others.

'Oh, we'd better just get on with things,' he muttered. 'Move as I direct you. Don't push things any further by trying to join in the service. And whoever advised you on gold leaf for your face will surely burn in Hell!'

I'd been passing the Great Church several times a day since July. I'd been dropping in for services as often as I'd thought necessary for keeping up appearances. Now, what to say about the place?

If you've never been out of England, think of the biggest and most lavish church you ever saw and try to imagine it beside the Great Church of Constantinople as a lit taper next to the sun. If you know Rome, you can do better. Think in that case of the Prefect's Basilica, but make it bigger and taller, and replace the barrel vaults of its roof with a dome that has means of support you only see if you know something of engineering.

The Great Church had been consecrated over seventy years earlier, with Justinian himself in attendance. This was after a Circus riot that had left much of the city centre in smoking ruins. His intention was to stamp his authority on the Empire once and for all with a building that would outdo the efforts all his predecessors and Solomon himself with its size and magnificence.

With no shortage of cash in those days, and architects of genius, Justinian had succeeded in spectacular fashion. Every stone quarry in Greece and Asia Minor had been worked double-time to supply the columns and interior furnishings. Every temple in Syria still untouched by centuries of closure had been ransacked for bronze doors and other fittings. The artists had faced problems hitherto unimagined to decorate the interior with mosaics that were in proportion to the whole.

The result was the largest covered space ever built. From the outside, it is impressive in its mass but looks rather like a giant mushroom. It's on the inside that it comes alive. The overall shape of the Great Church is a cross with arms of equal length. Its central space is a rectangle of about eighty yards by seventy-five. This is divided from the nave by great columns which take the weight of the galleries and, sixty yards above the floor, of the central dome.

Our procession had set out from the Legation and crossed the square into the wide atrium of the church. At the main door, we'd been met by the Patriarch. Now, he was leading the way past the Imperial Throne towards the high altar. The interior was brilliantly lit by a constellation of lamps that were suspended from points high above.

Though conducted in Greek, and with variations of music and incense you'll see nowhere else, the Eastern ritual for the dead is pretty close in essentials to our own. It has all the same prayers and readings and hymns. There is the usual dwelling on the frailty of life and the vanity of worldly things – the usual directing of hearts and minds to the Incomparable Value and Infinite Blessings of the Life to Come.

Presiding in a vague sense over all this, Phocas sat on his throne a few dozen yards from the altar. He glowered at the congregation as he made sure that the representative of his good friend the Pope received the send-off he deserved.

As if to show who was really in charge, the Greek Patriarch's plans were changed without warning. As he readied himself to turn back from the coffin for another sermon, a deacon plucked at his sleeve. There was a whispered exchange that ended in a look in my direction from the Patriarch that Medusa might have envied. Then I found myself propelled to the front of the church.

'You're to give the final reading,' a voice murmured in my right ear. 'Have you got your text ready?'

'What the fuck? . . .' I gasped, luckily unheard in the shuffling around me. No one had told me I was to do other than watch and look pretty in the robe I'd finally bullied those tailors into working like galley slaves to produce.

I stood looking down at the immense congregation lining both sides of the central area of the church. The assembled thousands stood looking expectantly back at me. I recognised Philip and some of the other students, all dressed in a most fetching black. There was Baruch, standing beside one of the supporting columns, a golden cross hung prominently round his neck. I noticed the Faction leaders close together. It seemed that Priscus had managed after all to settle their difference.

I saw the Patriarch, breathing hard and looking down at the floor. Beside him, with a seniority I'd never been able to work out, stood Sergius. He looked at me, his face diplomatically blank.

Over beside the Emperor, I saw Priscus. He took a surreptitious handful of something I rather fancied for myself at that moment, and washed it down with a swig from his flask. He smiled as he might at a public execution and blew me a kiss.

Theophanes, standing far behind him, seemed nervous. Next to him, I could see a look of horror on Martin's face that outdid anything he'd yet managed. It was as if he expected the dome of the church to cave in on us.

Swathed in purple and gold, Phocas sat in his full hieratic mode. The house might belong to God. But he was its Master. For him, all was as it ought to be.

I felt the full blast of the expectant hush around me as I pulled open the heavy bound volume of the Gospels before me.

'My reading today' – my voice caught with sudden nerves. I hadn't realised how the acoustics in that place would magnify and deepen it. I pulled myself together.

'My reading today', I began again with forced confidence, 'is' – I looked down at the page that had fallen open – 'from the First Letter of St Paul to the Corinthians.'

I swallowed and began: 'Though I speak with the tongues of men and of angels, and have not charity . . .'

Oh Jesus! I thought with a stab of terror, I couldn't read the words in Greek. The lamp in front of me wasn't up to showing the tiny script. Besides, it was of the crabbed, ecclesiastical type I'd always left to Martin when I came across it in the Patriarchal Library.

I squinted as I recited the opening clause. It was useless. I couldn't read a fucking word. It was as if a spider had crawled out of an inkpot.

I paused. I swallowed. I resisted the temptation to stage a fainting fit. Instead I improvised, continuing in Latin:

'*Factus sum uelut aes sonans aut cymbalum tinniens.*

'*Et si habuero prophetiam et nouerim mysteria omnia et omnem scientiam et habuero omnem fidem ita ut montes transferam caritatem autem non habuero . . .*'

I got no further.

'Blasphemy! Blasphemy!' a voice screamed behind me. 'The Great Church is become as Babylon!'

Fucking cheek! I thought. I wasn't doing that badly. As for the Latin, I was Acting Permanent Legate to His Holiness in Rome. If I chose to read the lesson in the Empire's official language, that was my right.

I turned to see what the commotion was.

A young deacon had broken free from the throng around the altar and was rushing up the steps to my lectern. Knife in hand, his face carried a look of wild fanaticism. He reminded me of the monks I'd occasionally seen running about the city when they'd heard there was heretical talk in the Baths.

'The Latin dog blasphemes!'

A few elderly clerics had made an effort to restrain the maniac. Of course, they'd failed. I heard the clatter of armed men over by the Emperor. But they'd have to push their way through a sea of bodies to get to me.

I was on my own.

I waited at the top of the bronze steps, ready to overpower the man. He had a knife, but I was much larger.

It was now that I got a closer look at the knife. It shone dull in the light of the overhead lamps. Some dark gel was dripping from its point. It had been steeped in poison. One nick of that thing, and I'd be a dead man.

'Let the Temple be cleansed!' the deacon bellowed as he reached the top of the steps.

'God help me!' I cried in terror. Would there be no limit to the horrors of the past few days? Unless I fancied jumping twenty feet, there was no way off this lectern but past some maniac who was flailing about like the scythe on a war chariot's wheel.

'Fuck you to hell, Greekling shit!' I screamed at him with a recovery of nerve. I hurled the Gospels at his head. They missed, but caught him on the shoulder. He wheeled back. For a moment, I thought he'd fall backwards down the steps. But he caught himself on the rail with his free arm.

The Gospels crashed heavily on to the stone floor, where the binding burst into a cascade of parchment sections.

'Die, Blasphemer!' the deacon cried with a stab in my direction.

He missed me, thank God. But he did open a great rent in my lovely new robe. As he came at me again, all wild eyes and slashing knife, I found time to observe that I wasn't having the best of luck in this City where clothing was concerned. I'd had to hand over a pile of gold for that purple border, and I wasn't sure it would be chargeable to expenses.

There was nothing else for it. Through the gash in my robe, I pulled out my sword. In normal circumstances, I wouldn't have thought to bring it into church. But you tell me, dear reader, when I'd last seen any of those.

I pulled it out and thrust it at the deacon's body. It glanced off, the hole I ripped in his robe showing the chainmail underneath. For a moment, he gripped again at the rail to get his balance. Then he was back at me.

I finally got him down the steps with a knock of the sword handle to his face. Anyone else would have paused to wipe away the blood that gushed from the wound I opened on his forehead. Not this lunatic deacon. His mouth foamed. His eyes glared at me with pupils contracted almost to the size of pinheads.

He didn't even cease his cries of 'Blasphemy! Blasphemy!' They echoed horribly round the now silent church.

As he started up the steps again, I took the sword in both hands and swung hard. With a dull thud and a recoil that almost pitched me off the lectern on to the floor far below, I had it half through his neck and deep into his collarbone.

And it would have gone further but for the mail collar.

The deacon crashed sideways against the rail. His eyes bulged, the pupils now expanding as they looked fixedly into mine. He opened his mouth for one last cry but in place of any human sound, there was only a gurgling from his severed windpipe.

Blood gushed from his neck in dying spurts. But, still in command, he stepped backwards in good order on to the lower steps. I thought he might be so far gone in piety and whatever he was on, he'd try another slash with his knife.

I was taking no further chances. I kicked him hard in the stomach and sent him spinning to the foot of the steps, where he fell in a now silent heap. The knife, though still in his hand, was underneath the body.

'And may God have mercy on your soul,' I rasped, suddenly recalling where and who I was.

As I reached up to mop the blood from my face, a most annoying shower of gold leaf dropped down on to my robe.

'That was a most lucky blow, my darling Alaric,' said Priscus. 'Was it not a Sign from Heaven that you never got to say "*nihil sum*"?'

He stood at the foot of the lectern steps with a couple of armed guards for company and aimed a kick at the motionless body. 'A shame you had to finish him off, even so,' he said. 'It would have been interesting to watch an interrogation according to your own custom. As it is, we'll never know who put him up to this.'

'I quite agree, my dear Priscus,' I said, breathing hard. 'But' – I quoted – ' "Not all that men desire do they obtain." '

He smiled, nodding acknowledgement of the line from Euripides. It eclipsed his finishing the verse from St Paul.

I sheathed my sword and walked down to Priscus. Blood had turned the bronze steps as slippery as ice. I had to grip hard on the rail to avoid falling.

I looked around. The church was absolutely silent. The congregation stood exactly as I'd last seen it. Several hands were still raised in prayer. Some of the people in the front row of worshippers were splashed with blood.

So was I. More importantly, the slash in my robe was marked all the way down by a dark smear of poison. I'd have to be careful as I took it off.

Behind me, the Patriarch lay nestled in the arms of one of the younger clerics. He had passed out from the shock. An elderly bishop fanned him gently with one of the leaves from the Gospels.

There was a sound of quiet weeping.

Now the Emperor was on his feet. 'This has been a day of considerable sadness, my Dear Brothers in Christ,' he said, enunciating slowly.

All heads turned in his direction.

'However, unless anyone has anything to say to the contrary, I suggest that the service should continue. We can at least commit the body of our Dear Brother the Permanent Legate to God with some attempt at decency.'

Phocas pointed at one of the clerics who was still on his feet.

'Might I ask if My Lord Bishop of Nicaea has any objection to officiating in place of His Excellency the Patriarch?'

44

'It was fucking brill – the way you all but took his head off! I haven't seen better since my fighting days.'

His regalia stripped off and piled on the floor, Phocas spoke in Latin. He refilled my cup and took another draught from his own.

'Fucking brill!' he repeated. 'Just like the good old days, I'd say.'

It was later in the evening. We sat in the palace together with Theophanes. Martin had been carried home under armed guard. I'd insisted the slaves should double-bar the door to my suite and sit with him while he tried to sleep.

None of the guards nor any other outsiders were to be admitted.

I'd again resisted the offer of drugs from Priscus, but Theophanes had fixed me up with something nice from his own box of potions and berries. I don't think anything could have wholly refreshed me this far into what seemed the longest two days of my life, but I was able for the moment to sit drinking and taking a coherent part in the discussion.

Now in jolly mood again, the Emperor had told Theophanes to investigate what had happened in the Great Church. That was a hard one. The Greek Patriarch had suffered a stroke during the disturbance.

It was hoped he would recover his speech by the morning. In the meantime, the other clerics were running about like a flock of terrified sheep.

'The deacon', said Theophanes, 'was one Dioscorides, an Alexandrian of rising fame as a preacher. His life till tonight had, so far as I can tell, been blameless. His only eccentricity seems to have been a prejudice against the male use of cosmetics.'

'A little too much premeditation there', Phocas broke in, 'for the gold leaf to have sent the fucker mad – we'd all have overlooked the Latin.'

'I agree,' Theophanes replied. 'The knife was steeped in something highly toxic. One of the slaves who helped young Alaric out of his robe managed to smear some of it on his forearm. He's already in a sweating fever. The doctors say he is unlikely to survive the night.

'As for Dioscorides, I believe he was high on a drug called *ganjika*. This is used in Egypt as a harmless sleeping preparation. In high doses, though, it can cause delusions and wild excitement. I would say that he was a lone assassin, prompted by a dislike of the Western Church. But there are certain attendant circumstances that do not incline me to that view.'

There was a slight pause after the words 'attendant circumstances' and Theophanes shot me the briefest glance, before continuing:

'Your Majesty has already remarked on the degree of preparation. There is also the question of how Dioscorides knew he would be able to get close to Alaric. Had we not changed the order of service at the last moment, he would have observed the proceedings as a member of the Imperial Party. How could Dioscorides have known that Alaric would be alone and exposed?'

'I ordered the change,' said Phocas. 'You took the orders and passed them on in the church. Who else could have known?'

'That, sir,' said Theophanes, 'is something I will investigate in the morning.'

Phocas nodded.

We moved on to the question of the Permanent Legate's murder and what I'd been able to find out since our meeting earlier in the day. Phocas also showed much interest in the death of Authari. He'd already had a brief report from Priscus and wanted amplification of the main points.

There was little to report on either front. I'd now interviewed everyone in the Legation I could lay hands on. The mass of notes Martin had taken added to what I knew already, but nothing likely to transform the investigation. It would have been useful to know where Demetrius had got himself to. I'd had the Legation combed by the Black Agents once it was clear that he was missing. No one without a permit from me or Theophanes had entered or left the Legation and certainly no one matching any reasonable description of Demetrius.

As for the Permanent Legate, the bloody robe he was wearing had been discovered in an out-of-the-way latrine. But the body had vanished.

The Black Agents had taken my instructions literally. They'd spent the day ripping the Permanent Legate's room apart. The whole corridor looked like a demolition site.

But no hiding place had been found. No weapon of murder. Even the poison cup was a mystery. It matched nothing in the kitchens or elsewhere in the Legation. It had probably been brought in from outside.

And what about those silent monks who tended the garden? Someone claimed to have seen one or two of them around even though they never worked on Sundays. I needed to see their abbot about this.

'As for the Permanent Legate's last known movements,' I concluded, 'I only know that he was visited on his last afternoon by His Excellency the Illustrious Theophanes.'

'That was while everyone else was enjoying the races,' Theophanes hurriedly explained. He flashed me a brief but intense glare to keep me in careful limits. 'I was on business for the Master of the Offices, trying to tempt His Excellency the Permanent Legate to attend dinner at the palace.'

'You did meet the Permanent Legate?' I asked, playing along. 'Or did you only deal with him through Demetrius?'

'Of course I met him,' Theophanes said with a careless wave. 'A low creature like Demetrius might keep you away, and even senior messengers from the Ministry. No one – the Augustus excepted – is indisposed when I grace him with a visit!'

'How did he seem when you spoke with him?' I asked, deciding not to gratify him with an apology.

'He was polite but distant,' Theophanes said. 'He spoke of you – I regret to say in rather slighting tones, for all I insisted on your many excellences. He called you, if you'll pardon the words, a drunken, tow-headed barbarian promoted out of place.'

With a temporary loss of control, I flushed red with anger. The fucking cheek of it! Here was a dirty old priest, with a really low taste in porn – and he dared to sneer at a person of *my* quality? If any incentive remained to find the killer, it was only so that I might shake him by the hand.

Phocas saw my discomfiture and laughed. 'I'm told', he said with a stretch of his arms, 'there is no wine in England. Can this be true?'

'Vines do grow in Kent, sir,' I answered with a forced recovery of composure. 'I believe the Province of Britain did export wine in its final days. But my people prefer beer.'

'Well,' said Phocas with a flourish of his cup, 'drink deep while you can.'

Irrespective of any letter to Ethelbert, I had no intention of ever going back to the place. For all I cared, Richborough itself could fall into the sea. But I drank up as I was told and accepted the offered refill.

I turned back to Theophanes. 'Did the Permanent Legate show any fear for his safety?' I asked.

'None whatever,' said Theophanes.

He turned the question: 'Had you any reason to think the Legation unsafe?'

Was that a smile lurking behind the lead paste?

'The doorkeepers were drugged,' I answered. 'There was a dinner last night at the Legation. My own people shared in the pork, but kept mostly to the beer. This being said, the wine served at the feast doesn't seem to have been contaminated. I've had all the opened wine there sent off for testing by an apothecary of my own choice. He'll report back sooner than your own people at the Ministry,' I added hastily to Theophanes. The tiredness was coming back and I was beginning to wander in my speech.

Phocas saved me. 'You've had a long day,' he said. 'Go home to bed. Continue with your investigation tomorrow. See me again the day after next.

'Theophanes has already had the crowds cleared from the square outside the Legation. With guards posted inside and out, you'll sleep more secure than I shall here in the palace.'

O sleep! What a glorious thing it can be. I'd been looking forward to the moment when I could slide safe and warm into my own bed. There was a brief interval of joy as I sank into the mattress and felt the smooth silk of the sheets. Then the soft blackness swept over me, and I was gone from the world.

45

I woke to a smell of frying sausages. It was late in the morning, though the shuttered window gave me no indication of the time. I had the most awful headache, and white flashes attended my every move as I staggered out of bed. The scabs over my wounds had come off in the night, and I'd bled into the bedclothes. Pulling myself free of the sticky silk added to the chorus of pains.

I shambled round in the light that poured through a single chink in the shutters, looking for some clothes. Then I gave up. I unbolted and dragged the door open.

'Authari,' I almost called, before remembering all that had happened.

'Oh fuck!' I groaned as the horrors of the past day or so came crowding into my mind. I didn't even try to pretend that they might have been a dream.

I called for Martin. He was already waiting outside the door with Maximin in his arms. Gutrune, he said, was still overcome by the death of Authari. In the past few months, she had lost the father of her child and the child itself. Now she had lost the man who, Martin told me, was planning to ask me to sell her to him so they could be married.

Poor cow! I thought. I'd see her right if Maximin made it to his first birthday.

For the moment, though, there was work to be done. I took up the jug of wine Martin had placed on a table in the corridor and drained it without acknowledgement of the little cup set beside it. Too late, I found it was the sour, greenish stuff favoured by the Greek higher classes and I nearly choked on it. But it was enough to bring me back to a pale semblance of humanity.

'Martin,' I said, taking Maximin into my own arms and feeling almost ready to bask in the radiance of his smile – 'Martin, we need to press on with the investigation. I think we should concentrate on finding out how that bastard Agathius got into my room.'

'I quite agree, sir,' said Martin. 'I suggest first, however, that a bath might be in order. I've had one prepared. All else aside, I'm afraid to say that Maximin has had an accident.'

That he had. With Gutrune out of action, no one had changed him, and the tight hug I'd given the boy had squirted a stream of yellow shit all over my belly and legs.

'Jesus and the Virgin!' I groaned, now noticing the smell. I handed him straight back to Martin, who held him out at arm's length.

'You'll remember that the main gate was unbarred when we got down there,' I said in Celtic, 'but the doorkeepers were drugged. That makes it fair to assume my attacker was let in as part of a conspiracy that involved people trusted by the doorkeepers.'

Martin stood back to let me go first on to the balcony from my bedroom.

'You may be right,' he said. 'But might it not be that some outsider crept in and hid during the day, until he could drug their wine unobserved, and then open the gate?'

'Possible,' I replied, 'but not likely. Remember – except it was drugged, their wine was the same as that served to everyone else in the Legation household that night. That makes it most likely that the wine was drugged by whoever served it, and that he was known to the doorkeepers. Of course, we can settle this when we speak to the men directly. Without Priscus around to interfere, we can ask whatever questions we like.'

With Martin keeping hold of my tunic – I was still a little unsteady – I climbed on to the railing and pulled myself up to look at the ledge that ran along to the dome. It was impossible to tell if anyone else had been up there since my escapade in the summer. But the spikes of the railings at the end were now covered in a film of rust. Any intruder would surely have rubbed off patches of this and left traces of their clothing on them.

I could have walked along to inspect these at close quarters but Martin was holding on to me as a sailor his ropes. I jumped back down beside him.

'Agathius didn't come from above,' I said. 'That means he must have come up the stairs from the gardens. Now, since we've never been able to get out of the garden these stairs lead to, it's worth asking how he got into it from the main hall.'

That was a mystery easily solved. When we'd last sat there in the summer, the walls of the garden were lined with thick shrubbery. Now, enough of the leaves had blown off to reveal a small door that had been unbarred from the other side. This led into the much larger central garden, where I'd seen those monks go about their clipping and watering and which, in turn, led to various parts of the main building.

It was now that I saw the previously hidden warren of offices and corridors where the main work of the Legation went on and which had once been the state rooms of the palace. The builders had done a good job with the walls and doors, and had even lowered the ceilings to maintain a sense of proportion. It was the mosaic floors that told the story. Where these had been dug up to make way for new walls, the spaces had been crudely filled with concrete.

I was beginning to learn quite a lot about the work of the Legation. This included handling petitions and arranging loans to the Emperor, setting up appointments with him, and promoting the exchange of information that was too confidential to be conducted through the Exarch's chancery in Ravenna. No wonder the virtual shutting down of the Legation since my arrival had raised so many concerns among those not in the know.

When I had asked for the Permanent Legate's bedroom to be taken apart by the Black Agents I had rather hoped that the rest of the Legation would be subjected to a less thorough inspection. The broken doors and smashed furniture that the Black Agents had left in their wake proved otherwise. Some of the small band of officials and slaves who were busy cleaning up the mess gave me hard looks as we passed. They were doing their best, but restoring any kind of order would take days.

From here, it was a straight walk through the lower storey of the Permanent Legate's suite to the now open door that led into the main hall.

'It was Demetrius,' the elder and apparently less stupid of the doorkeepers told me when I repeated my question. 'Slaves got us the meat. He brung the wine.'

He was able to show me the jug and wooden cups in which the wine had been brought since these had still not been collected owing to the chaos of the previous day. The cups were of the sort I had already seen in the slave quarters of the Legation – the sort, that is, that didn't match the one given to Authari. I handed them to Martin with the request that they be sent to my apothecary for testing.

No point in further questioning. The doorkeepers had settled the one matter on which they were competent to give information. In doing so, they had saved us from a mass of speculation. They claimed not to have seen Demetrius since he had brought the wine and to know nothing more about the Legation than the others since they had both been bought only about a month before my own arrival.

Now, the fact that so much effort had been put into getting at least one intruder through the main gate raised a problem. I'd taken it as fair to assume that there was some alternative way in to the Legation. This would explain how Demetrius and the body of the Permanent Legate had been able to disappear without leaving any trail. What I had now learnt indicated that there was no secret entrance.

'No one has seen him since we were called to the Emperor,' Martin reminded me. 'It may be we were the last to see him.'

As we walked back to the end of the hall, and I prepared to knock on the barred door to my own suite – Radogast would never be able to understand how I was asking to be let back in without having first gone out past him! – the gate of the Legation swung open behind us and Theophanes was carried in. As ever,

Alypius walked beside the chair, a purple bag hanging from his shoulders.

'Ah, there you both are!' Theophanes cried, prodding at the slaves to carry him over to us. He flashed us an almost natural smile. 'I have some progress to report.'

46

Theophanes sat in my office. The little sofa creaked beneath his bulk as he shifted around for comfort. He beamed with genuine pleasure as he looked at the ebony cot from where Maximin stared back with solemn interest.

'No wine for me, as you know,' he said, 'but I have a supply of my *kava* berries. Let us have boiling water brought up, together with a silver jug, and join together in a cup of the brew that cheers but does not inebriate.'

When the slaves had withdrawn, I bolted the door. Then I went out on to the balcony and into my bedroom and bolted the door to that. Just to be thorough, I looked along the ledge.

'I can promise you', I said, coming back into the office, 'we are alone. So long as we keep our voices down – and I speak from experience here – we can't be heard from the corridor. If anyone tries to creep up from the garden, we'll hear the steps creak.'

I sat behind my desk. Martin sat on a low stool to my left. Alypius stood close by the door to the balcony. If a bird so much as landed on the steps, it would be noticed at once.

'A fine set of precautions,' Theophanes observed. 'Persons of our quality should always take advantage of such privacy as can be obtained. I do not think, however, we have much to say that requires total security.'

I smiled, but said nothing.

He called Alypius over to pour two cups of the steaming dark liquid – Martin having excused himself from the novelty with a cup of apple juice.

This done, Alypius went to his bag and drew out a sheaf of

documents. One of these, I could see from across the room, carried the seal of the Greek Patriarch.

'The office of His Holiness remains in some disorder,' Theophanes explained, 'but I have managed to procure the personal file of Dioscorides. Combined with his security file, held in the Ministry, a most interesting picture emerges.'

It *was* an interesting picture. As said, the man was an Egyptian. But, after completing his studies in Alexandria, he'd been attached to the small permanent mission which the Alexandrian Patriarch kept up in Carthage. There, he'd learned Punic – reasonably similar to Coptic – and made a nuisance of himself as a preacher to the common people of the country districts. By his endless and heated denunciations, he had revived past heresies and re-awakened people's fears of them. From there he'd been sent packing by the Exarch, and had turned up in Constantinople about eighteen months earlier. You can imagine for yourself his maniac solicitation of the rabble here.

What Theophanes had also discovered was that Dioscorides had an elder brother who had attached himself to the Heraclian side in Egypt. He was now a bishop in some out-of-the-way town in Upper Egypt that he would never have to visit, and was, so far as could be known, with Heraclius himself just down the Straits at Abydos.

'Well,' said I, leaning back in my chair for a stretch, 'let us proceed to the matter of Demetrius. Since he's nowhere to be found, I think it most likely he was involved in the Permanent Legate's murder. If so, he also helped remove the body. If so, he also murdered Authari. We have learned already that he has a talent for serving doctored wine.'

I leaned forward again to ease the pressure on my sore back. Martin had assured me there was nothing unpleasant to worry about, and the *kava* berries were quickening my wits very nicely.

'Is there anything on him in the Ministry files?' I asked. 'The drugs aside, what motivated Dioscorides is easily guessed. But Demetrius? He was the Permanent Legate's personal secretary in all senses. It now seems he was also working for Heraclius. I imagine his file must be as fat as a Syrian whore.'

'Not really,' said Alypius, speaking in place of Theophanes and looking rather nervous. 'He is an Armenian, taken directly into the service of His Excellency.'

'An Armenian?' I said, with a bright smile. 'That would explain the weak Latin, yet also the poverty of his Greek. Can you say when he arrived in Constantinople?'

'He appeared shortly after His Excellency had sent all the regular officials and slaves out of the city,' Alypius replied.

'I've had Priscus circulate his description to everyone it may concern,' I said. 'Let's hope that he is found soon – and preferably brought to me in one piece. I think my instructions were reasonably clear, even to the Black Agents.

'Every mystery involving the Permanent Legate seems to begin with Demetrius. With or without the help of Priscus, I'm sure I shall find much to discuss with him when he does reappear. Such a shame, though, don't you think, that there is so much on file about a relative nobody like Dioscorides, and so little on a man who has for months now been Number Two to the Pope's representative?'

'Have you not considered', Theophanes answered, with a look at Alypius, 'that there might be a supernatural element to the killing?'

I smiled again and chose my words. 'Theophanes,' I said, 'there are undoubtedly miracles on the record. Most undoubtedly, there are those recorded in the Holy Scriptures of Our Lord Jesus Christ and of His Apostles.' I thought for a moment to stop and cross myself. But it might have spoiled the cool sarcasm of my tone. I continued: 'But in our own corrupted age, we cannot accept that a miracle has occurred until we have exhausted all other natural possibilities.

'Let me assure you,' I finished, 'that the Permanent Legate was killed by a natural person. I don't yet know why he did it. But I think I know how it was done and who did it. And I'll further assure you that – unless I'm stopped by naked force – I'll know within the next few days *why* it was done.'

Theophanes looked again at Alypius. His face had taken on the stiff tension of a gambler at the races. Looking out of his depth, Martin sat very still.

I turned to the boxes of confidential files piled up on the far side of the room from Maximin.

'Martin went properly through these this morning,' I said. 'We've both since had another look. As Martin thought yesterday, the Permanent Legate's papers have been carefully sorted. Many things are missing that we reasonably believe ought to be there. We are missing all correspondence for this year with the Dispensator in Rome. Also all correspondence whatever between you and His Late Excellency since his arrival in the city the year before last. We are certain of this last correspondence because the empty filing racks still carry the inked labels of description. This gives us further reason to believe that the sifting of papers was both hurried and unpremeditated. Given luck and boldness, murder is easy. It's the attendant circumstances that are harder to control.'

As I spoke, I could see that Theophanes was beginning to sweat under the paint. For the first time ever, I'd broken his composure.

'What I have, though' – I held up my hand for silence – 'what I have is *this*.'

I took a small sheet of papyrus from the file that Martin held open for me. The pattern of folds and weakening in one of the corners told that it had once been pinned to other sheets. Now, sliced in half down the middle, it had been reused on the back.

'This is interesting for what it says on both sides,' I announced to Theophanes. 'The reverse of the sheet carries a list written, I think, by His Excellency himself. If so, he was dealing with some very large sums of money – far more than the Legation accounts indicate were at his disposal.

'You will see references to my own banking house. I may visit Baruch in the next few days, but will not trouble him with this. He's a banker and – until recently, at least – a Jew. I am convinced that even three days with Priscus under the Ministry would not reveal what services he provides his other customers. And such is as it ought to be.

'The sheet was used originally, however, for the draft minutes of a meeting in Ephesus. You will see that this took place in April. I

295

wonder why His Excellency might have made a spring visit to Ephesus? And who else might have attended?'

I asked the question with a lightness that no other face in the room reflected. Theophanes was on his feet. He snatched furiously at the sheet as I stood over him with it. He looked at the list. He turned to Alypius. Eyes blazing, he launched into a flood of blame in their own bleak language.

Alypius defended himself as best he could. But Theophanes was almost out of control with rage. He even forgot to keep his voice down and every so often his gaze wandered to the open door to the balcony. It was only with extreme effort that he pulled himself together and turned back to face me.

He looked at the upper side of the sheet and I could see traces of anger on his face under the paint give way to relief.

'But my dear Alaric,' he said with a return to Greek, 'you have only the right-hand side of the sheet. There are no names here. As for the date, this could be any April – the regnal year is missing.'

He spoke now with forced lightness, but his hands shook as he dropped the sheet on to my desk.

'Of course, you are right,' I said, enjoying myself. 'I really should have seen that for myself. As for what I can read of the minutes, they do seem to concern matters of doctrine that were quite within His Excellency's competence. I cannot see why he had to travel to Ephesus to discuss whether the Lombard King might be won over to Orthodoxy. But what I can see of his probable comments is most uplifting. Perhaps the sheet is useless after all. Shall I throw it away?'

'Do allow me to take that duty from you,' said Theophanes with the glimmering return of his charm. 'It would never do to disturb the serene tidiness of your office.'

He took the sheet back and buried it in his robe. Then he sat down and, with still shaking hands, sipped at his *kava* juice. Martin gave me an even more scared and uncomprehending look.

At that moment Maximin began to cry. I turned to Martin with a sigh. 'Can you see if Gutrune is yet up to changing some shitty clothes?'

But as Martin rose, so too did Theophanes.

'In one of my numerous pasts,' he said, 'I was an acting nursemaid. Nothing would give me greater pleasure than to bring comfort to your most beautiful son. If Martin would be so kind as to fetch fresh clothes and hot scented water for my hands . . .'

47

Maximin again lay in his cot, happy in his fresh clothes. For all I knew, Theophanes hadn't touched a baby in fifty years. But he hadn't lost an ounce of a very considerable skill. He could have given lessons to Gutrune on how to clean shitty bottoms and then tie the clothes on.

Martin and Alypius had danced attendance with bowls of water and lengths of fine cloth. Then Theophanes had spent an age praising the boy's present and future qualities. He had evidently enjoyed himself with Maximin but it was also clear that he'd been eager for any excuse to change the subject. But if I was willing to let him recover his composure, there was much more ground to cover.

'Now, Theophanes,' I opened, 'let us deal with this matter of an apparently insoluble murder. We have the Permanent Legate's body in a locked room, with neither weapon nor murderer. I have no doubt you were highly pleased with yourself when you set it up. But I am not one of those two-legged sheep wandering about the streets of this city.

'The main enemy of truth is not ignorance. If perceived, that can be the beginning of wisdom. The real enemy is false assumptions.'

I leaned forward and dropped my voice lower still. I now spoke in Latin.

'What reason,' I asked Martin, 'have we to believe that the Permanent Legate's room was bolted on the inside?'

'I watched three powerful Northerners smashing the door in,' he answered in a whisper. 'That surely tells us something about the room's security.'

'It tells you that the room was secured,' I said. 'It doesn't tell you that the door was secured from the inside. We both saw Demetrius

298

fussing with his keys. Can you remember how many times he pushed them in and out of the lock? I think it was twice. Before that, Legation slaves had been trying to get in. Once would have unlocked a door unbarred on the inside. Twice would have locked it again for us to have a go.

'And when we did break in, did you bother to check which way the bolt was drawn? I know I should have. But I didn't. By the time I realised what must have happened, the Black Agents had done their work, and it was too late to tell.

'Let us assume, though, that the door wasn't bolted when we broke it down – that it was only locked – and that part of the mystery is solved. Demetrius drugged the doorkeepers. He let Agathius in. Perhaps they killed the Permanent Legate together. Agathius then came looking for me.

'The Permanent Legate's body lay undisturbed until Demetrius went back into the room and made a commotion just before we returned from dumping the now unfortunate Agathius, and then came out and locked the door. Everyone accepted that the murder had taken place later than it did. That would explain why the body was already stiff when Martin and I moved it. It would also explain why it was removed after it was known that I'd called for a medical examination.

'Do you not think, my most Magnificent Theophanes, this provides a natural explanation of your alleged miracle? You will pardon me if all this escaped my notice yesterday. As you can imagine, I was somewhat overcome by the pressure of events – and by the drugs you had Alypius slip me in the Circus.'

Theophanes reached up and dabbed gently at his face. He looked down at a shaking and now white finger tip.

'Was it out of *some* regard for my safety', I asked ironically, 'that you tried to ensure I'd not fall asleep that night? Or was it because you'd set Agathius up? You had him kill the Permanent Legate. Then he was supposed to come round and finish me off. You made very sure I'd be in bed, by twice getting me away from Priscus. But you also made reasonably sure that it was Agathius whose corpse lay on my bedroom floor.

'And bearing in mind the contents of the letter you gave him to plant by me, you knew there'd be no fuss about a body. That would have left you with a dead Silas and a mystery that no one could have unravelled. Isn't that how it happened, Theophanes?'

I leaned back again in my chair and twisted slightly to deal with the itching of my sore back.

'Would you think it a breach of our friendship,' I asked, with a wiggle of my index finger, 'if I were to ask you what the fuck is going on?'

Theophanes swallowed and looked at Alypius. If Martin could have squeezed himself through a gap in the floorboards, I'm sure he'd have stirred from his utter immobility.

'Aelric,' he said, moving out of Latin, 'do you recall how dexterously I juggled those heads in the tent of the Great One? That could stand as a metaphor for how well I had arranged matters in the city. But any juggler will tell you how, on account of some overlooked defect in his objects, he will need to step sideways to avoid dropping something. He must then step back to catch those things that remain in their appointed course. Before long, his performance will have been destabilised. His efforts must now be turned to a less elegant set of improvisations as he endeavours to regain his original equilibrium.'

'If I can decode your utterance, Theophanes,' I said with a bleak smile, 'you've lost control of your plot, and you're now having to make things up as you go along. Any chance you might care to explain yourself in plain Greek?'

Visibly recovering, Theophanes was for the moment inspecting his face in a little bronze mirror and touching up the paint.

'It was not my choice', he began, 'to put you in charge of the investigation. I had been expecting Priscus to handle that. He could safely have been left to rack his way through the Legation staff while everyone else agreed on some demonic intervention. And yes – it was at least partly from the great love I bear you that I made sure the odds would be moved in your favour. Luck may be a philosophical absurdity. But you are possessed of it well enough to use whatever improved odds are given you.

'This being said, I am not at liberty to tell you more than you have uncovered for yourself. There are matters that cannot be revealed to you without the gravest possible consequences, as I have already explained. Let me assure you, however, that I had no part in the murder of your freedman. I am sensible to my own debt to him, and I truly deplore his murder. Beyond guessing that it was Demetrius who served the poison, I cannot say more. And do not ask what has become of the body.'

He ignored my reply and continued: 'I must warn you that if you have any regard for any person in this room, you will say nothing more of your most interesting theory. You have been appointed to investigate the murder of His Excellency the Permanent Legate. This does not mean you are required to solve the case before Heraclius arrives in the city.

'Please rely on Priscus for as much help as he offers you. Do not continue with your own speculations. They will serve no useful purpose.'

I looked over at Maximin, who was now sleeping peacefully, then turned back to Theophanes.

'What chance', I asked, 'of another murder attempt the moment I set foot outside the Legation?'

'None,' he assured me. 'With both Agathius and Dioscorides out of the way, Heraclius has lost his only men of any ability in the City. In your new eminence, you are above any law that bars the carrying of arms in the street. I have no doubt you can handle any casual attempt that may be made against you.

'Stay inside the Legation as much as you can,' he said with quiet emphasis. 'Wait for the moment when the blockade has been lifted and you – and yours – can make your escape.'

As Theophanes made his excuses for getting away, I poured out the remnants of the pot. Since no one else wanted any, I took the lot for myself and crunched on pulverised berries.

'My dearest friend Theophanes,' I said as Martin helped fasten his cloak, 'I have business myself at the Ministry later today. Depending on how long Priscus or his secretary have need of me, might I have the pleasure of a visit to your office?'

48

'How could you do that to the old eunuch? Don't you realise what he could do to us?'

I stopped and turned to Martin. He was still pale and shaking. A passer-by, finding himself between us, stood smartly back and bowed his apology to me before continuing his journey.

At first, those tailors had disappointed me. 'No new clerical robes possible before the middle of next month,' they'd insisted. This was a shame, as the robe cut up by that demented cleric Dioscorides wasn't safe to wear – the slave had died, just as Theophanes said he would. But they had managed to fit me into some plain senatorial robes they had picked up at an auction of confiscated goods.

I was wearing one now in the street, and looked pretty lush in the white silk with a purple border when I stopped to admire myself in a shop window.

From the wording of the Imperial Warrant, the grant of senatorial status was independent of my position as Acting Permanent Legate. If I ever got out of the city alive, I'd have more to take back to Gretel than an adopted foundling.

'Martin,' I replied in the Celtic of his question, 'I had to interrogate Theophanes in the best approximation we'd get to privacy. Short of putting him on the rack, there was nothing I wasn't willing to try to get far less information than he eventually gave us. Now, do stand out of the way. There's a munitions cart coming that looks set on splashing mud all over you.'

At first, I'd felt cautious about taking to the streets after Theophanes' words of warning, but the Greek Patriarch was failing and the churches were laying on special services. As I'd had something to do with his stroke, I was wondering if I might collect any of the blame.

I needn't have worried. That witticism of Priscus about how I'd never got to the 'I am nothing' of the reading from St Paul had been circulated round the city. I wasn't just a favourite of Saint Victorinus; everyone was now saying I had God Almighty Himself on my side.

I can't say how many benedictions I'd had asked of me once out of the Legation. But I can say that I wasn't once stopped at any of the barricades going up at street corners and made to show identification. Whether in Green livery or Blue, the pickets just stood smartly back and let us both through. This meant that, while it was on the far side of the city, getting to the Monastery of St John Chrysostom took only half the time Martin had set aside.

A grey building, abutting directly on to the Golden Horn, the monastery stood in one of the outlying commercial districts. In one of those slow, semi-tidal movements that carry business around a great city like Constantinople, the smarter establishments had long since moved towards the Bosphorus side. What remained were mostly the second-hand markets. Crowded with Jews and un-washed paupers, the streets might have been in another city. But, as you ought now to realise, Constantinople is a world in itself – a city of many cities.

'Your Excellency will surely not object to the removal of his sword within this House of God,' the clerk said, rising from his bow as I stepped through the opened gate.

'Of course not,' I replied, reaching for the buckle. 'I'd have been surprised had you asked anything else.'

I passed my sword to a monk who'd been washing the floor. He put his mop down and bowed silently before hanging it on a peg for outer clothes.

As we passed down a shabby corridor that stank of boiled cabbage, I wondered how many monks there could be in this Order. The monastery must have been bigger than the Legation, but was absolutely silent.

Unless their foundations exist to bother God in earnest, abbots in the West tend towards the jolly. Think of my dear Benedict here in Jarrow. The Abbot of this monastery sat slumped at his desk, glowering in the Greek fashion into his huge, scruffy beard.

'Reverend Father,' I opened in my most courtly manner, 'I represent His Holiness the Patriarch of Rome, and come with the full authority of His Most Sacred Imperial Majesty—'

I got no further. The Abbot continued looking down at his desk, breathing hard. Instead, the clerk who'd brought me in struck up:

'Your Excellency must be aware that the monks of this Order are under a vow of perpetual silence. The Reverend Father cannot possibly respond to anything you say.'

'What?' I asked, astonished.

The clerk took up an oratorical pose and continued: 'Our Patron Saint said everything that needed to be said. He said it as well as could be said. It would be a disservice to Him if the monks devoted to His Most Glorious and Eloquent Memory were to try speaking for themselves. They may use their organs of speech to give quiet thanks to the Heavenly Father. But there can be no profane use.'

This was a novel excuse for not trying to speak proper Greek. It was a bit of a conversation stopper, though.

I smiled and tried again:

'I would ask the Reverend Father to consider that, in the fullest possible sense, I represent the successor of Saint Peter Himself. Our Lord and Saviour said to him: "And I will give unto thee the keys of the kingdom of heaven: and whatsoever thou shalt bind on earth shall be bound in heaven: and whatsoever thou shalt loose on earth shall be loosed in heaven."

'In virtue of this,' I continued, 'I release you from your vow for the purpose of my audience with you.'

At this, the Abbot looked up. I thought for a moment he'd open his mouth and scream obscenities before attacking me. Instead, he clasped his dirty fingers harder together and looked back down.

'We are aware that His Holiness of Rome stands at the head of all the Patriarchs,' the clerk replied smoothly. 'By law, he has primacy of place. And you have full authority on his behalf to make such a release. However' – the clerk was beginning to enjoy himself – 'Constantinople is not Rome or the West. You are within the jurisdiction of another Patriarch. Any communication from His Holiness in Rome must be passed through the office of our own Patriarch, who will, I have no doubt, be pleased in due course to send it down for our own miserable attention.'

Dear me – how very troublesome that the Greek Patriarch was indisposed!

I tried yet again: 'Then you will surely accept that I speak also with the authority of our Most Sacred Emperor. I need to ask questions of the Reverend Father. He would not wish to impede the urgent business of the Empire?'

'Indeed not!' the clerk exclaimed, raising his hands in mock horror. 'We are loyal citizens of the Empire. As such, we must without question obey every lawful command of His Majesty. If we choose not to obey commands unlawful to our faith, we are still obliged as citizens to stretch our necks meekly forward for the sword of execution. But we are convinced that His Most Sacred Majesty would never issue an unlawful command. You might therefore wish to return to him to seek a clarification of your warrant.'

I gave up on the Abbot. It was hard to imagine how he could run a monastery without opening his mouth. But there was no shaking their story in the time I was willing to give them before Heraclius broke into the city and the murder investigation was redundant.

'Then perhaps you, sir, might be able to assist me,' I said to the clerk. 'There are several monks from your Order who with great kindness and diligence have been looking after the garden at my Legation. The last time they were definitely there was on the day before His Excellency the Permanent Legate was brutally slain. I appreciate that they cannot answer any questions put to them with regard to what they might have seen that day. But it would be most useful if I could have their names and if I could at least see their faces.'

'I do regret', the clerk replied in a voice that sounded only just the wrong side of genuine, 'that I am not at liberty to comment on any aspect of our internal management. Only the Reverend Father can do that.'

I looked again at the Abbot. Had I misjudged him? Was that anger he was suppressing, or the urge to burst out laughing?

'That wasn't very productive,' said Martin in Celtic. We stood in a second-hand bookshop that I hadn't yet seen. It was coming on to rain, and I'd decided to take shelter there until a chair could be procured.

'On the contrary,' I said, 'it was most productive. I fail to see how Demetrius could have slipped out of the Legation unless dressed as one of these monks. It may be the same with his accomplice. My suspicion that he is inside those walls isn't yet confirmed. But it has been strengthened.'

'But, surely,' Martin asked, 'if he thinks you know that, he'll now move on.'

'Look over there,' I said, pointing at a Black Agent who was trying without much success to look inconspicuous in a doorway. 'I've had one stationed near every known entrance to the monastery. Demetrius might get out through some hidden tunnel. But with Black Agents combing the city for him, there's nowhere else for him to go.

'What I do next is get a permit out of Theophanes or the Emperor for a search. Give me Demetrius and I'll have the truth out of him. Then I'll pass him to Priscus to die under questioning.'

I turned to the bookseller. 'Now, you listen here, my good man,' I said, back in Greek and holding up a battered, crumbling roll of papyrus, 'I know exactly how much these old things are worth. For this and the five others I'll give you one quarter *solidus*. I'm doing you a favour to take them off your hands. Have you bothered opening any of them to see what loathsome blasphemy they contain? Sell them to me, and I will compose a refutation of their contents before destroying them. Keep them, and I will denounce you to the Prefect.'

The bookseller sniffed at my threat and told me that he might have other things of interest to me in his back rooms. He'd picked up a senator's entire library at auction. He shuffled away, in the certain knowledge that I'd follow him.

As we haggled over the price of what I had found, Martin darted around to try and stop one of the chairs. But I was hardly thinking of the rain now coming down in sheets. I was thinking even less of the investigation.

As I pulled out roll after roll – no modern books here with pages bound in sections – the bookseller raised his prices. I just couldn't keep the look of greed off my face. When I got to Porphyry's banned attack on the Christian Faith he began demanding a solidus per roll.

But you should never not buy a book. You might never see it again. I negotiated hard, but I did so from an obviously weak position. In the end I got everything for twenty-five solidi, and the bookseller threw in as a freebie some of the anti-Christian writings of Celsus – one of the last big Epicureans, you know – that I'd already seen in the University Library but hadn't, dared pass over for copying.

The second-hand book trade, the man assured me as I hesitated, was completely unregulated in Constantinople. You could buy what you liked, he said, and no record was taken for the authorities to add to your file. I'd heard this before, but had never bought any books such as these.

By the time I'd arranged for their delivery, Martin was soaked and the chair-men were muttering about their waiting charge. But I was content. I wiped the book dust off my hands on the curtain of the chair and settled back for the journey home through the wet, militarised streets of the city.

Martin might be grumbling as he walked along beside me. But it had turned out so far a very productive day.

49

The light was gone. So too the rainclouds. The stars again looked down from a perfectly clear autumnal sky. The bright crescent of a new moon was climbing among them.

Yet another shift in the wind, and the cold spell had come to an end. Woollen overclothes and a jug of warmed red wine were all that were needed to sit outside. For light, we had an enclosed lantern with glass sides.

Martin had found the roof garden on one of his tours of the Legation. It was a railed square, about ten foot by ten, cut into the roof. You reached it by going to the end of the corridor which ran past the Permanent Legate's rooms. Here, a door just like all the others led not to another room but to a staircase leading straight up.

It was a fine discovery. Sitting up there by day gave an unbroken view of the city. Look in one direction and you could see straight over to the Great Church, and in the other the main public buildings. Look aside from the central area, and you could see right over the city, either to the bleak countryside that stretched beyond the old suburbs outside the land walls, or to the sea and then to the shores of Asia.

At any time of day, it was about as private as could be desired.

Martin was first to break the long silence. 'Antony tells me', he said, 'that every division in Egypt and every Syrian division not actually fighting the Persians has been brought in for the siege.'

He waved over the rooftops at the continued darting of lights on every stretch of water we could see.

'There won't be an assault,' I replied, quoting Priscus. 'The walls are impregnable. The question is when and how the gates will be opened. But this brings us to the matter in hand,' I added,

308

reaching into my bag. I pulled out a single sheet of papyrus, rolled and held in place by a leather band. I handed it to Martin and waited for him to read it.

He looked up, confusion on his face. 'What are you trying to do?' he asked.

'You'll see that it bears both the legatorial seal and that of Theophanes,' I said. 'His seal gets you out of the city. Mine will get you through the Heraclians and across the water to Chalcedon. I've made up a purse for your immediate needs, and I've had Baruch make out drafts in your name.

'I want you and Maximin and Gutrune to be at the Eugenian Gate first thing tomorrow. You'll show this permit to the guards. They'll have had instructions from Theophanes. Then you approach the most senior officer outside the walls for help with the onward journey.

'You get into Chalcedon. If possible, you move on to Nicomedia. You wait for things to settle. If they've gone badly back here, you get yourself, Gutrune and the child to Rome by whatever route you think the least unsafe.'

Martin waved impatiently at me. 'There's pestilence outside the walls,' he said. 'I was looking over them earlier. I could see the bodies being carried away from the main camp – dozens at a time. Will you expose Maximin to that?'

'And do you suppose', I retorted, 'it will be any safer here once I've winkled Demetrius out of that monastery? Theophanes likes me far too much to kill me unless he must, but I am pushing rather close to that "must". Besides, nowhere in the city will be safe once the street-fighting starts.

'You go without me, and you go tomorrow.'

'I won't leave you.' Martin's voice was shrill. 'With no one around you to trust, you'll be dead within a day.'

I sipped at my wine and chose my words. 'Martin,' I said, 'I wish you hadn't raised the question of trust. But now that you have, I really must ask what trust I can have in a man who's been spying on my every move since we arrived in Constantinople? Spying on my every move and reporting it to Theophanes!'

If I'd punched him hard in the stomach, he'd not have looked more winded. I refilled his cup.

'No, Martin – you just sit there and listen to me,' I said, cutting off a weak attempt at interruption. 'I could list dozens of occasions when Theophanes knew what we were about before I told him. But I can't be bothered. I decided a long time ago that you were feeding him information.'

I stood up and looked over the rail at the build-up of forces. Little as I knew then of war, I wondered at how feebly the City was defended. Phocas had no navy for open-water fighting. But he had enough ships to block the Straits to this sort of operation. It was going ahead without interference.

I turned back to face Martin. He was slumped forward in his chair and crying softly. I took his hands in mine but he turned his head away and continued crying.

'Martin,' I said softly, 'there was one mystery in this City that I did clear up almost at once. I still don't know who was behind the curtain in the Great One's tent, but I'm sure I know who was breathing down my neck two months ago in the Ministry.

'I don't suppose you could see how I was nearly pissing myself with fright as I sat there with Alypius, half expecting at any moment to be dragged to the basement. Afterwards, as I walked home, I realised I'd been got there so that Alypius could pass on a warning from Theophanes against further snooping.

'But it was the note from Theophanes next morning about that cot for Maximin – that plus your own uncharacteristic behaviour with the wine and opium – that aroused my suspicions.

'You killed the old Court Poet, didn't you? Theophanes knew you'd done it, and put the frighteners on you by shoving me in that room. I imagine you told him you could brave any horrors he might subject you to in the dungeons. But you couldn't face me, and he had me there ready at hand, just in case that was needed to break you.'

But for the occasional breeze and the faint sounds of the city and those passing and re-passing ships, we sat in silence. Martin looked at me and opened his mouth. Then he looked down again. At last, he found his words.

'The old eunuch threatened to expose me in front of you. He said you might be roped into the trial. He said he couldn't guarantee your safety or that of Maximin. You've seen for yourself the terrible looks and words he can manage when he isn't trying to charm.'

'The man was Court Poet under Maurice,' I said. 'I suppose he had a hand in smashing you and your father up.'

I poured out more wine for us, and drew my cloak about my legs. Martin looked up at me and smiled.

'You know,' he said, 'I didn't want to come back to Constantinople. I knew it would be a disaster. Even so I really did hope, before we arrived, that I could stick close by you and behave as if I'd never been here before. Then the eunuch had us to lunch and made me dig up all those memories of what happened before.'

'You mean', I asked, 'that Professor of Rhetoric done over on some more than usually inventive charge of treason?'

'That's the one,' said Martin. 'He led the pack against my father. It wasn't all his own money he put up to pay off our debts. But he collected it. He issued the bankruptcy petition when we couldn't pay. You should have seen his face when we met in court.'

Martin closed his eyes and thought back to that dreadful day. He wasn't up to explaining the details of the case as it unfolded. But I managed to reconstruct for myself that the Anthemius petition had been an excuse to involve the tax authorities. Without Anthemius to push them, they'd have waited, reasonably sure the tax bill would be paid. With the matter in court, they had to hurry forward to grab what they could. That had allowed the ban on enslavement for debt to be set aside.

They'd got their cross petition granted without a hearing and without any hope of appeal or delay of execution.

Martin and his father had gone in as free men. They emerged as bound slaves. People they knew turned from them as they were marched along the street to the market. His father had collapsed and died as he stood on the slave block. Anthemius had made a derisory bid for Martin – the sort of bid that pulls down the final selling price.

'I couldn't get Anthemius,' Martin continued after another reverie, 'but I could make a start on the others. I might never have acted at all, but for an accident.

'I was called in by Theophanes a few days after your first brush with Priscus in that restaurant. We met in his office, where he told me of his concerns for your safety. We agreed that you were still very young, and without any experience of City ways. He asked me to keep an eye on you – not spying, you understand. I'd never have spied on you. He just wanted me to guide you away from trouble and report any possible dangers to him in advance.

'When I was still considering whether I could in conscience do as he wanted, he was called out of the room. I'd seen my security file on his desk as I sat down. He forgot to take it with him. So I had a good look.

'We'd already discussed the bankruptcy, and he'd explained that there was nothing he could do after so long to ensure any restitution of property. But I knew the file must contain the names and addresses of the people Anthemius had got on his side. I committed all the details to memory and then rearranged the file so it wouldn't look as if I'd touched it.

'I was lucky. I'd no sooner got everything right than the eunuch came back into the room.'

I took another sip of wine. Where this sort of thing was concerned, there must have been more intelligent lapdogs than Martin. He'd waited, he explained, until Theophanes 'must have' forgotten his carelessness with the file. The evening after he brought Maximin to me, he'd put his plan into execution. He'd followed the Court Poet as he went out on the pull, and bashed his head in with a half-brick.

Afterwards, he had shambled round the outer central districts of Constantinople, covered in blood and doubtless apologising out loud to God, before tripping over the bundle that turned out to be Maximin.

Somehow – Martin swore he couldn't think how – Theophanes had known he was the killer.

Their next interview I'd already guessed. Once Martin was broken down by all the terrors Theophanes could imply with a turn of his mouth, it had been agreed that the murder would be overlooked. Of course he'd also impressed on Martin the need for much closer surveillance of me and regular reports. So it had all gone from there.

I should have been outraged. But one has to be reasonable. No harm had been done. Perhaps Martin had even kept me out of danger, which might not have been the case if I had been spied on by some copying clerk who might actually have stumbled on something.

'Tell me, though, Martin,' I asked with a sudden thought. 'Did Authari know about the killing?'

'He grabbed me as I came back into the Legation,' he said. 'He helped me get the blood washed off. It was then that we noticed you were missing. He was a truer friend than I'd ever realised,' he added mournfully. 'And we had so little time to be friends . . .'

'Very well,' I said, fixing Martin in the eye, 'I am hurt. But I forgive you.'

He swallowed. 'Thank you, Aelric,' he said. 'That does mean much to me. I know that God will be less forgiving. I have committed the most unpardonable sin. That means . . .'

For a moment, he had lost me. I'd forgiven him for the betrayal. But now that he'd mentioned it, I thought to pull rank and give general absolution. Then again, Martin had never really accepted me as the Pope's representative in anything. But it was only for a moment he'd lost me.

'Oh, as for the killing,' I said, cutting off his talk of hellfire, 'I shouldn't worry about God. The man was fair game by any custom. And having looked through some of his poems, I can't say you deprived the world of genius or even taste.

'Is the work finished yet?' I asked. 'Are there any remaining on your list?'

'Two,' he said. 'Theophanes did say he would see to them. But nothing has happened yet.'

'Well,' I sighed, 'you'll have to leave them until your next visit. This time tomorrow, you'll be with Maximin across the water in Chalcedon.'

'I'm not leaving the city without you,' Martin insisted again. 'It was my prayers that got us out of the Yellow Camp. I committed my soul to God and myself to His service. I don't yet know what that service must be, but I feel it concerns you. As you said to me outside the walls, we came together, and we go together.'

Its oil exhausted, the lamp suddenly went out. We sat a while silent in the darkness.

I gave up for the moment. There was no point trying to reason with a man in the grip of religious mania. I changed the subject.

'We bury Authari tomorrow morning,' I said. 'Is the body prepared?'

'Yes,' Martin answered. 'I've explained to Gutrune about the need for a sealed coffin. She was upset – her people like the more showy Arian ritual, where everything is on view. But I told her it was your will.'

Since Authari had stood in for the Permanent Legate, Theophanes had given me the body of the slave who'd been poisoned by the stuff on my robe. He'd stand in for Authari. No one would ask what had become of his body.

'How about flowers?' I asked. 'I want the church alive with the things.'

'I scoured the city this afternoon,' Martin assured me. 'Everything is arranged.'

At least that would go right. I thought.

50

I stepped out the following morning into a fully militarised City. The Ministry guards around the Legation had been withdrawn. They no longer served any good purpose, and were needed elsewhere. But the street junctions were now barricaded and guarded by the Circus Factions. Shopkeepers and craftsmen strutted about in makeshift armour, carrying swords of varied provenance. Those without swords carried whatever could be adapted into weapons.

It wasn't an army for trusting in the field – not against the forces massed outside the walls. But it might lend itself to days of vicious street-fighting.

Whatever his other failings, Priscus did seem to know his military stuff. He even won a couple of battles, Martin had told me. One of them, to be sure, he'd won by reporting the opposing general to the Persian King for treason. He'd delayed his attack until the man was being impaled with his sons.

Still, credit where it was due – Priscus was a better man on the battlefield. Perhaps Phocas should have trusted him with an army.

With Martin, I pushed my way through the crowds and stood on the sea wall looking across to the Galatan shore.

At last, a heavy chain had been stretched across the entrance to the Golden Horn. Nothing would be able to get close to the least impregnable stretch of defences. Even so, the size of the army Heraclius had positioned at all other points was a dispiriting sight. Tents covered the Asiatic shore. A steady stream of boats struggled back and forth across the choppy waters to the unwalled suburbs of Galata. There, among the trees and houses, the sun glinted on armour and bright swords. In the far distance – I had to strain to see against the sun – a whole body of mounted troops cantered off towards the Thracian suburbs.

Someone beside me turned and asked if I knew how much food had been stockpiled against a siege. I gave a noncommittal answer. I knew that Martin and Authari had made sure to fill our own lower rooms with enough dry goods and beer to last for months. The Legation itself could have supplied a small town from its storehouses.

Fuck the City. Whatever else happened, I and mine were unlikely to go hungry.

Someone else said he'd come from the land walls. The army there was even larger, he said. He added that the guards had been issued with orders to let no one out. The City gates were now barred against a siege. No exit permits were being honoured. Even a party of missionary monks had been prevented from leaving.

'That can't possibly be true!' the man beside me said. 'The work of evangelising the barbarian is a duty for the whole Empire. No civil war can interrupt the Godly Work.'

'Are you calling me a liar?' snarled the man who'd volunteered the news. 'Because if you are, I've got a bigger sword than yours, and I know how to use it. I tell you – every fucking gate is shut. The whole world is sealed off from us.'

'My dear Brothers in Christ,' I intervened, eager to see if my status had more than token meaning, 'my poor colleague the Patriarch Thomas is lying on his bed of sickness even as you speak. In this moment of sadness, we have more than a duty of love to each other.'

The man pursed his lips and carefully chose his words.

'My Lord,' he said with a little bow, 'I regret to inform you the Patriarch is not long for this world. He took a turn for the worse last night. Not even wine steeped with a single hair from the head of Saint Andrew could revive him. The doctors have abandoned hope.'

'I am fully aware of these tidings,' I lied. I looked down my nose at the man, and continued:

'In these last days of the world, the Dark One himself dares to walk the streets of the city. Yes!' I cried as I pointed at a conveniently black slab of granite cemented into the battlement – 'The Dark One himself is abroad!'

There was an impressed murmur at this, and several members of the crowd stepped back from the slab.

I would have said more. With my dramatic gesture, though, I'd caught sight of flabby old Nicias in one of the gibbets. Still dressed in the robe he'd worn in the Imperial Box, false teeth rammed upside down in his mouth, his horribly twisted body swayed in the breeze.

'And so,' I ended lamely, 'it is the duty of all good citizens to utter no words that may contribute to demoralisation of the people. Come, Martin,' I said, eager to get away. 'We have work of the highest importance.'

The wine shops were still open for business. All other trading was at an end. The University was closed. Even the bookshops were shuttered and barred.

'No exit from the City, after all,' said Martin. He was quietly pleased with himself. I ignored him.

Going back past the Great Church, for the first time I was required to prove my identity.

The funeral was over. We'd managed a good showing in the church. There had been all my people – and these now included the Legation staff. Theophanes had turned up in time for the interment. Even Priscus had sent flowers.

Overawed by the crowd, Gutrune had confined herself to silent weeping beside Martin. A dab of opium juice on his lead comforter, Maximin had sat quietly in her arms.

Now – the gate securely fastened – we were back in the Legation. I sat at the Permanent Legate's desk, going through his papers again. On the third day of the investigation, I was no longer put off by the volume of papyrus and parchment. It was no longer a question of examining each document, but of what nuggets of information could be extracted from the whole.

'It's the accounts from February onwards that are missing,' Martin said, looking up from his own pile of boxes.

317

I pushed the documents into a pile and reached for my cup. 'There's no point in going through all this again at the moment,' I said. 'I need to sit down alone for a while and think it into a pattern.'

No such luck!

'Pardon me for intruding, My Lord.'

It was Antony. Now that I'd given him the routine business of the Legation to direct, he was looking almost cheerful.

There was an Imperial messenger downstairs. Should he show the man in?

51

Phocas sat down heavily and waved me into another chair placed opposite his own. I was back in his private office. As if he found its mockery too great in his current situation, he sat with the map of the Empire behind him.

'I came as soon as I received the message, Your Majesty,' I explained. 'It was the strip searches that held me up.'

The Emperor threw me a bleary scowl. 'That'll be my eunuchs,' he muttered. 'They must have something to do to justify their salaries.'

He straightened up and pointed at the secretary who was hovering over by the desk.

'Get out of here!' he snarled. 'I'll sign the death warrants later. The victims won't complain at the delay. And shut both doors.'

We were alone. I took up the wine cup set before me and drank. Phocas took up another of his parchment sheets.

'You were shopped late yesterday evening to Priscus,' he began. 'Some bookseller says you were buying blasphemous writings.'

I nearly choked on my wine. I thought of Nicias in that gibbet.

Phocas squinted at the writing on the sheet. It was a very big sheet, and the writing was very small. Someone had been busy, it seemed.

'I have better things to do than fuss about the contents of your library,' said Phocas, looking up. 'But Priscus can be very persuasive in the matter of my duties.'

He dropped the sheet on the floor and looked at me.

'Sir,' I began, trying to look and sound untroubled, 'I am, as you know, here on Church business that requires me to consult a wide range of writings. Many of these are heretical, as they will allow us more effectively to counter heresy in the West. Some are atheistical writings from ancient times. Some are defences of the Old Faith. They are deeply shocking to anyone of delicate sensibilities. But it is my sorrowful duty to read them, in the hope that I may help steer others from the path of deception.'

I would have said more along those lines. It usually went down well. But I could see that Phocas wasn't really interested. Even so, I'd see that fucking bookseller hung from the city walls at the first opportunity. And I'd bribe the pick of his books out of the Black Agents.

'I'm told all these books mean more to you than just the service of Holy Mother Church,' said Phocas, pulling out another sheet from the box beside his chair. 'Let me see—' He raised the sheet close to his face but the tiny writing was too much for him in his present condition. That too landed up on the floor.

His voice now took on an edge that was alarming.

'Priscus has got hold of a list of all the books you've been consulting in the University Library,' he said. 'My son-in-law tells me you've been having many of them copied. These can't all be for Church business. I'm told some of them shouldn't exist, let alone be available for any barbarian to march into the city and inspect.

'I suppose I should ask what your game is. Have you been sent here as a spy?' He leaned forward and looked me close in the face.

'As you know, Caesar, I am from a province currently under barbarian rule,' I said. I was trying desperately hard not to shit myself on the spot.

Espionage accusations – and from Phocas!

'My people are fast accepting the light of Holy Mother Church,' I said. 'Nevertheless, they are an unlearned race, and our ancestors took no care of the libraries that once flourished in the cities of Britain. Those cities are all passed away, and we live in mud huts roofed with straw.

'It is my ambition to help my people to a perfect understanding of the Imperial languages of Latin and Greek, so that they can more perfectly understand the doctrines of our Most Holy Faith. Perhaps it will also bring them to an acceptance that True Religion means obedience to God's Political Representative here in the City.'

Phocas tipped his head back and roared with laughter. 'If I'm still Emperor when all this is over,' he jeered, 'I'll certainly make you an ambassador. You'd do better with the Persians than some of the morons I've sent out.'

That was a promise I didn't fancy having remembered. I thought of what had happened to the envoy he'd sent to the Great One. But I made sure to look flattered.

Phocas leaned forward again. As the laughing fit passed, his face sagged back into semi-drunken blankness. 'Do you know what I want most in the world?' he asked. 'And how you might be able to help me get it?'

I'd been wondering when he'd get round to this. I'd been turning responses over in my mind for three days.

'I suppose, sir,' I answered, 'it has to do with a formal denunciation of Heraclius.'

'It might,' he said, a faint sneer on his face. He leaned back to reach for his cup. 'I've made you Acting Permanent Legate. That means you have all the powers of His Holiness in Rome. You could sign an excommunication here and now. I could send it outside the walls under a flag of truce, and then sit back while all hell broke loose around Heraclius.'

'Indeed, sir, I could,' I said. 'If you put the document before me, it would be my undoubted duty as a citizen of the Empire to sign it. However, would it be in your present interest to ask such of me?' I paused.

'Well, get on with it,' said Phocas with a slight, though not wholly genuine, impatience. 'Let's see how you too can wriggle out of paying back all the favours I've done those shitbag clerics in Rome. Let's see just how good your diplomatic skills are.'

I thought again of Nicias. No reply was plainly the wrong reply.

'Sir,' I began, 'if I were to sign a formal excommunication of Heraclius, it would serve no useful purpose in your present circumstances. It might cause problems for Heraclius in Africa and in the West as a whole. But this would take months to have any effect – even if we could get it out of the City.

'It might tip the Eastern Churches solidly behind Heraclius – and it is Easterners who are presently with him outside the walls. So far as I can tell, his main army out there is Syrian and Egyptian. They don't like Rome at the best of times. Their reasonable inference would be that a deal had been done, under which you would declare His Holiness to be Universal Bishop.

'I repeat – I will sign anything you put in front of me. I suppose it would be accepted in Rome, bearing in mind my present status. But would it be of any immediate use?'

Phocas gave me another of his terrifyingly blank looks. Then he laughed again. He began softly, but soon, in his drunken state, ran out of control. He was now laughing so hard that tears ran down his face. He drained his cup and refilled it.

'No,' he said – 'No, you aren't anywhere near so stupid as my dearest Priscus assures me. Well said, my pretty boy. And do have another drink.'

I said a prayer of thanks as he turned to discussing the Greek Patriarch. Had I, as representative of the Pope, any recommendations as to a successor, should poor Thomas not come back to life?

'I may not be the most authoritative source on these matters,' I answered with another stab at diplomacy. 'The only person I can think of who is both holy and learned enough for such preferment is one Sergius, who is an associate of the Professor of Theology.'

Phocas grunted and wrote the name on the back of one of his death warrants.

'I'll have to think about that,' he said. 'I suppose you are aware that Sergius has been nagging me to have you killed? He hates all Westerners and didn't welcome your presence at all. Still, turn the other cheek and all that!

'Do you suppose you'll ever see Rome again?' he asked suddenly.

'I have a woman there,' I said, a renewed cold tingle in my guts. 'I have a woman there with child. I may already be a father by now. It is my wish to return to Rome at some point. But I am a citizen of the Empire and a servant of the Church. My duty is to go where I'm sent and do there as I'm told.'

'And my present wish', said Phocas, 'is that you should be here, and that you should continue investigating the death of the Permanent Legate.'

He stretched in a manner that indicated he'd had enough of my company. As I rose and began the perfunctory bow he said he didn't want, but always seemed to enjoy, he leaned forward again and caught my sleeve.

'What did you find out at the Monastery of St John?' he asked. For all his other problems, the man knew my movements pretty well.

'I have some reason to believe the place is harbouring Demetrius,' I explained. I added that the Abbot had refused my dispensation from his vow of silence.

'Well, that's as it should be,' Phocas said, giving me another of his blank looks. 'The Fathers of St John are good friends of His Holiness in Rome. They have his full confidence. That, of course, means they have my full confidence. Don't go back there ever again.'

'No, Caesar,' I said.

'I've already ordered Priscus to get those men withdrawn,' he said after a long belch. 'It's a fucking insult to the Church, wouldn't you agree?'

'Without any possible doubt, Caesar,' I said.

I was back in my own office with Martin and with Maximin. A light dinner had been served and cleared away. The sky outside the window was darkening. To the best of my knowledge, we were alone. For the moment, we spoke softly in Latin.

'Oh, what can this mean? What can it mean?' Martin asked in a stunned voice, going back to the main point.

'It means', I said, 'that something is going on far beyond our guessing. Demetrius and Agathius seem to have killed the Permanent Legate. Agathius was almost certainly working for Heraclius. Theophanes helped set it up. Now Phocas is protecting Demetrius.

'It's possible that Heraclius wanted the Permanent Legate dead to prevent any deal between Pope and Emperor. Then again, it's possible he wanted such a deal so the East would rise against Phocas.

'Theophanes, we can be sure, is up to something that secures his own interest. But I don't think he'd act without at least the knowledge and tacit consent of Phocas or Heraclius.

'What Phocas is up to is beyond me. If he really wanted an excommunication, getting rid of the Permanent Legate and replacing him with me was a step in the right direction. But he wasn't that keen this afternoon to ask anything beyond my advice on clerical appointments.'

I explained the denunciation Priscus had made of me to Phocas. 'I can't begin to imagine what his interests could be beyond succeeding Phocas. But it's quite obvious that he wants me dead. That, or he wants me as a friend. Or perhaps he wants both. They seem interchangeable in his mind.'

We lapsed into silence.

'I prayed hard this afternoon while you were at the palace,' said Martin. 'I prayed for your safe return. And I prayed for understanding of the mystery.'

' "Half only he granted, half he denied him," ' I said, now in Greek, quoting Homer. 'I got safely back from the Most Sacred Presence. But we're neither of us any closer to the answer we want. We still have the mystery to solve.'

I looked over at Maximin. So long as they get regular feeding and changing, it doesn't take much to keep a baby happy.

'Perhaps,' said Martin, 'we are labouring under one of those false assumptions you always warn against?'

I looked at Martin. It could be that praying had sharpened his wits.

'Perhaps Theophanes killed the Permanent Legate,' he suggested.

'That might explain the murder itself,' I said. 'But where's the motive? Also, we know the Permanent Legate's papers were sifted. That must have been done before the body was found. I can't comment on the intelligence of His Late Excellency Silas. But I think most people would notice a fat eunuch pawing over their private files.

'Now' – I checked Martin's reply – 'now, it is possible that the Permanent Legate was already a corpse when the papers were sifted. We're no longer committed to believing in a murder shortly before dawn. That body might have been lying there half a day at least. Theophanes could have murdered the Permanent Legate even while we were all in the Circus.

'But this stretches the timing until it undermines the only hypothesis that appears to make sense. We've decided that Agathius and perhaps Demetrius killed the Permanent Legate shortly before Agathius came looking for me. Of course, if proven facts demand it, we must reject the hypothesis. Even so . . .'

I trailed off. We sat a while in glum silence.

'If it weren't for Authari,' I said flatly, 'I'd suggest going slow on the investigation, and waiting to see what happens with the siege. You don't investigate murders when an Emperor crops up among the suspects.'

'But we must avenge Authari,' Martin said with sudden insistence. 'His soul won't rest easy until we know the truth and act on it.'

I didn't recall reading that in any of the Scriptures. The sentiment had more to do with my own people or even with the Old Faith. But I wasn't inclined to disagree. I'd put the poor bugger in danger. It was up to me to make the blood sacrifice.

'We have our duty to Authari,' I agreed. 'That means we press on to the end – wherever that may be and wherever the path may lie.'

As I got up, Antony knocked on the door again. Another messenger – this time from 'His Magnificence, the Lord Eunuch', he sniffed, with a comment on the late hour. The man had left a note, then gone off again.

I broke the seal and scanned the familiar wording.

'Here's a change of direction,' I said eagerly. 'He's arrested Demetrius, and is effectively inviting me to help turn the rack before anyone can intervene.'

52

Antony's point about lateness had been worth making. Even in the City, there comes a time for business to wind down. I walked out of the Legation into almost empty streets. No moon shone down from the now clouded sky. All was silent. Were Heraclius to break in by night, the presently unmanned barricades might still slow his progress. No one seemed to worry, though. And probably Heraclius too was abed.

From my first visit, I recalled that Theophanes had his palace about fifty yards down a side street that curled past a church built in some Oriental style. It was all just outside the zone of street lighting, but I could see the church looming ahead, a greater darkness against the dark sky.

'Would that be Your Honour, come to see the eunuch?' a voice called out of the darkness in the whining Greek of an Easterner.

A cloth came off a lantern about a dozen feet away.

'What might that be to you?' I asked in a voice steadier than my insides. The message had said to come alone. For once, no chair was provided. Bearing in mind the need for secrecy, that had made sense back in the Legation. It was the first time I had been invited to visit Theophanes at his palace rather than his office in the Ministry. That also had made sense in the safety of the Legation.

In its general form, the message had looked genuine. I now kicked myself. If only the message hadn't told me what I so wanted to be told, I might have waited till morning.

'Who are you and what do you want?' I asked again.

The lantern shook slightly as a whispered conversation began. I strained to see who was there but whoever was holding it was dressed in dark clothes, and the dim light was all thrown in my direction.

'Did you bring any money with you?' another voice called out of the darkness. It had a greedy edge, but also sounded pleasantly surprised.

'That depends on how much you want, and on what you might care to give me in exchange for it,' I answered, reaching inside my cloak for the reassuring feel of my sword.

There was more whispered dialogue. I could hear it was in Syriac. There were one or two phrases, though, in Greek – just as you'd expect with long-settled immigrants.

'Orders is plain,' was the main phrase I caught.

Another cloth came off a lantern. This was brighter than the first, and it threw a pool of light reaching as far as the wall of the church. I could now see that there were four men. Two of them were armed with short swords. They stepped towards me.

'If I were armed myself', I said in a casual tone, 'you'd be unwise to come too close.'

They both stepped smartly back. I folded my hands placidly across my chest and stared back at them. You never show fear with people like these. They had the small size and darting movements usual of Syrians. I'd seen others like them hanging about the main squares. If you could manage the right opening words, they'd agree to any contract of murder.

But there were only four of them, I told myself over and again. Almost certainly, there were no others lurking round corners. And if those swords were their only armament, I had nothing to fear so long as I kept my nerve.

'It's turning rather chilly again, don't you think?' I observed. 'I want my bed. I'm sure you want some of my money.'

I reached down and patted my right hip. There was a gratifying chink of gold. I smiled and put my hands together.

The two men who'd so far stood behind the other two now put their lanterns carefully on the ground. The pools of light grew smaller and the almost cheerful glow they had cast outside the church disappeared.

All the men took out short swords of their own and moved towards me.

'It's hardly a friendly act to come at me with four swords,' I said, still conversational.

'Too right, you fucking piece of Latin trash!' one of the men snarled. He stood against the light and I couldn't see his face. But I could hear the triumphant hatred in his voice.

'Well!' said I. 'If I had thought I was coming here to listen to such words, I might have ignored your fake summons and stayed at home. You may be aware that I am a man of the cloth. That surely entitles me to a certain delicacy of address. However, I'd still insist that the four of you would be an unlikely match for someone like me, were I to pull out a sword. I'll give you double what you've been promised.'

Another of the men waved his sword quite close to my face, though he didn't chance his luck by coming too close.

'Don't you worry your pretty little blond empty head,' he sneered. 'We'll be sure to take double – double and treble from a Chalcedonite fucker like you.'

'And fuckall good of it you'll have', I said, 'if I run you through.'

'Let's get this over and done with,' the same ruffian said. He waved at the others. They spread out around me, and then began to close in.

There was a shrill cry and the clatter of a dropped sword as I got one of them. Still cautious, he'd stretched as far towards me as he could without falling over. As his sword-point came within inches of my cloak, I'd pulled out my own sword and lunged forward and up.

I thought at first I'd taken his hand off at the wrist but discovered later that I'd only sliced off the right knuckles. Still, that must have hurt worse than a mere amputation. Certainly, he was now out of action – down on the ground, twisting and gasping at the unbearable pain.

I kept my sword up. Though my heart was racing, and I felt an almost irresistible urge to jump forward, slashing to right and left, I stayed put and kept my voice as calm and neutral as before.

'There's surely no need for more unpleasantness,' I said. 'The offer's this – you tell me who sent you and I give you twice what he paid you. Can I say fairer than that?'

One of the men lowered his sword and stood back again. 'Have you got sixty *solidi*?' he asked in a doubtful tone.

'That and more,' I said reassuringly. 'Put your sword away and go and stand by the lanterns.'

'You stupid cunt!' another of the men snarled at him. 'This ain't no usual contract. I haven't told you the half of what's behind this one. We kill the bastard and then take his gold. Count of three, we go at him.' He opened his mouth to count down the numbers.

No point in hoping for a parley. They had their orders, and there was no shaking these. I'd have to kill some of them, and I'd find myself with another nice robe fit only for giving to the poor.

Such a waste, I thought. I lifted my sword and wondered who would be the easiest to dispose of first. Even as I arranged my cloak to catch most of the blood, the square behind the men filled with torches and shouting.

'I want them alive!' I roared above the commotion, realising what must have happened. 'I'll personally kill any man who injures them.'

'Throw those swords down over there,' I said curtly to the confused ruffians. They were looking open-mouthed at the little army that blocked every exit from the square. 'And you will sit by your wounded friend, hands spread in front of you. Try anything fancy, and I'll start by having your toes nipped off. Do you understand me?'

As one of them nodded, Theophanes came into view.

'My dear Aelric,' he cried plaintively, 'I can only ask what on earth you thought you were doing? I praise God that I had need of Martin's company tonight.' Was that a blush? Hard to say in the torchlight.

Dressed in black, a shawl over his head, Theophanes tried to look military. Torch in hand, Alypius stood beside him. I smiled grimly, but could think of nothing to say. For what it was worth, I'd show him the message soon. Theophanes, I had no doubt, would be astonished by the signature it carried.

Yes – Priscus had gone too far this time. That forgery, plus whatever testimony we could get out of those Syrians, would give him much explaining to do at his next meeting with the Emperor.

A shutter overhead flew open and a flickering light seeped out. The occupant looked down at us, realised this was state business, and closed it again with desperate force.

'If you please, do bring that torch over here,' I asked of Alypius.

I peered into the faces of the three sitting men. There's something about Syrians – especially bearded ones. They all tend to look alike. But I was fixing on any peculiarities of expression. I wanted to remember those faces

The one I'd injured was in some kind of spasm from the pain. But a mild jab with a sword-point got him to look up. There was little worth remembering in the contorted expression. Instead I looked closely at the mutilated right hand. I noted the dark tattooed crosses on his remaining two knuckles.

I drew Theophanes over towards the church. 'Please,' I said, speaking low, 'I'd like all four put in solitary under the Ministry. I want each one deprived of all sound and light. No food. No water. Naked and chained. No medical attention for the one with the wounded hand.

'I want the cells guarded by your own people. No one goes into them except you or me – *no one else at all*. We'll interrogate them tomorrow evening. Any sooner, and I'm not sure if they'd give us the truth.'

'It will all be as you ask,' said Theophanes. I could see the questioning look on his face.

'It was', said Theophanes, cup in hand, 'the neatest double ambush you could ever have wanted to see. One moment, our hero was confronted by four low ruffians. The next, they were grovelling at his feet and blinking in the light of a dozen torches.'

Martin grunted and looked over to the sleeping Maximin. I could see he still wasn't pleased that I'd gone without thinking into the night. Had Theophanes not turned up to demand a sudden report on me, I might be lying face down in a gutter.

'Don't worry,' I'd said. 'Really, I was never in the slightest danger – and we might be able to reduce the number of our enemies because of this.'

He'd paid no attention as he fussed over an inkpot.

'Have some wine, Martin,' I now said, leaning forward with the jug.

'No thank you, sir,' he said, still very stiff. He looked away.

'Suit yourself,' I said with a clumsy attempt at lightness. I waved to Gutrune to fetch some more of the spiced melon pulp for Theophanes.

'Martin,' said Theophanes with a slight emphasis, 'you will be aware that at least our present game is approaching its end. Heraclius has nearly thirty thousand men outside the walls. Thirty thousand men – and barely enough food and shelter for half that number. If he doesn't make his move in the next two days, he might as well not bother. But you and I know he will attack – don't we?'

'Yes,' Martin said flatly.

I pretended not to notice the indirect warning. My own game was nowhere close to finished.

'There will be an attack,' Theophanes continued. 'It may fail – in which case we shall have many more jolly parties ahead of us. If not, all that we have so far gone through together must be the whole sum of our relationship.

'We shall meet again tomorrow in the course of business, and perhaps also the next day. But there may be no more of these little gatherings from which I have come to draw so much honest enjoyment.'

He turned to me. 'Aelric,' he said, 'when the attack does come, I advise you to lock the main gate and barricade yourself in here. Do not advertise your presence. Pray that no one who might break in tries to set fire to the building. Wait patiently – in this beautiful home you have created within a drab official residence – wait until, one way or another, order has been restored. What you do then must be for you to decide in the circumstances prevailing.

'But why give thought to the things of the morrow? Now let us drink and make merry.'

To Gutrune: 'My dear woman, I will take just a little wine. Do please add plenty of water.'

She had enough Latin to understand 'wine'. 'Water' was outside her vocabulary.

'Do you remember, Martin,' I asked, 'the look on the Great One's face as Theophanes began juggling those heads?'

So, keeping our voices down for Maximin, and for any spies who might be listening, we caroused till dawn.

53

Going out of the Legation next morning, I bumped into a band of about a dozen students from the University. One of them was wearing a breastplate far too large for his body. Another had perched a bronze helmet on his head that looked so like something in an ancient bas relief, he must have got it from a tomb.

They told me they had asked if they could join the first line of defence down at the docks, and had been honoured with an acceptance. Would I bless their weapons? one of them asked me. All the Greek priests they'd met had made excuses and scurried away.

And quite properly too, I'll say. Men of God should only get involved in civil wars when it's clear which side has won. I called an ambiguous blessing on the arms of the Emperor and continued about my own business.

I didn't get far in the crowded streets. At the first main barricade, I met Priscus. He was patiently drilling some members of the Blue Faction in how to discharge their slingshots in a slow volley.

'Oh, my darling vision of beauty!' he exclaimed as I tried to sidle past. 'How we insult your dignity by allowing you to wander about the City on foot and unguarded. I was only mentioning this to His Majesty yesterday – how we should keep our most distinguished guest out of danger.'

'The time you spare from your own duties to think of me, dear Priscus,' I said, 'warms my heart. Is it true the Charisian Gate was open all night?'

Priscus scowled. He took hold of my arm and drew me aside. 'Of course it fucking wasn't,' he snarled. 'If ever I find who started that rumour, I'll flay him with my own hands.'

He took out his leather pouch and began fussing over its many compartments.

'One rumour I can promise is true', he went on, his selection made, his mood restored, 'is that Thomas snuffed it earlier this morning. He cursed all Latins and their ways, and then made a noise that reminded me of two mating hyenas. I can tell you this is so. I was there.'

'So we have another clerical vacancy,' I observed.

'Sadly, you'll not be filling that one as well,' said Priscus with one of his charming smiles. 'I've already recommended Sergius,' he added proudly. 'Phocas will have the announcement made at evening service.'

We stopped for yet another column of armed citizens to straggle past. These were wearing armour made from dismantled wine vats and carried bronze railings they had stripped from one of the parks to serve as spears.

Priscus took their salute and made a brief speech about the duties of patriotism.

As the great wooden gate of the Legation swung shut behind us, Priscus sagged straight out of his military pose.

'Fuck me, Alaric!' he moaned. 'Much more of this and I'll join a bloody monastery.'

He threw himself on to the couch in my office and breathed a handful of yellow powder up his nose. As ever, I refused to join him and reached for the jug of heavily watered wine that had appeared on my desk.

I could hear Gutrune down the corridor. She was singing something mournful to Maximin in her own language. I couldn't tell through the two shut doors if it was cheering him, but he wasn't crying.

'We're up Shit Creek, you know,' said Priscus in conversational tone when his convulsions had moderated. 'Do believe me that no gates were left open last night. But if the gates do open – correction: *when* they open – there'll be two days of bloodshed on the streets.'

'If it does come to that,' I said, looking round the settled comfort of the room, 'it might be hard for you.'

Priscus pulled himself up and went over to look out on to the balcony. He turned back to me.

'It won't be too good for anyone closely associated with His Majesty,' he said with an odd laugh. 'How do you suppose you'll get out?'

'I believe I have full immunity as the Pope's representative,' I said.

Priscus laughed again. 'I'd look more to the strength of those gates – or, better still, a fast ship out,' he said.

I got up and pulled on a bell cord I'd recently had fitted. This would bring up a slave from the kitchen with the bread and cheese I'd earlier specified for lunch.

'You'll join me for some food, Priscus?' I asked. 'I can't promise anything special, but you'll surely find it wholesome.'

'Now when did you last see me do anything wholesome?' Priscus responded with a nasty grin. 'I've got a vial somewhere of my special black liquid. I think I can chance a few drops of that in some wine – though, mind you, only in white wine. Red with this stuff is bad for my stomach.'

He asked if I'd found any hidden ways into the Legation from the street. I gave a noncommittal grunt. I wasn't telling Priscus that Martin was at this moment on an intensive search for some other way out in an emergency.

'I used to come here quite a bit when the Permanent Legate was still receiving guests,' he said, 'but I never went beyond the state rooms. Still, it wouldn't surprise me if there were some passage-way. As it might save your life at the right moment, I suppose I'd better help you find it.'

A very good reason, I thought, for not accepting his offer. But I smiled. 'You are always so good to me, Priscus,' I said.

'Once a friend, always a friend, is my guiding motto,' he replied.

We made our way down to the main garden and headed left towards the back buildings of the Legation. I'd agreed with Martin that the most likely hidden exit would be close by the Permanent Legate's own quarters. So I wanted Priscus as far away from that as possible. It would never do to let him hear Martin rummaging through the cellars.

335

As we crossed the gardens, we were joined by two of the Black Agents. One of them handed Priscus a sealed message. He frowned as he read it.

'It seems that greasy old eunuch has sealed off the Ministry to my people,' he said, passing the message back. 'I regard this as an act of open war against me. I'll tell as much to Phocas when I dine with him this evening. Even at this late stage, there's always room for one more under the Ministry.'

I wondered how Martin might be doing.

We stopped at the pigsties. Priscus was beginning to sweat heavily. It was a warm afternoon, but that and the trembling probably had more to do with his idea of lunch.

The pigs were happy. A slave was ladling acorns out of a bucket, and they squealed and grunted with pleasure as they nosed through the carpet of liquefied shit to get at them. As we leaned on the gate to watch the pigs feeding I noticed that Priscus was breathing heavily, his face the colour of new papyrus. I began to hope he might have a seizure. That would remove one complication from my life. But he recovered himself with an effort of will and turned to me.

'Wonderful things are pigs, you know,' he said.

'Yes,' I added. 'I've always found them more intelligent than dogs.'

'I wouldn't go that far,' said Priscus. 'But, certainly, they know what's up when killing-time comes round. When I was a boy, and out for innocent fun, I used to hide the knife behind my back. Still, I'd see the fear in their eyes as they backed away. And they taste good. Every body part has its own flavour. Do you ever have cups of blood brought to you when one is freshly killed?'

'Not a pleasure I've yet sampled,' I said, 'though my people do make the most gorgeous blood sausages – much better than I've had outside England.'

'Oh yes, you're from there,' said Priscus, sounding bored. 'Phocas once gave me a lecture on the place when he was more than usually pissed. He said it was full of blacks and headless dwarves. Did I hear aright in the Circus that you came here with letters of submission from one of the local kings?'

I gave a noncommittal sniff and turned back to the pigs, who'd started fighting over some rotten cabbages.

'They'll eat anything, of course,' said Priscus, stepping back to avoid getting splashed. 'When I was carving the Persians up back in the days of Maurice, I once fed some live prisoners to the pigs I had with me. They were Syrian double agents, you see, and I wanted to make an example of them. Like Jews and Egyptians, many of them have a horror of pork.

'Well, they wouldn't eat pigs. But the pigs ate them. They'll eat their way through flesh, guts, bone – you name it. They have trouble with teeth and hair, but everything else—'

Priscus stopped suddenly. We looked at each other and then back at the feasting pigs.

'Do you suppose—?' I asked.

'It's a possibility – a distinct possibility,' said Priscus.

'You there,' I called to the slave, 'when was all this shit last raked out?'

Not for a while, came the answer. If it didn't rain again, it was something for the day after next.

'Get wide-meshed sieves from the kitchen,' I ordered.

We watched as the slave, down on his knees, began work in one corner of the sty. Two big handfuls of shit scooped up and pressed through his sieve into a bucket. The remaining straw and other residue carefully picked through. The bucket taken out and emptied. Then back on his knees.

'This will take for ever,' Priscus said.

'It might take all day,' I agreed. 'The problem is, I don't want the household alerted yet to the possibility. But we do need more hands.'

The two Black Agents read the look in my eyes and stepped back, horror and disbelief stamped on their faces.

I pulled out a scented cloth from my robe and held it to my nose. 'Priscus, I have a request to make of you,' I said lightly.

54

As if I were playing dice, I rattled the box as I emptied it on to the Emperor's desk. Five indisputably human teeth bounced on to the polished wood. Phocas took up the least decayed of them and held it against the light.

'Without seeing them in the Permanent Legate's head,' he began, 'I wouldn't like to guess whose these might be. But it's an interesting possibility.

'So, my two brave champions, you've started bringing me answers. Indeed, I think it calls for drinks all round.'

We drank deeply.

Priscus had met unexpected resistance when ordering his men into the pigsty. Orders hadn't worked. Threats hadn't worked. He'd eventually had to borrow gold from me for a bribe, and then offer more as a bounty. At last, though, they'd joined in the fun.

'Dear me, no,' I'd said after enough teeth had been recovered, 'I couldn't possibly have your men in my bathhouse.'

So off they'd been sent to sit in the chill waters of a fishpond. Their uniforms would have to be burned. Unless they could find their way into a steam room, their bodies would stink for a month.

Priscus now sat happily beside me, basking in the sun of Imperial approval.

'Young Alaric is sharp,' he said. 'He almost got there before me.'

'The question remains, of course,' said Phocas with a leer at Priscus, '*who* fed His Excellency to the pigs?'

'I am convinced, sir, that it was the official Demetrius and some other person as yet unknown,' I answered.

'So you assure me. But have you found this Demetrius?'

I looked at Priscus.

'My dearest Father-in-Law,' he said, 'even in its present chaos, I've had the City searched and searched. No one fitting the description given has been found. Perhaps if we could do as Alaric suggests, and search the Monastery of St John Chrysostom . . .'

'I've told you both already,' Phocas snapped with a sudden turn of ill humour, 'that the Holy Fathers of St John are not to be troubled with any enquiries. You'll find no one called Demetrius in their house.'

Priscus bowed and changed the subject. He spoke now about the treble ring of defence he'd organised for the streets.

A secretary entered with a pile of documents. A slave carried more behind him.

Phocas sighed. 'Alaric, go back to your searches,' he said.

He looked over at Priscus. 'And you have your own work that needs attention. We'll talk properly about the defences over dinner.'

'We make such a wonderful team, don't you think, my great blond stunner?' Priscus asked.

I looked down from our position on the land walls to the vast army encamped in the old suburbs. A man wearing the purple stripe of a senator caught my eye. He was standing well out of artillery range while, beside him, a slave was flashing a coded message with a mirror against the sun. It might have been for any one of the thousands of men who looked silently back from the safety of the walls.

'What do you think he might be saying?' I asked, avoiding the question.

'It could be orders to their people inside the walls,' Priscus said. 'Or it might just be a bluff to demoralise an already demoralised people.'

He was right about the changing mood within the City. The excitement of putting on makeshift armour and strutting about with weapons was beginning to wear off. So far as anyone could tell, the whole Empire was now behind Heraclius. And these were fighting soldiers, all taken from the frontiers.

It no longer sounded so comforting to hear that Heraclius would have to move fast before pestilence and hunger arrived in earnest in his camp – or before the denuded frontiers wholly collapsed. We now expected that there would be an attack very soon, and knew that, whatever might be said of Heraclius himself, he had some good generals around him to lead it.

The flashing went on and on. If instructions were being sent to the city, they were frighteningly detailed.

Priscus kissed his hand and waved at a man who sat on horseback behind the Senator. 'I was at school with him, you know,' he said cheerfully. 'He and his friends beat me to pulp when I put the word round that he was fucking a wax image of the Patriarch. How about a little drinkie? Just a small one to guard against the coming chill? There's a nice establishment by the Church of Saint Anna. And I have a proposal that may interest you.'

We sat in a cosy upstairs room in the wine shop. The owner fussed silently round us with glass pitchers of white wine and dishes of toasted bread covered in olive paste.

'This can't be as long as I'd like it to be,' said Priscus when the man had left. 'I'm about to engage in urgent business. What I want to ask is if you'd like to share that business.'

I looked back at him in silence.

'It seems the fucking old eunuch has won for the moment,' he said, heating his knife over a candle. 'When I married my charming Domentia and became Heir to the Empire, I thought I'd won the biggest prize in the universe. "Priscus," I told myself, "you've jumped straight over those tossers who held you back in military and civil life. You'll be Number One in no time at all. In the meantime, you're just one down from the top." Then I found that Theophanes stood in my way at every move. He's the one who made sure I didn't get made Commander-in-Chief of the field armies. He saw to it that my roving commission through the Eastern Provinces didn't get me farther than Ancyra. For years now, he's had the ear of Phocas. He's been watching me and reporting on me, and dropping poison with each honeyed phrase about my abilities. Fuck him!'

340

Priscus squeezed a pinch of another powder on to the hot knife and breathed in the fumes. His gasp of ecstasy over, he looked up again.

'Fuck the old eunuch,' he repeated. 'I wish he'd burst from all the food he shovels into his gullet.'

'He is, I'm told, a most remarkable administrator,' I said, rubbing in the salt.

'Administrator?' Priscus spat with venomous contempt. 'If I had my way, he'd still be singing in the travelling brothel that brought him to Constantinople. Yes, that's a talent I'll not deny him – "Watchman at the Gates of Love": a fitting description of someone whose balls were rotting in some Bostra cesspit before I was born!'

He paused with a little smile as my mind went into motion. Martin and I rarely spoke of what had happened in the Great One's tent. Neither of us had mentioned it again to Theophanes. He himself would never have breathed a word. That left . . .

'Yes, my dearest boy,' said Priscus with an expansive wave – his cheerful mood was restored – 'I was there. Sadly, I had business outside the tent that deprived me of your own most remarkable performance. But I had a fine view of the musical cabaret. For the first and probably the only time in my life, I was impressed by the old eunuch's abilities.'

Cup in hand, I sat still. I was aghast at the revelation.

'I never once thought it was *you* behind the curtain in the Great One's tent,' I said. 'I thought it was one of Heraclius's men.'

'And you may be sure, my dearest Alaric,' Priscus said with a stretch of his arms, 'that it was someone from Heraclius. I was there on business relating to the captives and their eventual release. It was quite a surprise when you were all marched into the Monstrous One's presence. I barely had time to get behind that curtain.'

'So it was you who was negotiating with Theophanes outside the tent,' I said. 'In exchange for his life, he agreed to help you kill the Permanent Legate. He was the only one with access. And that would get you in deeper with Heraclius.'

'Brains and beauty.' Priscus smiled, raising his cup in a mock toast. 'Of course, I needed you and your freedman dead. I couldn't risk even the slightest chance that you'd spotted me. The eunuch was very persuasive when it came to getting his own skin spared. You two, however, were decidedly surplus to requirements.'

'I suppose that explains why you've been so eager to have me killed since I got back to the City,' I said.

'Oh, that was nothing personal, dear boy,' Priscus said with a smile. 'That little scene in church was merely tying up loose ends. I got the old eunuch to kill the Permanent Legate. When you got the job, you had to go the same way. There's no point in bumping off a Permanent Legate if he's immediately replaced.

'Getting you murdered in the Great Church, and in the Imperial Presence, would have dropped my Divine Father-in-Law right in the shit with everyone.'

'Are you not forgetting, My Lord,' I asked mildly, 'your attempt on me via Agathius in the Legation, your attempt via those Syrians last night, and your efforts with the Emperor?'

'I don't know anything about last night,' came the airy reply. 'As for Agathius, I'd like to know what became of him. My guess is that he's holed up with Demetrius. If only we'd been able to get hold of either of them, it would have been a sword held right over the old eunuch's head. With him neutralised, I could have gone through with my plan of surrendering the city once the gates were open. As it is, killing the Permanent Legate will have been my latest service to Heraclius. That alone should keep me in his good books.'

I looked at him. Was he telling the truth? He appeared to be. Having admitted to a murder attempt in the Great Church, he would hardly deny anything more seemly.

But Priscus continued: 'My latest service unless, my dearest, you've managed to learn what Theophanes was up to with Justinus of Tyre. I thought for a while he had the means to betray me to Phocas. It seems he had other information – information Heraclius was willing to pay through the nose to get.

'Any ideas about what he did know? Did His Magnificence ever take you into his confidence on that one? Do you fancy a meeting with the next Emperor? I'll be with him come dusk.'

I ignored the invitation. 'What I can't understand', I said, 'is why you've changed sides. You might be useful to Heraclius at the moment. Do you really think, though, that he will spare your life once you've helped make him Emperor?'

Priscus looked thoughtfully over to the closed door and then to the shuttered window.

'There are many things you don't understand,' he said quietly across the table.

I had to lean forward to catch his further words. 'The deal is that I give him the City', he said, 'and he gives me an army to use against the Persians. Be assured I'll soon be turning on him.

'The best I can hope for while Phocas lives is to be a glorified chief of police. The way he carries on, he'll live for ever. Long before then, he'll have no Empire left to hand over. All things considered, Heraclius is a much better bet.'

I scarce knew where to begin. It seemed to me then that he was a walking illustration of what too many mood-altering substances, consumed over too long a period, can do to the understanding.

I changed the subject. 'Why do you ask me to defect with you?' I asked.

Priscus smiled again. 'Because, my darling little god,' he said, 'now you're in the know, what else can you do but stick with me?'

'That begs the question, My Lord,' I said, 'why you have put me in the know.'

I thought for a moment of killing Priscus but soon dismissed it. He was also armed, and he might be no fool with a sword.

He spoke again: 'Why don't you join us? I'm sure I could put in a word with Heraclius. He's not very bright, you should be aware. Once I'm Emperor, I'll reopen the University and make you its chancellor.'

Seeing the scorn I couldn't keep off my face, Priscus continued: 'And, of course, there are other openings for you at my court. You know that we make a great team. Relieved of the duty to have you killed, I'd find you even more madly attractive than I have so far.

I'm not as young as I used to be, but I can still teach a thing or two about mattress acrobatics.'

This really was too much!

'My dear Priscus,' I said when I'd recovered use of my voice, 'you should be aware that the only bodily fluid I might want to discharge near you is vomit.'

As if I'd spat at him, he shrank back in his chair. A look of rage passed over his face. Then he was all smooth serpent again.

'Be that as it may,' he said, 'you've lavished enough tenderness these past few months on some of my spawn.'

I felt as if I'd had a stiletto of ice pushed into my stomach.

'And what in the name of shit,' I snarled, 'do you mean by that?'

'Isn't it obvious?' Priscus said slowly and emphatically. 'Your darling Maximin is one of my bastards. You say he was picked up near dawn outside the Mary Magdalene Church? It's surely no coincidence that I had a boy child left in the same place at probably the same time – I'm sure we'd agree on the date if we bothered comparing notes. I let the bitch slave-girl carry her belly-load about until she shat it out. When I saw the scrawny thing, I had her throat cut and the baby dumped.

'Yes, my darling boy – I'm the father of the thing you love most in this City. And when I'm Emperor, I may have to take it back from you. It might not do to have a grandson of Phocas as my heir.'

'You're a fucking liar, you shitbag Greekling!' I shouted in Latin. Because he spoke it, I suddenly found Greek too dirty a language for my lips.

'But you know I'm telling the truth – don't you?' he said, still in Greek. 'Now you go back to your Legation and look on your beautiful adopted son. If you want to spare yourself a whole mountain of grief – and him too once I'm Emperor – you'll throw him to those pigs.'

Priscus got up. 'I'm sure we still have much to discuss. Perhaps we'll continue this conversation when we next meet. Perhaps it will be in circumstances similar to those I intended on our first meeting. But for the moment, I have other, more pressing business to attend to.'

By the time I'd gathered myself sufficiently to follow him from the wine shop, he'd vanished.

As I staggered through the gate to the Legation, I heard the first word on the streets that the Caesar Priscus had somehow found a way out of the City, and that he'd gone over to Heraclius.

55

Martin looked at the child again. 'There is a certain resemblance,' he said in a doubtful tone.

'Of course there's a resemblance, you dickhead,' I hissed. With his eyes shut, Maximin was a smaller version of Priscus. It was astonishing how I hadn't noticed this before.

'Where's your God now? The moment you found that child by the church, you sealed our death warrant.'

'Shut up, or you'll wake him,' came the reply. Martin carefully pulled the covers back. He turned to face me. For all the concern he showed, I might have been telling him about a crate of spoiled papers.

'Besides,' he added, 'I only picked him up. I recall it was you who insisted on adopting him. And you did adopt him,' he continued with a sudden intensity. He'd switched into Celtic. 'Under the laws of every nation, including even yours, the father of a child is the man who takes it as his own. Fatherhood comes from acknowledgement, not from fucking. That child is yours and yours alone.'

'That isn't the point,' I said. I'd not let Martin see the tears I was forcing back as I repeated his point again and again to myself. 'The point is that we're in the deepest shit you can imagine. This is the natural child of the second biggest traitor in the Empire. In a few days, he may again be the child of the second biggest man in the Empire. Where does that leave him or us? Now, do please shut up about your God. If He had any hand in this, it shows at least an unorthodox sense of humour.'

'Fuck them!' Martin spat. I looked up in shock at the unexpected obscenity. 'Do you suppose it was mere chance that I went

346

to that place and at that time? Had I ever been there before? Had I ever taken notice of a foundling before? Was it chance that I brought him home? Was it chance that you adopted him on the spot? Was it chance that you called him Maximin without the shadow of a thought?

'Was any of this chance? It was the Will of God, I tell you!

'It was God who willed me to send the Court Poet early into His Presence. Once He had arranged for me to be in the right time and place, all else followed with the same certainty as a branch struck by lightning crashes from a tree. You can laugh at me with your mind full of the muddy thoughts of the ancients. But you know I'm talking sense.

'I tell you' – he dropped his voice as the child stirred – 'I tell you that God is guiding our every move towards some Holy Purpose. You can forget Phocas and Priscus and all the rest of them. If God be for us, who can be against us?'

If Martin had thrown the wine jug out of the window, and slapped my face and called me names, it wouldn't have had the same sobering effect as this latest outpouring. But what reply was there to it all?

We looked silently at each other for a long moment. Then I walked out on to the balcony and sat at the little table, trying to think through the practicalities of the situation.

'Drink this.' Martin pushed a cup of warmed fruit juice to my lips. 'You'll get cold out here otherwise.'

We sat for a very long time without speaking. The sky turned from purple to black. Dogs barked in the distance. The wind blew softly on my face.

At last, I got up and went back inside. Maximin was now awake. He smiled as I approached him, lamp in hand. I looked down at him. I put the lamp on the table beside his cot and took him into my arms. I breathed in the slightly shitty smell of the only son I'd ever managed to hold.

I tried to control the spasms, but wept uncontrollably. The tears burned my eyes and I buried my face in Maximin's blanket.

'You're mine, you're mine,' I said again and again. 'You're mine, and I'll kill anyone who tries to take you from me.'

After what seemed another age, I felt Martin beside me. 'Aelric,' he said softly in Latin, 'I've sent down for hot water. There's a messenger from Theophanes. You must wash your face.'

There was an armed guard outside the Ministry. The few clerks who'd bothered turning up for work had all been kicked out into the street, where some of them now fraternised with the demonstrators. These had now taken to singing hymns and looking hopeful.

'He'll be coming out soon, you know,' said the old woman who'd spoken to Theophanes in the summer. 'The time of retribution is upon us. My son will come home again.'

I evaded her attempt to catch hold of me and slipped past. A silent crowd had gathered to watch the demonstrators. It was impossible to tell from their faces what they were thinking. Dressed mostly as if for church, they stood and watched, and waited for whatever might happen next.

As I finished threading my way through the crowd, Alypius came forward to meet me. He waved me past the guards and into the darkened hall of the Ministry. Lamp in hand, he led me up to Theophanes.

'I already know the truth,' said Theophanes, cutting off my account of Priscus. 'I climbed on to the walls before darkness and saw the man riding up and down and calling on the City to surrender. He's had quite an effect. About half the remaining nobility has now slipped out of the City, together with most of the senior Ministers. A few were caught and hanged as they tried to leave. Most bought their way out. I regret we are losing control over the garrison in charge of the land walls.

'But tell me, Aelric,' he said, changing the subject, 'what did you discover from Priscus? You were seen going together into the wine shop. You came out separately – he to open treason, you back to the Legation.'

'I know that you and he reached an agreement outside the Great One's tent,' I began. 'I know that you conspired to kill the Permanent Legate. And I know that you both agreed on my death.'

348

Theophanes checked me. 'You know that Priscus agreed on your death,' he repented with a laboured formality. 'That you are still alive and in good health should tell you the extent of my agreement.

'I have no doubt Priscus told you many things. But there are many other things far beyond his knowledge. For all you see it as your present duty to uncover these things, I must remind you yet again that knowing them would do you no good.'

'Theophanes, I will have the truth about the Permanent Legate's murder – and about everything else,' I said.

'Then you will have none from me,' he responded. 'However, we are meeting here to get one set of truths that you may readily have. Though, since they concern Priscus, they may come too late.'

I thought of those four Syrians down below, now a day into their solitary confinement. I'd been looking forward to showing Theophanes the benefits of an interrogation that didn't involve the rack and red-hot pincers. It no longer seemed such a fine idea, but it was already arranged and I could think of nothing else to do instead.

'Because I know this building better than I know the wrinkles on my own face,' Theophanes said, 'you will pardon me if I insist on leading the way.'

I followed Theophanes down the stairs from his office to the main hall, and then across to a locked doorway. As he unlocked the door and pulled it open, my stomach turned at the waft of cold, filthy air.

In all the ages during which the Ministry had stood, I wondered as I followed him down that endless spiral of worn-out steps, how many wretches had been dragged through this or the other entrance, and never come out again?

We passed into the entrance chamber I recalled from my first visit. It was a low-vaulted circular room with another set of steps on the far side. Equidistant between these two entrances, a wide passageway led into the endless and regular network of cells.

As before, the lamps flickered dimly in their niches. The reception desk was covered with much the same jumbled mass of papyrus. But—

'Where can they be?' Theophanes asked, looking round the empty room. 'The guards knew we had an appointment. I was here myself earlier to see that all was in readiness.' I strained to see into the network of corridors but heard and saw nothing. The whole place might have been evacuated.

'Do you know where the prisoners were put?' I asked Theophanes.

He nodded absently, still looking around the unexpected stillness of his own private Hell.

'Then we'll start with the big one,' I said. 'I mean the one with the scar on his left cheek that stops his beard from growing right. I think he was their leader.'

Theophanes fussed a while over the heavy ledger on the reception desk, turning the pages. He reached up to a board studded with what looked like hundreds of numbered hooks and lifted off a single set of keys. He tutted impatiently as he saw they were all out of sequence and searched again for the ring that carried the right number. Then he turned back to the ledger and made a series of neat entries.

'Order in this world begins with small things,' he said, blotting the parchment.

Then, without so much as a pause to get his bearings, he took up his lamp again and stepped into the passageway. I followed close behind, trying not to retch at the smell of the place. It was far worse than I remembered.

I tried at first to take note of the turns we made and the secondary corridors we passed. But I noticed the complex stretched under the whole Ministry building – even under the surrounding streets and squares. It was immense. But for Theophanes leading the way with the unthinking assurance of a native, I'd soon have been lost.

As we turned into another corridor, I saw two dark figures standing in the gloom of the far end. One was gigantically tall. The

other stooped. There was something furtive about their appearance. It was as if they'd been caught in some malevolent act.

We stopped. I fingered my knife. Theophanes smoothed his
robe in a gesture of confusion.

'Fancy meeting you here,' a voice rasped loudly. 'As ever, we
can dispense with prostrations. With these floors, you'd never get
the muck off your clothes.'

56

Phocas inspected himself in the long mirror Theophanes kept in his office.

'I don't suppose the blood shows too much against the purple – not in this light, anyway,' he said.

'If you please, Your Majesty.' Theophanes handed him a large cup of wine. Phocas drained it and let out a long sigh of contentment. He handed it back for a refill.

'Do I need explain myself to you?' he asked me.

'No, Caesar,' I said, trying not to look at the red smear that ran from his trailing robe to the door of the office.

'Then if you'll take advice from an older and wiser man,' he said, 'let me give you one of the main secrets of effective leadership. As an officer on the Danube, I never believed in giving orders I wasn't prepared to follow myself.'

'Clearing my accounts' is what he'd called it when stopping halfway up the spiral steps for a tipsy giggle. I didn't see what business it was of mine to ask how many prisoners had been held down there. It was enough to know that he'd gone down and ordered the dungeon guards to kill all of them. He and the huge black slave he'd brought in tow had then turned on the exhausted guards. It *was* my business that some of the prisoners had been mine. But there's nothing in the books of etiquette to cover protests to an Emperor for this sort of thing.

I was glad I'd taken care to put on common leather boots before coming out. Anything else would have been ruined by all the blood I hadn't seen on the floors.

'I see that fucker Priscus has shat on me,' said Phocas, still looking at himself in the mirror.

'Your Majesty will surely agree', Theophanes said, 'that Priscus has served his purpose remarkably well since we discovered his intentions. Everything we told him was passed back, and was implicitly believed by Heraclius.'

'I suppose he'll be more of a danger to Heraclius outside the City than he was to me inside,' Phocas said. He sank heavily into a chair covered in white kid leather. I could almost hear the squelching of his robe. I could certainly see the dark stain on the chair-back when he leaned forward.

He looked at me. 'Now, I find a vacancy has emerged at the head of the City defences. Bearing in mind the defection of almost all the qualified candidates – and the unreliability of those remaining – I am minded to appoint you to the position.'

'Sir,' I cried, aghast, 'I – I. . . .'

I trailed off. I was too young. I was a barbarian. I was the Pope's representative. I knew fuck all about the military. I didn't want to die. All I wanted was to go home.

'If I might be so bold as to suggest—'

Phocas cut Theophanes off. 'You suggest nothing,' he snarled in sudden anger. 'I'm Emperor yet. I still say what goes in this City. I'm keeping to my side of the bargain. You will therefore keep your mouth shut.'

A strange look on his face, Theophanes did as he was told. He turned back to me.

'I remove you from the post of Acting Permanent Legate,' he said. 'I now appoint you Count of the Palace Guard, which includes the newish post of Duke of the Sacred Defence.'

As he spoke, he splashed wine from his cup over the black slave who was nodding off on the floor beside him. He too was sodden with blood. Like water from a squeezed sponge, it oozed from his clothing on to the floorboards. The man jerked into life and handed up the leather satchel he'd been cuddling. From this, Phocas produced yet another of his parchment sheets.

'This gives formal effect to my wishes,' he said. He tried to wipe a spot of blood from the sheet. Instead, his finger only made a broader dark smear over the writing. 'I brought this along on the off-chance I'd catch you. How lucky we ran into each other downstairs.

'With immediate effect, you are transferred to duties of equal rank to those from which I relieve you. I appoint you Count of the Palace Guard and so forth, with supreme power over all life and property for the purpose of your commission,' he intoned. 'You will see there is no mention of appeals to me from any decision you make. You have the same rank and powers as dear Priscus.'

I struggled to find the words to extricate myself from this latest horror.

Phocas flashed me a thoroughly evil smile. 'Oh no, my lad,' he said, 'you don't get out of this at all. You get yourself off to the palace where you'll be kitted out in armour of gold and silver, and then greet your men. If you refuse my order, I'll have you impaled before morning.

'If you lose the battle on the streets, you either die or make whatever submission you can to Heraclius and Priscus. But let's be reasonable – that means you die. If you win, you become my champion. Play things right, and I'll think of chucking in my daughter and the succession. Since there's no one else left, it might as well be you.

'With hindsight, I can see that Priscus wasn't the right man for Domentia. He didn't use her well. You, on the other hand, will make an ideal husband. She might even fancy you. Certainly, you'll need to give her another son. I can't have a son of Priscus continuing my line.'

Unable to think of anything remotely better, I stood in front of the Emperor, bowing my obedience to his will.

'Go, my boy,' Phocas called, with a return to full good humour. 'You've a busy night ahead of you. I expect to find everything up to scratch on the streets tomorrow when – or if – I decide on my eve-of-battle inspection.'

As I bowed out of the room, I threw a final glance at Theophanes. He looked ninety if he was a day.

'It suits you better than the clerical robes,' Martin agreed. 'It's a shame they've finally arrived.'

Radogast untied the golden breastplate and I let out my first natural breath since leaving the Imperial Palace. Martin hadn't missed the scale of this latest disaster. Given any choice in the matter, he'd have had the Legation gates locked, with us on the inside and the keys dropped into a sewer. On the other hand, I could sense some relief that the blasphemy of my position as Acting Permanent Legislator was at an end.

But my new appointment – and I can't sufficiently emphasise the fact – was a fucking disaster. All else aside, I knew as much about military tactics as I did about the laying of mosaics. Whatever plans of defence I might take over would have been already betrayed by Priscus. And that was assuming his plans were any good in the first place.

On the other hand, the shock of the appointment had wondrously settled me after that horrid time with Priscus. Men often dull the pain of torture by biting their tongues. One pain cancels the other. So it was with me. Back in the Legation earlier, I'd thought the pain of that truth about Maximin would never pass. Now, it was almost forgotten with this latest turn of the page.

And I looked absolutely lush in the suit of armour that had been waiting for me at the palace. It had been so skilfully adapted that it might have been made specially for me.

I scooped Maximin out of the cot from where he'd been solemnly regarding me, and carried him triumphantly about the room. I'd taken many things from Priscus – his job, his armour, his son. None of them might do me much good, but I might as well try to enjoy them.

'So he killed them all?' Martin asked, now in Celtic.

'Every last one of them, it seems,' I replied, giving Maximin my helmet to pat. 'On the way out, I'll swear I saw blood dripping down the walls. They must have gone through each cell in turn. Even with the guards to help, I can't say how the Emperor and his slave could still stand afterwards.

'For what it may now be worth,' I added after another look in the mirror, 'I know it wasn't Priscus who hired those Syrians. It was the Emperor. I had a good look at his bloody footprints in the

Ministry. They were the same as the ones in the Permanent Legate's bedroom. The left foot was decidedly shorter than the right.'

God forgotten for the moment, Martin's face turned grey.

'I find it reasonable', I went on, 'to assume he had everyone under the Ministry butchered to save himself the embarrassment of being revealed as the man who hired those assassins. Having me put to death would itself have been embarrassing, bearing in mind what he'd appointed me to represent. But he was so eager to cover any trail that led to Demetrius that ordering me and Priscus to back away wasn't enough.'

'So Phocas killed the Permanent Legate?' Martin asked. 'And Authari?'

'No,' I said. 'That was still probably Demetrius. But Phocas was in the Legation to help get rid of the body. If two monks really were seen there last Sunday, Phocas was one of them. That raises any number of new hypotheses to test against the facts. However, the investigation is ended – at least, for the moment.

'Now, to other business,' I said. 'I'm going out shortly to see what forces I might have for tomorrow. I'd like you to start supervising the packing of boxes. I want all the more important papers and books safely stowed in the official areas of the Legation.'

There was a knock at the door. Antony entered the room.

'My Lord,' he said, 'I've drafted the documents you asked for. All is in order.'

He'd been quick about his business. I'd only instructed him a while earlier in the main hall as I came back in.

'Excellent,' I said. 'Martin, be so kind as to assemble all the slaves in this office. I have an important announcement to make.'

All my slaves stood before me, including Gutrune. With them were the three slaves Theophanes had passed over to me to keep the bathhouse in order. These had been kept away from anything confidential and, having been watched on and off over the past few days, seemed to fit nicely into the household. I didn't know what they could have heard of the latest news, but they looked worried.

'Martin,' I said, 'I shall make my announcement in Latin. I'd like you to interpret straight into Lombardic. That should make what I have to say comprehensible to everyone.'

I stood up. 'Dear friends,' I began, 'you will be aware that everyone expects an attack on the City tomorrow or the day after at the latest. It is now impossible to believe that a gate will not be opened to Heraclius. I cannot say what will happen when he enters the City. But I must act now so far as I can to ensure the safety of those who look to me.'

I raised my voice and spoke slowly, stopping after every clause to make sure I was clearly followed.

'By the authority vested in me by His Imperial Majesty, I believe that the safety of the Empire and of the City requires me to free certain persons from the servitude to which they were born or to which they have been reduced by the fortunes of war.'

I named all the slaves present. As I did so, Martin took up the relevant deed and passed it to me for signing. I had no seal ready but Antony had assured me that a signature would be sufficient. As I signed each document, he added the seal of the Legation. I no longer had any right to this, so had passed it to him for safekeeping.

'To those of you who know something of the law,' I continued, 'I say that this is an Act of State. Being so, it requires none of the formalities that must attend a private manumission. It is a legal and an irrevocable act. However, should anyone be inclined, once order has been restored, to question the legality of my act, each deed here granted is witnessed on behalf of His Holiness the Universal Bishop in Rome.

'You are each, as of this moment, free. You are free to go when and where you please. In a moment, I must leave you on official business. When I am gone, Martin will give each of you a purse of gold and silver to start you in your new lives. It is my advice that you should stay in this Legation so long as it remains safe. If, in defiance of all law and all religion, it is entered by any hostile force, I advise you to leave at once. You must offer no resistance.

'Gutrune' – I turned to her and spoke in the simple Lombardic she was happiest with – 'if it is necessary for you to leave the

Legation, I want you to take Maximin with you. If possible, you will return him to Martin. If this is not possible, I wish you to bring him up as if he were your own child. Martin will make additional financial arrangements to cover this eventuality.'

I raised my hand for silence. I had no time for extended thanks. Besides, I have never encouraged emotional scenes where they could be avoided. I had cleared my own accounts, and that would have to be an end of the matter. I embraced each free citizen as I handed out the deeds.

In a babble of 'God be with you!' the room emptied.

'Can you help me back on with this thing?' I asked Martin, pointing at the breastplate. 'I have no idea how to tie all these leather straps.'

'Can't we just run away?' Martin asked with a shaking voice. 'Surely we can disguise ourselves and hide out in one of the Latin districts. We can come out again when all this is over. Can't you see that Phocas is sending you to your death?'

'That seems to be part of his intention,' I agreed. 'Perhaps he wants to make a better job of it than he made last night with those Syrians. More likely, though, he just wants someone to slow things down in the streets while he prepares his own Thermopylae in the Imperial Palace.'

I silenced whatever comment Martin had begun.

'Listen,' I said, dropping from pure habit into Celtic, 'Phocas tells me he's armed his eunuchs, and plans to lead them in a fight to the last at the entrance to the Throne Room. For the moment, he has enough control in the city to be able to track me down if I try making a dash for it. Once Heraclius is through the gates, however, I doubt I shall be the only defender buggering off out of sight.

'Now, Martin,' I went on, fixing him in the eye, 'what I said to the slaves goes for you as well. I want you out of here at the first smell of trouble. Take whatever you need to get back to Rome. If you can get the child back to Gretel, so much the better.'

'You have very little respect for my courage,' he said, his exalted tone returning. 'Perhaps I don't always acquit myself well in the presence of the unexpected. But I know my duty.'

I cut him off. 'Your duty', I said, 'is to take that child back to Rome. Beyond that, you look to your own safety. We don't know for certain it's all up for Phocas. If it is, I'm more likely to get out safely if I'm alone. We'll have dinner in Rome yet. I'm sure you can persuade Sveta not to poison me.'

Martin ignored me. 'I bought a relic of Saint Victorinus when we got back to the City,' he said. 'It is attested by the Holy Fathers of his own monastery. I want you to wear it when you go out on the streets. He saved you once before.'

'My dear Martin,' I said, trying not to laugh at the shrivelled finger he passed across the desk. 'Put that thing back in its box.'

'Then we shall all pray for you,' he said.

'I'm not going to my death just yet,' I reminded him. 'I'll be back at dawn.'

57

After several months in the place, I'd come to take the sheer size of Constantinople for granted. Now I was put in charge of its defence, I was brought back to my first realisation. There are nearly ten miles of wall to cover. As I keep saying, the City walls are impregnable; and, as hardly a decade goes by without one of more attempts to breach them, they are always kept in excellent repair.

My problem, though, was a shortage of men. Just about all the officers in the garrison and in the City Guard had now deserted. Phocas had caught a few and hanged them, but that didn't solve the immediate problem. Many of the common soldiers were staying at home, and there was no way of getting them back on duty in time for the expected attack. The rest made it clear to me that they'd do their minimal duty of holding the walls, but would do nothing to endanger their own lives.

I might be its Count. Bugger me, though, if I saw one member of the Palace Guard.

When Priscus had been told to recruit the citizens to mount an internal defence, that had been largely to keep everyone busy and take their minds off the coming struggle. No one had seriously expected that this line of defence would be needed. Now it was the only line of defence. The Green Faction, under old General Bonosus, was looking after the Main Harbour. The Emperor had dug his younger brother out of a brothel to muster the few regular troops who remained in the City.

As head of the City's defences I'd spent much of the night hurrying from barricade to barricade, inspecting them and giving little speeches of encouragement. The outer barricades had been largely deserted, and I'd moved the few armed citizens who were there back to a smaller line around the central areas. Some of these obeyed. Many others, I later discovered, had gone off home.

The only enthusiasm I found was among the university students. They had no commitment to Phocas or to anyone else, but the thought of a good fight was far more exciting than reading up for examinations. I bumped into them as I came away from the Eleutherian Harbour, where I'd been watching brightly lit ships darting about some business which the decrepit veterans assigned to my staff were unable to explain.

'Have any of you read much military history?' I asked after draining one of the wine jugs offered me. I'd paid little attention to battles myself, except in Thucydides and a few other historians, where they are integral to the text.

'No,' answered one with a piping voice – he looked about fifteen – 'but an uncle of mine did once write a poem about Saint Sebastian. It had lots of killing in it.'

'That will have to do,' I said. 'Now listen,' I told the whole group. 'I don't doubt Heraclius will get into the City. When he does come, it will probably be from two or more directions at once. Therefore, we don't go out of the main ring of barricades. Go outside, and we'll be cut off in no time. I want you gathered by the Great Church when news comes of an attack. We then go together to whatever place needs additional defence. We fight together. We stay together. We don't face the enemy at any time in open terrain. We pick them off half a dozen at a time, and preferably from behind.'

I knew nothing yet of generalship in the regular sense, but I had led that band of ruffians on the Wessex borders with reasonable success. Defending a gigantic city with a thousand miles of streets was beyond my present abilities, but I felt some comfort in having my own group of irregulars.

I made a literary speech about deathless glory. Then I sent everyone home to get some rest.

The Great Church was crowded when I arrived there. With bonfires to keep off the night chill, hundreds lolled on the pavements of the square outside, eating and drinking. It was hardly a merry occasion, but the drink had cheered everyone.

Theophanes caught up with me as I was admiring myself in a shop window. He was alone.

'Aelric,' he said, puffing at the exertion of having to move quickly around the City without his chair – 'Aelric, I want you to know that this wasn't any of my doing. All I wanted was for you to stay in the Legation and wait on events. My juggling has not worked out as expected.'

'What's done is done,' I said and waved dismissively. 'But what are your plans now? Have you come to volunteer for a place at the barricades? You're a neat hand with a dagger, as I recall.'

He smiled grimly. 'You don't seem to understand the seriousness of what is happening,' he said.

'I understand perfectly well what is happening,' I snapped. 'As ever, I don't understand *why* it is. Now, Theophanes, since I hardly think you've come here with any new revelations, I'll simply ask what I can do for you.'

Theophanes looked quickly around. There was no one in hearing distance. He leaned close to me.

'There is a little monastery by the Pantocrator Church – it's the one close by the old wall of Constantine,' he said. 'Go there if the need arises. The Fathers are all Monophysites but good people otherwise. They owe me much for the protection I've given them over the years. Show them this—'

With an effort, he pulled a black ring from one of his fingers. 'Give them this, and trust them. Once order is restored, dress as one of their own and set out for Pavia or Marseilles. So long as you don't show your face or hair, you can easily pass as a cleric of any theological persuasion. No one ever stops a monk.

'Go, and don't ever come back to the City or to any Imperial territory.'

I took the ring and held it up to the light. I'd noticed it outside the City, when it had been the only one not stripped from him by the barbarians. It was of heavily worn and pitted bronze.

'Why are you doing this for me?' I asked.

'I do it because I can,' came the answer. 'If I could do more, I would.'

'And what of you, Theophanes?' I asked.

His face closed over. 'Be assured', he said, 'that Theophanes the Magnificent has his own plans for when the moment comes. Only remember that I served the Empire to the best of my abilities when I could. The Persians may overwhelm you. If not them, some other race will finish the job. It could all have been so different if only this ghastly Religion of the Son hadn't come to divide citizen from citizen.

'You're a Westerner. Even if in Latin, you're trapped within the circle of Greek theology. None of you – Greek, Latin, barbarian – has ever realised that Easterners don't fundamentally care about the Son. For us, it has always been the Father and the Father alone. That isn't just the Jews – it's all of us.

'If Constantine had only realised this, he could have united the Empire for eternity. He missed his chance. No one else after him thought to repair the mistake. Now, if it ever is repaired, it will be from without your civilisation, and to the eventual ruin of your civilisation.'

The last thing I'd expected from Theophanes at this moment was a lecture on theology.

'Will I ever learn what you and Phocas and Demetrius were up to?' I asked.

'Pray that you can ask that of His Excellency the Dispensator in Rome,' Theophanes replied. 'He knows all.'

'Will the Emperor be joining me tonight?' I asked.

Theophanes laughed bitterly. 'His Majesty is currently so drunk, he can't hold a pen to sign the last death warrants. Pray you'll not see him again.'

He turned abruptly and walked away from me. Some old men squeezed into armour blocked his way at first. As he reached them, they suddenly stood back and bowed for him to pass. I watched him walk briskly across the square past the Great Church. At the far end, he turned not in the direction of the Ministry, but towards the palace.

I watched until he was out of sight. Then I turned back to the shop window. Inside, clearly visible in the torchlight, were some beautiful shoes. One pair I was sure would fit me. I had only to smash one of the panes and reach in for them. No one would stop me.

In the end I decided it would set a bad example. So I went home to catch up on sleep.

As the gate of the Legation swung shut behind me, I breathed a sigh of relief. The lamps were turned down but I could see that all was neat and orderly. I crossed the hall and rapped on the door to my suite.

'Who's there?' Martin hissed from behind the heavy wood.

'It's me,' I said. 'I've come for a break from leading my army of old men and schoolboys.'

Fully clothed, I lay on my bed. Martin sat beside me.

'I went out myself earlier,' he said. 'I know you told me to stay inside, but I had to get out for a walk. Everyone was talking of you as a future Emperor.'

I sat up. 'In the name of God!' I cried. 'Let's hope that doesn't get back to any of the Imperial rivals. Besides, the last thing I want is to rule over this mob of lunatics.'

I showed him the ring Theophanes had given me. 'This means', I said, 'we all have some means of escape. You can now stay here in good conscience with the others.'

'God spoke to me while you were out,' Martin said in a voice that he might have used for reminding me of a lunch appointment with Sergius. 'He told me you would be saved if I did my duty. He finally told me why I was spared in the Yellow Camp.'

I lay back and stared up at the plaster vaulting. Outside my window, all remained dark. I really should try to get some rest. Before leaving me, Martin passed on some thoroughly grim news that no one else had seen fit to share with me. Just before nightfall, the chain securing the Golden Horn had been let down from the Galatan shore.

The City was now indefensible on every side.

58

The attack started in the middle of the next morning. It was a fine day. A good south wind was blowing away the broken cloud above the City. We'd not be fighting in rain or cold. Nor, though, would it be too hot for action.

Bathed and oiled with unusual care, I stood in my fine armour on the dome of the Great Church. From here, I had an unbroken view of the whole City and of the seas and the countryside that lay beyond.

The smoke signals I'd arranged went up from four places at once along the land walls. They went up, and then vanished in the wind.

'The Second and Fourth Military Gates,' Martin said, pointing due west. 'Plus, I think, the Saint Anna and Charisian Gates.'

I doubted if there had been any military resistance at all. What surprised me was that anyone had bothered to follow my orders to signal that the gates were open. Perhaps every gate had opened.

All that mattered was that Heraclius was now inside the City. His forces would be marching up along those straight, wide streets, and they'd be on us in due course.

As we joined the crowds gathered outside the church I was met by the aged guard who'd stopped me all that time ago outside the Senatorial Dock.

'If it may please you, sir,' he gasped, out of breath from running, 'the Green Faction has betrayed the Main Harbour. They've declared for Heraclius and turned on the Blues.'

I looked at the Aged Guard. He looked steadily back.

'Is it worth fighting at all?' I asked uncertainly. Was this the excuse I'd been hoping for to call the whole thing off?

He smiled and drew himself more stiffly to attention. 'Duty is duty, sir,' he said. 'So long as you lead us, we'll fight for you.' He touched the blue cloth that covered part of his breastplate. 'In any event, sir,' he added, 'it's too late for any of us to back out. Our enemy now isn't Heraclius. It's them shitbag Greens. If we try dispersing, they'll pick us off in the streets. Those of us what escape won't never hear the end of it in the Circus.'

A younger and less military man spoke up from behind me:

'Too right, My Lord. It's battle or death for all on these barricades. It's already bloody murder down in the docks. We fight until Heraclius draws off the Greens and sends in his regulars. We go on fighting until he gives us terms.'

There was a murmur of agreement from the crowd that had gathered to hear the exchange. For the first time, I realised that everyone around me – and everyone I'd seen manning the barricades – was wearing something blue. The only ones not in blue were my students. I knew Priscus had recruited the Circus Factions. I'd been too wrapped up in my own business, and I was still too fresh to Circus politics, to realise that he'd recruited them as members of existing armies rather than of a citizen militia.

'Another thing, sir,' the Aged Guard added confidentially. 'Orders is that if you won't lead us, we're to hang you from the torch bracket nearest the doorway of the Great Church. You could, of course, countermand the order, was we to put you up for Emperor. You couldn't be worse than the last few we've had.'

I smiled and shook my head. I looked out over the sea of faces. Some were troubled. Most were expectant.

'Then we fight,' I said. I ignored the threat. I had no duty to Phocas. I had none to any of the Circus Factions. But I was their leader, and that surely meant something in this world of multiple betrayals.

As I spoke, a cheer went up. It began close by me, and spread backwards through the crowd. It was taken up by groups beyond the main crowd, and cheering rang back from the barricades in the streets beyond the square.

Women and children and very old men began pouring out of the Great Church. 'Is it victory?' I heard one calling. 'Is it victory?'

I realised with a shock they also were all wearing blue.

Now it was no longer a matter of Phocas against Heraclius, the priests in the Great Church abandoned all neutrality. To still greater cheers, blue banners streamed from the windows fringing the upper dome. Priests emerged from another doorway in the church with blue ribands tied to their crucifixes.

I didn't like the inattention to the approaching enemy. If the regulars still had a long way to go before they hit the centre, the Greens would surely be upon us at any moment. But the impromptu service and blessing of weapons put a fighting spirit into my men that I hadn't expected ever to see.

With Martin beside me, I crossed the square. Now the ceremonial part of the battle was over, non-combatants were struggling like mad things to squeeze into the still open doorways in the Great Church. One despairing old Senator who'd come late with his wife waved a bag of gold to buy his way in. He was ignored.

My student band let up a cheer as I came in sight. In an almost passable imitation of the Palace Guard, they raised their weapons in salute.

'Martin,' I said, 'go back and stand by the Great Church. It's too late to get you into the main area, but the priests will let you back up to the dome if need be.'

I turned from him. 'Right, my boys.' I shouted. 'Are we going to clear those fucking Heraclians out of this city? Or are we just going to show them how to fight?'

I tried to think of some battle cry that was both literary and relevant.

I was beaten to it.

'Blue – Blue – Blue – Blue,' chanted the true racing fans around me.

I'd expected the exit into Middle Street from the Forum of Constantine would be the weakest point in the defence. Though we had a stout wooden wall built across the street, there was a wide-open space beyond for an attacking force to gather. If you think of it in terms of a battering ram against a door, there was room here for a good, hard run.

The first attack on the wall came from the Greens. They poured into the Forum from the direction of the Main Harbour. I watched them from the platform that ran along the upper part of the wall and let us see over at breast height. There was no appearance of discipline among them. Their weapons and armour were as make-shift as those of my own men. Their big advantage was in numbers. We were strung out along a line that had to be held at all times. They could stay together in larger groups and make their attack at any point.

The Greens filled the wide expanse of the Forum. As they slowly came forward, they struck up one of their Circus chants. That low, rhythmical grunting a few days earlier had seemed part of the good-humoured badinage before the races. Now, it was in earnest. It had a sound about it of blood and death. At the back of the crowd, I saw pikes with heads stuck on them. It wasn't hard to guess, from the imprecations that began around me, that these were the decapitated heads of Blues picked off after the sudden change of side at the Main Harbour.

The Greens marked every downbeat of their chant by striking their weapons on the pavement.

The Blues around me began a chant of their own. Then – just like at the races, though now with malevolence – the ritual insults and curses flew back and forth.

As the Greens came within striking distance, my Blues took up their slingshots and let fly with volley after volley of the excrement they'd taken the trouble to collect from around the Great Church. The smell was overpowering. The Greens let out a howl of rage as it splattered all over them. Their fine green banners turned brown. Some slipped on the splashes of shit littering the ground in front of them and fell heavily down.

The Blues screamed with laughter. Some of my more vulgar men even took to pelting each other. Their betters called them to order with canes, and turned their attention back to the advancing enemy.

The Greens were now coming on fast. Then, with a last and terrible scream of hatred, they broke into a run for the last twenty yards of the advance. As their twisted faces grew clearer, I heard the panted aftersound of their war chant and the scuffing of leather on pavement as the massed attack of the Greens came closer and closer.

With a sudden shock, they crashed into the wall. The wooden planks shook horribly at the impact of so many hundreds of bodies. I clutched at the inner frame of the wall to hold myself steady. I thought at first it would tumble down, and we'd be into open combat.

But the wall held. Now into another of their Circus chants, the Green attackers grabbed hold of the walls where they could and rocked backwards and forwards. I thought to jump down before I was pitched off, but the Blues beside me now went into action. They poked the attackers with sharpened stakes and poured cauldrons of boiling water over their heads.

It was very light work to break the force of the Green attack. After taking a few dozen casualties, they drew back. They stood about ten yards from the wall, throwing stones and chanting more factional insults. The occasional severed head bumped against the outer planks. Shaking their weapons, the Blues chanted back. No one seemed inclined to engage in more bloodshed.

I climbed down from the wall. 'This all seems to be under control,' I said briefly to one of my students.

At that moment a message was delivered from the barricade by the Saint Julian Church. This was one of the strongpoints, but now it was under attack by regular troops.

59

We arrived just as the enemy was battering at the wall. In scarlet cloaks and pointed silver helmets, the soldiers had marched straight down the shopping street beyond, and were now attacking the wall more effectively than the Greens had managed.

The citizen defenders hadn't yet run away. But they stood nervously back from our side of the wall. Some of them were still throwing a few stones over the top. For all the good that did the defence, it might have been rain.

'On to the rooftops!' I shouted. I led the way up to the roof of the church. Some of the Blues already there were looking nervously over to the archers who stood further back from the attack force. Though not so dangerous in street-fighting as on an open battle-field, archers on the opposing side are bad news when you have none yourself.

I took up one of the cobblestones Priscus had made sure to put up there in great baskets. I threw it and hit one of the attackers straight on the forehead. He went down like a stunned ox. The soldiers beside him stopped their pushing at the wall and looked up.

'Come on,' I said encouragingly. 'They die just like the rest of us.'

I threw another stone and this time caught an officer on the shoulder. There was a shout of sudden confidence around me, and a whole volley of stones followed mine.

'Now for the glass,' I said. The small catapult that had been dragged up there went into action. Heaps of glass dishes and drinking vessels flew about thirty yards down the street beyond our barricade. These didn't hit anyone. Instead, their purpose was to hold the cavalry back. The enemy plan, it was clear, was for the

370

infantry to smash the wall down so that mounted troops could sweep straight along the street to the city centre.

That had to be avoided whatever the cost. Now their blood was fully up, my Blues were a match for any regular troops so long as we had some advantage of cover. There was nothing we could do against heavy cavalry. That would go straight through us.

Well, we did avoid it. That set of barricades wasn't going anywhere soon. And horses would now have to be led very carefully round those shards of glass.

I felt a surge of joy as I called the men back. The defence wasn't going too badly so far.

A hand brushed my cloak. 'My Lord,' someone said from behind, 'they are breaking through by the Urban Prefecture building.'

He was right. By the time we got there, they had already done so. Soldiers stood with raised shields to fend off our hail of slingshot, while Green volunteers cleared the far less solid barricade Priscus had put there.

'Charge!' I called to my students. My mouth had gone very dry and my sword arm trembled as I led them into battle.

We took the soldiers by surprise. They hadn't expected active resistance and we were on them before they could mount a defence. I struck one of them straight in his bearded face with the pommel of my sword. I drew its edge along his throat and pushed him back against another two. I snapped another's neck with the edge of my shield. Beside me, my students hacked and shouted their way through the soldiers as they pushed them back to the other side of the barricade. We moved away just in time to avoid the boiling oil that had begun to rain from the upper windows of the Prefecture.

With the soldiers in retreat, we turned on the trapped Greens and butchered them until the ground under our feet turned slippery with blood. I lost my sword in one particularly fat victim. It went in easily enough, but got stuck somewhere on the way out. He squealed and rolled his eyes as I pushed in and out of his body. It must have seemed rather comical to anyone watching.

'Take this one,' somebody yelled in my ear, passing over a much heavier military sword. The new weight and length took a bit of getting used to, but this one cut through flesh and bone as if it were a butcher's cleaver.

With a blast of trumpets, the soldiers were sent back to rescue the Greens. We now went for Greens and soldiers indiscriminately. The ground before us was a natural killing ground; we had the advantage of cover and a slight incline.

I picked up a spear and threw it at the fleeing soldiers. It caught one of them in the leg. As he went down, one of my students – the young man who'd spoken of Saint Sebastian – disregarded my orders and ran forward. He dodged past the pools of steaming oil that covered the ground and killed the man with a sword-thrust into his mouth. Waving a stolen shield above his head, he danced back behind the barricades, his face shining with joy.

I wanted to supervise the rebuilding of the barricade while the soldiers were in retreat but before I could do so another message arrived. We were hard pressed a few hundred yards down the line where someone had fired one of the buildings. I filled my lungs with clean air as we dashed into the cloud of smoke and felt our way towards the new threatened point. Buildings were burning around us. Missiles rained from the tops of burning buildings as we fought and killed and raced from one threatened point to another.

There were still no cavalry attacks, perhaps because the streets were so choked with debris. But the main danger now was arrows. It seemed that hundreds of archers had been brought forward to join the few I'd seen earlier. They stood out of range of anything we could send back at them, firing off volley after volley of arrows. Most of them fell spent around us, but they made getting about the streets inside the barricades increasingly slow and difficult.

The fighting had by now reached the stage when we were hard pressed everywhere. Blues fought back against Greens with murderous passion. When I and my students got to any one barricade, many of the Greens turned and ran, to be replaced by regular soldiers who usually waited for us to run at them sword in hand.

But we were untrained and outnumbered. The proper place for my Blues was on the City walls, fetching and carrying for the regular defenders. A leader of genius like Belisarius might have kept the defence going longer and more effectively. Had I known then what I learned many years later, I could have used fire and the safe lines of communication offered by rooftops to inflict cata- strophic losses on the enemy. But that day I had only the skills of a bandit and the dispositions made by Priscus.

And there were now so many threatened points. I knew that we were being pushed steadily back, but we had to hold the line we had. I'd already pulled everyone back to the innermost ring of defences. There was nowhere further to retreat to and regroup.

We fought with frantic energy. My sword twisted in my grip with blood and sweat and weariness as I hacked and stabbed at the soldiers. So far as I could tell, I was unwounded myself, but I tripped several times over the bodies that now littered the rubble-strewn streets – bodies both in uniform and in makeshift armour.

At last, that poor Saint Sebastian boy died in my arms. He'd taken an arrow in his throat. His face still shining, he choked with his last breath over the poem Simonides had written so long ago for the Spartan dead at Thermopylae:

> Here dead we lie because we did not choose
>> To live and shame the land from which we sprung.
> Life, to be sure, is nothing much to lose;
>> But young men think it is, and we were young.

As I looked down into the dead eyes of his still face, my mind began to clear. Simonides had known how to speak for the Spartans. Their heroes had died for a country that was worth any number of lives. What could I ever hope to say to that boy's mother? That he'd died to buy time for Phocas?

So far as I could tell, he hadn't even died for the Blue Faction. Perhaps he'd died for me.

I sat down heavily beside him and pushed his eyes closed. An officer in the attack force stood over me. I reached for my sword.

'Fuck off!' I said wearily.

The man looked at me and walked smartly off.

I heard yet another blast of the military trumpets and then a loud voice shouting in the distance: 'Put your weapons down. Stand against the walls. We give you quarter.'

I heard another voice from a different direction: 'Put your weapons down. Your battle is lost. You have full quarter.'

'They're right,' Martin spoke urgently behind me. 'It's all over. You must get away.'

I looked round. It was Martin indeed. I'd thought at first I was hearing things. He was nursing a cut to his arm but was otherwise unharmed.

What the fuck was he doing here? I hadn't noticed him during the fighting. So far as I'd thought of him at all, it was to assume that he was safe inside the Great Church.

He sawed at the straps of my breastplate with a broken sword until the thing fell away from my body. It was splashed with blood and dented all over.

I helped him pull the helmet off my head. This also was dented nearly out of shape. I let him throw a piece of cloth over my hair.

'Where are the others?' I asked, confused at the sudden silence around me. I coughed as the wind blew smoke into my face.

'Dead or gone home,' he said.

He pulled me to my feet.

'We must get out of here,' he said. 'There's no quarter for you. Before the Prefecture building fell, its defenders hailed you as Emperor.'

'Stupid fucking bastards,' I croaked. All of a sudden, I was thirsty beyond imagining.

I had by now recovered my senses as much as I needed them. One after the other, I stretched my arms and legs, expecting to feel a stab of white pain at any moment. But I felt nothing. I'd been in the thick of the battle and I hadn't picked up a scratch. Given time, I'd have started an argument with Martin about the power of his holy relics.

I looked around me. Except that there was no grass, the street looked like one of the tattier parts of Rome – all smashed wood and other things.

'Which way to the Legation?' I asked weakly.

60

I don't know how we got back to the Legation. There were soldiers everywhere. Citizens scurried around, searching for loved ones or loot. A few times, I saw soldiers looking at me. One raised his sword in a strange salute. But no one tried to stop us.

There were a few bodies in the square outside, and one or two piles of discarded loot. Otherwise all looked much as usual. The Legation was just inside the ring of defences but I didn't recall any fighting here. Smoke drifted into the square but from some distance away.

I approached the gate as if in a dream. It was shut. I prayed that it was locked and that all was well inside. As I drew closer, my head was pounding as if I were going into battle again.

'God be praised!' said Martin in a quivering voice when we reached the gate.

I touched it gently. No movement. It was surely locked. I pushed harder.

The gate moved and we both stood looking at the inch of darkness that had opened before us. Neither of us moved. It was like being in a dream. The faint sound of shouting from the streets behind us died away to an oppressive silence. The rest of the world might not have existed as we stood, stupidly, looking at that strip of darkness.

I pushed harder at the gate and we stepped into the gloom of the main hall. At first, everything seemed as it should be. There were the same patterns of light and shadow, the same dull quietness of the place. Then I saw the empty lodge just inside to my right. Where were the doorkeepers?

'We must go upstairs,' said Martin in an odd voice, but he seemed as rooted to the spot as I was.

I made a tremendous effort and stepped forward. 'Come on,' I said, taking Martin by the arm. I found my teeth chattering uncontrollably.

The door to my suite was off its hinges. The bars Authari had worked so hard to procure and fit were smashed with the force of whatever had been brought against the door.

Upstairs, everyone was dead.

We found Radogast first. He lay at the top of the stairs. He'd been almost cut to pieces in the desperate struggle. His severed right arm still clutched a military cloak.

Gutrune lay in the corridor outside my office. Her throat had been slit. She'd died with a bloody knife in her hand. The dent in the lead feeding bottle showed that she must have used it as a club.

The other dead bodies also showed signs of desperate resistance.

And Maximin?

We ran up and down the corridor, looking into each room.

Nothing.

There was no sign of looting. This had been a tight military operation. There had been a wild struggle but its outcome could never have been in doubt.

'Aelric,' Martin cried from my office. 'Aelric, it's Antony – he's still alive.'

Alive he was, though only just. He was sitting on the floor and he groaned as Martin lifted the cup of water to his lips.

'Men,' he whispered, 'armed men. They had the Emperor's authority. All was in order when I had the gate opened. Priscus' – he swallowed – 'he came in with full authority. The doorkeepers let him in. I protested the violation of our immunity. I tried to stop them from taking the dear child.'

He coughed and blood ran down his chin. I looked at the great spreading stain on his robe.

'The law says the authorities can enter in an emergency to secure the Legation. They have no right to—'

He coughed again. More blood. His face turned an ashen colour as his lips described the word 'right'. I took hold of him and held him during his last violent spasm.

Martin pulled the robe over his face as I drained the water jug.

'I should have been here,' I said flatly. 'I could have kept Priscus out.' I imagined Priscus holding up Maximin to see the work of butchery against the only family he'd known. I could see the look on the man's face and hear the triumph in his voice as he took possession of his alienated property.

He hadn't killed Maximin. That much was certain. If the child's body wasn't here, it was repossession that Priscus had in mind. He'd thrown Maximin out before changing sides. Once he had changed sides, he'd needed another son and heir.

I shook my head to try and get it to focus on the immediate present.

'I could have instructed the officials not to open up,' I said in elaboration.

'No,' said Martin. 'You'd have ended like Radogast. If Priscus hadn't been let in, he'd only have broken in. Whatever else you may have done or not done today, you couldn't have prevented this.'

He stood up. He put his hands on my shoulders and steadied me as I began to shake again. Another moment, and I'd have lost control.

'Aelric, we've got to see if anyone is alive in the main Legation, and get the place secured. Come on. We need to find the others.'

We went back into the main hall just as a couple of soldiers Priscus had left behind as guards were returning from the Permanent Legate's side of the building. One was straining under the weight of the silver crucifix they'd taken from the chapel. Another carried a pile of jewelled icons.

'Fucking good stuff here, mate,' one of them began with a drunken wave of his booty. Then he remembered who and where he was, and felt for his sword.

I made short and brutal work of him. Once you're into a rhythm of killing, it doesn't greatly matter how tired you are. With the sword-thrust I made into his unprotected throat, he must have been dead before he hit the pavement.

377

I turned to deal with his colleague, but Martin had got there already. The soldier lay gurgling at his feet, a bronze pen straight through his windpipe. With the look of an avenging angel on his face, Martin stared grimly down at his work. How he had managed to get the better of an armed soldier was as far beyond me as how he'd managed to stand by me throughout the battle without being recognised or killed.

We found the Legation officials and slaves locked in one of the storage houses near the pigsties. We had no keys, but the lock was easy enough to smash from the outside. As they emerged blinking into the light, they confirmed what we had already guessed. Priscus had arrived on regular form but once in the Legation he had gone wild. The fact that he'd locked them up rather than killed them showed that he hadn't forgotten everything about Papal immunity, even under the influence of those shitty drugs.

Another reason to suppose Maximin was safe.

Martin took control of the Legation staff. He ordered the gates to be secured and had the bodies taken away to be prepared for a decent burial. He even set some of the slaves about cleaning the blood off the floors of our suite and righting the furniture. I could hear him scolding them as I sat in the lead bath and had warm water splashed over me.

'We'll get out of here once it's dark and you've had something like a rest,' he'd snapped before pushing me into the bath. 'For the moment, I'm assuming Heraclius has more to do than come looking for you here. We both need to get clean and change into different clothes. Stay here until I come for you. I'll get as much money as I can lay hands on. I don't suppose your parchment money will be worth anything after today. I can't say any good has ever come of it,' he'd added with a glance that managed to express his contempt of the financial world.

By the time we were dressed in clean but inconspicuous clothes, it was turning dark. Against my will, I'd dozed a long while in the bath which the Legation slaves had kept topped up with warm water. I emerged from the bath less exhausted than when I'd gone in, but was now beginning to ache all over from the strain of of the day's fighting.

After we'd eaten with the Legation staff – not a cheerful meal, but a good solid dish of pork sausage and stale bread, all washed down with beer – I was beginning to feel more like my usual self.

'I have to kill Priscus,' I said to Martin as we went back upstairs to my office. 'I can't save Maximin from him in any other way. I need to get close enough to him to get a knife into his throat.'

I looked round the office. Order had been restored. It was as if nothing had happened. I could almost imagine that I heard Gutrune's heavy tread on the boards outside as she went to attend to Maximin.

The Legation officials and slaves continued to act as if there had been no change in my status because they had no leadership to tell them otherwise. They were even sending up trays of wine and warm fruit juice for us.

But everything had changed irrevocably. Whatever I might be doing tomorrow evening, I would not be sitting here. I could no longer regard any of these things as mine.

'You'll do no such thing,' Martin told me. 'You'll remember that you have a natural child and a woman waiting for you in Rome. If you've lost Maximin, you must take it as the Will of God – "The Lord giveth, and the Lord taketh away",' he quoted piously.

'I've been thinking hard about what must be done. I think I can get Maximin back in my own way. Don't ask me how. I will get the child back or die in the attempt. But, remember – God is with us.'

I looked at him, but said nothing.

'I'm going out shortly,' he continued. 'I want you to sleep for a while. I'll have you woken later this evening. Then I want you to make your way to that monastery Theophanes told you about. If we don't meet there, I'm sure you know how to get yourself out of the City. Prayers aren't your thing, I know. But do speak well of me in the Lateran when you see the Dispensator. Do tell him I did my duty in the end. And do please talk to my wife. Sveta really does like you.'

He stood and walked quickly from the room. Before I could call after him, he was already pulling to the shattered door at the bottom of the stairs.

If Martin thought I could just lie placidly back and sleep, he was a proper fool. At the very least, I was staying here on borrowed time. How long before there was a price on my head and people came looking in the most obvious place? Perhaps because it was the most obvious I'd so far been left alone. But every additional moment here brought the danger closer of an official knock on the main gate.

I was no longer Acting Permanent Legate. Whatever residual immunity I might have had as a servant of the Church had gone when Phocas put me in charge of the City's defence. Having been hailed as Emperor by some of the Blues had surely put the lid on things.

It was time to make a getaway. I'd go and see if there was any safety to be had in the monastery by the Pantocrator Church. If there was, I'd consider what might be the best way to get even with Priscus.

Before leaving, I changed my clothing again and took a couple of the stimulants that Theophanes had left with me the day before yesterday for just such a moment. After the bath, I wasn't feeling as tired as I knew I ought to be, but that might change. Theophanes had told me the pills would have a gradual effect – nothing like the drugs Priscus used.

Then I took one last tour of my suite. Every inhabited room had its memories. Here was where I'd first set eyes on Maximin. Here was where Authari and I had got Martin so drunk that he'd consented to show us a Celtic dance and tripped over a chair. Here was where I'd entertained my whores. Here was where I'd sat long into the evening talking in English to Maximin about the life he'd have as my son.

No one was watching me so it hardly mattered if I blubbed uncontrollably as I took my leave of a home that had been so sweet to me. I gently forced the door back into its closed position at the bottom of the stairs. I kissed it reverently, then I turned and stepped alone into the main hall.

'I've just heard you were back here,' a voice called in good Latin from the far end of the hall. 'I must say you have a nerve polluting my Legation with your blasphemous and now treasonable presence.'

I strained in the gloom of the lamps to see who it was. He was standing by the main gate and had evidently been talking to the doorkeepers.

Was I surprised? Was I shocked? Not really.

'Welcome back, Demetrius,' I replied – 'or rather, welcome back, Your Excellency Silas. As I'm now of senatorial rank, and still haven't been formally relieved of my command, you'll surely not complain if I neglect to bow to you.'

61

Silas the Permanent Legate didn't look at all pleased as he inspected the wreckage of his private office.

'Four days out of the building', he sniffed, 'and I come back to find it looking worse than the chaos in the streets outside.'

He picked up an overturned chair and sat down. Somehow, he'd dug out one of his official robes from the chaos of his wardrobe. This was the less grand of the two he'd had for public occasions. The grander one I'd sent off as a model to the tailors.

Now that he'd cast off the stooping, arrogant servility that had been Demetrius, he looked every inch a senior dignitary of the Roman Church. And note my adjective – Roman. Compared with the officials of the Greek Church, he was like a senator among clerks. Silas wasn't some trash who'd done well through penances or fake miracles, or even hard learning. He was old Roman nobility. He knew it, and he expected everyone else to know it without being told.

I perched on the edge of his desk and looked at my fingernails. I'd managed to get most of the blood out from under them, but they'd need a good polishing before I could be seen again in polite company.

'I never did manage to explain', I said, speaking slowly, 'why there was no one but Demetrius here who'd seen the Permanent Legate – why the whole staff of the Legation was replaced before I arrived. It never crossed my mind that you and Demetrius were one and the same person.

'Of course,' I went on, 'now I know that you and Demetrius are one, I think I can explain everything – or nearly everything.'

'Go on then.' Silas gave me a haughty look. 'Let us see if you are really as bright as they say – and not only renowned for violence and low debauchery.'

I ignored the jibe and continued: 'I discovered a long time ago that you and Phocas were in this together. You were working together through Theophanes. You didn't arrange with Rome to get me here as an excuse for withdrawing from contact with the Imperial Court. It was arranged between the three of you as an excuse for getting you out of public sight.

'You weren't avoiding Phocas. You were scared of Heraclius – that he'd have you murdered before you could broker a deal between Phocas and the Pope. It was just made to look as if you were out of sorts with Rome.

'Things changed when Theophanes arrived back in the city. He knew Priscus had been ordered to have you killed one way or the other. He couldn't stop an attempt on your life but he did arrange things to make the attempt look successful.

'He intercepted the killer that Priscus sent after you and directed him to my rooms. He did so knowing I'd finish the killer off and probably keep quiet about it. At the same time, you and Theophanes arranged your own fake murder. I was racking my brains about the double coincidence of murder attempts in the Legation. But all Heraclius and Priscus knew was that someone had been sent to kill the Permanent Legate, and the Permanent Legate was now dead.

'By the way,' I asked suddenly, 'whose body was that in your bedroom? It wasn't yours.'

Silas wrinkled his nose. 'How should I know?' he said. 'Why should I care? It was provided by Theophanes – and a creature in his position can always lay hands on a body when it's needed. This whole plot was his idea. I thought it was all far too elaborate. But I suppose that's what you get from Oriental eunuchs.'

He shrugged. 'Theophanes came up with the idea of the locked-room mystery,' he went on. 'He expected Priscus would be appointed chief investigator of the "death". That would keep him busy, but utterly in the dark. It was also useful to cast a certain ambiguity over the time of the murder. The body wasn't that fresh, you see. We covered it in pig's blood to disguise this but a medical inspection would have raised awkward questions.

383

'The Emperor put you in charge of the investigation because he didn't think we could get rid of the body before Priscus arrived. Priscus, you see, knew me well enough to see at once that the body wasn't mine. That would have split everything wide open. The old eunuch said you were dangerously competent and suggested removing the head, but Phocas and I agreed otherwise.

'Having you appointed to my own position and wearing my robe was the Emperor's idea as well. He said you would provide a convenient target for Priscus and Heraclius. If they were hard at work on trying to get you, they might not bother looking for holes in the account of my own alleged murder.'

'And that's why you killed Authari, isn't it?' I asked quietly. 'Priscus arrived before you expected he'd be out of bed. You had to move quickly. Authari was guarding the body. So you killed him. Did you do it with your own hands?'

'Most certainly!' Silas said with pride. He got up and stood before me, his neck pushed out, a leer on his face. Without cosmetics or wig or any change of costume, he was Demetrius again. An artist would have seen through the pretence immediately. Most other people, who are more concerned with the endless small accidentals of expression, would never have noticed the unchanged substance of underlying features.

'The Master sends word that you'll be needed here a while yet,' he rasped in the common Latin of Demetrius. 'But he also sends a cup of wine to keep you company – good red wine, thickened with something special.' He held out an imaginary cup to an imaginary figure sitting against the wall, then turned back with a complacent smile and sat down again. It was a fascinating if repulsive transformation.

I wanted to kill the bastard on the spot. More than that, though, I wanted the truth.

'Who helped you remove the body?' I asked. I already knew the answer but it might be useful to have it confirmed.

'Wouldn't you just like to know?' Silas answered with another gloat. 'I'd like to see you try bringing *him* to justice.' He rearranged his features and became the Permanent Legate again.

384

'Oh, and a word of advice, my little Alaric – I hear you've been unlucky these past few days with your attempts at freeing slaves. Well, if you put honey on shit, it's still shit. You really should bear in mind that God Almighty made us all and set each in his place. It doesn't do to try altering His Dispositions.'

I'd have the truth out of him before we were finished. For the moment, I chose to ignore a vulgarity of expression unbecoming his station. I moved on to another question, one he was willing to answer.

'I know you got out of the Legation dressed as a monk,' I said. 'I guessed the Emperor had you put up in the Monastery of St John Chrysostom.'

'Theophanes told me you and Priscus were pressing for a search warrant,' Silas answered. He stood up and began digging through his leather bag. He pulled out various items of toiletry. One of these was a little bronze mirror I'd bought back in July and lost almost immediately. afterwards – that was before Authari had closed my suite to outsiders. Was he doing this to annoy? Or did he just assume that anything in the Legation was his property?

'That was why Phocas tried to have me done away with the other night, wasn't it?' I asked, pulling myself back to the subject in hand. 'But can you tell me why he didn't just have me killed when he still had the power? Why go through the farce of appointing me head of the city defences?'

Silas turned back from his heaped-up items of toiletry.

'I don't regard these things as worth discussing,' he said with an abstracted look. 'If you don't know what kept the Emperor from putting you to the death you richly deserved, I can't be bothered to enlighten you.'

'I asked in the hope that you might give me a better reason than I'd already worked out,' I said with a smile. 'But let us go back to your exit from the Legation. Priscus had the place surrounded, and he wasn't on your list of accomplices – not unless I much underrate him – so how did you get out?'

'No one ever stops a monk,' Silas said with a happy flourish of things that included more of my possessions.

I didn't need to continue. The answer was obvious. The Black Agents had ignored orders and let them past. They had lied about this when it became important that no one should be allowed access.

'Well,' I said, looking at the sealed roll of parchment Silas was pulling from a leather case, 'is that your formal patent for His Holiness in Rome? Does that confirm him as Universal Bishop?'

Silas smiled happily at me. 'It is, and it does,' he said. 'It's sealed and dated as of last night. I suppose I should be impressed that you knew its contents without needing my explanation. Perhaps Theophanes wasn't just under your spell. Perhaps there are some glimmerings of intelligence.'

Again, I ignored the sneer. Time was pressing and I wanted as much truth as I could get from him.

'And you think', I asked with a sneer of my own, 'this will make you a big man back in Rome?'

'Of course it bloody will!' he exclaimed. 'You know as well as I do that this has been the main objective of Church policy for at least a generation. We wanted it. Now I've got it. Can't you imagine the looks on every face when I flash this about in the Lateran?'

'You might even get to replace Bishop Lawrence as head of the English Mission,' I observed drily.

'Oh, very witty, I'm sure,' Silas snarled at me. He glanced at the sealed roll of parchment. 'When I turn up with this in Rome, I shan't be satisfied with a bishopric in somewhere like Naples or Rimini. It certainly won't be anything in some shithole barbarian land like yours. That's a place for sending others to, not for visiting.

'I suppose you know that Pope Gregory the Saint was once Permanent Legate here,' he continued with a change of tone. 'It's often been a good step towards the top job.'

'If you're after the Papacy itself,' I reminded him, 'you'll need Heraclius to confirm it. And will he do that for a man who's lately made life harder for him all over the East?'

'Heraclius will have no choice but to accept the unanimous decision of the Roman Church,' Silas said with a snigger. 'Phocas has left him with problems that leave no Imperial room for manoeuvre in the West.'

'Tell me, Silas,' I asked suddenly, 'tell me – why shouldn't I kill you here and now and trade that patent with Heraclius for my life?'

Silas did an excellent job of keeping a look of alarm off his face. 'Because, my stupid little barbarian, I represent His Holiness in Rome. Lay violent hands on me, and you'll go to Hell. Besides, you haven't any sword with you.'

A fair answer, the second one at least – though I did have a very sharp knife under my cloak.

'And,' Silas went on, with a cheerful wave of his hand, 'because Heraclius would need rather more than a scrap of parchment to convince him that a rival for the Purple shouldn't be killed on the spot. Some of your "soldiers" were so drunk towards the end of that glorified street brawl you led that they were still hailing you as Emperor even after order was restored.

'I wouldn't trust any promises he made to the likes of you. Even if we leave aside the little matter of the Purple, you're a barbarian. I know you don't like Greeks. I don't much like them myself if truth be told. But they've always known how to deal with barbarians.

'Let me tell you – back when your people were first smashing up the Western Provinces, there were immense numbers of you settled here in the Eastern cities. In the West, we spoke piously of integration and assimilation. We rejoiced over the prospect of your conversion to the Orthodox Faith of Nicaea and of Chalcedon.

'In the East, they knew better. You can take a barbarian out of the forest, the Greeks said to us. You can't take the forest out of a barbarian. Getting a few of the Creeds by heart doesn't make a savage into a citizen.

'The authorities sent out a message to every barbarian in the East to assemble in certain places on a certain day. There they should all receive some token of Imperial favour.'

Silas paused for a gloating smile, then continued:

'They killed every last one of you – men, women, children. They had you surrounded in the public squares. You people stood there, as trusting as beasts on their way to slaughter. You never saw the archers until they were on every rooftop.

'As the West fell away, a province at a time, the East was renewed in the blood of the barbarians. The Greeks have kept an eye on you lot ever since. Therefore the need for residence permits.

'Don't suppose any deal you made with Heraclius would last the blink of an eye beyond his setting hands on this document.'

Silas sat back and laughed unpleasantly as he doubtless recalled the massacre of barbarians all over the East.

'Don't think of killing me, my silly Englishman,' he said at length. 'Come back with me to Rome. Only I can get you out of here, and you'll be useful to me there as an unfriendly but truthful witness to what I've done here in the city.'

'That's all very well, Your Excellency,' I said with a mock bow at his genius. 'There is, however, one matter that still perplexes me. Phocas has saved your life. Phocas has given Holy Mother Church what it wanted most in the world. He has made you the agent of communication to Rome. This will perhaps advance you to the Papacy. But what's in it for him? Phocas has never struck me as a particularly charitable man. Back in his early days, he may have given a lot to Pope Gregory, but he always made sure to get flattery and hard cash in exchange. So what's in it for our former Lord and Master and Ruler of the Universe, Phocas?'

'You may ask that of the Dispensator in Rome,' Silas said with an attempt at the enigmatic. He wasn't to know that Theophanes had already given the same answer. Hearing it a second time rather spoiled the effect.

Again, I didn't pursue the question. The answer was now pretty obvious. The moment I saw the patent, all those odd conversations with Theophanes and with Phocas suddenly made sense. It was like one of those bursts of enlightenment the very religious sometimes report. Instead I moved on to the question of what had occurred in Ephesus late the previous spring. That was something I still couldn't fit into the puzzle.

Silas was going into an orgasm of evasion when we were disturbed by a knock at what remained of the door. One of the Legation officials looked in.

'Demet— My Lord, rather,' he said in evident confusion, 'there are armed men to see you.'

62

The official stood back. Immediately, three soldiers stepped past him into the room.

'Ah, do come in, my good men,' Silas said in halting Greek. Now he was no longer Demetrius, it would never do for him to soil his lips with the common Greek of the streets. Like most of his sort, though, he was too grand and too idle to have paid much attention to learning the pure language.

He turned to me and switched back into Latin. 'You know I said I'd take you to Rome with me? Well, I lied.'

He sat back in his chair and hugged himself.

One of the soldiers stepped forward. He was a big man with black hair on his hands and wrists and a massive black beard broken only by the occasional battle scar. He looked nothing like the men of the City Guard I'd taken as typical of the Eastern armies. He cleared his throat and held up a slip of papyrus.

'We are here', he said in the deep, flattened Greek of the Mesopotamian provinces, 'to see the so-called Permanent Legate of the Roman Patriarch.'

He looked at Silas. 'Are you that person?'

'I am indeed, my good man,' Silas said, patting his official robe to emphasise his status. 'To be precise, I am the Permanent Legate of His Holiness the Universal Bishop. I represent His Holiness and, through him, Saint Peter himself.

'Now, to business. I want to thank His Imperial Majesty Heraclius for the speed of his response to my message. You will find that this loathsome and obscene barbarian child—'

The soldier held up an impatient arm for silence. He looked decidedly sour at Silas's mention of the hated title.

'You tell me you are the Acting Permanent Legate?' he asked. Without bothering for a reply, he turned to his subordinates. 'You will note', he said, 'the malefactor confessed his blasphemy and treason.'

The other two nodded. One fingered his sword.

Silas got to his feet. The easy smile had gone from his face. He looked nervously around the room. The windows were still shuttered after my orders for the room to be sealed. Soldiers blocked the doorway.

I cast my eyes demurely down and tried to look part of the battered furniture.

'My good man,' Silas opened, with another, but failed, attempt at jollity, 'I think we are talking at cross purposes. I said I was the Permanent Legate. If you want the *Acting* Permanent Legate—'

He got no further. The soldier reached forward and struck him hard in the face with a fist that looked about the size and weight of a lead club.

'Silence, you piece of Latin shit!' he said, barely changing either tone or volume.

Silas fell gasping to the floor. He put his hands to his face and drew them away covered in blood. Then he fell silent, looking up with growing horror at the dull, official faces.

The soldier held the slip of papyrus close to his face and began intoning his orders from Priscus.

'You've misunderstood,' Silas gabbled, now in Latin. 'The one you want is the yellow-headed barbarian. He's the one you want.'

'Silence, pig!' the soldier rasped in Greek, showing his fist again. He was growing impatient at the sounds Silas was making. It was plain he knew no Latin.

He turned to the other two soldiers. 'Get him on his feet,' he said curtly. 'Each of you – take an arm. Hold him steady.'

He drew his sword.

'No!' Silas screamed. 'Please, in the name of God. You must take me to Heraclius. I have a deal with him. He'll confirm you've made a mistake. Please—'

He got no further. His voice was choked off by a hard sword-thrust into the guts. The soldier pulled it smartly out, wiped the

391

blade on a cloth and sheathed it again. It was one of those smooth strokes you only see from professionals.

Silas was on his knees again. He held up his hands, bloodier than before. He looked up at me, terror and shock stamped equally on his white face.

'No,' he croaked, still in Latin. 'Not like this. I've come so far. You must tell them—'

He fell on to his hands and tried to crawl towards me. But every move was suddenly an effort. Then he fell forward on to his face and tried ineffectually to drag himself across the boards. I continued staring down.

The soldier looked at me for the first time. 'Do I know you?' he asked.

'I am, sir,' I replied in the smooth, unaccented Greek that I'd long since perfected, 'Fourth Secretary to His Holiness Sergius, Patriarch of Constantinople. I was here on business at the Legation when this impostor tried to extract money from the officials.'

The soldier softened. 'You know, people like you shouldn't be out on the streets on a day like this,' he said. 'There are some wicked people about.'

He gave me an appreciative look that went straight through my outdoor clothing. But then he remembered what I'd said about the Greek Patriarch. It didn't do to go about propositioning clerics, even on the Imperial frontiers.

I gave him a charming smile and said something about how the work of Holy Mother Church must go on even during a civil war.

We all crossed ourselves at the mention of the word 'holy', then the soldier turned back to Silas, who was still groping his way across the floor in my direction. His bloody robe clung to him as after a heavy downpour and its delicate silk snagged on the floorboards. Strength failing, he gasped with pain at every move. But he somehow wanted to be beside me.

The soldier waved at his subordinates. 'Let's get this over and done with,' he said.

One of them took hold of Silas by what remained of his hair and pulled his head up. There was a hiss of steel through air and a dull thud as the head was parted with a single stroke from its shoulders. Spurting blood which the soldiers moved smartly back to avoid, the body fell to the floor with a heavy thump. For a moment, it lay twitching – then it was still.

'Excuse me, sir,' I said, standing forward. 'May I?'

I took the severed head from the soldier's hands. He stood back with a bemused respect. I held the head up carefully to avoid getting blood on my clean clothes. I'd often wondered how quickly a beheading killed its victim. Does the mind die at once when the head is severed from its body? Or does some vestige of life remain like the cooling of a stone taken from a fire?

There were other matters, I'll admit, more deserving of my attention. But this was a chance of knowledge that might not come up so conveniently again. I pushed my face within about six inches of the severed head.

'Can you still hear me, Silas?' I cried softly in Latin. I tapped hard on the closed eyes with the fingers of my left hand. There was a fluttering movement.

'Silas,' I repeated.

The eyes fell open. I swear they focused for a moment on my face.

'Silas, you've lost,' I said triumphantly. 'Now that I know everything, I'm going to make sure that what you schemed to achieve will come to nothing. In a few moments, you'll wake in Hell. Take this as the beginning of your torments.'

I watched in fascination as the eyes dulled and the twitching of the already slack lips died away.

There – I'd learned something. I'd also done something to get even with that worthless fucker. No one calls me a barbarian without coming seriously to grief, I can tell you.

'I was placing a curse of the Church on the impostor,' I explained to the soldier. He nodded, still respectful, and put the head into a black bag.

'Was any of that stuff his?' the soldier asked, looking at the pile of things on the floor.

'The document belongs to the Church,' I said, avoiding the matter of which Church.

He grunted and took the bronze mirror for himself. It was a very nice object. Martin had gaped at the price.

I went with the soldiers down to the main hall to make sure the door was secured behind them. Before it closed, I noticed another detachment of armed men in the street. They didn't stop to compare notes, but marched straight past each other.

When there came the inevitable knock on the Legation door, I was ready for them.

'His Excellency the Permanent Legate begs your indulgence, kind sirs,' I said through the grille, 'but your presence is no longer needed. The emergency has been handled from within the Legation.'

I closed the grille and waited until, at last, I heard a shuffling outside and a few muttered obscenities. Then there was the tread of booted feet marching off in disciplined fashion.

This might have been a happier day for me. But I couldn't complain about my luck.

'Please, sir,' the official asked with a despairing look at the headless corpse, 'can you explain what is going on?'

'It has been a trying day for all of us,' I said soothingly, patting the man on the shoulder. I turned back to rolling up the Patent of Universality I'd been inspecting. It was wholly in order. I put it back into the retaining band and then into the leather case.

'Just get Demetrius ready for a decent burial.'

'He told us', the official said – 'he told us he was really the Permanent Legate. He was ever so angry with us when we let him in. He was angry when we didn't believe him. He was angry that you were here. He was angry about everything. He said he was going to send us all to Thessalonica to be massacred once the barbarians broke in.'

'The Permanent Legate died last Sunday morning,' I reassured him. 'We all saw the body. We don't need to ask what Demetrius was up to. He was a strange one, even without this latest pretence.'

The official nodded. That much was undeniable.

I looked at the body. Someone like Seneca might once have taken all this and worked it into a farce to amuse the Imperial

Court. Here lay the Permanent Legate in place of me. Someone else of utterly unknown name had lain in the room next door nearly five days back in place of the Permanent Legate. In place of him, Authari had been buried in the Great Church. In place of Authari, some slave of unimportant name had been buried in another church.

Now the Permanent Legate would be buried under the name of a Demetrius who had never lived at all. Rather, his body would be buried. The head would be thrown down a sewer the moment Priscus caught sight of it.

I changed the subject. 'Other men will be here before morning. Don't let them in. Tell them I've gone away. Tell them also to remember that the Legation has full immunity from entry and inspection. I'd be grateful if you could eventually get all my books and papers back to His Excellency the Dispensator.'

'Is it true, sir,' the official asked, 'you are wanted for treason?'

'Probably,' I said. 'Though I doubt if anyone will publish the details until tomorrow morning at the earliest.'

'Why not stay here, sir?' the man asked. He spoke with sudden eagerness. 'There are many places in the Legation where we could shelter you.'

I looked at him. He really meant it.

'I thank you, but no,' I said. 'When order is finally restored, you will need to open the gates to the Emperor and do so with a clean conscience. When I do make it to the "wanted" list, Heraclius will not be pleased with anyone who might have given me sanctuary. You've risked enough already.'

When I'd changed again in what had been my suite, we walked back together down to the main hall. The lamps still burned as they always had. I took one last look around me.

'Once I've gone,' I said, 'do make sure to lock and bar the door. Remember what I told you about not letting anyone else in.'

We shook hands. Then, on a sudden impulse, we embraced.

I paused in the chill outside the gate and listened for the heavy click of the bar. This time, I had a sword under my cloak.

63

All was quiet in the square outside the Legation. A small but bright moon shone down from the clear skies above the city. In its pale brightness, I could see one or two dark patches on the pavements, which I took to be blood. But the bodies had been long since cleared away.

The Great Church, far opposite, was now in darkness. With quarter given, it was no longer needed as a place of sanctuary. The Blues had taken up their movable wealth and gone home.

A few streets beyond the square, it was all different. Here, the Urban Prefecture was still on fire, and the fire had spread to the surrounding buildings. It was too late to save the Prefecture building. The flames had spread far within, and would burn unchecked for days to come. But the city slaves and sundry volunteers ran noisily back and forth with buckets to try and save the surrounding buildings. Men I'd never seen before stood in fine clothes, encouraging the slaves with words and the occasional handful of silver.

A dark hood covering my face and hair, I moved carefully through the running, often frantic crowds of fire-fighting men. So far as possible I kept close to the walls of buildings to avoid drawing attention to myself. I picked my way down a street still littered, except for the bodies, with the refuse of battle. I passed a set of barricades that now amounted to a pile of broken masonry and some burnt wooden spars. Was it here, that dozens had fought desperately to hold off an army – and that army had been held at bay for the better part of half a day?

Now all was silent and silver in the moonshine. A dog cocked its leg on one of the spars and went back to licking at the dark smears on the pavement.

From two streets away, I could see that the Ministry building was on fire. Great tongues of flame shot from the upper windows and licked cruelly around the lower reaches of the central dome. No one was trying to quench these flames. Instead, an immense crowd stood silently watching as the building in which generations of Constantinopolitans had been terrorised, and from which so many had never again emerged into the daylight, was consumed by flames that were themselves fed with the files that had enabled the despotism.

As I watched the Ministry burning I was reminded of that official, back in the time of Julian. Now his plan was being realised. Take away the records, you see, and you rule by consent or not at all.

I didn't know if anyone had searched those awful dungeons. In the flickering light, it was hard to recognise anyone among the crowds but I turned away. After all the killing and pain I'd seen, I couldn't bring myself to witness the despair of those who'd waited so long outside, only to find a catacomb at the end of the Terror.

Constantinople, as I keep saying, is a huge city. There had been a fierce battle in the centre. Buildings were burning in all directions. An invading army had taken control of the city in its entirety, but you'd never have known that from a walk outside the centre. Once past the Ministry, the streets grew steadily quieter. A few people staggered drunkenly past. One or two who were plainly up to no good darted furtively away as I approached. When one man tried to insist that I should remove my hood, I showed him the blade of my sword and it had the desired effect.

Passing into a deserted street, I came upon bodies hanging limp from the torch brackets. Some of them wore the uniforms of the Black Agents. A few wore common civilian clothes. One had a sign hung round his broken neck: 'Informer' it said. I didn't look too closely at the bodies. It was enough to imagine the furious mobs that had flushed these creatures out of their hiding places and hunted them through the streets. I thought of the crunch of breaking bones, of the cutting and gouging – of the terrified screams of hunters turned by circumstances beyond their control into prey.

397

I passed into the square before the Law Courts. Here, the outdoor restaurants were in full swing. A forest of torches burned around me. Carrying heavy dishes and trays loaded with jugs of wine, the waiters ran from kitchens to tables and back again. Except that everyone should long since have been abed, it was as if there had been no battle that day – nor even the smallest disturbance to the life of the city.

Then, as I walked round the edge of the square, I heard it:

'Well, I'd stand with him again, any day. So would every man of us.'

It was the high, clear voice of well-bred youth and I identified it as coming from a table close by one of the monuments. Braziers stood around the diners to keep off the autumnal chill, and a canopy was stretched over them in case of rain.

I recognised the speaker as one of the students I'd led into battle. He had a bandage over his head and his right arm in a sling, but he was alive and still jubilant. At the same long table, and on the table beyond that, I saw that the majority of my students were gathered. Even Philip was there, and I was sure I'd seen him take a knock on the head. Martin had been wrong. The students weren't mostly dead. Though rather battered from the hard fighting, they were mostly still alive. And now they were celebrating.

'It was like fighting by God-like Achilles,' another said, with a garbled attempt at quoting Homer. He got a nasty look from an elder sitting opposite him.

'Oh, I shouldn't worry about all that stuff – the Tyrant's dead,' he called, choosing to interpret the look as nothing other than a reflection on his learning. 'We've all got our amnesty. Besides, isn't Uncle Flavius planning to be first out of the city to welcome Heraclius when he shows up?'

'There's no amnesty for your Golden Alaric,' the elder said with a knowing sneer. 'There's a price on his head – its weight in gold.'

'I'd like to see anyone try to collect on that!' the first student interjected. 'I saw him get away right at the end. There wasn't a single scratch on him.'

'Then pray the bugger is dead before Heraclius gets hold of him,' the elder replied. 'He'll regret the hour that riff-raff of veterans by the Great Church put him up for Emperor. I saw the exception list published beside the amnesty. His name was just below that of Phocas' – the man turned and spat elegantly at mention of the Emperor.

'As for you' – he turned back to the first student – 'you've had your fun. From tomorrow, it's back to the University. If you want that posting to Rhodes, you'll need to pass those examinations.'

At this, the table fell silent. Then someone recited a long snatch from *The Iliad* – one of the bits full of fighting and blood – and the whole gathering joined in with varying degrees of recollection and competence.

On the far side of the square, I noticed several men pulling on ropes at an equestrian statue of Phocas. It buckled at the legs, but was too strongly set into the plinth. The bronze would have to wait until day for breaking up into sections and dispatch for coining into money or melting into a more fashionable shape.

I noticed more bodies hanging from torch brackets as I moved on, but the stimulants Theophanes had given me were now having their full effect, and I felt thoroughly jaunty. It was disturbing to be reminded that those idiotic Blues had put me outside the scope of the amnesty. But I was still alive and in one piece. And I had every intention of staying that way.

As I walked from the square into the shadows of a street obviously inhabited by persons of quality, I caught a brief exchange about the whereabouts of Heraclius. Someone suggested that he was already in the palace.

'Not so,' came the reply. 'He's on his flagship in the Golden Horn. He'll not be coming ashore until the mess is cleared away.'

In the dim light that showed in the upper windows of most of the houses it was possible to see the hasty messages of devotion and greeting for Heraclius that had been daubed on sheets and hung from each heavy gate.

64

The Jewish district was in uproar when I arrived there. Men were arguing bitterly in the streets. Slaves went about tearing crosses and enamelled icons from the shop signs. Others were fighting to keep them there.

One old Jew caught the hem of my cloak as I walked past him. 'In the name of our Common Father,' he cried in despair, 'can you say anything about what Heraclius intends for us?'

I looked back at him from within the folds of my hood. 'I am perhaps the last person in the city able to answer that one,' I said with a gentle laugh. 'But my advice, for what it may be worth, is to gather a big sum in hard cash and go indoors to wait on events. There may be a return to toleration. Or there may not. It depends on whether Heraclius listens more to his priests or to his money people.'

I turned to go. But someone else came from behind and pulled my hood back. 'I thought I recognised your voice,' he said.

I reached for my sword. But Baruch grinned and touched the blue amulet on his turban.

I'd been amazed by the display of blue over at the Great Church. It had never occurred to me that even the Jews had joined the Circus Factions.

'This is the one, Rabbi,' said Baruch. He hugged me and kissed both cheeks in his ebullient, Eastern way. 'If I hadn't been there myself, I'd never have believed it. He fought like Samson with his ass's jawbone. He smote those Green dogs good and proper. They ran like the Philistines at Lechi. I killed three myself.'

Baruch looked set to drift into a reverie of smiting but the Rabbi dragged him back to the present with a high-pitched reprimand in what I can now say was Aramaic. Jews in the City all speak common Greek on the streets, you see, but many of them can also speak a couple of Eastern languages which they use when they want to talk privately among themselves.

'No,' said Baruch firmly, pulling the conversation back into Greek. 'No one grasses on the Hero of the Blues. He led us to a draw with the Imperial Army. Besides, he's a good customer – well, good on the whole.'

He turned back to me. 'See that piece of offal up there?' he asked.

'Yes?' I said, giving a polite but hurried look at the torch bracket.

'That was my Chief Clerk, that was,' he said. 'I don't grass on people. People don't grass on me.' He dropped his voice. 'Are you in need of shelter?' he asked. 'My bank is safe as any fortress, and I could get you away in the morning. So long as no one looks under your tunic, you can—'

'Thanks, but no,' I said. 'I do, however, have something in mind that would benefit from your help.'

I took him next to a wall and quietly explained what I had in mind. Baruch listened gravely. His eyes widened when I mentioned certain documents that might be of interest. He raised only one objection, and I changed my plan to accommodate this.

'If you want to help your people,' I ended, 'that is probably the best way of doing it.'

'I'm in,' he said as soon as I'd finished. 'Let me go in for a sword.'

'And get a cloak,' I hissed after him. I pulled my own hood back on but, noticing a very pretty young woman looking out of a window at me, quickly pulled it half back again and smiled up at her. It may have been the drugs, or it may have been the thought of sodding everything up for several people who deserved no better, but I was feeling in the mood for devilry this evening.

Sadly, the girl was almost at once jerked back from the window, and the shutters were pulled across.

★   ★   ★

Over by the shore of the Golden Horn, some of the Greens had broken into a wine depot and were drinking their way through several dozen vats of the best wine in the city. Hundreds of them crowded into the narrow streets that ran down to the water. Blissfully happy, their dirty, often hideous proley faces softened by drink, and the knowledge of a betrayal well made, they pissed and belched where they sat. A few, lying in odd positions, looked dead from over-indulgence. Rather more of them were still up to dancing with each other for support, as they croaked a discordant hymn of triumph over the Blues.

A detachment of regular troops stood by the shore, just in case of any disturbance.

Come dawn, whatever trash had survived the celebrations would be cleared off the streets and driven back to their workshops or whatever filthy burrows they inhabited by day. For the moment, they were left to enjoy the fruits of their victory.

'See how the Greens would make an easy target,' Baruch whispered in my ear. 'Shall we not cut a few throats?'

'We have other work to do,' I reminded him.

For away from any of the troubles, the Monastery of St John Chrysostom lay in silence. We took up our positions in the doorway of a derelict shop nearby and waited. Baruch muttered a few times about his rheumatism and breathed garlic in my face every time he moved for a scratch. But, dressed in black, we stood still enough to be invisible.

Then, just as the dawn was breaking, the main gate opened slightly. A face looked cautiously out and peered right and left. Once it was clear the street was empty, the gate swung half open, and a procession of the younger monks emerged. They strained and grunted as they carried out great containers of the previous day's excrements for casting into the Golden Horn.

The Clerk had no time for more than the opening words of his protest as I smashed the pommel of my sword against the side of his head. He went down stunned. I pushed him into a broom cupboard, and we walked straight into the interior of the Monastery.

'This way,' I hissed to Baruch, pulling him just in time from a turn into the chapel. For the moment, we had the advantage of surprise. We needed to keep it that way.

The Abbot was rolling up a letter as we walked into his office.

'What in God's name? . . .' he asked, jumping to his feet.

'Excellent,' I said in my easiest tone. I shut the door softly. 'I take it you are now dispensed from your vow of silence?'

I told him what I wanted. His response was to dash for a window that opened on to the courtyard. How he'd ever have got through it, and then where he'd have gone, were questions Baruch saved him from having to answer. With a single blow of his fist, he had the Abbot floored.

'You can make this easy on us, or hard for yourself,' I said, looking down, my voice conversational.

'I don't know what you mean,' the Abbot spluttered. He gasped in horror as Baruch stepped heavily on his right hand. I could hear the bones cracking.

'You know exactly what I mean,' I said, pulling him back to his feet. 'Now . . .'

There was a banging on the door.

'Reverend Father, Reverend Father,' a voice called urgently. 'Are you all right?'

'Oh shit!' Baruch muttered. He spat on his sword blade for luck and added something about 'corpse-eating Nazarene dogs'.

I pulled the door open. For monks, the three men outside were well-armed. I walked towards the doorway, the Abbot now held before me, right arm twisted high up his back, my sword at his throat.

'If you don't do exactly as I tell you,' I said, still conversational, 'I'll kill your Reverend Father. And then, if you resist me, I'll kill you. And if you make a noise while trying to avoid being killed by me, you'll have some soldiers straight from Heraclius banging on the gate.

'Which is it to be?'

'Do as they say,' the Abbot cried.

'An excellent choice,' I snarled in his ear. I stepped into the corridor. Still holding their swords, the three monks moved away from us.

Baruch covered me from behind as I followed the Abbot's directions and pushed him down the long main corridor of the building. Doors opened before us, and pale, scared faces looked out from the tiny cells. But no one else was armed. As we approached, the faces pulled back and doors were slammed again.

'In there,' the Abbot gasped, indicating a smaller doorway near the end of the corridor.

'In there – and may God punish your blasphemy.'

'We'll see about that,' I said coldly. I held my sword tighter to his throat and stared at the armed monks, who'd followed us closely down the corridor. For a moment, they stared back. Then, with a gesture of submission, they put their swords down. For them, the game was over. What point in wagering now?

'Get me the keys to this door,' I said to no one in particular. His use as guide and hostage now at an end, I pushed the Abbot so he fell sprawling to the floor.

'Keep your sword up,' I said to Baruch as keys rattled somewhere in trembling hands. 'We'll need to look overpowering.'

My voice shook as I strained to hear any sound from inside. Was that the rasp of a sword from its scabbard?

For me, the game wasn't over at all.

65

Though still hardly into the eastern sky, the sun had risen with almost summer-like heat as we set out upon the Golden Horn.

'That one, over there,' I said to the boatman, pointing at the largest of the ships that rode at anchor in the narrow bay.

I emptied a whole vial of perfume on to my sleeve and raised it to my nose as the oars began turning over the filth that lurked just beneath the sparkling water. Common sense told me I should sit in the boat but dignity was more important. I steadied myself against each gentle pitch of the boat and remained standing.

I'd thrown off my dark cloak and was showing off the dazzling white and purple-fringed robe of a senator. That, plus my golden hair and the general dignity and assurance of my pose, must have fixed every eye on those anchored ships.

I couldn't be sure. If the sun shone full on me, it was also in my eyes, and I could see damn all of what might be happening ahead of me.

'Who goes there?' a voice cried from the flagship as we came within hailing distance.

I waited until we were close enough for me not to have to strain my voice with shouting.

'I am the Senator Alaric,' I called back at the second hailing, 'formerly Acting Permanent Legate of His Holiness the Roman Patriarch, and lately Count of the Palace Guard.'

There was a long silence. We came alongside the flagship and skirted round the banks of oars to the wide stern. I remained standing, my head held up proudly for anyone to see who was inclined to look.

A face peered over the stern of the flagship. 'What do you want?' a voice asked uncertainly.

'I have come to pay my respects to the Emperor,' I said mildly.

The face retreated. There was a subdued conversation several feet above me. Then, instead of the rope ladder I'd expected, there was a clumsy squeaking and a whole wooden staircase swung over the side, its lowest step just above the waterline. I stepped across on to it.

'Wait here,' I muttered to Baruch. 'Do exactly as I say.' He looked at me, suddenly doubtful. His free hand tightened on the leather satchel that contained the promissory notes made out to bearer.

As I came on deck, it was like stepping into one of the grander mosaics you see in the Great Church. In full dress and all in proper place before me stood what looked like the whole of the new Imperial Court. Here were the generals, the priests and bishops, the scholars, the ministers, and all the other leading men of the New Order of Things. They stood before me grave and silent, glorious in their robes of many colours. I had no idea what they had been about before I came aboard, but they were as fine a reception committee as anyone short of an emperor himself might have wanted.

Right at the heart of the gathering sat Heraclius. I recognised him from the purple robe, and from the fact that he was sitting while all the others stood. He was just approaching his thirty-fifth birthday when I first saw him. Tall and thin, his light hair cut short, his face close-bearded, he looked barely older than I was. He stared back into my face, confused and perhaps a little annoyed.

A eunuch just to the left of Heraclius coughed gently and looked meaningfully at the purple carpet that lay between us. I stepped forward into my best ever prostration. Every movement was exactly as it ought to be. I could hear a whisper of admiration around me as I tapped my head a third time on the carpet and then rose in a single movement.

'You will be aware', someone who looked rather senior began, 'that you are excepted from the amnesty, and that you stand ready condemned as a traitor.'

'I am so aware,' I answered in a firm voice. 'But His Imperial Majesty may be assured that I neither sought nor accepted an election that was made in my absence.'

Suddenly, just behind Heraclius, I noticed Priscus. How I hadn't spotted him at once is beyond me. Perhaps he only came forward when I was deep into my grovel. Perhaps it was the white lead that had blurred and softened his features. Even through the paint, though, I could see the rage on his face.

'That may be the case,' the senior official replied – I discovered shortly afterwards that he was the new Master of the Offices. 'You still stand condemned. Will you beg for mercy?'

'I will never beg before the Great Augustus', I said, 'for the justice that is mine by right.'

As a murmur of astonishment rose around me, I turned and walked back to the stern of the ship. About a mile away, far within the City, a pall of smoke hung over the centre. The Ministry and Prefecture buildings were still ablaze, and even if the flames had been contained, they would continue to burn for days to come.

I looked down at Baruch and jerked my head upwards. Without a word, I went back to stand before Heraclius.

'Caesar,' I said, looking him in the eye, 'there are many things you will want in the long reign that stretches before you. Many of these will be granted to you. Some will be withheld. At this moment, however, I give to you the thing you want most in the world.'

I took the bound figure swathed in black from Baruch and pushed it forward, to land clumsily on the deck about a yard from Heraclius.

Now Heraclius stood. There was a general shuffling and impromptu bowing as people crowded back to get out of his way. He was a big man. Standing, he fell more into proportion, so that he didn't seem so thin.

He pointed to Baruch. 'You have a knife, I have no doubt,' he said. 'Let me see this alleged gift of my heart's desire.'

As the black folds of the cloak and the restraining thongs fell away, there was a wail of terrified shock at the sight of Phocas. Still wearing the monkish robe in which he'd hoped to escape the city, and in which he'd come and gone at will from the Legation, he stood cowed and suddenly somehow shorter than he'd seemed only a day or so earlier. He winced at the sudden strain on his broken wrists and looked round, squinting in the brightness.

'Vile ruffian!' Heraclius cried in the loud and dramatic voice that I later found he used whenever he hadn't the foggiest idea what to do next and was hoping for inspiration. 'Foul beast!' he added.

Phocas looked past him to the silent crowd. 'See how the pigs gather at the new-filled trough,' he said. 'You all accepted my honours when they were worth having. You all swore loyalty when there was no likely test of it. As for you' – he turned to me – 'I should never have listened to that fucking eunuch. You were trouble from the moment you turned up in the City. I should have had you killed long ago.'

'You flatter me,' I said gravely. 'But I may have done you quite a favour. You'd have hated Canterbury in the winter. Forget the blacks, the headless dwarfs, the lack of wine. It's the weather that rules England out as a fit place of asylum.'

'I suppose Theophanes sold me out,' Phocas snarled at me. 'Or was it Silas? Never trust Latins. Never trust the fucking Pope!'

'Not at all,' I said, raising my voice so all could hear me. Those stimulants were wearing off but my mind was still like glowing charcoal. 'You praised my investigatory skills just a few days ago. It was only a question of using those skills to uncover your whole sordid conspiracy against the Empire.'

As I fell silent and turned to face him, Heraclius piped up again: 'Is this, O villain, how you have ruled the Empire?'

He waved at the City and at the smoke that was now billowing towards us on a shift of the breeze.

Phocas walked over to the side of the ship and looked long towards the City. He turned back with an easy smile. He now had all the assurance as if of restored power. He threw a sardonic glance over the hushed, crestfallen band of courtiers, then he turned to look Heraclius in the face.

'And will you, my young man, rule any better than I did?'

It was a brave answer. As if he'd been rehearsing for this moment, Phocas was preparing to die better than he'd lived.

And there was only one possible end to the conversation. Heraclius raised a hand and nodded. A soldier stood forward. He bowed as he handed over his sword, hilt forward.

As the soldier moved out of the way, I got a sudden view of Martin. He stood over by the other side of the ship, looked tensely back at me. Maximin was in his arms.

'My dearest friend,' Heraclius said after the second embrace, 'before I met you, I was prepared to grant you only your life. Now that you have performed so worthy a service and shown me such loyalty and devotion, I grant you the friendship of your Emperor.

'Yes, my Golden Alaric – and let all the universe be my witness – you are my Special Friend from this moment forth, and I will find some position in my government worthy of your talents.'

That Priscus didn't collapse from horror is testimony to his diplomatic skills. As it was, he waited his turn with the others to kiss me.

'Perhaps you'll be Whoremaster General,' he whispered in my ear. 'That's about the level of your abilities.'

'So long as you don't get to mix the wine', I replied, 'I'll take what I'm given.'

Slaves were already scrubbing away at the splash of red on the deck. The body was perhaps ten yards away, floating about an inch below the filthy waters. I could see its position only from the outer layer of clothing that broke the still smoothness.

The head was set on a pike and tied to the prow of the flagship. Phocas would precede us into the Senatorial Dock. It was the last precedence he would ever enjoy.

Phocas would precede us, his head to the right of the prow. To the left, his severed head also on a pike, would be Theophanes. As in life, so in death, their fate was joined.

'I thought I'd know where to find him,' said Martin once we'd broken for drinks and a bite to eat. 'I found him with his bags already packed. He and Alypius were planning to get themselves out of the city dressed as monks. They'd have been halfway to Damascus before anyone would have missed them. They'd have been across the frontier into Arabia before anyone could have caught up with them.'

Somewhere behind me, Baruch was lecturing a slave on the dietary requirements of his restored faith. They seemed to exclude most of the breakfast buffet. Luckily, Moses had said nothing in particular against wine.

I looked at the severed head of Theophanes. Without his animating spirit it was just one more saggy ball of flesh and bone. The eyes were already dull. The worn teeth poked forward above the drooping lower lip.

Phocas still looked like Phocas. Theophanes was already gone.

'What threats did you use?' I asked.

'None,' said Martin. 'I simply described the situation and asked for his help.'

'And he came?' I asked again. 'He simply came at your request?'

'He sat thinking a while,' Martin said slowly. 'We discussed what else might be done to get you and the child reunited and out of trouble. In the end, though – and there was a big argument over this in their own language – he ordered Alypius to go off alone. Then he came with me down to the shore.'

'Was it a fast death?' I asked. The head was neatly severed, but gave no indication of what might have been done first to the body.

'As fast as anyone could wish,' said Martin. 'The deal I brokered was that Theophanes handed himself over. In return, Priscus surrendered the child, you got kicked out of the Empire, and Theophanes was put to death without torture.

'Unlike with Phocas, Heraclius didn't strike the killing blow himself, but it was done with so much skill, I didn't realise at first the sword had passed clean through his neck.'

'He gave me a message to pass on to you,' Martin continued after a pause. 'He said to remind you of the promise he made. He also said: "If I now give my body to be burned, I do so with charity".'

I said nothing, but continued to gaze at the head. You shouldn't weep for a man like Theophanes. How many tears had been shed over his actions? That labyrinth under the Ministry had long since been his second home. His company was fine enough from across a dinner table. It must have been something else from the bed of a rack.

And his final service to the Empire might well have served to divide it. In exchange for that roll of parchment, all made out in proper order, he'd arranged for Phocas to be shipped out of the city under Church protection and set down in one of the monasteries outside Canterbury. There, Phocas would have been a standing challenge to Heraclius. The Church would only have had to say the word and there'd have been rebellions all over the West.

To avoid the possible loss of Italy and his native Africa, Heraclius would have been tied to Rome in all matters of doctrine and authority.

How long the Eastern Provinces would have stood for that – especially with the Persians running wild – is anyone's guess. Perhaps the Phocas challenge would have sunk without trace. But it might have split the Empire, leaving a Greek core, the other parts moving off in different directions.

That this had now been achieved by the Saracens, from whom Theophanes was snatched as a child, is one of the curiosities of history.

Perhaps it would have been better for the world if the inevitable that I've spent much of my life trying to put off had happened at one stroke. Perhaps Theophanes was after all a faithful servant of the Empire.

I couldn't know that as I stood looking at his severed head. While you shouldn't weep for a man like that, I had to fight myself not to. How he must have dreamed of a return to the burning wilderness of his childhood – free to pass the remainder of his life without lies or betrayal. He'd come so close to that. Then he'd given it all up for the child of his own worst enemy and for a barbarian who'd tried his hardest, without knowing what it was, to wreck his plan.

I reached forward and pulled the eyes shut. Then I took Maximin in my arms.

Now that the sun was up, a whole flotilla had set out from the shore. It was obvious even to the most cautious or foolish of the better classes who was the undisputed victor. I could already hear the salutations and cries of loyalty.

Whether they now raced against each other not to be last on that purple carpet, or stayed on shore to greet the Saviour on his entry into the City, all would be welcomed – with a few named exceptions, and a slightly larger number of others who would be disposed of before the coronation.

Behind me, I heard Baruch offering round his ivory cards and explaining the precise location of his bank. There can be advantages, you'll agree, in being the first.

66

Once again, the Dispensator avoided looking me in the eye.

'I wanted you there', he said for the third time, 'to secure the best outcome for the Church.'

All over Rome, the bells were ringing for Christmas Day. A steady drizzle since dawn had taken the fun out of the processions. But there was feasting and dancing and general good cheer within doors.

Or there was in all places but the Lateran. The great spider that lurked at the centre of the extended web of the Roman Church was taking no rest from its continual watch over the whole, or from its spinning of new threads to secure still more power for itself.

'You cannot imagine, my dear Aelric,' the Dispensator said, 'how those coded reports I kept getting from Silas alarmed me. I agreed in principle that any price was worth paying to get our Patent of Universality. But the deal Silas proposed was potentially ruinous. It would have been ruinous had it come unstuck. It might have been still more ruinous had it succeeded.

'Holding Phocas might have been useful for us – but not in England.

'I hardly need remind you that England belongs to the Church as a religious asset. With England as a direct province of Rome, the whole of the West can be ours until Judgement Day. We can hold it against all heresies that exist or may arise. It is therefore important that England should not be embroiled in merely Imperial politics.

'There was no chance that Heraclius or any other Emperor could invade England. But the use of England as a place of refuge for Phocas would have worked a diplomatic revolution throughout

413

the West. The Lombard and Frankish courts would have swarmed with Imperial agents – and, for all I know, agents of the Persian King. The northern kingdoms of England would have been locked into the new diplomatic system. Even the Irish would not have been left out.

'We needed the title of Universal Bishop – but not at the expense of losing all that made it worth having. England is ours. We will not share it with anyone. We will not risk having to fight for it. We will compromise in nothing – not even for the considerable short-term advantage we might have obtained.'

The Dispensator paused and looked again at the Patent of Universality I'd put on his desk.

'On the other hand,' he said with a change of tone, 'Silas had actually opened a negotiation that seemed likely to give us the title. For the first time, we were told that no declaration against Heraclius would be required. Phocas had abandoned hope of saving his throne. All that interested him now was finding some place of refuge beyond the reach of Heraclius.

'You don't refuse a bargain just because the price is not currently the one you are willing to pay. And this was a price that might, with proper management, be wholly avoided.

'As you know, I travelled to the East earlier this year. That it was a long and dangerous journey you won't need telling. Its inconvenience was all the greater because I had to travel in absolute secrecy. Heraclius, the Persians, and anyone else who might be interested, all had to be kept in the dark. That is why the meetings were arranged in Ephesus.

'I met there with Silas and with Theophanes, and we agreed the main terms of the bargain. This was the bargain that you uncovered in your usual way.'

'So why send me to Constantinople?' I asked. 'You could hardly expect me to vary the terms of an agreement of which I knew nothing until nearly the end of my time there.'

The Dispensator gave me one of his joyless smiles.

'In Ephesus,' he went on, 'it was agreed that Silas must withdraw from all official business in order to save himself from assassination by person or persons unknowable. Sending out someone from Rome of low status to perform some of his functions was an excellent cover for this.'

I frowned at the words 'low status' but let the Dispensator continue:

'When I met the old eunuch, I realised at once he was nobody's fool. He spoke of saving his Imperial Master from the punishment he richly deserved. It was obvious he had some wider agenda in his mind. From what you say, it was bolder than I imagined. You tell me that he had no other master, but was serving an idea? That he was aiming at a shortening of the Empire's frontiers to make it both more orthodox and more defensible?

'Without some positive statement of his to that effect, I am not sure what to make of your inference. If that was his intention, it might not have been inconsistent with our own interests. Such an Empire would be at once less able to intervene in our own sphere of influence, and a more reliable friend. And it would ultimately bring the Greeks to a better understanding of their place in the order of things.

'I could know nothing of this at our meetings but it was obvious that Theophanes would not be easily deceived. Any ordinary agent would have been flushed out in no time at all. I needed someone in Constantinople who could be trusted to look after the essential interests of the Church, and not be suspected of any double game.'

'You could hardly trust someone to look after your essential interests', I reminded him, 'unless he'd been told what they were.'

'Not so!' the Dispensator replied. He smoothed his white robe and righted some pens on his desk. 'You, Aelric, are less intelligent than you think yourself, but you always succeed. Some would call that luck. I prefer to think of it as something less vulgar.

'Whatever the case, I needed someone in Constantinople who could be trusted to do the right thing at the right moment. I had no idea when that moment would come, or what that thing would be. I only knew that you were that person.

'And now' – he looked again at the Patent – 'and now, everything has worked out as it should. We have the title that is rightly ours. We have none of the embarrassments that Silas had arranged as its price.'

He stood up to file the document. Later, he'd already told me, it would be taken out again and copied and sent all over the West with the usual attestations.

I smiled and leaned forward. I'd been waiting for this moment.

'Not so fast, my Lord Dispensator,' I said. 'You seem to have overlooked the fact that all the official acts of Phocas were annulled by Heraclius. It was the first act of his reign. You can hardly believe that the last document Phocas ever signed will be accepted as valid anywhere. That sheet of parchment has about the same value as the draft of a broken banker.'

The Dispensator froze. He came back to his desk and stood over me.

'Young man,' he said with cold menace, 'if this document is of no value, why have you brought it to me?'

'Because', I said, leaning back in my chair, 'I have full authority to make it valuable.'

I pulled the Imperial Warrant from my bag. It gave the Senator Alaric authority to validate any grant of the late reign involving the transfer of property or other valuable assets that could be shown to have reached its recipient before news of the Revolution. In these circumstances, anything bearing my own seal of attestation would be regarded as of equal validity to a grant from Heraclius himself.

The nice thing about this arrangement was that the Pope would get his title, and the Eastern Churches could be told that its validation was an act of unavoidable secular justice. Heraclius would get hardly any blame for that. The Roman Church would never dare accuse his man of perjury, as that would only invalidate the grant.

And what of Heraclius? Why should he be willing to let me perjure myself? On what basis might I be permitted to declare that a document I'd carried there myself had somehow preceded me?

The Dispensator nearly fainted as I recited my list of demands. The money was easy for him. Heraclius was in urgent need of all the gold we could lay hands on. But for the Church, it would only

416

mean working the slaves on its Sicilian estates double hard for a year, and keeping the Roman mob short of bread.

It was the theological demand that had the Dispensator's eyes bulging with horror. I wanted the Church to drop all objection to that heresy in Ravenna. The position agreed at Chalcedon of One Person and Two Natures for Christ would, of course, be untouched. But it was to be an open question whether this implied One Will and One Operation. The deacons were to be let off memorising the whole library of nonsense I'd prepared for them.

Sergius and I had come up with this one together the night before he was invested as Patriarch in Constantinople. The Monophysite dispute had been grinding away for a hundred and fifty years. Some obscure Western clerics had managed to fall over a compromise that might reconcile all opinions on the Trinity. We'd need to develop the position, drawing on the whole technical apparatus of Greek theology. Whether it would lead where we wanted remained to be seen.

In the meantime, we didn't need any crude formulations of the Orthodox Faith from Rome.

'Get these signed and sealed', I said, pushing the prepared documents across the desk, 'and I'll apply my own seal to your document.'

For the first time since my return, it was the Dispensator and not I who was lost for words. He glared horribly at me, then muttered something about taking advice from his legal counsel.

As our meeting ended and I stood silently by the closed door, the Dispensator looked quizzically over at me. Then, as if remembering an unfamiliar fact, he got up and crossed the office to open the door for me himself.

'My Lord Dispensator,' I said, embracing the old bag of sticks, 'it has been an honour to be with you on this joyous day.'

'The honour has been mine entirely,' he rasped back at me – 'My Lord Senator.'

Just as Martin and I bumped into each other, it came on to rain hard again. We took shelter under the portico of the Temple of

Jupiter. The place had been closed for worship for two hundred years and, while it hadn't yet managed to fall down, it was increasingly torn apart by tree roots and human depredation. But the roof was still intact in those days, and we found reasonably dry places on the steps for sitting down.

'I would have come straight to see you,' Martin said. 'You got my message?'

I nodded.

'But as soon as I got home, we had to go off to celebrate Christmas outside the walls. You know how Sveta can be . . .' He trailed off.

'I was grateful for the message,' I said. 'There were many others, but yours meant the most to me.'

I looked down the Capitoline Hill to the derelict Forum, and over the jumble of blackened buildings to the larger structures beyond.

'She was brought to bed at the end of September,' I said, trying to keep my voice level. 'Marcella had her lawyer there at the confinement, and made sure to free Gretel as the child began to emerge. Mother and child were freed together. It was a boy.

'The trouble started the following day. Gretel took some kind of fever. She rallied. Then the child stopped breathing. Then she too died. She died early in the morning on the last Sunday of September.'

Martin thought back. 'That was the night the assassin broke into your room.'

'Yes,' I said. I'd just come away from my daily visit to the grave. Marcella had paid for the funeral and had commissioned a stone of surprising elegance. Three times a day, she was assuring me that the child had been baptised before it was cold.

I'd been crying again, and I didn't want anyone to see that. I might let myself go with Martin, but I'd rather not.

'I'm told you will go back East,' Martin said. 'I don't suppose you have any choice in the matter, bearing in mind your appointment.'

'Not so, Martin,' I said, glad of the changed subject. I'd been on the point of telling him about my dream on the night of the

418

attempted assassination. Best I didn't, though – it would only have provoked his superstition.

'I can go where and when I please. If I want to go back to Constantinople, I will. If I want to stay here, I will. No one can command me at this distance. My will is free.'

I looked again down to the Forum. The great houses and other buildings that had once lined the Sacred Way were all without roofs and had fallen into further decay since my first arrival in Rome. Through the misty rain, I could see down to the silent waters of the Tiber. Or I could look the other away across the whole desolation of what had once been the Capital of the World.

The Forum remained, impressive even in decay. Now the golden statue of Phocas had been toppled from its column, the one last splash of colour down there had gone. But the Forum remained. It was – and will remain – the noblest sight that ever moved the imagination of men.

'I will go back,' I said. There could be no doubt of that. For all that can be said of Rome, it has nothing to compare with Constantinople. When I'd first come here with Father Maximin, I'd been overpowered by the amenities of Rome. Now I'd seen Constantinople, and Rome seemed a dull, ruinous place – bereft of wealth and of learning. It was no place for me or for the baby Maximin.

I'd been granted the nice palace Theophanes had owned, together with all his other non-monetary goods. Set beside that, the house I'd been offered in Rome was a decidedly low-class place.

A chill wind was blowing up. Martin and I huddled closer together on the steps of the temple for warmth.

'Yes,' I repeated, 'I'm going back. I expect my business here will be over by the New Year. Then it's south again. There's that business Heraclius wants me to oversee in Catania. That should keep me busy until the weather allows a sea crossing from Syracuse. I might even see Athens this time.'

'Can I come with you?' Martin asked with sudden intensity.

I looked at him.

419

'If you think Maximin can manage the sea voyage,' he added. 'I see no reason why my own family should fear for anything. Surely the Lord Senator Alaric will be in need of a confidential secretary?'

He did have a point there. I'd not find anyone in the city more trustworthy. And, of course, I wanted him with me. But I had wanted the offer to come from him, rather than having to suggest it myself.

'And', he concluded, 'you may be assured that Sveta will keep me from walking the streets at night.'

For the first time since the awful day of my homecoming, I laughed . . .

EPILOGUE

I did go back to Constantinople after leaving Rome. I went back with Maximin and Martin and his family. I went back to Heraclius and Sergius. And, yes – I went back to Priscus. I went back, and all that happened between then and my eventual return to Jarrow you can read about in the histories.

Alexius and his colleagues are long since departed from Jarrow but I have stayed behind. If the Empire is under threat again, it must be without my advice and direction that it fights off the Saracens or the Slavs or whatever other race has lit fires outside the city walls.

In a moment, Bede will come in for one of his Greek lessons. After that, we shall go out for our afternoon walk. Summer has come at last, even to Jarrow. The sun shines bright outside the walls of this monastery. The fruit ripens on the trees. My hand in Maximin's, I shall pick my slow, unsteady way down to the great river that empties into the sea. And the boy will press me with his endless questions, any one of which is a joy to answer.

He's got his way. I shall die among my own.

I will not go back again. But I have only to look away from the dark, shrivelled paw that holds my pen and I see myself again in all the strength and glory of manhood – and feel again some ghost of what I have been.

Death alone can rob me of the memories that now, like the waters of the Mediterranean, warmly lap the fringes of my mind.